GO WEST, YOUNG MAN

Look for these exciting Western series from bestselling authors William W. Johnstone and J.A. Johnstone

The Mountain Man

Luke Jensen: Bounty Hunter

Brannigan's Land

The Jensen Brand

Preacher and MacCallister

The Red Ryan Westerns

Perley Gates

Have Brides, Will Travel

Guns of the Vigilantes

Shotgun Johnny

The Chuckwagon Trail

The Jackals

The Slash and Pecos Westerns

The Texas Moonshiners

Stoneface Finnegan Westerns

Ben Savage: Saloon Ranger

The Buck Trammel Westerns

The Death and Texas Westerns

The Hunter Buchanon Westerns

Tinhorn

Will Tanner, U.S. Deputy Marshal

GO WEST, YOUNG MAN

WILLIAM W. JOHNSTONE
AND J.A. JOHNSTONE

PINNACLE BOOKS
Kensington Publishing Corp.
www.kensingtonbooks.com

PINNACLE BOOKS are published by

Kensington Publishing Corp.
119 West 40th Street
New York, NY 10018

PUBLISHER'S NOTE
Following the death of William W. Johnstone, the Johnstone family is working with a carefully selected writer to organize and complete Mr. Johnstone's outlines and many unfinished manuscripts to create additional novels in all of his series like The Last Gunfighter, Mountain Man, and Eagles, among others. This novel was inspired by Mr. Johnstone's superb storytelling.

ISBN: 978-0-7860-4915-8

First Kensington trade edition: May 2021
First Pinnacle mass market edition: August 2022

ISBN: 978-1-4967-3450-1 (ebook)

10 9 8 7 6 5 4 3 2 1

Printed in the United States of America

Chapter 1

John Zachary walked into the post office in Springfield, Missouri, hoping a letter he had been waiting for might have arrived. The postmaster, Sam Gunter, answered his question before John had a chance to ask. "Howdy, John. That letter you've been looking for came yesterday." He went over to a box that held all the mail for the farms out James Bridge Road and sorted through it until he came to the one letter addressed to John Zachary. "Must be important," Gunter remarked, hoping John might share the content.

"Much obliged, Sam," Zachary replied. "Yeah, it's kinda important—some information a fellow is sendin' me about growin' better corn." That was not entirely untrue, but he wasn't ready to tell Sam, or anyone else he knew in town, what he had in mind to do. And as if on cue, Sam then brought up one of the main reasons.

"You know, if you're gonna be in town later this evening, the mayor's holding a meeting to discuss the future of our town, what with there being more and more talk about the possibility of the southern states seceding from the Union. A lot of us think it'd be a good idea to know where everybody stands if it comes to war."

"I reckon I already know where I stand," John said. "I won't be at the meetin', but you can tell the mayor I stand for the Union and against war. So I sure hope it doesn't come to that."

"I suspect that's where most of us stand," Sam allowed. "But there's liable to be some trouble in Greene County 'cause there's lots of folks with southern ties."

"You may be right, Sam," John said and started walking toward the door. "Well, I'd best be gettin' back. Emmett's waitin' for me at Simpson's."

"Tell him about the meeting," Sam said.

"I will. I'll tell him," John assured him. He left the post office and went directly to Simpson's General Merchandise where his friend Emmett Braxton was waiting with the wagon. The two men had been best friends since their school days and for the past five years had worked to raise crops on adjoining farms. When he reached the store, Emmett was sitting on the wagon seat, waiting for him. John's son, Johnny, and Emmett's son, Skeeter, were chasing each other around and around the wagon. Seeing the boys playing caused John to think, *I don't want their future to promise nothing more than to be sent off to fight a war as soon as they're old enough.*

"Did you get your letter?" Emmett asked.

"Yep," John answered, holding the letter up for him to see.

"Ain'tcha gonna open it?"

"Yep," John answered again. "You drive the horses and I'll read it on the way home." He called the boys then. "Hop on, boys. We're headin' home."

"It looks like a helluva letter," Emmett commented. "How many pages is that?"

"A lot," John answered, already reading and not bothering to stop and count the pages.

Emmett pulled the empty envelope out of John's hand and read, "From Mr. Clayton Scofield. Is that the fellow that leads the wagon train? The wagon master, I guess you call him."

"Yeah, he's the guide." After reading the first three pages, John started informing his friend of the contents. "Boy, he didn't leave anything out. It's all right here in this letter, everything you need to make the trip; how to equip your wagon, what supplies and how much of 'em you need to take you through, how far you go each day, and everything else."

Emmett shook his head, marveling at his friend's excitement over the prospect of traveling in a wagon all the way across the continent to Oregon country. He couldn't really say John was making a bad decision. He couldn't blame him for leaving his poorly producing farm here for land in the fertile Willamette Valley the emigrants talked about. He wondered if he shouldn't pack up his family and go with him. John had talked so enthusiastically about it for the last couple of months, it was hard not to catch some of his excitement. He wouldn't admit it to anyone, but sometimes he felt a little resentment for the fact that John didn't consult him about the wisdom of dumping everything here they had worked so hard to build before making a final decision. But they were best friends, so he had to wish him well.

They stopped at Emmett's farm first and unloaded his purchases. "Why don't you and Sarah and the kids come on over to the house with me?" John suggested. "We can all tell Marcy she can start gettin' ready 'cause we're goin' to Oregon for sure."

"I don't know, John," Emmett said. "You and Marcy might wanna do some serious talkin' or something."

"Nonsense," Sarah commented in her typically blunt fashion, "we'll go and help you get excited." She paused and gazed at a grinning John Zachary, then added, "It may be too late for that, judging by that silly expression on your face." So, Sarah, Skeeter, and Lou Ann scrambled up on the wagon with Johnny behind John and Emmett, and they continued on to the Zachary farm.

"Evenin', Marcy," Sarah sang out when the wagon pulled up by the back door and Marcy came outside to meet them. "John invited us all to come to dinner, so I hope you're cookin' something good."

"I'll just pour another quart or two of water in the soup and that'll have to do," Marcy answered, accustomed to Sarah's japing. "What is the occasion for this visit?"

"We've come to help you celebrate," Sarah replied. "John got that letter you were waitin' for."

Marcy's eyes lit up in excitement upon hearing that news. She looked at once toward her husband. "The letter came?" He answered with a nod and a grin. "Well, hallelujah," she declared, "I guess we're goin' to Oregon!" She took hold of Sarah's arm. "Well, come on in the house. It's cold out here."

When he saw John deliberating over whether or not to unhitch the horses, Emmett said, "Come on, I'll help you unhitch. We'll just walk back home. Those two women get to gabbin' and there ain't no tellin' how long we'll be here. No sense in lettin' your horses stand hitched up." It was not a long walk back to their house, anyway. It was just a matter of cutting across a corn field that separated the two homesteads. When they returned to the house, they found the two wives chattering away about the adventure of the cross-country trip and the new life to be anticipated in that faraway land of Oregon. They also noticed that Marcy had seen fit to bring out one of the apple cider jugs for the celebration.

While the women were shuffling through the pages of Clayton Scofield's instructions and recommendations, and the kids were chasing all over the house, only Emmett had concerns about his friend's decision. While he forced a smile to stay in place on his face, he was troubled by his own indecisions during the months before when John talked about it so much. He now found himself regretting his hesitancy and thinking that maybe he should have followed John's lead once more. When his wife noticed his seeming lack of enthusiasm, she asked, "What's wrong, hon?"

He looked at her and shook his head, then spoke softly, so no one else would hear, "I don't know. I think maybe it woulda been smart if we had signed up to go with 'em."

"Maybe you should take a look at this letter and see all the things you would need and what you'd have to do to our wagon, and how long that trip would be," she suggested. When he showed no incentive to do so, she asked Marcy for the first few pages, since she had already read them. She handed the pages to Emmett. "Might as well see what you're missin'."

Emmett shrugged and started reading the first page. It started out: *Dear Mr. Zachary, I'm happy to hear that you and your family, and the Braxton family, have decided to join our train, leaving Independence, Missouri on April 1, 1860.* That was as far as he got before he looked up to find all conversation stopped and all eyes upon him, faces waiting expectantly. He looked at his wife, who was grinning ear to ear. He looked at John then, whose smile was equal to that of Sarah's. "You son of a gun. You signed me up, too."

"Hell, I knew you'd wanna go. It just takes you longer to realize what's best for you. And I knew—hell, we all knew—you wouldn't let me ride off without you."

Emmett's grin was now wider than anybody's. "I oughta let you go out there by yourself and see how you make it without me to keep you straight. Gimme the rest of that letter. There's a heck of a lot to do between now and April first." He paused then when he remembered. "'Course, I'll have to talk this over with Sarah first. She might not wanna make a trip like that."

"Shoot," John scoffed, "she's the one who told me to put your name on my letter."

The drop-in visit from the Braxtons turned out to be an all-day affair that lasted well into suppertime and the sudden demise of two fat chickens that ended up in the pot. Cornbread to go with the chicken required a good portion of the cornmeal just purchased at Simpson's that morning as well. It would be the first of many days the two families would work to prepare for the journey of their lives. Paying strict attention to the letter from Scofield, the two men fixed their wagons just as he recommended and followed the specified guidelines for quantities of food and provisions. Over the two-month time before the first of April, they sold their farms and furniture. Selling the furniture was the hardest part, but there was no room in the wagons for anything beyond clothes to wear and things necessary to eat and prepare meals. Sometimes it was difficult to believe they could accomplish everything that had to be done. However, three days prior to April first found the two families driving their wagons into the town of Independence, hoping their decision was a sensible one. They had made an appointment to meet Mr. Scofield on the morning of the twenty-eighth, at the Henry House Hotel, to finalize any agreements and pay any advance charges.

Chapter 2

While the Braxtons and the Zacharys were bedding their families down for the night, the man they had come to meet was passing his time in a card game in the Gateway Saloon. "I swear, sonny, I know I've had a helluva lot to drink since I sat down at this table, but I don't reckon I could get drunk enough to where I couldn't see that card come off the bottom of the deck. I ain't sore enough to wanna shoot you for cheatin', but that's the reason I've just throwed my cards in the last few times it's your deal."

"What the hell are you talkin' about?" the young gambler exclaimed. "You'd best watch who you're callin' a cheat, old man. I don't take that offa nobody."

"Like I said," Scofield responded, "ain't no use gettin' your feathers ruffled. I'm just tryin' to give you a little friendly advice, that's all. But if you're thinkin' about makin' it as a gambler strictly by sleight of hand, you've got a helluva lot more practicing to do."

"Why you old drunk, I'm thinkin' 'bout puttin' an extra air hole right between your eyes. A man don't accuse another man of cheatin' unless he's ready to back it up. You're wearin' a handgun, so I'm givin' you a chance to prove you can handle one." With his eyes locked on Scofield's, he stood up and pushed his chair back. The steady din of saloon conversation stopped immediately as it became apparent to everyone in the room that a challenge was about to be issued. A duel between two card players was not an uncommon occurrence in the Gateway Saloon, so the regular patrons remained silent in anticipation of the challenge to follow. They were not disappointed. "Old man," the young gambler pronounced clearly, "you're a no-account drunken liar and a damn yellow-bellied coward to boot. I'll have you take a knee and beg my forgiveness or stand up to me and go for that handgun you're wearin'."

"Now, there you go, tryin' to make a name for yourself by shootin' me," Scofield responded. "If you're as bad at gunfightin' as you are at cheatin' at cards, you ain't likely to last long enough to ever get to my age. And if you shot me, what good would that do your reputation? Hell, I ain't got no name as a gunfighter. You just called me a no-account old drunk. You ain't gonna get very famous for shootin' an old drunk." Scofield got up on his feet, holding onto the edge of the table to steady himself. "Damn," he swore, "that likker's hit me harder'n I thought. I might have to set down again to keep this saloon from rockin' back and forth." He looked the young gambler in the eye and said, "I'll not draw on you, young feller, so go on and find yourself another game."

The young man was not to be denied, however, and was not willing to be bluffed by the wobbly old man. No matter what Scofield had said, a kill was a kill, and that's all anybody would talk about. And this would be so easy he'd be a fool to pass up the opportunity. He stepped up in Scofield's face and poked his shoulder with his forefinger. "You ain't talkin' your way outta this, big mouth." The last word had barely dropped from his lips when Scofield's Colt Navy Model six-shooter landed solidly against the side of his face, knocking him unconscious and breaking his jaw in the process.

Clayton Scofield plopped back down in the chair and shook his head slowly, as if afraid it might roll off his neck. "Damn" was his only comment when Pete, the bartender, walked over to take a look at the unconscious man on the floor.

"I declare, Scofield, it's been over a year since you were in here," Pete said. "Don't look like you've changed a helluva lot." He paused to see if Scofield was even aware of his comment. When it appeared that he wasn't, or that he didn't give a damn, one way or the other, Pete shrugged and asked a couple of the spectators to give him a hand. He directed them to carry the injured man out the door and deposit him on the front porch of the saloon. Back to Scofield then, he said, "Best pick up your money and let somebody else take that chair." He glanced at the remaining two card players and they both nodded vigorously. Scofield looked to be a handful, drunk or sober, and the recent altercation with the young gambler verified it.

Scofield didn't protest. He was well aware of his incapacity after consuming such a large quantity of rye whiskey at a single sitting. He struggled to his feet once again, and with Pete to give him a helping hand, he made it over to a small table against the back wall. He settled heavily into the chair and smiled up at Pete. "'Preciate it. I'll just set here a little while. Do I owe you any money?"

"No, you're paid up. You need me to bring a spittoon over here for you?"

"Nope," Scofield answered with certainty, knowing that the sick part of his drunk would strike him in the morning, most likely. "I won't be here long." He felt confident in saying that, thinking that Clint was probably looking in all the saloons for him already.

"Might be a good idea to get outta here as soon as you feel like you can make it," Pete advised. "You clobbered that feller pretty good, but when his head stops ringin', I expect he's gonna be lookin' for you. And you ain't in no shape for a shoot-out."

"Ain't that the truth?" Scofield responded with another foolish smile. "I'll just set here and rest a spell."

On the street in front of the saloon, young Clint Buchanan pulled up to a stop at the hitching rail when he saw a black Morgan tied there. Seeing the prone body lying on one side of the porch, he at once thought his chances looked favorable for finding his uncle inside. He stepped down from the saddle and tied his horses up at the rail. Then, out of habit, he drew his Henry rifle from his saddle sling. He liked to keep it with him because the Henry rifle had just been manufactured and it was not easy to come by one. He stepped up on the porch, where he paused for a moment to observe the man lying there. After a few moments, he saw signs of life as the man struggled to come to. *I hope you ain't got nothing to do with Uncle Clayton*, Clint thought as he walked past him and went into the saloon.

Pete glanced up from the bar when the tall, strapping young man walked in. He was a stranger, but there was something familiar about him. He looked more closely as he approached the bar. Then it struck him. He pointed to the little table in the back. “He’s settin’ right back there at the table, Clint.”

“Much obliged,” Clint said. “Has he caused any trouble?”

“Well, maybe a little bit,” Pete replied, still marveling at how a year had served to complete the rugged image of a competent young man.

“That fellow lyin’ on the porch?” Clint asked and Pete nodded. Then he quickly told Clint about the incident during the card game. “And the other two players, they didn’t say anything about that fellow cheatin’?” Pete shook his head. “You reckon he was?” Clint asked.

“I expect that he was,” Pete admitted. “But the other two fellers in the game are in here playin’ cards all the time and ain’t neither one of ’em likely to call anybody on it.” He shook his head and grinned. “But not ol’ Scofield. I expect you’ve got a fulltime job tryin’ to keep him outta trouble, don’tcha?”

“No, for a fact, I don’t,” Clint answered, “just between runs. Uncle Clayton won’t usually take a drink of whiskey when we’re on the trail. All the way from here to Oregon, he’s sober as a judge. Oh, there are some places when he feels the need to have a drink, but even then, he won’t take more than two shots. That’s just his way. The only time he wants to tie one on is when we get back here and then he makes up for all that time he’s done without.

He'll be sick as a dog tomorrow and we're supposed to meet with some people who wanna go to Oregon with us. I expect I'd best get him back to the hotel. Does he owe you any money?"

"No, sir," Pete said. "He's all paid up. You need any help gettin' him outta here? He drank an awful lot of whiskey."

Clint thanked him just the same, then walked back to get his uncle. Scofield opened his eyes when he heard his nephew approach the table. Seeing who it was, he fashioned a satisfied smile and announced, "Clint, I'm drunk as a skunk."

"I expect so," Clint replied. "Can you walk?"

"I'll give her a try," he answered and tried to stand up, but found he needed help from his nephew to get up from the chair. "I ain't so sure," he confessed and tried to take a step forward, only to start to fall face forward. "When they built this dang saloon, they shoulda used a level on the floor. It's hard to walk when it's on a slant like this floor's on."

"No matter," Clint said as he quickly laid his rifle on the table, ducked down and caught Scofield on his right shoulder, then straightened up. He settled his load on his shoulder, then picked up his rifle and headed for the door.

"Good night all," Scofield slurred cheerfully over Clint's shoulder, as he was carried past the bar.

"I want you to be real quiet now," Clint told him. "Don't say another word until I get you on your horse. Can you do that?"

"Anything you say, Clint," Scofield slurred.

When Clint walked out the door, he found he didn't have to worry about his uncle making a sound. Scofield was fast asleep. The injured gambler was now up on one knee, gingerly feeling his broken jaw with his fingers. When he saw Clint, he managed to spit out, "Is that him?"

"Yep," Clint answered. "That's the old coot who busted your jaw. He's dead, so you might as well go get that jaw fixed up. I'll take care of this'un."

"Whaddaya gonna do with him?" The gambler forced through clenched teeth.

"Bury him," Clint replied and slid his uncle off his shoulder to lie across his saddle. Wasting no more time then, he rode away from the saloon, leading Scofield's horse toward the hotel and the stable behind it.

Morning arrived a good bit earlier than Scofield had planned to greet it. He woke Clint up with his frantic efforts to pull his trousers and boots on in his haste to make it to the outhouse behind the hotel. He didn't waste a moment to consider the thunder-mug under the bed, knowing every evil he had trapped inside his body the night before would not be denied its escape. Clint had to get up to close the door his uncle had left wide open before he could go back to bed and try to go to sleep again. He finally dozed off, thinking how much he missed the freedom of sleeping on the open prairie.

Much to Clint's surprise, he was allowed to sleep until well past sunup when Scofield, fully dressed, roused him out. "Time to crawl outta them blankets, sleepyhead. Breakfast is cookin' and you're still layin' in the bed."

"Well, if you ain't somethin'," Clint replied, rubbing the sleep out of his eyes. "When did you come back in to get dressed?"

"About two hours ago. You was sleepin' like a baby. I

went down to the washroom and cleaned up. And right now, I feel like I could eat half a buffalo. They got a nice outhouse, a two-seater, and that worked out real nice for me, because I was shipping outta both ends at the same time."

"I'm mighty glad you're feelin' so good this mornin'," Clint commented. "'Cause I was a little worried about you last night. I thought for a while there that I was gonna have to do the talkin' to these fellows from Springfield. And talkin' ain't my strong suit."

"Well, get your boots on and we'll go get us a big breakfast," Scofield said. "I mean your moccasins." Clint didn't wear boots. "We're supposed to meet those fellers at ten o'clock at the Henry House Hotel."

For their breakfast, they went to the same place they had eaten supper the night before, a tiny little establishment called Mama's Kitchen. The hotel they spent the night in was small and offered no dining room, but Mama's Kitchen was only a short walk away. They considered having breakfast at the Henry House but decided their dining room might be too fancy for a couple of trail-hardened adventurers like themselves. The food at Mama's was to their liking, as Scofield put it, and it was bound to be a helluva lot more reasonable in cost. So, after a leisurely breakfast, they returned to their hotel. It was time to go to the meeting with the two men from Springfield.

"Mr. Scofield?" John Zachary asked when they walked into the Henry House lobby. He had been standing near the front door, watching for the wagon guide. When Scofield pleaded guilty, Zachary introduced himself and they shook hands. "It's a pleasure to meet you in person, sir," Zachary said. Then he signaled a man standing near a side entrance and he immediately hurried over to join them. "This is Emmett Braxton, Emmett's the other party I wrote you about."

"Glad to meetcha," Scofield said. "This young feller with me is Clint Buchanan. He'll be ridin' scout on this crossin'."

"Mr. Zachary, Mr. Braxton," Clint said politely and stepped forward to shake their hands.

"Why don't we go over there where we can sit down and talk about this trek across the country," Braxton suggested, knowing there were a great many questions he and Zachary wanted to ask. They went across the parlor to a sitting area, and the meeting began. "To start with, John and I have definitely made the decision to make this journey. Right, John?"

"Absolutely," Zachary replied. "We're goin', for sure, and accordin' to your letter, you're gettin' ready to lead a wagon train out to Oregon Territory any day now."

"Well, sir," Scofield replied, "that's a fact. We've got some folks that are ready to go, waitin' on the prairie across the river. Some of 'em have been there for a week, but I'm just waitin' to give the grass a little time to grow. I set a date to leave on April the first and that's day after tomorrow. I'll be mighty happy to have you join our train, if you can get your wagons ready to roll by then." He paused to glance from Zachary to Braxton, trying to make a quick judgment of the seriousness of their intent. "Where are your wagons now? And your families, are they here in Independence?"

"Both families are packed up and ready to go," Braxton answered him. "They're parked down at the river, near the ferry slips. We were waitin' till we talked with you before we crossed over the river. So, I reckon we'll go ahead and cross over as soon as we leave here and join your wagons on the other side of the river."

Scofield had to chuckle. "I swear, I thought you were stayin' here in the hotel."

Zachary laughed with him. "No, I just suggested we meet here because it was the only hotel I knew the name of here in town."

Scofield laughed again and declared, "Me and Clint, here, will try to get you and your families out to Oregon as fast and as safely as we can. But you need to understand, this ain't no pleasure trip. There's gonna be hardships and maybe dangers we might have to face. But if a family's strong and willin' to make some sacrifices, there ain't no reason they can't make it. And what's waitin' for you on the other end of the journey is worth it. I sent you a list of everything you'll need to make it for four to six months. I hope you treated that list just like a Bible, especially the part about the wagons. On the route we're takin', a light farm wagon does the best job over the flat prairie land we'll be travelin'. And like I told you in my letter, my trains are with horses or mules. Lotta folks say oxen are better, they got stronger pull and they can go longer without water, and oxen are cheaper to buy than horses or mules. But on the route I'll be leadin' you on, horses do just fine, and there's plenty of water along the way. Oxen are too slow to suit me. Most trains that use oxen make about fifteen miles a day. That's the same as we'll make with our horses, maybe a little more. The difference is it'll take oxen all damn day and half the night to do it. We'll make our fifteen and stop at five o'clock in the afternoon for supper and rest. It'll make your journey a whole lot easier to take."

"You don't have to sell us on that. Emmett and I are both drivin' horses. How many wagons do you think you're gonna end up with?" Zachary asked.

"The same number I start out with," Scofield replied, then quickly chuckled to show he was joking. "Right now, I'll have twenty-seven wagons, counting you and Mr. Braxton. We might pick up a few more before we pull out day after tomorrow and we might not. But twenty-seven is a good manageable number. I've led trains of a hundred-and-fifty wagons, and I'd a heap druther go with a smaller number. I think you and your family will find it a lot more comfortable, too."

The meeting continued for quite some time until Zachary and Braxton ran out of questions. In the end, they shook hands with Scofield and Clint, and assured them they would be ready to join them on the day after tomorrow when the wagon train would roll out of Independence.

"Well, I expect John and I best get back to the wagons," Emmett declared. "Marcy and Sarah will be wantin' to get everything ready to travel."

Scofield and Clint walked them to the front door. "Seem like nice people," Clint commented to his uncle as they watched them depart.

"You'll find out for sure after they've been on that trail for a few weeks," Scofield replied.

Chapter 3

Scofield and Clint showed up that afternoon on the prairie where a couple of circles of wagons were in camp. Off to the side, they saw the two wagons belonging to Zachary and Braxton. "I'm tickled to see they've got the right kind of wagons and horses to pull 'em," Scofield said. "That's a good start. If they'd showed up with oxen pullin' them wagons, I'da told 'em they couldn't go with us. We'll go over and meet their families." Clint didn't bother to respond to the comment, knowing his uncle's dislike for the slow-moving oxen. This, in spite of the fact that a lot of wagon masters would argue that oxen were superior to both horses and mules when encountering rough spots in the trail. He wheeled the Palouse gelding and followed his uncle toward the new members of Scofield's train.

Standing next to his father, Johnny Zachary asked,

"Why did they park 'em in a circle like that, Papa? Are they afraid of an Indian attack this close to Independence?" Overhearing his question, his mother, also curious, looked to her husband for his answer.

Zachary couldn't help chuckling. "No, son, I don't reckon they're worried about Indians around here. I expect they're more concerned about corrallin' their stock, so they don't go wanderin' into town."

Scofield pulled his hat off and waved to acknowledge their presence, as he and Clint rode across the wide campground to join them. Emmett Braxton walked over to join John and his son. "Well, at least he knows we're here. Reckon he'll tell us if we're supposed to circle up," he said to Zachary.

"I reckon," Zachary answered. "But I don't see any sense in puttin' everybody to the trouble of movin' their wagons just for a couple of nights. I suppose we could go ahead and make our camp right where we set," he said, but made no move to do so.

"Maybe he's wantin' to see if we can circle two wagons," Emmett chortled.

"I see you got your wagons across the river all right," Scofield said as he and Clint pulled up before them. "I thought we'd come over and meet your families." He and Clint stepped down from the saddle as Marcy and Sarah walked over to meet them. "Clayton Scofield, ma'am," he said to Marcy as he shook her hand, then repeated the same to Sarah. "This young feller is my nephew, Clint Buchanan. He'll be scoutin' for us on the trip. We're right happy to have you with us." Clint nodded to each of the women and smiled politely. After the women introduced their children, Scofield continued his instructions. "First off, you might wanna move your wagons over by that circle of wagons over yonder on the other side of the clearin'. This one, here, ain't headin' for the same place we are and you might have to change your religion if you go with them."

"Why do you say that?" Marcy asked.

"'Cause they're Mormons," Scofield answered. "Ain't nothin' wrong with 'em. They're just a different religion. Wouldn't be no harm a-tall if you was to camp right here, but we've had a little change in our plans. Since you folks showed up ready to go today, we're gonna pull outta here in the mornin', instead of day after tomorrow. I figure we might as well get on the trail ahead of the Mormons. It'll be a little easier for you to start out in line, if you're camped over there with the rest of us. And maybe tonight you'll get to know some of the folks you're fixin' to spend the next few months with."

"Well, that certainly makes sense," Sarah said.

The Zacharys and the Braxtons were welcomed cordially by the other members of the train. Although some of the wagons had traveled a great distance just to get to the jumping off point in Independence, none of the party were experienced in traveling in a wagon train. Realizing that, there was a general sense of cordiality and cooperation. Scofield told them they would all be well indoctrinated in the military-like rules of the trail by the time the train reached the Kansas River crossing. He explained that by adhering to a strict daily routine, it would make the journey better for them as well as their animals. "We'll get started early in the mornin'. You'll hear my bugle at four o'clock every mornin'. That'll give you plenty of time to graze your horses and cow, if you brought one. Then you can pack up, eat breakfast, and hitch up the horses. You women can clean up your breakfast dishes while the men are hitchin' up. Then we'll be ready to get on the road by seven. We'll make one stop at noontime to eat and rest. Then we'll be back on the road till five o'clock when we'll camp for the night. You can have your supper, and afterward, you can enjoy your evenin'.

"One of our members, Doc Meadows, plays a fiddle," Scofield continued. "Another one, Buck Carrey, plays the banjo, and there are several others who play guitars. So if it's like every other train we've led, there'll be singing and dancing almost every night, helping the journey seem more pleasurable." While Scofield felt it important to keep a positive spirit, he felt it his responsibility to remind them that they could expect harsher conditions ahead, the farther west they traveled. "After we leave Fort Laramie, the trail will gradually get a little harder as we travel up toward the Continental Divide, but by that time, you'll all be experienced wagoners," he said.

As they had been warned, the camp was awakened the next morning by several long raucous blasts from Scofield's bugle. "What the hell is that?" John Zachary exclaimed, sitting suddenly upright in his blanket. Then remembering the warning from the night before, he looked at his pocket watch. "Four o'clock," he muttered. "Time to get up." He had expected to hear a bugler playing reveille but realized now that Scofield couldn't blow a bugle call. He could only make an un-Godly noise with his bugle. It was effective enough to save him the trouble of arousing his family. They were all awake. He got

Johnny out of his bed and took him with him to round up the horses and the cow, since they had been allowed to graze during the night. Marcy, with Sarah's help, cooked a breakfast of bacon and corn porridge. Afterward, the women washed the dishes and pans while the men took down the tents and packed them in the wagons. Everyone had a job that would soon become routine for them after a short time on the trail. When it was time, Scofield announced the order of travel and rode back and forth along the line on his black Morgan gelding to ensure the proper order of the column. The wagons belonging to the Zacharys and the Braxtons were both somewhere in the middle of the column. The wagons pulled out for the start of the long journey west at seven o'clock on the nose.

The first few days on the trail gave the new travelers time to adjust to the wagon train. And by the time they were approaching the Kansas River Crossing, they felt they were old hands at it. Riding far in advance of the train, Clint Buchanan scouted the crossing to determine its condition since he and Scofield had last crossed at that point. It was a narrow section of the river with gentle sloping banks on both sides that made it easier to enter the water and for the horses to pull the wagons out of the water on the opposite bank. There was sand on the far side, but no quicksand, and the deepest part of the river was a twelve-foot channel that curved around close to the other side. Satisfied that the sandy bank showed no signs of deteriorating, Clint went back to report to Scofield with his recommendation to cross the river there again. "Nothing's changed since we were last here," he told his uncle. "I checked the deep part and it's still about twelve feet across. The horses will have to swim when they hit that, but they'll find solid footin' again almost as soon as they start swimming. And the wagons won't have to float but a minute or two before their front wheels touch the bottom again. The tide ain't too strong, and if we head 'em across at an angle, I don't think it'll bother the wagons for that little bit of time they'll be floatin'."

"That sounds good enough to me," Scofield responded. "We'll cross over in the mornin'. I'll tell 'em after supper."

When supper was finished and the women went to work cleaning up the pots and pans, the men congregated near the fire to smoke and talk. Buck Carrey got his banjo from the wagon and started picking a lively tune. A couple of the men limbered up their guitars and tuned up with Buck's banjo. That was enough to cause Doc Meadows to fetch his fiddle, and pretty soon, the chilly evening air was filled with the old tunes that everybody was familiar with. And those who could dance were inspired to do so.

When Marcy Zachary finished the dishes, she came to find John where he was sitting with Emmett and Lonnie James, a big bull-like man with whom they had become quite friendly. Lonnie and Susie, a tiny woman, had a boy Johnny Zachary's age and he soon became a pal to him and Skeeter Braxton. "Listen to that music," Marcy said when she walked up to join the men. "Can't you feel that music?" She danced a few steps with an imaginary partner in time with the music. When it failed to motivate her husband to join her, she pestered, "Come on, John, you used to like to dance with me."

"That was back before I found out I had two left feet,"

John replied and drew a chuckle from Lonnie and Emmett. "I found out I look a lot more graceful settin' down and puffin' on my pipe."

They were joined by Susie James then. In time to hear John's reply, she said, "That's the same thing Lonnie used to say. Then he'd get out there and show off what he calls his fancy steps. Trouble is, as big as he is, he'll crush you if you ain't quick enough to stay outta his way."

"As tiny as you are," Marcy commented, "that could be fatal for you."

"Don't let her fool you," Lonnie responded. "She's tough as a female badger." He looked at her fondly. "Besides, she don't fight fair."

"You waited too long now," Susie told him and nodded toward the other side of the circle of wagons. "Pat Shephard's showin' out now." Pat Shephard, a tall, bone-thin man with a full head of white hair to match his mustache, did indeed know all the fancy steps and he delighted in entertaining the folks with his buck-and-wing.

"That settles it for me," Lonnie declared. "I ain't gonna get out there with Pat puttin' on a show."

"That goes for me, too," John said to Marcy. "Wait till the boys play a slow one and then we'll take a spin."

"I'm holding you to that promise," Marcy said. "And I've got all these witnesses that heard you say it."

As the evening wore on, they did dance one slow dance, as did Emmett and Sarah, but as usual, the men retired back to the fire after one dance. After that, the women danced together, with Sarah Braxton leading. Before folks started to retire to their sleeping arrangements, Scofield interrupted the music to make his announcement.

"I wanna remind you that you'll hear my bugle blast at

four o'clock in the mornin'. Get your breakfast cleared away and the horses hitched up, ready to roll at seven o'clock. Right at the start, we're gonna make our first river crossin'. If you ain't done it already, you need to use that wax I gave you to seal up any cracks in your wagon boxes. The Kansas has got some deep water, but Clint has scouted out the crossin' and he says the channel ain't very wide, where we'll be crossin'. So your wagon won't be floatin' very far before the wheels find bottom again. We'll get you all across safe and sound. Then we'll be headin' on our way again. So, go on back to your dancin' and I'll give you a wake-up in the mornin'."

His statement caused a pronounced pause in the entertainment for only a short time before the fiddle cranked up again. Everyone had known they would have to make a lot of river crossings on their journey. But now, they were aware that their first major crossing was upon them with the coming of morning. And there was some concern about the floating capability of their two-thousand-pound wagons.

Morning came, announced by the blast of Clayton Scofield's bugle at four A.M. precisely. The order of travel was kept by Scofield, changing daily, so that no wagon had to eat all the dust every day. Of course, Scofield's was the lead wagon every day, since he was the wagon master. Spud Williams, a round little man with a completely bald head, drove Scofield's wagon, although Scofield took the reins, himself, frequently. Spud also acted as Scofield's cook, having driven a chuckwagon for many years before going to work for Scofield. On this morning,

John Zachary's wagon was third in line and Emmett Braxton's was twentieth. A rope line was strung diagonally across the river for the wagons to follow as a precaution. The tide was not strong, but Scofield thought it better to angle against the tide, instead of subjecting the wagons to its full force. The tide proved to be of little consequence, especially for the first wagons to cross. Since the deepest part was not that wide, Clint had suggested hooking up two teams of horses to each wagon. The one extra team would have to swim when deep water was reached, but the horses behind them would still be on solid footing on the bottom. When they started to swim, the lead team would be on solid footing again. And when the wagons started to float, all the horses had reached footing on the other side and were able to pull the wagon for the short distance it was actually floating onto firm bottom. The one extra team of horses was enough to make the crossing trouble-free for the most part.

It was a little more difficult for the last wagons to cross, however, starting with wagon number twenty. Eleven-year-old Skeeter Braxton elected to swim across to lighten the load, because this was what Johnny Zachary had chosen to do. Since his mother was a woman who prided herself in handling the reins of their team of horses, she convinced Emmett to swim across with Skeeter and let her drive the wagon. "That'll lighten the load on the wagon with your big carcass out of it," Sarah told him, only halfway joking.

Emmett and his son followed their wagon into the water, holding onto the back of the wagon box as they waded through the shallow part until the horses had to swim. Skeeter's seven-year-old sister, Lou Ann, went across in the wagon, since she couldn't swim. She took great delight in standing in the back of the wagon to taunt her brother in the chilly water.

"Watch out, now," Emmett cautioned Skeeter. "She oughta start floatin' any minute and she'll shift downstream a little." This was what had occurred with every wagon preceding theirs. What no one had foreseen, however, was the gradual softening of the sandy bottom on the other bank, due to the constant plowing of the horses' hooves before them. The result of this was the sudden collapsing of that sandy bottom with no solid footing for the horses. This forced the horses to continue swimming with no leverage to pull the wagon after them. When the front wheels mired down in the shifting sandy bottom, the tide swept the floating wagon sideways and shifted it downstream, threatening to overturn.

Emmett's natural reaction was to try to grab the wagon to save his family's belongings, but his first concern was to pull Skeeter upstream from the wagon to save the boy from being caught under the two-thousand-pound wagon. He was able to clutch Skeeter's collar and pull him clear of the wallowing wagon while his wife continued to encourage the horses to pull. Much to Emmett's relief, the wagon managed to remain right-side-up when one of the rear wheels lodged against the bank. "Thank the Lord!" He fairly shouted, having seen what he thought was going to be the loss of their family possessions. Some of the men were already rigging up a third team of horses to pull the wagon up the bank.

It was only after the chaos of almost losing the wagon, that Sarah Braxton had time to look back in the wagon to see if Lou Ann was all right. The seven-year-old was not there! In the midst of the excitement, no one had noticed when the little girl fell into the river. "Lou Ann!" Sarah screamed and jumped from the wagon seat into the shallow water, thrashing about in a desperate attempt to find her daughter. With no sign of the little girl anywhere, she waded out toward the middle of the river where Emmett was already searching the deep water. Men and boys from the other wagons came running to join the search. All of them in too great a panic to notice the horse coming toward the wagon from the bank above.

"Does this belong to anybody up here?" Clint Buchanan asked.

Sarah looked up to see the young scout astride his Palouse gelding with a thoroughly soaked Lou Ann sitting in the saddle in front of him. "Lou Ann!" Sarah exclaimed, this time in sheer relief. She immediately made her way back to shore.

"I found her bobbin' in the river about fifty yards downstream," Clint said. "I thought she was a muskrat at first," he joked, "but she didn't try to run when I went after her."

Emmett and Skeeter had managed to hurry out of the water by then to join Sarah. Emmett held his arms up toward Lou Ann. "Here, I'll take her now. Come to Papa, darlin'. You're all right now." Lou Ann came to him, almost reluctantly. Looking up at the smiling young man then, Emmett said, "Mr. Buchanan, my family owes you a great deal for this. Don't know if it's possible to repay you. Lou Ann can't swim a lick. If you hadn't come along . . ."

"She's a fighter," Clint interrupted. "She was flailin' away so strong, I expect she mighta taught herself how to swim, if I hadn't picked her up."

Holding his daughter close in his arms, Emmett laughed and declared, "She takes after her mama, I reckon."

"When we get to wherever Mr. Scofield says we're gonna camp tonight," Sarah announced, "I'd be pleased if you would take supper with us tonight, since we didn't lose anything in the river today." She reached up and gave Lou Ann a playful tug of her wet hair. "Including this mischief."

"That's mighty kind of you, Mrs. Braxton," Clint replied. "But I'd hate to have you waste your provisions on me."

"I insist," Sarah informed him. "We'll worry about running out of provisions when we get to Fort Laramie. Right, Emmett?"

"That's right," Emmett responded. "You oughta come on and eat with us. It's best not to argue with the Missus."

"Well, in that case, it'd be my pleasure to take supper with the Braxtons tonight," Clint accepted. "Now, I expect I'd best go back across the river to see if I can help the rest of the wagons across. Since the bank has give way on this side, I expect we're gonna have to raft the others over." He left them then to help prepare the seven wagons still on the other side of the river.

When he crossed over, he found Scofield in the process of explaining to the remaining families how they were to go about making rafts out of their wagons. "We're lucky there's plenty of good timber in this spot, so's we can choose the right size to fit your wagons and we'll just go ahead and float 'em all the way over. And we ought not have any more trouble like Braxton's wagon. It'll cost us a little time, but we'll get everybody across and get back on the trail."

Saws and axes were immediately in action as the men went to work cutting the trees that Scofield selected. Clint went to work with them and soon he and Scofield were showing them how to fit them to their wagons. Still with some skepticism, the others watched as the first wagon started across the river. A cheer went up on both sides of the river when it floated safely across to the other side. Then the rest of them were anxious to be next. With new confidence that nothing could stop them, they set out again, nourishing their visions of the fertile land of the Willamette Valley waiting for their plows.

Chapter 4

The wagons continued west with no major problems for animals or emigrants for the next three weeks. Some wagons experienced minor wheel problems, usually loose rims when the wooden wheels shrank. But there was promise for help within the next day or so when the train would reach Fort Kearny. As they had hoped, the grass was growing with the spring rains. Much of the present trail followed along Little Blue River, so there was plenty of water at each campsite. Fort Kearny would provide the opportunity to replenish supplies that were running low, as well. And according to Scofield, the fort was well-stocked on stores of all kinds and by government mandate, it was sold at special low prices to help the emigrants on the trail. Everyone was looking forward to reaching the fort.

Three members of the train who had become fast

friends were talking about Fort Kearny with great interest, but not for the same reason their mothers and fathers did. "You know they built the fort to protect us from the Indians," Skeeter Braxton insisted, as the three young boys walked along beside the Zachary wagon.

"What Indians?" Johnny Zachary asked. "We ain't seen no Indians."

"That's right," Sammy James said. "We ain't seen no Indians. Where are they?"

"I don't know," Skeeter replied. "But I hear tell they're watchin' us all the time. They stay hid, so you can't see 'em, then they attack when you don't expect 'em to."

"Who told you all that?" Marcy Zachary asked, walking a few yards in front of them.

"Lemuel Blue," Skeeter answered. "He said they might be waitin' till we're all asleep one night."

"Pshaw," Marcy responded. "You boys pay no attention to what Lemuel Blue says. I'm sure your mamas would tell you to stay away from Lemuel. He's liable to tell you anything." She turned to point her finger at her son. "And you mind what I'm saying, Johnny." She was not at all comfortable with the thought that he had anything to do with Fancy Wallace's hired man. A large brute of a man, he was almost a mute in the presence of other adults, keeping to himself except whenever Fancy called out for him to do some chore. Even in the evenings after supper when everyone was enjoying the social time, he would watch the singing and dancing from his bedroll under Fancy's wagon. Marcy supposed the only reason he talked to the young boys was perhaps because his brain had developed no further than their age. "Anyway," she continued, "the Indians who live here are peaceful Indians. They're not going to attack anybody."

She turned her attention back to her other child, Mary, ten, who was walking along in front of her. She cautioned her again not to walk too close to the horses, but her mind drifted back to Lemuel Blue. Fancy Wallace, alone, was enough mystery to wonder about. An outright brazen woman, she had no husband and drove her wagon herself. She employed Lemuel Blue to do the heavy work and to take care of her horses. That was the extent of his obligations, as far as the other folks in the wagon train could determine. One woman alone, Fancy didn't use a tent when they camped. She slept in her wagon. Lemuel slept under the wagon. John told her that, even in the middle of the night, the men on guard duty had never seen Lemuel's bedroll under the wagon empty. So, there was no speculation that Fancy called on him to take care of any personal desires she might have. Judging by the few words that had passed between Fancy and herself, Marcy had decided the woman cared not a fig about anyone's opinion of her. Of uncertain age, she walked with a swagger and talked in a confident manner. When Marcy and John joined the wagon train in Independence, John questioned Scofield on the advisability of a woman alone driving a wagon across the country. Scofield assured him that Fancy was up to the challenge and would offer no hindrance to the progress of the train. He also reminded John that Fancy was not alone, since she hired Lemuel to do her heavy lifting. John told Marcy later that he got the impression that Scofield had known Fancy for quite some time before this excursion.

"I've watched her and Lemuel unload that wagon she's drivin'," he had commented to Scofield. "And she ain't haulin' the first piece of farm equipment that I could see. You figure she's gonna buy it all after we get out there?"

His question had brought forth a laugh from Scofield. "I believe that's her plan, all right. She'll be buyin' what she needs, but she won't be spendin' any money on plows or hoes. She'll be lookin' into buildin' a saloon. She was in that business ever since I've run into her—had a partnership with some English fellow, and I think Fancy was the one really runnin' the business. I was surprised when she contacted me about goin' west with me. She said she wanted to be one of the first to open a good saloon out there."

After John had told her about that, Marcy had a better understanding of the woman's tendency to get along with the men better than their wives. She was still a little puzzled about Lemuel's place in the picture. She could understand his usefulness working a farm. But he seemed too slow-witted to function in any business that required him to meet the public. In view of that, she couldn't help feeling a bit sorry for the dull young man, for it seemed likely he would be out of a job as soon as they reached Oregon. And then what would he do? She couldn't imagine he had anything to offer in the running of a saloon. That was as far as her thoughts of Lemuel Blue went for the moment, distracted then by the sight of Clint Buchanan's spotted horse approaching the lead wagon. She could guess by his gestures as he talked to Scofield, that he had selected a good spot to camp for the night. *What an inspiring figure he strikes*, she found herself thinking, *sitting tall and handsome on that big horse he rides*. A strange-looking horse, John said it was called a Palouse because it was bred by the Nez Perce near the Palouse

River. She looked quickly away then, as if someone might read her admiring thoughts. *Oh, to be that young again,* she thought, shaking her head. She walked up beside the wagon seat then to talk to her husband. "Looks like Scofield is getting ready to call it a day."

"Yeah," her husband replied, "and it ain't gonna be too soon to suit me. I'm needin' to head for the bushes just as soon as we get unhitched. Blamed if I don't think that cornmeal we brought has gone bad."

"I don't think so," she replied. "It looked fine to me."

"Somethin' we ate at noontime has got my bowels in an uproar," he insisted.

Thank you, dear, for bringing my romantic fantasies back to earth, she thought. Like young Clint Buchanan, her husband was also dashing. *The only difference is John is usually dashing for the bushes to ease his pains,* she told herself. She immediately felt guilty. *I ain't exactly the shy little girl he married, either, I reckon.*

After a few minutes more, Clint wheeled his horse away from Scofield's wagon and rode back down the line of wagons following to let them know they were going to circle the wagons for the night. When he reached the Zacharys' wagon, he wheeled the big gelding around to keep in stride with the wagon while he delivered his message. "'Bout a mile ahead, Mr. Zachary, we'll circle 'em up. There's good grass and water."

"I'm ready, Clint," Zachary replied. "Won't be a minute too soon. I hope there's some bushes nearby." He was not in a position to see his wife cringe when she heard his comment to the young scout.

Clint responded with a knowing smile. "Yes, sir, there's plenty of bushes. Just remember to go downstream." He reined his horse to a stop, then wheeled it again to inform the next wagon.

"I declare, John, did you have to tell him that?" Marcy complained when Clint was gone. "I doubt he's interested in your bodily functions."

Puzzled to think she would care what he said to Clint, he replied, "Well, I'm sure he's had occasion to feel the same way."

"Maybe so, but I expect he's got manners enough not to come telling us about it," she said.

"Climb aboard, old girl," he said. "Your feet must be sore and it's makin' you cranky."

"According to Clint, it ain't but another mile, so I might as well keep walking with the kids." When they had started on this journey, she hadn't planned on walking clear across the country, but it seemed now that she might. The only springs on their wagon were the ones under the driver's seat. The constant bumpy ride in the wagon box was downright uncomfortable, and she was soon driven to walking, as was everyone else in the other wagons. Walking served another purpose, as well. It lightened the load for the horses. And there was no trouble keeping up, for the wagon traveled at a man's walking pace. It was thought to be generally better for the children for certain.

After supper that night, when many of the folks began to gather for the usual social hour, Scofield announced that they would strike the Platte River the next day and would be camping at Fort Kearny that night. His announcement was met with cheers of enthusiasm and a lively reel by Doc Meadows on the fiddle, enough to entice Pat Shephard to set his feet to the rhythm of the instrument. The stage was his alone for a few minutes until Marcy Zachary pleaded, "Come on, John, let's show 'em how it's done in Springfield."

"Not me," John responded, "not with ol' rubber legs out there showin' off. Lonnie's the one who says he can dance. Take him out there, if Susie will let him go."

"You're welcome to him," Susie volunteered, "but you're goin' at your own risk."

"That's just what Pat Shephard wants," Lonnie said. "I hate to pass up the invitation, Marcy, but I ain't ready to get out there so he can make a fool outta me."

"Ah, come on," Marcy begged. "Nobody? Everybody afraid to take on big bad Pat Shephard for champion dancer of the wagon train? I reckon I'll have to challenge him by myself." She started moving slowly toward the bony white-haired man in the center of the circle, performing a little two-step creation of her own in time with the fiddle. Pat looked up and saw her. He grinned, raised his arm in the air, and motioned her on. Accepting the challenge, Marcy grabbed her skirt in each hand and raised it almost up to her knees, so she could better show off her steps. Pat howled like a wolf, kicked it up to another gear, and slowly advanced toward her. And the duel was on, much to the delight of the folks gathered there. Even John found himself grinning and clapping for the performance. Not to be left out, Buck Carrey broke out his banjo and fell in with Doc's fiddle.

"How 'bout you, young fellow?" Susie James asked when Clint Buchanan stopped to watch the dancing. "I'll bet you could show that old pair a step or two." She, along with Marcy and Sarah, had discussed the almost graceful way the tall young scout moved, both on his feet and in the saddle.

"Ah, no, ma'am," Clint replied. "I never was much for dancin'. I'll leave that to Mr. Shephard. He's doin' a pretty good job of it."

"I'll bet you'd be good at it," Susie insisted. "You oughta give it a try. I can show you a few steps, same as I taught Lonnie. If he can do it, you surely oughta be able to." She looked at Sarah and laughed. "Teachin' Lonnie was more like teachin' a mule to dance."

"I reckon not," Clint responded. "Thanks just the same. I'd best see about my horse." He tipped his hat and walked toward the river.

"You sure scared him away," Sarah said to Susie, causing them both to chuckle. "Won't do you any good flirtin' with him, anyway," Sarah informed her. "My daughter has already told me she's gonna marry Clint just as soon as she's old enough. She decided that the day he pulled her out of the Kansas River. So, I reckon all the women can stop eyeballin' our fine Mr. Clint Buchanan."

"Oh, fiddle, Sarah," Susie charged. "You're always spoiling our fantasies. Who are we gonna talk about now? There aren't that many young men on this train." She paused to giggle. "And I already know all I wanna know about the old men."

That remark caused a spontaneous giggle, loud enough so it was overheard by their husbands sitting several yards away. "What are you old hens cacklin' about over there?" Lonnie James asked.

"Oh, cookin' and raisin' young'uns and such," his wife answered him. "Nothin' you boys would be interested in."

Not ready to abandon the subject, Sarah remarked, tongue in cheek, "'Course there's always Lemuel Blue. He ain't got a wife and Fancy Wallace ain't usin' him for nothing but hitchin' up her horses."

"Bite your tongue, girl!" Susie exclaimed. "That man has got a sickness between his ears. Marcy told me she already had to tell the young'uns to leave Mr. Blue alone. He's been fillin' their heads with stories about the Indians waitin' to attack us. Besides, how do you know he ain't doin' other things for Miss Fancy Wallace when nobody's lookin'?"

"'Cause if he is, Fancy ain't as particular as she lets on," Sarah answered. "There's somethin' funny about his eyes. They're too close together, or something. And you ever notice he won't look straight at you. Just sorta turns his head to the side."

"I must notta talked to him as much as you have," Susie remarked but didn't continue to tease because the music stopped, and Pat Shephard led a beaming Marcy back to her husband.

"Let me return your lovely lady back to you, John," Pat said gallantly. "I must say, I had to work hard to keep up with her." He turned toward Marcy again and said, "That was a real pleasure. Thank you, ma'am. And thank you, sir."

"You're welcome," John replied. "I'll cool her down and water her, then I'll give her a portion of oats and she oughta be ready to hitch up in the mornin'."

Pat hesitated, not certain if John was japing him or Marcy, so he just said, "You folks have a good evenin'," then turned and walked back to the other side of the circle.

"If I had a stick, I'd give you a lick with it," Marcy scolded him. "That poor ol' man doesn't know you well enough to tell when you're serious and when you're cuttin' the fool."

Amused spectators, Emmett and Lonnie enjoyed John's

comeuppance for teasing the dancers. "It's a good thing you've already et supper," Lonnie said. "Else, you might notta got any tonight."

"It ain't a sure thing he'll get any breakfast in the mornin'," Marcy threatened. "Pat's such a nice old man. He's not used to puttin' up with roughnecks like you three buzzards."

"Well, he'd best get used to it," John said, serious now, "or this country will eat him up."

"I reckon there's a good chance it'll eat us all up," Lonnie remarked.

"Looks like we caught up with the folks raisin' all that dust we been ridin' through," Junior Fry saw fit to comment upon catching first sight of the wagons ahead of them. "I figured we was about to catch 'em 'cause it was gettin' thicker." He waited for his partner to comment, and when he didn't, he questioned, "We gonna take a wide swing around 'em?"

"Hell, yeah," Hamp Evans managed to reply, although it irritated him that his partner forced him to speak. It pained him greatly to try to talk and Junior should know they'd ride around the wagons, rather than riding right up the middle of them. With his broken jaw clamped shut, he grunted and pointed to the north, since what breeze there was came from that direction. He turned the buckskin gelding's head in that direction and grimaced as the horse took an unanticipated hop over a deep rut. Hamp had gone to the doctor in Independence, and the doctor did what he could for him. But he couldn't stay there with his jaw wrapped shut for no telling how long, waiting for it to mend. He and Junior were still two days behind the rest of the boys that took that herd back east. The doctor gave him some laudanum for the pain and told him, if he couldn't stay till it healed, he'd just have to learn to keep his mouth clamped shut all the time. He supposed he should be grateful that Junior stayed with him, but the slow-witted cowpuncher was quick to get on his nerves.

"I expect these folks will be at Fort Kearny tonight," Junior speculated. "They ain't got that far to go."

Hamp agreed with him, but he didn't bother to give him a grunt. His thoughts were centered upon reaching the fort himself. He'd had a long day in the saddle, so his horse was ready for a rest and he needed to find something to put in his stomach that didn't require chewing. He hadn't had anything but water and some coffee since starting out that morning, and the growling in his stomach increased with each mile they covered. Leo Stern's road ranch was one mile beyond Fort Kearny, and he figured he might persuade Lulu Belle to make him some soup or broth to quiet the hungry jackals in his stomach. He scowled when he thought about the misery that big drunk in the Gateway Saloon had caused him. He was only sorry he had not made sure he was dead. The fellow that carried him out of the saloon said he was dead. At the time, he chose to believe him because it was difficult to think straight, with his jaw shooting sharp pains through the top of his head. After it was too late, when Junior came looking for him, only then did he think to wonder why the old drunk was dead. What killed him? Thinking about it now threatened to drive him into a rage. He glanced over to cast an accusing eye at Junior. *If you'd been back from that whorehouse when you said you would . . .* he thought.

Chapter 5

It was called “the Gateway to the Great Plains.” Fort Kearny had been built in 1848 to provide protection for travelers on the western trails. The fort was built here where Scofield’s wagon train left the Little Blue River and struck the Platte, a starting point for all the various western trails across the plains. The Oregon, the Mormon, the Bozeman, and other trails followed the Platte River Valley directly west before reaching their various break-off points. The members of Scofield’s train were excited about reaching Fort Kearny because it seemed to signify proof that they were veteran travelers, well on their way to Oregon. It would also provide an opportunity to replenish basic supplies that they may have underestimated. And there were blacksmiths and tradesmen to help with repairs to their wagons. Scofield announced that they would go into camp a short distance from the fort where a creek flowed into the river and they would stay over for an extra day. It was the favorite camping spot for travelers because the creek water was sweet. And they were early enough in the season to find the grass plentiful. This was where the first-time travelers on this trail found out about the poor quality of the Platte River water. It was silty and had a poor taste. They would be using it only when other water from streams or creeks was not available. "The Platte and North Platte, which we'll be followin', are wide and shallow, and muddy," Scofield told them. "You ain't gonna see no boats travelin' up the Platte. There's too many little islands and crooked spots where it'll go plumb shallow—so much so that a canoe will go a-ground. Don't get me wrong. It ain't gonna kill ya if you have to drink or cook with water outta the river. It just ain't gonna taste good. We'll be able to find good water most every place we camp, though, 'cause there's plenty of streams feedin' into the river."

"Damn," John Zachary swore. "That don't sound too good, does it?" He smiled at Marcy and added, "Maybe you can get some fresh cornmeal at the fort."

"If I do, do you want me to tell Clint Buchanan about it?" Marcy taunted sarcastically.

"What would you wanna tell him for?" John asked, puzzled by the question.

She just shook her head in disbelief that he had already forgotten. "No reason, I guess. And there's nothing wrong with my cornmeal, but there are some things we need at the post trader's."

"We'll take the wagon over," John said. "I know the kids wanna see the soldiers. Emmett and Sarah are gonna go with us. No sense in takin' two wagons."

Not everyone wanted to visit the fort that first night, preferring to wait until the next day, so those remaining in camp agreed to keep an eye on the camp for their neighbors.

After the camp was settled in for suppertime, Scofield walked back to his wagon to find his nephew busy roasting a couple of strips of smoked venison over a small campfire. Clint looked up when Scofield appeared around the back of the wagon. "Didn't know when you were thinkin' about gettin' some supper," Clint said. "Spud said you told him he didn't have to cook anything for supper tonight. But I was kinda hungry, so I thought I'd roast a couple of strips of meat to keep from faintin' while I was waitin' to find out when you're ready to go." They generally ate together at Leo's Road Ranch, but oftentimes the wagon master was invited to eat with one of the families. And since he had gotten them safely to Fort Kearny, Clint thought his uncle might have an invitation. "Thought you might be invited to supper with one of the families, and I'd have to go to the hog ranch by myself."

"Matter of fact, I had an invite to take supper with Pat and Ginny Shephard," Scofield said. "I thanked 'em just the same, and told 'em I had to go to a meetin' over at the fort tonight. Said it was just a routine report to the army that all wagon masters had to make."

"Is that so?" Clint replied. "You turned down a regular home-cooked supper?"

"Hell," Scofield responded, "you ain't took a good look at Pat Shephard, have you? Skinny as a hoe handle, it don't look like that woman feeds him enough to keep a turtle alive. I thought I'd go over to Leo Stern's place and get some beans and biscuits like ol' Lulu Belle cooks up. Might even take a drink of likker, if I feel like it. Ain't many places on this trail where a man can get vittles like Lulu Belle cooks up. You're goin' with me, ain't you? You ain't gonna get fat on that skinny little strip of deer meat."

"Well, I was gonna cook up some hardtack, too," Clint replied with a chuckle. "But I reckon I could save that for breakfast." Actually, he would have been disappointed if he didn't hear his uncle say he planned to go to Stern's for supper, but he would have gone by himself regardless. It was worth the trip to Fort Kearny just to eat at Lulu Belle's table. He pulled his venison off the fire and offered Scofield one of the strips. "Here," he said, "something to hold you till we get to Stern's. We walkin' or ridin'?"

"Hell, let's walk," Scofield answered. "It ain't even a mile from here, and it'll give me a chance to stretch my legs. Settin' in that wagon seat too much, it's a wonder my legs don't shrivel up and fall off. You set in a saddle all day, you could use a walk, yourself."

"You're startin' to sound a helluva lot like an uncle," Clint said with a chuckle. "As long as Biscuit has four good legs under him, I don't need mine." He put his fire out and they went to check with whoever had guard duty that evening to watch the horses.

"How'd you come to name that Palouse Biscuit?" Scofield asked, as they walked toward the horses grazing near the creek.

"I was gonna give him an Indian name, considerin' the Nez Perce bred him, but I couldn't think of a good one that fit him. Matter of fact, this is the place where Biscuit got his official name, when we stopped here last year. We took supper at Leo's, but if you remember, we rode the horses over there. When we came out to go back to camp, I stole a biscuit off a fresh platter of 'em when we were walkin' out the door. When I was untyin' Biscuit's reins, he started sniffin' around to see what I was holdin' in my hand, so I opened it so he could see. Before I could close my hand again, he stole my biscuit—just like that, it was gone. So, I started callin' him Biscuit. He didn't seem to care what I called him, so that's what the two of us settled on."

It was a nice night for a walk as they followed an often-used path up the creek toward Leo Stern's Road Ranch, as he called it. It was called a Hog Ranch by the soldiers stationed at the fort, since there were half a dozen soiled doves who resided there as well. A large woman, significantly past her youth, by the name of Lulu Belle, was thought to be the acting mother-hen for the younger "working girls" at the ranch. Clint had never heard anyone use Lulu Belle's last name, so he had assumed she was Leo's wife until his uncle told him she was definitely not. Most likely Scofield knew her last name, but Clint wasn't interested to the point where he would ask. Clint's only interest in the road ranch was Lulu Belle's cooking. She took great pride in it and was generous with her servings.

The hog ranch appeared to be fairly humming with business on this early April evening. And judging by the horses tied at the hitching rail, Leo's customers were not all soldiers from the fort. There was a side door that led directly to the saloon, but Clint and Scofield went to the front door, which led into the parlor. Scofield liked to look at the merchandise, as he passed through it, even though Clint had never known his uncle to purchase any of it. They paused just inside the front door to look the room over before passing through to go to the bar room. All of the doves were not engaged with a customer upstairs, and the two who were sitting in the parlor took a moment to check Clint and Scofield out. Clint was young enough and fair enough to warrant a longer look as well as a friendly smile. "We're just here for supper, ladies," Scofield said and headed for the barroom door.

"Ladies," Clint nodded politely and followed Scofield.

"Damn," one of the women said to the other one, "if he'da played his cards right, I mighta paid him." Then she yelled after him, "Hey, if you're lookin' for a wife, I ain't married." Both women cackled with laughter over that.

Inside, they paused while Scofield decided if he would have his drink of whiskey before or after supper. Clint didn't care one way or the other, so he left it up to his uncle. They paused before the bar long enough for the bartender to recognize them. "Well, howdy, Scofield," Floyd Trainer called out. "You and Clint makin' another run west?"

"Howdy, Floyd," Scofield replied. "As a matter of fact, we are." Floyd's greeting was enough to help Scofield decide. "Pour us a little drink of whiskey before we go get us some supper." He turned toward Clint then. "That all right with you, partner?" Clint said that it was, but one was all he wanted. "That goes for me, too,"

Scofield said. He watched while Floyd poured the two shots, picked up his glass right away, and said, "Here's to good weather and peaceful Injuns."

"Amen," Clint said and raised his glass, but instead of clinking his glass against Scofield's, he whipped his arm around and threw the glass as hard as he could at the man behind Scofield. It had happened too fast to think, but his aim was good enough to hit the man in the face with the glass. It caused him to pull the trigger on the pistol in his hand, sending a .44 slug into the floor. The gunman released a sharp yelp of pain when the whiskey stung his eyes and he tried to cock his pistol and raise it again, but he could not move fast enough to prevent Clint from charging into him and taking him to the floor.

Alerted to what was happening then, Scofield knelt down on the gunman's arm, pinning it to the floor. Then he wrenched the pistol from his hand and turned it on him. "All right, Clint, let him up and we'll see what's ailin' him." Then, getting his first good look at his would-be assassin, he blurted, "Well, I'll be damned . . ." Holding Hamp Evans' gun in one hand, he grabbed a handful of Hamp's shirt and pulled the hapless man to his feet with the other. "You just don't ever learn, do ya? You ain't only the world's worst card cheat, you can't even shoot a man in the back." He glanced at Clint. "You remember this young gentleman, don't you, Clint?"

"I do now," Clint answered. "I didn't get a good look at him when I saw him out on the porch at the Gateway Saloon." He took a good look at him then and realized why he wasn't saying anything. He couldn't, but he was saying plenty with his eyes. "I don't think he likes you. Whaddaya gonna do with him?"

"I don't know. I can't let him keep runnin' around waitin' to take a shot at me." He hesitated then when Leo Stern came in from a back room to investigate the shot he had heard. "Here's a man who might know what to do with him. Leo, you reckon the army would send some soldiers over here to put this little back-shooter in the guardhouse?"

"The army ain't gonna bother with trouble we've got unless there's soldiers involved in the trouble. And if that was the case, what they'd most likely do is close me down," Leo said. "You oughta know that, Scofield. Hell, you're the judge and jury for any crimes that happen on that wagon train. It's up to you what you're gonna do with him."

"Yeah, I reckon you're right," Scofield admitted. "I reckon it's gonna be up to me to take care of him." He cocked the hammer back on Hamp's pistol. "Easiest thing would be to execute him with this here weapon he was fixin' to use on me. Most times, we give 'em a trial then hang 'em, but I don't wanna spend a lot of time havin' a trial for him before we hang him. Gunshot in the head is a lot easier. Better for you, too, back-shooter. Be over real quick." He paused then when he heard a noise from the prisoner. "What?" Scofield blurted. "What are you tryin' to say?"

Not sure if he was going to face the grim reaper of wayward souls within the next few minutes or not, Hamp Evans felt helpless to save himself. His only hope of salvation was for Junior to come downstairs in time to put a bullet in this big blowhard's back. And prospects of that happening didn't seem likely when that gunshot didn't rouse him from his lady-friend's arms. So he tried the first thing he could think of. The problem was trying to speak so they could understand what he was saying. He slurred his statement through his tightly clenched teeth, but Scofield pretended that he still could not understand him and bent down closer to hear. Hamp forced his teeth a little more open, bringing sharp stabbing pain to his injured jawbone. "I was just japin'," he managed. "I wasn't gonna shoot nobody."

"Oh, all right, then," Scofield exclaimed and turned to look at Clint and Leo to explain. "It's all right. He was just japin', wanted to give us a start. No harm done." Back to Hamp then, he said, "Sorry about that little drink of whiskey Clint wasted on you. No hard feelings? Here, here's your gun back." He reached over and dropped the gun in Hamp's holster. When he stepped back, he whispered quickly to Clint. "Get ready!" Back to Hamp then, he asked, "Anybody here with you?" Hamp shook his head. "Then I reckon you can have a drink with us."

Hamp nodded, took a step back, and made a show of tucking his shirttail in while Scofield favored him with a friendly smile. Hamp returned the smile with the best attempt he could through his clenched teeth, seconds before he dropped his hand to rest on the handle of the holstered pistol. In the next instant, the hand came back up, holding the pistol leveled at Scofield's gut. Clint's .44 was out in another instant, but not before they heard the click of Hamp's hammer on an empty cylinder. As startled as Hamp, Clint hesitated to shoot when he realized Hamp's gun was empty, as Hamp pulled the trigger two more times with the same result. Not surprised, however, Scofield drew his pistol unhurriedly, took deliberate aim and put a bullet in Hamp's chest. Looking at the startled faces around him, Scofield shrugged and said, "I gave him a chance to walk away, but he didn't take it."

"When did you empty his gun?" Clint asked.

"When you was all lookin' at him after I picked him up off the floor. He was lookin' back at you." He reached in his pocket and pulled out five cartridges and dumped them on the bar.

"He kinda gave himself a trial and came up with a guilty decision, didn't he?" Leo said. "Made it a lot easier, didn't it? Floyd, get somebody to carry his body outta here. He's blockin' the bar. Better check his pockets first. He probably owes us some money."

One spectator, a little more interested in the execution than most, watched from the top of the stairs. "What you waitin' for?" Sally Brown asked when she came from her room and found him still standing there. "You ain't thinkin' 'bout takin' another ride, are you? That first one was kinda short." She was pretty sure he didn't have any more money and she hoped he wasn't going to try to play on her sympathy for the short duration of his ride. Like so many cowhands who spent the little money they had with her and the other girls, he was like a backward child with two left hands. But it wasn't her job on this earth to suckle them like babies. He only shook his head in answer to her question, distracted as he was by the scene below in the saloon. She looked down toward the bar then and saw the body on the floor. "Is that what the gunshots were about?" He answered with a nod, seeming to be overly interested in the activity around the dead man. "Is he somebody you know?" she asked while craning her neck in an effort to see if it was anybody she knew. Again, he nodded, trying to make up his mind if he should do anything about it or not. "That's the fellow you came in with, ain't it?" She recognized him now. "The fellow with his jaw clamped shut," she said. "What you gonna do about it?"

Junior didn't answer her right away. He was still trying to decide, and when he did, his answer was short and blunt. "I ain't gonna do nothin' about it," he said and hurried down the steps. When he reached the bottom, he walked around behind the spectators and went out the door.

"Lulu Belle," Floyd sang out when he stuck his head in the kitchen door, "is Slim in here?"

"He's in the storeroom," Lulu Belle answered. "Slim! Floyd wants ya."

In a few seconds, Slim walked into the kitchen, and Floyd told him Leo wanted him to carry a body out of the saloon.

"Who is it?" Slim asked.

"Nobody we know," Floyd answered. "Just take him down to the hollow and plant him with the others down there. He came in with another feller. I expect he'll give you a hand—might even take care of him, himself. If we find him," he added. "If we don't, I'll give you a hand carryin' him out." Then another thought struck him. "Him and his friend rode in on a couple of horses and a packhorse, too. So, we need to claim them before somebody else does." He started to go back to the bar but stopped when he remembered. "And, Lulu Belle, there's two fellers from the wagon train that are wantin' supper."

Back in the saloon, Leo Stern questioned the spectators. "Somebody said this man came in with another man. Where is he? Anybody know?"

"Yeah, Leo, I know," Sally answered. "His name's Junior and he took off when he saw what happened to this fellow."

"I expect their horses are gone already," Leo said when he saw Slim behind Floyd. "Go out and check, anyway. They were leadin' a packhorse, too."

Now spectators, themselves, after the execution took place, Clint and Scofield stood idly by until Slim and Floyd hauled the body out to the porch. "Well, that's enough activity to spark my appetite," Scofield announced to Clint. "Let's go see what Lulu Belle cooked for supper." They walked over to a back corner of the saloon where a long table was set up for folks who were there just to eat. It was close to the kitchen for Lulu Belle's convenience and she appeared with two cups of coffee as soon as they were seated.

"Clayton Scofield and Clint Buchanan," she sang out cheerfully, "two of my favorite customers. How are you doin', boys?"

"Howdy, Lulu Belle, darlin'," Scofield responded. "You know me and Clint ain't gonna pass this way without comin' to see you. Whatcha got on the stove tonight?"

"I got a big kettle of chicken and rice and beans and biscuits," she answered. "Oughta be just what two handsome men like yourselves need."

"As long as you've got biscuits, I'll be satisfied," Clint said.

She laughed. "That's right, you do like a hot biscuit."

"Not just any hot biscuits," Clint said. "Your hot biscuits. They're the best biscuits in the whole territory."

She laughed again, openly pleased. "I swear, you're a sweet young man. You always say that."

"Tell her, Uncle Clayton," Clint insisted. "I tell everybody you bake the best biscuits in the country." She shook her head and blushed outright as she spun on her heel to get their food from the kitchen.

Leo came over from the bar then and sat down at the table with them. "How come that fellow was fixin' to shoot you, Scofield?"

"'Cause I broke his jaw," Scofield said. "It was just bad luck we ended up in the same place here at Fort Kearny." He went on to tell Leo the circumstances that caused the friction between them. "I never counted on ever runnin' into him again. Sorry it had to happen in your saloon."

"Hell, it don't look like it caused much trouble beyond that piece of wood his bullet tore outta the floor," Leo said. "That's close enough to the bar to just set that spittoon over it. He sure as hell ain't the first one to get shot down in here—and won't be the last, I reckon." He got up then to return to his office. "You boys enjoy your supper."

"Much obliged," Scofield replied. "We'll enjoy it, right, Clint? I might drop over for a little drink to help me sleep after I get my camp settled down for the night. Depends on how I feel." He tried to disguise his glance toward Lulu Belle as she delivered two heaping plates of food to the table. She returned it with one of her own. Clint wanted to chuckle, but pretended not to notice, turning his attention to the chicken and rice, instead.

When they had finished supper, they lingered only a short while to compliment Lulu Belle on her cooking because Scofield declared that he had to get back to make sure all was well in his camp of settlers. It served to impress Lulu Belle with his sense of responsibility for the welfare of his people, Clint supposed. In a more practical vein, Lulu Belle placed a biscuit in Clint's hand as they were leaving. "You said you like 'em so much, I thought I'd give you one in case you get hungry later on." It was wrapped neatly in a napkin and was inspiration for Scofield to tell her how Clint had named his horse. The story delighted Lulu Belle. Clint thanked her for the biscuit, not in the least embarrassed by the origin of Biscuit's name.

Walking back along the creek bank, they could hear the music and the singing from the wagon train as soon as they left the hog ranch. "That's a happy sound, ain't it?" Scofield asked. Clint said that it was. "I just hope they're all that happy after we get to the high plains and the mountains beyond."

"Ain't much we can do but the best we know how," Clint said. "The rest is up to something we don't have much control over."

"I declare," Scofield said with a chuckle, "that was downright philosophical. I didn't know my sister could raise a boy with brains like that."

"Go to hell," Clint fired back at him, laughing. "I knew from the beginning you hired me for my brains."

"Oh, was that the reason?" Scofield japed. "I thought I was just doin' your mama a favor by keepin' you outta jail." The japing back and forth was typical for them. But Scofield had no doubts concerning the reason he hired his nephew to work with him. Clint was strong and steady. He had no fear, and he lived with a tribe of Crow Indians for three of his teenage years, which endowed him with hunting and tracking skills few white men possessed.

When they reached the camp, Scofield said he was going to take a look around to make sure everything was all right. "You can go with me if you want. Or you can visit with the folks and watch the dancin' and singin'. It don't make no difference to me. Then I might turn in, I'm kinda sleepy tonight."

"Since it's all the same to you, I'll watch the folks dance for a while. But I ain't that sleepy, so I think I'll saddle Biscuit and maybe take a wide circle around the camp later on." He knew that would reassure Scofield that someone was watching over his camp, even though they were this close to the fort. It would ease up on his uncle's conscience as well, while he was back at Stern's, visiting Lulu Belle.

After leaving Scofield, Clint walked over close to a group including Lonnie and Susie James and Walt and Ellie Moody. They were encouraging a duel between Buck Carrey's banjo and Pat Shephard's feet. Buck was hammering out a tune popular at most square dances, his fingers flying on the strings with his own style of three-finger picking. Pat was displaying his intricate footwork with each step right in time with the banjo. Pretty soon everybody but Lemuel Blue, under Fancy Wallace's wagon, was gathering around. And Lemuel was straining his neck trying to see. It was such a show that Clint almost failed to notice Scofield walking hurriedly toward the creek and the path leading to Stern's. He brought his attention back to the duel in progress in time to see Buck throw his hands in the air and declare, "I can't wear him out! He's a danged machine." Pat, his shirt dark with sweat under his arms, performed a little tap dance sign-off routine and admitted he was just about to surrender to Buck's fingers. Everybody cheered and applauded.

"You better go get you a dry shirt, hon," Ginny Shephard said, "else you'll catch your death of cold out here in this night air."

"That's right, Pat," Lonnie James called out, "I'll show the crowd some dance steps you ain't learned yet while you're gone." That brought a laugh from the crowd when most of them tried to picture the huge man attempting to emulate the lithe Pat Shephard.

As the gathering started to drift back to their individual little groups, Clint thought about going to the horses grazing by the creek. Before taking a step, however, he was stopped by Walt Moody. "Say, Clint, what was that about Scofield gettin' mixed up in a shooting over at that hog ranch? You were with him, weren't you? Fellow at the post trader's store told me about it—said Scofield shot somebody."

Clint stopped to explain. He didn't want the people in the wagon train to get the wrong idea about their wagon master. "Yeah, that's right, Walt. Scofield and I went over there to eat supper. The fellow that owns the place, Leo Stern, has a jim-dandy cook, so we like to take supper there whenever we pass through this way." He unwrapped his biscuit and held it up as evidence. "We were just unlucky enough to pass through the bar room when this jasper was there. He was crazy, or jacked up on whiskey, or both. I don't know which, but I reckon he decided he didn't like my uncle's looks. Because he decided he'd just shoot him in the back. He pulled his pistol and aimed it at my uncle's back, but Scofield turned in time to shoot him down. The fellow got off a shot, but it went into the floor." That wasn't exactly the way it had happened, but Clint was afraid the actual version might cast Scofield as a cold-blooded killer.

"Dad-burn," Lonnie uttered. "It's a good thing he turned around when he did, ain't it?"

"That's a fact," Clint agreed, "else you mighta had to depend on me to lead you to Oregon."

"Nah," Lonnie cracked, "we coulda hired Lemuel to find Oregon for us."

"Hush your mouth," Susie scolded. "Don't let the young'uns hear you making jokes about him."

Walt laughed. "Better listen to your wife. Fancy finds out you make fun of Lemuel and she'll come after you with that big ol' Colt revolver she wears."

"Now, don't you start," Ellie Moody scolded her husband. "You don't know anything about that woman. We just ain't had a chance to get to know her."

"Ellie's right," Susie said. "And we've got a long way to go before we see the Willamette Valley. We might all be relyin' on each other before we're done." She looked around her to see where the children were. "And you know Sammy and Skeeter Braxton repeat everything that comes out of your mouth, Lonnie."

Clint shook his head in disbelief and said, "Anyway, that was just an unfortunate thing that happened at Stern's—don't want you to think Scofield gets mixed up in bar fights." He left them then to get his horse. When he stopped by the wagon to get his saddle and bridle, he smiled to think his uncle thought he wouldn't know that he had gone back to the hog ranch. He thought it was amusing that Scofield tried to keep his relationship with Lulu Belle a secret. Scofield didn't have a wife, so why should he care what anybody thought about his personal pleasures? Thinking about his uncle caused him to consider the fact that, had he not hit Hamp Evans in the face with a shot glass, Scofield might be dead. That thought caused him to wonder anew about the friend of Hamp Evans, the one called Junior. The first time, in Independence, when Hamp suffered a broken jaw, there was apparently no one with him. But he couldn't help wondering now if there was a possibility that Junior might have plans in mind to avenge his friend. He pictured his uncle walking the dark path beside the creek, going or coming to the hog ranch. It was enough to make him decide to patrol that path until his uncle returned safely.

Chapter 6

As soon as he saddled Biscuit, he rode the path to the hog ranch to satisfy himself that Scofield had not encountered an ambush on his way to visit Lulu Belle. After that, he rode back to the camp and took a wide circle around the wagons, as he had told Scofield he would. He planned to watch the path for Scofield's return, but he knew he had some time before that happened. This was not the first time his uncle had paid the lady a late visit when they had camped at Fort Kearny on other trips. He rode Biscuit back to the horse herd and took his saddle off. He pulled his rifle out when he put the saddle in the wagon and started back toward the hog ranch. His thinking was that he could move more stealthily on foot and do it faster on the opposite side from the path. He crossed over the creek and moved parallel to the length of the path to Stern's, trying to determine the best ambush spots. It was hard to pick the most likely spot because there were any number of likely places. He tried to pick a spot he would decide on, had he been the bushwhacker waiting for his victim. He still couldn't pick one, so he decided to simply keep on the prowl, up and down the creek, until he saw Scofield safely back to camp.

After a couple of trips along the path, using the trees on the bank for cover, he saw no sign of anyone else on the path side of the creek. Taking that as a good omen, he took a knee about midway the length of the path and just listened. In a few minutes, a full moon made its appearance over the tops of the trees to be greeted by the sound of crickets at the creek. *Damn, Uncle Clayton, you're staying longer than usual,* he thought. *You must be having a nice visit.* As soon as the thought occurred, he heard the soft sound of his uncle's boots on the path. He inched up a little closer to a large cottonwood for a better look across the creek. There was no mistaking that walk. It brought a smile to Clint's face as he watched his uncle move past a point directly opposite the tree he hid behind and proceed on down the path. *I'll let him get a little farther before I move again,* he thought moments before he saw a dark figure step out on the path behind Scofield. A faint glint of moonlight bounced off the barrel of the rifle when the man raised it to take aim. There was no time to think, Clint jerked his Henry rifle up and fired a split second before the assassin's rifle fired then dropped to the ground. The man was down, but Scofield went down, too.

Fearing he had not been quick enough, Clint splashed across the creek, cranking another cartridge into the chamber as he ran. When he came up the bank to the path, he found Junior lying flat, straining to reach for his rifle. Clint quickly grabbed it by the barrel and jerked it well out of his reach. Junior grimaced and groaned, "You've kilt me."

"Not yet, I ain't," Clint complained bitterly and fired another shot into Junior's chest. "Now, I've killed you." He turned then and yelled, "Scofield! It's me, Clint! I'm comin' to help you!" He ran down the path to find Scofield lying on his side, his pistol in his hand. "How bad are you hurt?" Clint asked anxiously.

"I ain't hurt a-tall," Scofield answered. "I just hit the ground when I heard that shot whippin' through the leaves over my head. Who the hell shot at me?"

"I expect it's that friend of the fellow you shot in the saloon. I reckon he figured he wasn't gonna stand for you shootin' his partner tonight. I didn't see him till he popped out on the path behind you and I wasn't quick enough to keep him from gettin' off that shot."

"What were you doin' out here, anyway?" Scofield asked.

"What? Oh, just lookin' around."

"How come your pants are wet? Damn-near up to your crotch," Scofield continued.

"I was on the other side of the creek. I had to wade across after I shot that fellow and that's how deep it is right there. So, if anybody asks you how deep it is at that spot, you can tell 'em it's crotch-deep." He offered that bit of sarcasm in an effort to end Scofield's questions.

"What was you doin' on the other side of the creek?" Scofield persisted.

"I told you. I was just lookin' around, and I hadn't ever

took a look at what was on the other side of that creek before."

"Liar," Scofield said. "You was spyin' on me, tryin' to see if I went back to Stern's to get another drink of likker."

"The hell I was!" Clint exclaimed. "I know where you went, and it wasn't to get a drink of likker. I just wanted to make sure you got home all right." The breeze freshened enough then to move some leaves aside to permit a ray of moonlight to display the wide grin on Scofield's face. Clint realized his uncle was japing him. "I shoulda let him shoot you," he said.

"No, no," Scofield responded, laughing. "You don't never wanna let that happen. So, you knew about me and Lulu Belle, huh?"

"Hell, I expect everybody at Stern's knows about you and Lulu Belle."

"Well, maybe you don't know, but me and Lulu Belle are just friends," Scofield declared. "And Lulu Belle ain't one of the workin' girls. I mean, I don't pay her for visitin' with me. She ain't a whore. She's the cook."

"Hell, I know that," Clint responded. "It ain't nobody's business but yours and hers, anyway. I just thought about that fellow havin' a partner who might be sneakin' around lookin' for a chance to take a shot at you."

"Well, partner, I'm mighty glad you did. I 'preciate it." He reached up toward Clint. "Here, gimme a hand and let's go look at that son of a gun and make sure he's dead." There was little doubt about the condition of the late Junior Fry. The initial shot in his side tore through his lung. It was fatal and promised a long agonizing death. The final shot in his chest took him out of his misery. "Well, I reckon we oughta drag him off the path." He paused and looked all around him. "He oughta have a horse around here somewhere."

The only place to hide a horse was in the trees that lined the creek, so they figured it couldn't be very far away. They walked back toward the hog ranch, hoping Junior hadn't left his horse tied up at the hitching rail because they wouldn't know his from the rest of the horses tied there. They were saved from that problem when they found a bay and a roan saddled, as well as a sorrel carrying a pack saddle about fifty feet from the end of the trail. Clint gave Scofield a look that asked, *How could you walk by them without noticing?*

"I had my mind on other things when I walked by here," Scofield answered the look.

They led the horses back along the trail, and when they reached Junior's body, they threw it over the saddle and led the horses on toward the wagon camp. Before reaching the camp, Clint led the bay across to the other side of the creek and found a gully to leave Junior in. He returned to the path then, and he and Scofield continued on to the camp. "I'd best go talk to John Zachary and Emmett Braxton to make sure they've got the guard set for tonight," Scofield said. "Even though we're still at Fort Kearny, it don't pay to get too careless." Scofield had held an election on the second week on the trail and John and Emmett had been elected as captains on the train. Scheduling the guard roster was one of their duties. The social hour was still in full swing since there would be no wake-up blast from Scofield's bugle in the morning.

On the morning of departure, the camp was alerted at four on the nose, and promptly at seven, they said farewell to Fort Kearny. Clint rode along beside Scofield's wagon until the train was in line and once again on the commonly used trail. When the buildings of the fort dropped out of sight behind them, he nudged Biscuit gently. The Palouse gelding broke into a gentle lope that soon carried him out ahead of the wagons. They were now following the Platte River. The river, primarily the north fork of it, would be their guide for the next month or so, until they left it to strike the Sweetwater. As a rule, the people in the wagons seldom saw Clint as they followed Scofield along the flat, well-defined Platte road. Only occasionally, he would appear on the trail ahead to signal Scofield, oftentimes to detour around a bad spot ahead. On some days, however, they saw him only twice—at noontime and five o'clock, when he was waiting to lead them to a camping spot.

It was the second night after leaving Fort Kearny, that Scofield identified a weak link in his party of emigrants. He was awakened by a rare middle-of-the-night call from Mother Nature. Looking over at Clint, fast asleep in his bedroll, he was careful not to wake him. Everything seemed peaceful enough as he walked outside the circle to answer nature's call. He took out his pocket watch and held it up so the moon could shine on the dial. *Two-thirty,* he thought. Since he was wide awake, he decided he'd take a walk around the circle to see how the men on guard duty were doing.

He encountered the first guard, Walt Moody, when he had walked about a quarter of the way around the circle of wagons. "Hold on, Walt! It's just me," he called out when Walt first saw him and raised his rifle to a ready position. "Didn't mean to come up on you all of a sudden like that, but I didn't see you till you passed the tail of that wagon."

"Damn, Scofield," Walt swore. "I'd hate to get hung for shootin' the wagon master."

"It'da been my fault," Scofield admitted. "I'm glad to see you're alert. Who's on guard with you?"

"Ralph Tyson," Walt answered.

"Is he across, next to the river?" Scofield wanted to be sure he didn't startle Tyson, like he almost did with Walt.

"I reckon," Walt answered after a moment's hesitation. "I ain't seen him since we came on."

Scofield thought he detected a definite note of concern in Walt's tone and he got the feeling Walt didn't want to say much more about it. "All right, Walt, you keep your eyes open. I'll walk on around the circle on my way back to my wagon, then I'll go back to bed. Good night." Walt returned the good night.

Walking very carefully now, wary of startling Ralph Tyson, and possibly getting shot, Scofield walked around the bottom half of the circled wagons, seeing no sign of Tyson. He was beginning to become irritated, thinking that possibly Tyson might have returned to his bed. When he approached Tyson's own wagon, he discovered he had been over-cautious for no reason, for he found Tyson asleep behind his wagon. When he walked up to him, where he was sprawled on the ground, he kicked the bottom of Tyson's boot, but Tyson did not stir beyond a few grunts. Several feet away, Scofield saw an empty whiskey bottle and realized Tyson wasn't just sleepy. He was passed out drunk. *You're lucky my pistol is back on my bedroll,* he thought. The next best thing was the bucket hanging on the back of Tyson's wagon. He grabbed the bucket and strode angrily down to the edge of the river, where he filled it from the muddiest spot he could reach.

When the bucket of water showered down on Tyson's head, it brought the drunken man sputtering and blubbering to life. Enraged then, Tyson stumbled drunkenly to his feet, only to be shoved back down on the ground again by the angry Scofield. "You son of a . . ." was as far as he got before Scofield grabbed him by his soaked shirt and jerked him to his feet.

"I oughta shoot you," Scofield threatened, "you no-good drunk. You put the lives of every person in this wagon train at risk. When we start out in the mornin', you can turn your wagon around and head back to Fort Kearny. I can't take a chance on men like you. And make no mistake about it, if it wasn't for the sake of your wife, I'd hang you."

Tyson had no reason to think Scofield was bluffing, he was convinced the wagon master meant what he said. So, he changed his tune and made a desperate plea for another chance. "That wasn't my fault, Scofield, I swear. I got hold of some bad whiskey back there at Fort Kearny. It made me sick. I thought I could do my guard duty, but it knocked me down again. I ain't got no drinkin' problem. I was sick."

"Is that so?" Scofield demanded, reached down, and picked up the empty whiskey bottle. "Then what the hell is this?"

"You got it all wrong," Tyson pleaded. "That was before supper, when I poured almost that whole bottle of bad likker out on the ground. My wife will tell you." Ruby Tyson opened the back curtain on the wagon then, having been awakened by the altercation. "Tell him I poured that likker out on the ground, honey."

"He poured it out, Mr. Scofield," Ruby obeyed, timidly.

"And I ain't got no more," Tyson said. "So there ain't no way this could happen again. Like I've been tellin' you, I got hold of some bad likker. And I've sure as hell learned my lesson. As God is my witness."

Scofield could not really accept Tyson's word, but he felt dreadfully sorry for the pitiful woman who was his wife. "Mrs. Tyson, has he got any more whiskey?"

"No, sir," she spoke up right away. "That one bottle was all he had."

"Listen to me, Tyson. Against my better judgment, we'll forget this happened tonight. But I'm gonna give you another chance only because of the respect I have for your wife. I'll stand guard the rest of this night because the people on this train, your wife included, deserve to have a sober man standin' guard."

"You ain't got to do that," Tyson pleaded. "I'm all right now. I can stand guard."

Scofield cut him off before he could say more. "I don't want you on guard. Just go on back to your bed and sleep it off. I'll keep an eye on the camp." Still fighting his anger, he stalked away toward his wagon to get his firearms.

The Platte was a wide river, shallow and muddy, with unpredictable channels and gullies where the trail passed close to the banks. There was a saying, by an unknown author, that the Platte was "too thin to plow and too thick to drink." But it was a flat road to travel, which made it easy on the horses. There was grass and occasional streams. The many islands in the river occasionally provided some wood. And when there was none, there were buffalo chips to burn. Most of the settlers were reluctant to believe Scofield when he told them they would need to collect the dried buffalo and cow dung on the prairie near the river. But they soon learned the chips burned easily, too easily in fact, requiring a couple of buckets full of them to cook a meal. And, to the emigrants' surprise, they burned without releasing an unpleasant odor. The gathering of fuel soon became one of the primary responsibilities of the children. The trio of Johnny Zachary, Sammy James, and Skeeter Braxton were especially skilled at finding the natural fuel. It became the usual practice for the three dung harvesters to run on ahead of the wagons when Clint Buchanan appeared to lead the train to camp.

Not all of the wagons had children to search for fuel. Fancy Wallace, in particular, was not inclined to harvest the dried dung patties. She intercepted Skeeter Braxton when the boy ran past her wagon on the fifth day after leaving Fort Kearny. "Boy!" she yelled at him. "You, there, what's your name?"

"Skeeter," he answered, out of fear more so than politeness. "Skeeter Braxton," he said and walked along with the wagon. Looking under the wagon, he could see the legs of a man walking in pace with the wagon on the other side and assumed it was Lemuel Blue.

"You any good at finding buffalo chips to burn?" Fancy demanded.

"Yes, ma'am, I'm as good as anybody else, I reckon."

"You like peppermint candy?" Fancy asked.

"Yes, ma'am."

"Well, I've got a whole jar of peppermint sticks and I'm willing to give one stick to you for two buckets full of chips. You interested?"

Skeeter took another glance underneath the wagon. "Ain't Lemuel Blue gonna find you some buffalo chips?"

"Lemuel ain't no good at it," Fancy said. "He's better at choppin' wood. You wanna do it or not?"

"Yes, ma'am!" Skeeter exclaimed. "I'll get 'em for you!"

"One stick of peppermint for two buckets," she reminded him. "And I want them in time to cook my supper. When we circle up, you can get the bucket off the back of my wagon. Lemuel! Show him which one."

Skeeter stopped to let the wagon roll on and Lemuel came around behind it. He looked at Skeeter and grinned as if he was in on a great big secret. Then he pointed to a bucket hanging on the tailgate of the wagon. Skeeter nodded rapidly up and down and ran back to his family's wagon.

When Clint appeared at a bend of the river ahead and signaled, Scofield led his train toward his scout and gave the wagon behind him the call to circle. Well drilled in Scofield's procedures by this time, that wagon passed the order along to the wagon following him and the wagon train filed into the grassy flat to form their circle. Since Clint brought word back that he had seen some Indian sign farther up the trail, they brought all the livestock inside the circle. “What kinda sign did you see?” Scofield asked Clint. “Anything we oughta be worried about?”

“I don’t think so,” Clint said. “Looked like a small huntin’ party to me. Three or four, no more than that. They might wanna try to steal a horse or a cow, but that’s about all I’d worry about.”

“All right,” Scofield said, “let’s pass the word.” They moved back among the wagons to make everybody aware of the possibility of Indians nearby.

“We’re gonna need to pick up some buffalo chips to burn,” John Zachary responded. “You think we best not let the boys go out lookin’ for ’em?”

“I figure it’s about two hundred yards of open prairie between here and that low rise to the south, yonder. I’d be surprised if you didn’t find all the chips you need between here and there. Just keep your rifle handy and an eye on your young’uns and you oughta be all right.”

“I reckon you’re right,” Zachary said. “Okay, boys, go get some dung. Just stay close to the wagons. Don’t go wanderin’ off where I can’t see you.”

“Yessir,” Johnny replied. “Let’s go, boys.” His pals ran to get their buckets and started out on the prairie. But Skeeter turned and ran back along the circle of wagons. “Where you goin’, Skeeter?” Johnny yelled.

“To get another bucket,” Skeeter yelled back. “I’m fixin’ to find more turds than I can carry in one bucket.”

Johnny and Sammy looked at each other and shook their heads. “I wonder what’s got into him,” Sammy uttered.

“Well, he ain’t gonna outwork me,” Johnny said. “Let’s get goin’.” They were hard at it, searching the grass for fuel when Skeeter came to join them. “Where’d you get the extra bucket?” Johnny asked.

"You two are out here playin' at pickin' up chips," Skeeter boasted. "But this is a business for me. I've got a job to supply buffalo chips." He stuck his chest out and grinned.

"Yeah," Johnny said, "and I'm takin' Mr. Scofield's place as wagon master."

Skeeter snickered, delighted to see both of his friends confused. He couldn't keep it up for very long, though, before he had to tell them about his deal with Fancy Wallace. "How come she picked you to get 'em for her?" Sammy wondered.

"I expect it's because she recognized the best worker," Skeeter boasted.

"Wait till she sees who fills up their bucket first," Johnny said, already hustling between targets. "She might pick somebody else next time we stop." It served to motivate all three boys and soon they were scouring the prairie like hound dogs on a scent. The first buckets were filled almost in a tie and Skeeter started working on his extra bucket while his two friends ran back to the wagons to empty the first. By the time they returned, he was searching closer to the rise that Scofield had suggested as a boundary in their hunt. He soon filled his second bucket and returned to the Wallace wagon to deliver the two buckets of chips. Fancy shook her head, amazed by the quick fulfillment of her order. In keeping with her part of the deal, she presented him with one peppermint stick. He hung her bucket back under the tailgate, and with his one bucket and peppermint stick, he hurried back to the hunt, knowing he still had to fill that bucket twice.

Since all the wagons needed fuel for fires, the prairie between the camp and the low rise was getting crowded with women and children looking for the dried cakes for fuel. Johnny and Sammy were already approaching the high point in the rise to find enough cakes to finish their second buckets. Skeeter hadn't figured on that possibility, so it was with a mild panic that he determined he was going to have to range much farther afield to take care of his family's fuel needs. He looked at the high point in the rise. He had been told not to go over that rise where he couldn't be seen from the circle of wagons. *But Mr. Scofield didn't say not to go farther along the trail,* Skeeter told himself. *And I'm liable to get a licking if I don't get enough chips for Mama to cook with.* It wasn't necessary to give it additional thought. Carrying his bucket, he ran up the trail beyond the camp.

He was convinced right away that he had made a good decision, for he was barely out of sight of the wagons when he came to a broad grassy area that extended down to the river's edge. It was obviously another place where the buffalo had grazed, for they had left plenty of evidence behind. Thinking of his two pals, competing with all the other families, he happily filled his bucket with the dried cakes. When he had no more room in his bucket, he turned to carry it back but paused to consider something he hadn't noticed before. There was a small island close to the edge of the river, and there was a sizable clump of willow trees on it. He went down to the water to get a better look and noticed some pieces of dead limbs had washed ashore. *Maybe,* he thought, *there is wood for the fire here!* He dropped down on his hands and knees so he could pick up some of the dead limbs to show his father. Then they could come back with an ax and get plenty of wood. Filled with excitement now, he turned around to find himself facing the two front hooves of a horse. Still on all-fours, he raised his head to discover a paint horse and a solemn Indian rider, who was regarding him with open curiosity.

Skeeter froze, fearing for his life, for several yards behind the fierce-looking Indian, there were two more. All three sat their ponies, silently watching the young white boy on his hands and knees, a bucket of dried buffalo dung beside him. After a long moment, Two Bears turned to say to his two companions, "The wagons must be near, maybe on the other side of the hill."

"Maybe there are no wagons and he crawled all the way from the big river," Walking Fox answered him, referring to the Missouri. He laughed at his joke.

Back to the boy then, Two Bears spoke in English. "You are with wagons?"

Skeeter got to his feet. "Yes, sir. I'm with the wagons and there's a lotta men there and all of 'em's got guns." He was plenty afraid, but he was trying hard not to show it. He couldn't help thinking about some of the things Lemuel had told him and his friends about the cruelty of the Indians.

"Where?" Two Bears asked. He and his two fellow hunters had ridden up from south of this point, so he wanted to know if the wagon train was camped east or west of there. Skeeter pointed to the east. "Who is chief of wagon train?"

"Mr. Clayton Scofield," Skeeter answered boldly.

Two Bears looked back at his two companions and nodded. "Come," he said to Skeeter. "I take." He reached down with one hand and motioned for Skeeter to take it. Seeing as how he had no choice, Skeeter grasped the outstretched hand and was promptly lifted up to land on the horse behind Two Bears. The Indian wheeled his horse and started back up the trail to the east. Behind him,

Walking Fox reached down and picked up Skeeter's bucket and loped after Two Bears.

As soon as they reached the top of the hill, they saw the camp. Two Bears didn't hesitate but guided his horse straight toward Scofield's wagon. "Uh-oh," Walt Moody muttered when he saw the three Indians top the hill to the west of the camp. Immediately concerned, he hurried up to Scofield's wagon where he found Scofield talking to John Zachary and a concerned Emmett Braxton. "We've got company," Walt announced, "and they're headin' straight for your wagon." Scofield turned to see, squinting his eyes in an effort to see better.

"Ain't nothin' to worry about," Scofield told them. "That's ol' Two Bears. He's a friend, Crow. Clint lived with his people for a couple of years. And look, he's bringing Skeeter back."

"He must recognize your wagon," Walt said, "'cause he's headin' this way."

"I doubt he could tell the difference between my wagon and any of the others," Scofield said. "He just knows I always park with the wagon tongue pointed in the direction I'm gonna start out in the mornin'." He threw his hand up and waved a welcome to the three Crow hunters. After another few seconds passed, he said, "Don't reckon we'll need to go lookin' for your boy after all, Braxton, less Two Bears has started growin' a new set of arms and legs." When the Indians got a little closer, they could clearly see Skeeter's feet on either side of Two Bears' hips and his arms around his waist. When they got a little closer, Skeeter stuck his head out to give them all a grin.

"Two Bears!" Scofield called out in welcome. "I'm happy to see you, my friend. And Walking Fox, welcome. I don't think I ever met the other fellow."

"He is Keeps His Blood," Two Bears said.

"Well, he's welcome, too," Scofield said. "Step down and we'll cook some bacon and drink some coffee. I see you caught a little varmint in your traps. Maybe we'll get this fire going a little better and we'll cook him, too."

Skeeter, still sitting behind Two Bears, giggled at that, and his father walked up to take him off the horse. "They followed me home, Papa. Can I keep 'em?" Skeeter joked.

"I ain't sure I ain't gonna skin you for runnin' off like that," his father said. "You're mighty dang lucky you ran into three Crows, instead of three Sioux. And your mama had to borrow some buffalo chips from Sammy's mama to start cookin' supper."

"I got a whole bucket full of 'em right there," Skeeter said when Walking Fox put the bucket on the ground. "And that ain't all, I found a place where you can cut some wood for a real fire. Right over that hill," he said and pointed back the way he had just come.

Emmett looked at John Zachary and said, "Now, that might be worth goin' to take a look at." The prospect of a real wood-burning fire was mighty tempting after so many days cooking over dung fires. "Why don't we grab a couple of axes and see if he knows what he's talkin' about?"

"Sounds good to me," John replied, then looked at Scofield to see if the wagon master had any reason to object.

Scofield looked at Two Bears. "You seen any sign of Sioux?"

"No Sioux," Two Bears replied. The three Crow hunters had been on a scouting mission, trying to find the buffalo herds. They had covered a large area, they said. It was their sign that Clint had reported finding. So, Skeeter's efforts to earn his peppermint resulted in what turned out to be a mass attack on the tiny island in the middle of the Platte. The group of willow trees were reduced to stumps, their trunks and limbs sacrificed to enable a grand fire in the center of the circle of wagons. It would be remembered by the settlers on the wagon train as the night of Skeeter's willow fire. It was their first close encounter with members of the Crow Tribe.

Chapter 7

Two Bears was startled out of a sound sleep by a loud screeching sound that he could not identify as any critter he had ever heard before. He almost ran headlong into Keeps His Blood when he came out of his blanket, prepared to fight for his life against some form of creature he had never faced before. They both turned to Walking Fox, who was crawling out from under Scofield's wagon, his rifle in hand. Then in the darkness, they recognized Scofield, in the middle of the circle, silhouetted against the dark morning sky, his bugle pressed to his lips. While they watched, astonished, he took a deep breath and blew into the bugle, again producing a cry like one might hear if plucking the feathers out of a live crow. In a matter of minutes, the people in the other wagons began to come out of their sleeping places. "He is telling them all to get out of their beds," Walking Fox said.

"It's still nighttime," Two Bears said. "The sun has not come up yet." While they watched, astonished, the horses and cows were let out of the circle of wagons and driven to water. And the women began building small cookfires. "I think we should go now," Two Bears decided. "We should ride down the river and find a place to stop and wait for the sun to come up." His suggestion was met with grunts of agreement.

For another week, the wagon train followed the Platte River across flat prairie lands with each day a duplicate of the day preceding it. The terrain was not difficult as they continued to follow the many tracks of previous wagon trains, but the monotony of plodding along beside the lumbering wagons began to wear on the spirits of both children and adults. It was with this in mind that Scofield promised a day of rest and recreation to recharge lagging spirits. This day would come when they reached the North Platte at a place called Ash Hollow. To reach the north fork of the Platte, they had to cross the south branch of the river. That crossing was accomplished with only minor problems, then it was another full day from there to the North Platte at Ash Hollow, a deep, wooded canyon, about four miles long.

Upon reaching Ash Hollow, the travelers were met with the problem of getting their wagons from the higher table land they had been crossing, down into the river bottom. This was a drop of about two hundred and fifty feet and the problem was complicated by the steepness of the bluffs, most of which had rock ledges that defied the descent of the covered wagons. One slope was the best place to descend down into the hollow, since it had no rock ledges. Consequently, it was scarred with the ruts of many wagon wheels before them. A day was spent getting the wagons down the hill, one by one, with various ways of braking the wagons. The most commonly used method was to lock the rear wheels by tying them and easing the wagon down with ropes.

Once the problem of getting the wagons down into the canyon was behind them, the settlers were well in need of the day of rest and recreation Scofield had promised. After miles and miles of foul-tasting Platte River water and no wood for fires, they found themselves in a green canyon, lush with flowers, grass, and trees, and best of all, sweet spring water. They likened it to a Garden of Eden, and it lifted their spirits for the rougher road ahead of them. "I think I'll pull my wagon out of the train and build me a house right here," John Zachary joked.

"I reckon that would work out all right," Scofield commented. " 'Course, you'd have to learn to get used to a lot of company, with all the wagon trains comin' through here."

Still joking, John said, "Hell, that's even better. I'd charge 'em a toll for every wagon that slides down that hill."

Scofield laughed with him. "How 'bout the Injuns? I hear tell that every once in a while, there's whole villages of Sioux camped here. And Sioux don't pay no tolls. You ever hear of the Harney Massacre, when all them Brule Sioux were killed?" John said he had heard of it. " 'Bout five years ago," Scofield went on. "Happened right around here. So, this ain't a Sioux Injun's favorite place for a white man to put up a toll booth, I reckon."

As planned, everybody enjoyed a day to recharge their spirits, to refit, and to make repairs after descending the hill. To add to the celebration of reaching the entry to the North Platte Valley, Clint tracked two deer into the canyon and managed to kill both of them. The fresh venison was shared by everyone. They ended up spending two days in Ash Hollow, courtesy of Scofield's good nature, and the fact that he wanted to see if there were more deer in the wooded canyon. Several of the men had the same idea, and according to Clint, they resulted in scaring all the deer into hiding in the thick woods. The next morning was greeted with the unearthly squawking of Scofield's bugle and the train was on the move again.

It was their first sighting of Courthouse Rock, four days after leaving Ash Hollow, that brought a feeling of real progress on their journey. The North Platte Trail was decidedly more difficult as they continued westward. In the days following Courthouse Rock, they would pass Chimney Rock and other landmarks that had been made famous by those who traveled the trail before them. Thirty-five miles farther brought them to Scott's Bluff, and Scofield told them they had now traveled about one third of the trail to their destination. All thoughts now were on reaching Fort Laramie, which was approximately fifty-four miles away. Many of the wagons needed some repairs that would require the services of a blacksmith or a harness maker. This resulted in a metal rim separating from the wooden wheel. In addition to repairs, Fort Laramie provided an opportunity to restock on supplies that were running out, as well as new shoes for those horses that needed them. And there was also the feeling of security that a garrison of soldiers provided.

* * *

The wagons pulled into Fort Laramie, at the confluence of the Platte and the Laramie rivers, before suppertime after a short day's travel. Clint was waiting to guide them to the campground he had selected by the Laramie River. The travelers were in for a pleasant surprise when they discovered the Laramie, unlike the Platte, provided clean fresh water for drinking, cooking, and bathing. Once the wagons were in place, Scofield called on his captains, John Zachary and Emmett Braxton, to pass on some information concerning the fort and how long the train should plan on camping here before moving on. "First thing everybody's gonna wanna know is where the Post Trader's Store is," Scofield said and drew a little diagram on the ground to show them where it was located. "The Post Trader's name is Seth Ward. I've known him a long time. He's an honest man and he'll treat you right." He went on to show them how to find the blacksmith and the harness shop. "They can find every place by themselves," he concluded. "But they'll most likely ask you, so you can tell 'em. I don't wanna lay around here too long, so we need to get everything done that has to be done and get on our way to South Pass."

"I got a question one of my people asked me," Braxton said. "I want you to understand this ain't me askin' for myself." He shrugged before coming out with it. "This bein' an army post, is there a place where a fellow can get a drink of whiskey, like that place at Fort Kearny?"

His friend, Zachary, recoiled and raised his eyebrows in mock surprise. "Why, Emmett Braxton, what would Sarah think if she knew you were lookin' for a place like that?"

"Go to hell, John," Emmett responded. "I just said it wasn't me askin', didn't I?"

Scofield had to chuckle at Emmett's embarrassment, then he gave him the information he asked for. "There's a fellow name of Jake Plummer who has a saloon about a mile-and-a-half up the Laramie River. He calls it Jake's Place. That's where the soldiers go to get drunk. Who asked you about it?" When Emmett hesitated, as if he wasn't sure he should say, Scofield pressed, "Tyson?" He had already had reason to concern himself with Ralph Tyson and his drinking. Unlike the other families on the train, the Tysons had no children, and as far as anyone could tell, none on the way. Also unlike the others, Tyson drove mules instead of horses, which was of no significance. It was just one more thing that set him apart from the rest of the folks.

Scofield took him at his word when he said he had no drinking problem, but he had since had occasion to suspect he may have made a bad decision when he let Tyson remain with the train. There had been no more incidents when whiskey was involved. But that was more than likely due to the unavailability of the demon spirits. However, there was evidence of Tyson's demons even in the absence of alcohol. On more than a few occasions, folks in the wagons parked close to Tyson's reported hearing loud swearing and ranting, all from Ralph. The timid little protests from Ruby Tyson were almost lost in a typical storm of insults and complaints from her husband. Some of the other wives, fearing for Ruby Tyson's life, had taken their concerns to Scofield, and he had addressed the issue with Ralph. But at this point in the journey, there was little Scofield could do about Ralph and Ruby Tyson's problems. He always had the option of driving

Tyson out of the wagon train. But that would probably result in making Ruby's situation worse and might even endanger her life. For lack of any better solution to the problem, Scofield had told Tyson that he could remain with the train, but if he saw any evidence of physical abuse on Ruby, he was going to personally beat the hell out of him. Tyson had accepted Scofield's terms only because he wanted the protection of the wagon train to get to the Oregon country.

So now, Tyson was asking about the availability of whiskey. Little wonder why Emmett was reluctant to ask the question. "It doesn't make a lotta difference if you tell him where he can get a drink or not," Scofield said. "Any soldier, or anybody else, can tell him how to find Jake's Place." Scofield could not help feeling perturbed to hear that Tyson wanted to know where to get whiskey. And he felt like kicking himself for not sending him back to Fort Kearny, as he had first threatened. *Maybe I'm wrong,* he thought. *We'll just wait and see.*

"Well, I see you made it back again," Seth Ward greeted Scofield when the burly wagon master walked in his store. "I saw those wagons comin' in today and I thought that looked like Clint Buchanan leadin' 'em in. How many you got this trip?"

"Twenty-seven wagons," Scofield replied, "all headin' to the promised land. How you doin', Seth?"

"Fair to middlin'," Seth answered. "What's the news back east? Any more talk about war?"

"Yep, I'm afraid so. Everybody's pickin' a side, north or south. Ain't nobody stayin' neutral. And anybody with a lick of sense can tell you we'll end up two different countries. Ain't no way the north and the south will ever come together as one country. There's too much difference in the north and the south." He glanced at a couple of Indian men looking at a display of broad-brimmed hats. "Might as well try to get the Crow and the Sioux to come together and make one tribe."

"You may be right," Ward declared. "If they do get a war started, it's even gonna affect us out here."

"How's that? There ain't no north-south out here."

"Major Day, he's the post commander since the first of the year. He said they told him they would most likely be pullin' soldiers outta here, if a shootin' war gets started. You think the Sioux and the Cheyenne ain't gonna start gettin' itchy for some cattle to eat and some farms to raid?"

"You might be right," Scofield said then. "It might be a good time for me to just stay out there in Oregon."

"Maybe so," Ward said. "You mighta already heard, but if you ain't, I oughta tell you there have been a couple of Sioux raidin' parties on the trail between Scott's Bluff and the Sweetwater this past month."

"No, I hadn't heard that. The Sioux have been pretty quiet for a good while now. What got them riled up?"

"Who knows? It don't take much," Seth replied. He paused then when two men walked in the door and came over to the counter. "Howdy, men, be with you in a minute." When one of them moved over to stand next to Scofield, Seth asked, "These two of your folks, Scofield?"

"Yep," he answered. "This is Lonnie James and John Zachary. Go ahead and get what they want. I ain't in no hurry."

"Welcome to Fort Laramie," Seth said. Then, looking

at Lonnie, he exclaimed, "Danged if this'un ain't bigger'n you, Scofield."

"He sure is," Scofield replied. "We brought him along in case we have one of those Indian raids you were talkin' about."

"Is he an Injun fighter?" Seth asked.

"I don't know," Scofield answered. "We brought him along so the rest of us can shoot behind him." That brought a good-natured laugh in response.

"I got a list the boss gave me of the things we're needin'," John said and handed it to Seth.

"Me, too," Lonnie said and placed his list on the counter.

Seth chuckled and asked, "You got one, too, Scofield?"

"As a matter fact, I have," he said. "I ain't married, but I've got a list of things that Spud says he needs. I'll have to give you mine outta my head."

Seth took a look at the first list and commented. "I like it when the women write the list. You can read it."

"I expect you'll be seeing most of my people for the next couple of days," Scofield told him. "We've got a couple of wagons that need some work on the wheels and axles. I'm hopin' we can get that done in two days. I wanna get on up past South Pass with plenty of time left to get through the mountains."

"I'll be happy to have the business," Seth said as he scanned the lists. "I've got plenty of all these items I see here." He started to reach under the counter for some sacks but paused when Clint Buchanan walked in the store. "Well, here he is," he greeted him. "I saw you ride in on that fancy Palouse of yours. How you doin', Clint?"

"Howdy, Mr. Ward," Clint returned, "pretty good, I reckon."

"There was somebody in here the other day askin' about you," Seth continued. "Old Yellow Sky, he was askin' if you had come through recently. His village has moved back to the Laramie River again. He wanted me to tell you they're back. I think he'd really like to see you."

Clint smiled and nodded. "I'm glad you told me. I'll ride down that way to see him tomorrow." He turned to look at Scofield. "Is that all right?"

"Sure. Sure, it's all right," Scofield replied at once. "I ain't got nothin' you gotta do tomorrow." He gave a little chuckle then. "Just be sure you get back here day after tomorrow. Don't let old Yellow Sky talk you into goin' Injun again."

"I won't," Clint said. "I expect my Injun days are over." He waited around to help John and Lonnie carry their supplies back to the wagons.

Clint drained the last swallow of coffee from his cup as he chewed on the strip of smoked venison he had saved from the deer he killed in Ash Hollow. He thought about the biscuits he enjoyed at Lulu Belle's table. He'd like to have one now. Spud made biscuits, but they weren't in the same class with Lulu Belle's. Maybe in the morning he would wander past some of the families eating breakfast and someone would offer a freshly baked biscuit. He picked up his coffeepot and cup and walked down to the river's edge to rinse them out. He heard a horse's hooves in the high grass behind him and moments later, he was not surprised to feel the Palouse's muzzle against his back. He smiled as he thought, *you must have known I was thinking about biscuits*. He emptied the water from his coffeepot and started to stand up when he heard her swear. Had his hearing not been so sharp, he might not have heard it at all, so softly it was uttered. He looked downstream toward the place in the river where the women went to bathe. In the darkness, he couldn't see her at first. He started to call out to her because he knew she couldn't see him. Then he decided it best not to startle her, and she would probably think one of the horses had just come down to drink. So he remained where he was, kneeling at the water's edge, listening as the woman came up from the river, carrying what looked like a bucket.

When she started up the bank, she seemed to be struggling with the bucket. He guessed that it must be full of water. Still unaware of his presence, she tried to take a big step up the bank, but her foot slipped, and she took a tumble, dropping her bucket of water in the process. Again, she swore barely loud enough to be heard as she saw her bucket roll into the river. Instantly aware that the woman was going to lose her bucket if he didn't get it before the tide took it away, he sprang into action. Running past the startled woman, he said, "Don't worry, I'll get it."

She sank down on the bank, helplessly watching him as he ran into the water and grabbed her bucket. Before coming out of the river, he filled the bucket again and carried it up on the bank where she was sitting. Able to recognize her then, he said, "Mrs. Tyson, are you all right? You took a little fall there."

"I'm all right," Ruby answered. "I'm sorry you had to get your boots wet to save my bucket." She hesitated. "I mean your moccasins," she said when she remembered that Clint wore moccasins.

"It's no trouble," he told her. "They'll dry out pretty quick. I'll carry your bucket back to your wagon for you, if you'll carry my coffeepot and my cup."

"Oh, you don't have to do that," she insisted, lifting her face to plead with him. "It's not really that heavy."

"What happened to your eye?" He had not noticed until then that her left eye was bruised and swollen. "That looks pretty bad. You sure you're all right?"

She quickly lowered her head again. "Yes, yes," she quickly assured him. "I must have hit it when I slipped on the bank just now." She started to get up on her feet. "I've got to get back to the wagon."

He reached down and took her elbow to help her up, then he took a closer look at the bruised eye. "That didn't happen when you fell down," he said. "That happened a while ago."

"Of course," she replied. "I meant to say I bumped it on the tailgate of the wagon. I'm all right now. Don't you concern yourself with it."

It was obvious that she did not want to divulge the circumstances that resulted in her having a black eye. It didn't take much imagination, however, to make a good guess as to the cause. No doubt, it probably happened on one of those nights the neighboring wagons complained about the noise. "Here," he said to her and handed his coffeepot and cup to her. "I'll tote your water back for you." He picked up the bucket of water and started toward the wagons. She had no choice but to follow him. He had no idea what he should do about her abusive husband. In the first place, it was none of his business, and if something was to be done about it, it fell within Scofield's responsibility as wagon master. Still, he felt it was every man's responsibility to defend a helpless woman. He supposed it would depend on her husband's reaction when he escorted his wife home.

As it turned out, the confrontation with Ralph Tyson did not occur. For when they got back to the wagon, Ralph was gone. Ruby immediately looked relieved, having been afraid of what the young scout had in mind upon facing her husband. Ralph's saddle was gone from the back of the wagon, so she knew where he had gone and that he would not likely return any time soon. The thought of more of the little bit of money they had left being drowned in a whiskey bottle didn't even occur at that moment, so relieved was she. "He was talkin' about doin' some coon huntin'," she offered to explain his absence. "Ralph likes to coon hunt, and he said there were likely a passel of 'em in these trees along the river."

"Is that a fact?" Clint replied skeptically. "Well, I reckon he'll be gone a while, won't he?"

"I expect so," she answered. "I'll tell him you carried the water for me. He'll be pleased to hear you gave me a hand, Clint. Thank you."

"I don't have any right to stick my nose in anybody else's business, but I hope every woman on this wagon train knows that Clayton Scofield won't tolerate any one of you ladies gettin' rough treatment from any man. And that don't matter if you're married to him or not."

"I don't know what you're thinkin'," Ruby replied, "but there's no need for you to worry on my part. Thank you again for savin' my water bucket." She tried to smile for him.

"Whatever you say, ma'am." He took a quick look around him. "Have you got enough wood for your breakfast fire? Maybe I'd best cut some more for you."

"No, I've got another stack I cut after supper. It's stacked under the back of the wagon to keep it dry."

"Was that when you busted your eye?" Clint couldn't resist asking.

"What? Oh, yes, I think that was when I bumped my eye."

The usual singers and dancers were still gathered in the middle of the circle of wagons when Clint left Ruby Tyson and returned to Scofield's wagon. He found his uncle sitting on a stool, facing the folks enjoying the entertainment, his back leaning against the side of the wagon. "You look like you ain't got a care in the world," Clint said.

"Just settin' here listenin' to the music," Scofield responded. "They play the same tunes over and over every night, but I still like to hear 'em." He pointed to Clint's wet trousers and moccasins. "What have you been doin', goin' fishin' the hard way?"

"As a matter of fact," Clint answered, "and all I caught was a bucket." He went on to relate his meeting Ruby down by the river and the black eye she was sporting.

"That sorry piece of crap hit her," Scofield growled. "I told him what would happen if he got rough with that woman."

"Well, that's what I think happened," Clint said. "'Course, she says she hit her head on the wagon tailgate."

"That son of a . . ." Scofield started, then stopped abruptly to ask, "You feel like a drink of whiskey?"

"I wouldn't mind one," Clint answered, knowing what his uncle had in mind.

Chapter 8

The well-traveled path from Fort Laramie to Jake Plummer's saloon was easy to follow by the light of a full moon. Clint and Scofield slow-walked their horses the short mile-and-a-half to the solidly built log structure with a front porch across the width of the building. Clint suspected Plummer built it with defense against Indian attack in mind. There were half a dozen horses and one mule tied out front at the rail, so Clint and Scofield tied their horses to a porch corner post. When they went inside, they found the saloon was more crowded than they suspected. This was due to the fact that a good portion of the crowd was made up of soldiers. And the soldiers had walked down from the fort. There were no empty tables, so they walked up to the bar and ordered a shot of whiskey. Elmo, the bartender, remembered Scofield and gave him a warm welcome. "You leadin' another wagon train west?" Elmo asked. When Scofield said that he was, Elmo asked, "Is that one of your settlers?" He pointed to a figure sitting on the floor, huddled in a back corner behind an oak sideboard.

"Hard to say, with him all slumped over like that, but I believe he might be," Scofield said. "What's he been doin'? Causin' trouble?"

"He came in pretty early and started drinkin' till he ran outta money. Then he started shootin' off his mouth about how he could outdrink any soldier in here. Only catch was, they had to buy the whiskey 'cause he was broke. He started makin' so much fuss till Jake came out to see what was goin' on. Jake told him he was gonna have to shut up, or he was gonna throw him out. He started to put up a fuss, but two of the soldiers picked him up and dumped him back there in the corner and he's been sittin' there ever since."

Scofield looked at Clint and shrugged, telling himself that it wasn't worth getting all bent out of shape thinking about it. "Whaddaya say? One more for the road, then take him home?" Clint answered with a shrug, so Elmo poured another shot and they tossed it back, then went to the back of the room to get Ralph. "Come on, Tyson," Scofield said, "get your butt up from there. It's time to go."

Tyson looked up to see who was talking to him. When he saw who was standing over him, he stared for a long moment before responding. "I ain't ready to go yet."

"I didn't ask you if you were ready. I said it's time to go. Now get up from there before I jerk a knot in your neck."

"You ain't got nothin' to say about what I do when I

ain't in that damn wagon train," Tyson quarreled. "This is a public place, so get the hell outta here and leave me be."

Clint looked at Scofield and nodded his readiness. Scofield nodded in response, then they both reached down and grabbed Tyson under his arms and jerked him up on his feet. They started walking him toward the door, his feet barely touching the floor as they carried him. Before they reached the door, however, two soldiers stepped in front of them. "Hey, where the hell you think you're goin' with our friend?"

Surprised to hear Tyson had any friends in that saloon, Scofield answered him. "We're takin' him back where he belongs, soldier. Your friend's had enough for one night."

"The hell you are," the second soldier said. "We made a deal with that jasper."

Curious now, Scofield asked, "What kinda deal?"

"He's got a wagon down by the river with a pretty little woman in it. When we get done here, we'll buy him a bottle of whiskey and he'll take us to see the woman for as long as we want. That's the deal."

Neither Scofield nor Clint could even comment for a long moment. Both looked at Tyson in utter contempt and a strong urge to strangle him. But Scofield felt the soldiers were not really to blame, since they weren't aware of the actual situation, so he explained. "You boys have been suckered in on somethin' that ain't what you think. That wagon he says he's got is in a wagon train and the woman is his wife. He's so eat up by whiskey that he don't know right from wrong. So that's all there is to it. We're takin' him back now."

"Well, now, wait a minute," the first soldier protested. "It don't make no difference. If she's his wife, he can do what he wants with her. And a deal's a deal. We already bought the bottle of likker. Here it is right here." He picked the bottle up from the table.

"I swear, you ain't no better than he is," Scofield said. "Now, stand aside."

"Go to hell," the second soldier said and stepped up in front of them. They both released Tyson at the same time and before he hit the floor, Scofield planted his oversized fist flush on the second soldier's nose, knocking him through the open door. At the same time this was happening, the first soldier, holding the full whiskey bottle by the neck, swung it like a club at Clint. Clint ducked under the roundhouse swing and came up with an uppercut under the soldier's jawbone that effectively shattered several teeth. The young scout's reflexes were sharp enough to catch the bottle of whiskey before it landed on the floor. With one free hand each, they reached down, pulled Tyson up again, and backed out the door.

They had to be concerned about the reactions of the other soldiers in the room, but none moved to stop them. They decided there was no attempt to stop their abduction of Tyson because they must certainly have heard Scofield when he told the true story of the woman in a wagon. And there was a general strain of decency among them that wouldn't permit them to support their fellow soldiers—that and the Colt Navy six-shooter in Scofield's free hand. Tyson was little more than a dead weight, due to the fact that he must have had enough money to render himself dead drunk. The fact that he rode a mule was the only way they could have possibly known which mount was his. So, while they made a quick departure, Elmo and Jake were left to puzzle over the one set of wet footprints left across the floor.

The nightly social gathering had ended by the time Clint and Scofield returned to the camp, leading an unconscious Ralph Tyson on his mule. They rode directly to Tyson's wagon where they found Ruby, wrapped in a blanket and huddled next to a small fire. Clint couldn't help wondering if she might have been better off had they not brought her husband home. *But,* he supposed, *I expect he's all she's got in this world.* She got up to receive them as they pulled up by her wagon.

"Well, Clint, first you save my bucket, now you've found my husband," she said, attempting to make a joke of it. But she was unable to disguise the melancholy in her voice for the life she suffered. "If you'll just help me get him off that mule, I'll take care of him. I'm real sorry you both had to trouble yourselves to bring him home."

"We'll help you get him in bed," Scofield said. "I doubt he's gonna wake up anytime soon. We're not pullin' outta here till day after tomorrow, so he oughta have time to get himself straightened out tomorrow." He hesitated to ask, but he thought he had to, in light of the fact that the bartender at Jake's Place said Tyson had spent all his money on whiskey. "S'cuse me for askin', but how are you fixed for supplies? Do you have any money for anything you'll be needin' to go on from here?"

She bowed her head low, obviously ashamed. "I've saved a little bit of money that Ralph don't know I took outta his pants pocket. But we don't need much, just the two of us, with no children."

"Do you know where you're goin' when we reach Oregon City?" Clint wondered aloud.

"Well, no, not exactly. Ralph has a brother that went out to the Oregon country two years ago. We'll find him and get us a piece of land near him."

"Does Ralph's brother know you're comin'?" Clint asked.

"No, we haven't had any contact with him, but Ralph says he'll be glad to see us."

Clint and Scofield exchanged doubtful glances, feeling as helpless as they knew she was. "Let's get him on his bed," Scofield said, and he and Clint carried the unconscious man to the bed under the wagon. Then while his uncle helped Ruby settle Ralph in the bed, Clint unsaddled the mule and released it to graze with the horses.

When they were ready to leave, Ruby again expressed her appreciation for bringing her husband home. Scofield bluntly replied, "I don't know if we done you a favor or not, but right now, there ain't nobody else to drive them mules for ya." He reached down and gently lifted her chin so he could look at her face. "I told him what I was gonna do, if I saw any marks on your face."

"You shouldn't blame my black eye on Ralph," she quickly insisted. "I did this to myself when I bumped my head on the wagon seat."

"On the tailgate," Clint corrected her.

"Right," she quickly replied. "On the tailgate, I meant to say."

Scofield got deadly serious as they were leaving. "Ruby, you listen to me. I won't stand for no women to be mistreated on any wagon train I'm leadin'. If you have trouble, you come tell me and we'll do somethin' about it." She said that she would, but he doubted that she meant it. He had an idea that she was too fearful of what Ralph might do to her if she told someone about his abuse. The only way she would be free of him was if someone killed him. And that would create another problem for her, for she would be on her own. He wasn't sure she could make it on her own. She was no Fancy Wallace.

"You sure you ain't gonna need me for anything?" Clint asked as he tied a Sharps rifle that had belonged to Junior Fry down beside his own Henry in the saddle sling. He planned to give the Sharps to Yellow Sky, since he had nothing else for a gift. It was an 1853 Sporting Model, a good rifle, but he had no use for it. Junior had a full belt of cartridges, so he could supply Yellow Sky with some ammunition, as well. Walking through the camp early that morning, he didn't see any sign of activity around the Tyson wagon. So, he figured Ralph had most likely crawled up into the back of his wagon to ride out the morning-after sickness. Then he reminded himself that it was too early for breakfast, anyway.

"I don't know of anything I need you for," Scofield answered him. "I ain't plannin' to do much of anything, myself."

"All right, then. I expect I'll be back before suppertime." He climbed up on Biscuit and rode out of the camp. He was starting out so early because the spot where Yellow Sky usually camped was a good twelve miles down the Laramie River. He was planning to share a midday meal with his Crow friend while Biscuit was resting, then return to the wagon train in time to get supper.

Many memories returned to fill his mind as he rode the familiar trail down the river. He had spent three years in Yellow Sky's village and during that time, they had moved several times. But the place he had lived the most was the Laramie River campground, the place he was going to this morning. He had hunted along these riverbanks many times, his weapon a bow made of ash wood. He was fourteen when his mother and father were killed by a Sioux war party and he was left to die in a burning cabin with a Sioux arrow in his back. He could still remember the feel of the arrow shaft, like a heavy weight on his chest as he crawled across the kitchen floor, trying to get to his parents' room. The flames swirled about the roof over his head and down the outside walls, turning the inside of the cabin into an oven. He could hear the yelling of the Sioux warriors trying to get back in the house to take scalps, but the flames turned them back. Finally, he made it to his parents' bedroom, only to find they were both dead, having been murdered while they slept.

Faced with the choice of being burned to death or facing the warriors running around outside, still trying to get inside, he decided to die fighting. In his efforts to get out of the cabin, he was blocked by a wall of fire everywhere he tried. Getting weaker every second with little air left to breathe, he came again to the front door, which was half-consumed by fire. Then the bottom half of the door broke off, leaving a gap in the flames for just a few seconds. He didn't hesitate. He crawled through the gap and was outside!

Riding along the river, he consciously thought about that moment on the tiny porch of the cabin. He had escaped the flames, now he must prepare to die at the hands of the Indians. But the Indians did not shoot at him, and they were no longer yelling and running around the burning cabin. They only stood and stared at him as if he was a ghost. He felt his brain was still half-cooked from the heat of the fire, but it slowly began to function again. And he finally realized the apparently astonished Indians staring at him now were Crow. They had caused the smaller raiding party of Sioux to run. It was Yellow Sky who had led that hunting party. He shook his head slowly when he thought about that time. It was how he got his Crow name, *Crawls Through Fire*.

That was a long time ago. He might still be Crawls Through Fire had not his father's brother-in-law found him three years later in Yellow Sky's village. Clint laughed to himself when he remembered how hard it was for Scofield to convince him that he belonged in the white man's world. To this day, he was still not sure.

The sun was high in the sky when he saw the tipis in a wide grassy meadow that led down to the river. There were several women skinning two deer near the water's edge. They paused in their work to watch the young man ride by. Knowing the order in which the tipis would be erected, he rode directly to the center of the camp and dismounted. One of the men walked over to face him. "What is it you want, white man?"

The Indian asked him in English. Clint answered in the Crow language. "I am Crawls Through Fire. I have come to visit my father, Yellow Sky."

The young Crow warrior smiled at once. Like most of the young men in the village, he had never met Crawls Through Fire, but he was quite familiar with the name. "Welcome, Crawls Through Fire, I will tell Yellow Sky you are here." He turned and hurried to the tipi Clint was sure belonged to Yellow Sky's wife, Mourning Song.

Clint stood waiting while everyone within earshot of the exchange beamed their delight, especially when they realized who he was. Some of them had been at his father's cabin when he earned his name. They welcomed him, and he thanked them, calling some of them by name. In a few moments' time, Yellow Sky emerged from the tipi, his old eyes shining at the sight of one he had great affection for. His delight at seeing the young man he had taken into his family brought a wide grin to Clint's face. At the same time, he couldn't help feeling guilty for not having visited the old chief more than he had. "My son, it brings great joy to these old eyes to see you again."

"It brings me great joy to see you as well, my father," Clint replied. "I was happy to hear that your village was back here close to Fort Laramie, so I could see you again."

"You are still leading the white settlers through our lands with your big white uncle?"

Clint smiled at Yellow Sky's reference to Scofield. "Yes, Father, I'm still scouting for Clayton Scofield. He sends his regards to you." He didn't, but Clint thought it would be the nice thing to say. "I brought some things I thought Mourning Song might need, some coffee, some sugar, and some flour." He took the sacks off his saddle and set them before the tipi entrance. Mourning Song took them inside immediately.

"You have come at a good time," Yellow Sky said. "The hunters have killed two deer. We will cook some of the meat to go with the things you brought."

"I brought you something else I hope you will like," Clint said. He untied the Sharps rifle from his saddle and presented it to Yellow Sky. "There are some bullets, too," he added and handed him a full cartridge belt.

The old chief was obviously very pleased to get it. "After we eat, you must show me how to shoot this gun."

Mourning Song baked bread with the flour Clint brought her and made coffee to drink with their fresh venison. Yellow Sky talked of many things that had happened since Crawls Through Fire had returned to the world of the white man. It pleased him to see that Clint had retained some of the Crow influence, evident by the buckskin shirt and moccasins he wore. There were also questions that Clint was unable to answer truthfully. When the mighty Crow chief, Plenty Coups, had a vision when still a boy, the elders of the tribe interpreted it to mean the white man would eventually take over the entire country. So they decided it in the Crow's best interest to always remain at peace with the whites. "The Absaroka still keep that peace with the white man, and many of our young men ride as scouts with the army," Yellow Sky said. "At the big treaty at Fort Laramie, almost ten summers ago, the white chiefs ruled that all the land from the Big Horn Valley, east to the Powder River, and south to the Musselshell River, would be the land of the Crow. Yet they do nothing to keep the Sioux and the Cheyenne from moving into our lands. The wagon trains you ride with are only passing through our land, and that is good. They take the white man to the Oregon country. But there are other white men who stop here to stay and build their farms. Is the white man going to keep settling his family on our hunting ground? How long will it be before the white man takes all of the land for himself?"

"I don't know the answer to your question," Clint replied. "I have to be honest and tell you what I think. I think it is bound to come. Maybe not while you are still here, but they will come." The old chief only nodded solemnly in reply. Clint wished he could tell him that he would always have his hunting grounds, but he was sure

Yellow Sky already knew that was not to be. He was just hoping that Clint could tell him otherwise.

They talked on after eating the food Mourning Song prepared for them until Yellow Sky said, "Come now, and show me how best to fire this weapon you have given me." When they came out of the tipi and Yellow Sky was carrying the Sharps carbine, they immediately attracted an audience, anxious to see him fire it. They were impressed when Clint suggested they should walk down to the riverbank. After he showed Yellow Sky how easily the breechloading rifle was to load, he then picked out a tree on the other side of the river as a target. "That is a long shot to try," Yellow Sky commented.

"This is a powerful weapon. Line the sights up just like you do with your old rifle and pull the trigger," Clint said. "Just pretend that tree's a buffalo. See that knot a few feet up the trunk? Pretend that's a spot right behind the buffalo's front leg." He stepped away from him to give him room and was about to encourage him again when the rifle fired. Clint squinted at the tree for a moment before announcing, "Doggone if you didn't just kill that buffalo."

"I'm not so sure," Yellow Sky said, grinning in excitement. "My eyes are not as young as yours." Clint was not one-hundred-percent sure himself, but he imagined he could see a bullet hole in the middle of that knot. There was no need to guess, however, for one of the young boys standing by, jumped into the river and started swimming across. In a few minutes, he crawled up the other bank and ran to the tree. A second later, he stuck his finger in the bullet hole, turned around, and held his other hand up in the air while he released a triumphant yell. Clint looked at the old man, who was grinning like a young boy, and said, “You can hunt anything with that rifle. You know how to reload, right?” Yellow Sky showed him that he could. “You want to try it again to prove it wasn’t just luck?”

“No, not luck,” Yellow Sky answered. “Save bullets for real buffalo.”

When Clint said that it was time for him to go, Yellow Sky gave him a word of caution. Our hunters have seen sign of Lakota raiding parties on the Platte, west of the cliff where the wagon people stop to scratch their names. Clint knew he was referring to Register Cliff, where many of the emigrants stopped to carve their names in the soft sandstone cliff. “How far past the cliff?” He asked because Register Cliff was only a day’s drive west of Fort Laramie.

One of the hunters answered for Yellow Sky. “Maybe five miles,” he volunteered. Clint nodded his thanks, even though he couldn’t be sure the hunter knew how far a mile was. At any rate, he knew that he would be keeping a sharp eye when he rode out ahead of the wagon train in the morning.

He whistled a couple of sharp notes and Biscuit raised his head from the grass down by the river and trotted up to find him. The people gathered around him, admired the Palouse gelding as Clint saddled him. “Nez Perce,” Yellow Sky said and nodded. “Friend of Absaroka.”

“He’s a good horse,” Clint said as he climbed up into the saddle. “I’ll see you again when I am back this way.” He turned Biscuit toward the river again and rode out of the camp.

Chapter 9

The wagon train started out at seven o'clock, right on schedule the following morning, to continue their journey west along the North Platte River. Although Scofield felt the horses could have pushed on a few miles farther, he ordered the train to stop for the first night out of Fort Laramie at Register Cliff. The cliffs were actually sandstone bluffs along the south bank of the river that stood over one hundred feet high. It was a favorite camping spot for the trains on the Oregon Trail because it afforded water and lush grass pasturing for the animals. An equal attraction to the spot was the bluffs themselves, because many of the travelers took the opportunity to carve their names into the soft face of the sandstone bluffs to record their passage. There was also the added feeling of safety, since the campground was so close to Fort Laramie and the soldiers stationed there. All these factors combined to make for a casual overnight stop. Clint was not inclined to share that casual attitude, however, for he remembered what the young Crow hunter at Yellow Sky's village had said about seeing signs of Lakota warriors. Whereas he was not certain of the young hunter's concept of five miles, he had every confidence in the hunter's ability to read sign. So, he decided it a good idea to take a look around a little on the north side of the river. That would be the only place a raiding party following the wagon train could keep from being seen by the wagons.

"I'd be surprised if Sioux or Cheyenne raiders would be fool enough to strike us this close to the fort," Scofield said. "But you can't never tell."

"Won't hurt to take a look," Clint said.

"It'd have to be a pretty doggone good-sized party of 'em to come after us in this river valley. There ain't that much cover and they're sure to know there'd be a rifle in every wagon shootin' at 'em."

"I wasn't talkin' about that kind of attack," Clint said. "I'm just talkin' about tryin' to keep 'em from slippin' in on us tonight to steal some horses."

Scofield paused to consider that possibility. "You might be right. I'll have 'em bring the stock inside the circle tonight. Might be a good idea to see who Zachary and Braxton have got on guard duty tonight, too."

"Good," Clint said. "Now, I'm gonna take a little ride across the river before it gets too dark. See if I can find any sign there's anybody followin' us."

"Watch yourself," Scofield told him.

"Always do," Clint answered.

* * *

"What you lookin' at me like that for?" Clint asked the Palouse when he untied his reins from the tailgate of Scofield's wagon. "You thinkin', 'Why ain't he took my saddle off?' Well, we're just gonna take an easy little scout on the other side of the river. You ain't been worked that hard today." He scratched the powerful gelding behind his ears for a minute or two, then climbed aboard and headed him toward the river.

When he rode out of the circle of wagons, he passed between Ralph Tyson's and Peter Gilbert's wagons. He didn't see Gilbert, but Tyson was lying on his bedroll under the wagon while Ruby was cooking supper. She looked up at him and spoke, "Clint."

"Evenin', Ruby. Everything all right with you today?" She answered with a quick nod, then lowered her gaze back down to the pot of beans she was stirring. Clint smiled and gave Biscuit a nudge with his heels.

"What the hell was that about?" Ralph demanded as he rolled out of his bed. "Is everythin' all right with you today? What's he askin' you that for?"

"Nothin', Ralph," she answered. "He was just bein' polite, that's all."

"Polite," he repeated. "I'll polite him and you, too. Maybe I need to remind you you're my wife. You ain't got no business talkin' to any of the other men in this wagon train, especially that sneaky dog."

"Why do you talk like that?" She had to protest. "Clint Buchanan is one of the most decent men I know."

"Oh, he is, is he? How come you say that? Have you been whinin' about how hard you have to work? Maybe he was wantin' to know how you got that black eye. Well, it ain't none of his business what happens in this wagon. He's as bad as that uncle of his, wantin' to tell everybody what's right and what's wrong, like he's God Almighty."

Fearing that he was working himself up for another one of his frequent bouts of violence, Ruby took a step back, trying to stay out of his range. "Ain't no use to go tellin' yourself things are happenin' that ain't really happenin'."

"Is that a fact?" He leered at her accusingly. "You think I don't know what's goin' on behind my back. But ain't it kinda strange that with twenty-seven wagons parked in this circle, Buchanan rides outta here right by my wagon? Where you just happen to be cookin' supper?"

"He rode out this way 'cause it looks like he's headin' across the river. And he most likely rode by our wagon 'cause there's a good-sized gap between our wagon and the Gilberts' wagon." Already afraid she had said too much, she didn't go on to say the gap was big because Peter and Effie didn't want their children to hear all of Ralph's blasphemy. That thought sparked another that had occurred to her many times during the four-plus years of their marriage, and that was her gratitude that she had never conceived a child. In her heart, she had to believe that God, in His wisdom, would not permit an innocent child to be subject to Ralph Tyson's evil temper. Ralph, of course, blamed her, calling her a barren slut. "Supper's gonna be ready in a few minutes," she said then, in an attempt to get his mind off Clint Buchanan. "I'm fixin' these soup beans like you said your mama used to fix 'em."

"The last time you fixed 'em, they didn't taste nothin'

like my mama cooked 'em. Too bad your mama didn't teach you how to cook. I wish you'da told me that before we got married."

I wish I had told you, too, she thought, *if it really would have stopped you from marrying me.* She thought of the brutal assaults upon her body that Ralph considered his right as her husband. Somehow, he even blamed her for his failure to keep up the parcel of land his father had given them as a wedding present. His obsession with the whiskey bottle began to take precedence over even the most minor of chores. Finally, his father told him he was taking the land back. To be fair, he had told him, he would buy the land back, leaving Ralph with enough money to start somewhere else. It was Ralph's father who suggested the idea of going to Oregon where land was said to be there for the taking. She had prayed that the Willamette Valley held the cure for her husband's failure as a farmer. She wondered now if he really cared enough to make the effort. As for herself, she no longer feared what might become of her. She had no choice but to hope each new day would be better than the one just passed and speculate upon what she must have done for God to punish her so severely.

"It's Rides Ahead," Lame Horse said, pointing to the rider that just rode out of the circle of wagons. This was the name the three Lakota warriors had given Clint, for he was the man who always rode ahead of the wagons to scout the way. They had followed the wagons when they had left Fort Laramie that morning. It was the first train they had seen since coming to scout the white man's road over a week before. "He's coming out by the river. Maybe he saw us."

"He didn't see us," Wounded Buffalo said. "If he did, he wouldn't be coming after us by himself. He's just trying to see if there is anyone watching the train."

"If he turns this way when he gets to the bottom of this bluff, we're going to have to move back where our horses are, or he'll see us," Lame Horse said.

"If he does that, maybe I'll stay here and put an arrow in his belly," Pony Walks remarked. "Then I'll take that Nez Perce horse he rides."

"Then they would know we were here and be ready to watch their horses tonight," Wounded Buffalo said. "And instead of driving off many horses, we would ride away with one horse."

"Wounded Buffalo is right," Lame Horse said. "We have come to take their horses. If we wait until they are all asleep, we can take many horses and Rides Ahead's horse, too."

"Maybe they might bring all the horses inside the circle for the night," Pony Walks replied.

"Then we'll slip inside their circle of wagons and drive the horses out through the wide gap Rides Ahead just rode through," Wounded Buffalo boasted.

"I don't like the look of that man," Pony Walks commented as they watched Clint ride slowly around the wagons, stopping occasionally to estimate the age of a random footprint here and there. "He looks more like an Absaroka than a white man."

In a short while, darkness settled over the camp. They were disappointed to see the men come out to drive the horses and cows inside the circle of wagons. But they were not discouraged. "Maybe they go to sleep now," Pony Walks said.

"There!" Lame Horse exclaimed and pointed. "Rides Ahead is back inside the wagons." Having watched the camp while they ate supper and the women washed the cooking utensils afterward, the three Indians assumed the camp would now go to their beds. They were startled then when Buck Carrey walked out to the center of the circle, sat down on a stool and started picking out a tune on his banjo.

"What is that thing?" Wounded Buffalo asked, startled when he heard the sounds emanating from the strange weapon. In a few minutes, Buck was joined by Doc Meadows and his fiddle, and the waiting horse thieves realized thc camp had no intentions toward going to sleep. They had no choice but to wait out the social hour.

Lame Horse suggested it might be in their favor for the white men to tire themselves out and they would sleep much more soundly. "We have to wait until they are all asleep, so now it is plain to see that it will be much later before they are. So, there is no need to sit up here on this bluff to wait. We might as well go back to our horses and cook something to eat. We have plenty of time." His two companions readily agreed with him, so they withdrew from the bluff, knowing they could hear the noise from the singing and dancing where their horses were tied. When the noise stopped, they planned to wait an hour or so, to give them time to go to sleep.

Clint walked over to the fire and poured himself another cup of coffee. Then he sat down beside Scofield to drink it. "I think I'll ride back outside the wagons for a while, now that the dancin' is startin' to peter out." When Scofield asked why, Clint told him that he just had a feeling and he wanted to look around. "Who's on guard duty tonight after midnight?"

"Tim Blake and Ron Settle," Scofield answered. "You'd better let 'em know you're gonna be snoopin' around outside the wagons. Either one of them boys are liable to take a shot at you."

"I'll let 'em know," Clint assured him, then dumped his coffee and went in search of Blake and Settle, leading Biscuit to plod patiently along behind him. He found the two guards with several of the other men who had started driving the horses and cows up from the river's edge. After he told them he might be on the prowl later that night, he climbed on Biscuit and helped herd the stock inside the circle of wagons. One of the wagons was turned out like a gate, and after the horses were driven through it, it was pushed back in place. Concerned about the size of the gap between Tyson's and Gilbert's wagon, Clint decided he'd best take some rope and make a temporary fence between their wagons. The gap was big enough that it might potentially attract some of the horses to wander.

"Tyson!" Clint called out when he rode up and dismounted. There was no answer from Ralph, but Ruby came from the back of the wagon where she had been putting away her cooking utensils.

"Howdy, Clint," she said, talking softly. "Ralph's already gone to bed. You want me to wake him up?"

Clint lowered his voice, as well. "No, no need to wake him up. I was just worried about the size of the gap between your wagon and the Gilberts'. I brought some rope, and I thought I'd run a couple of lengths between the wagons, in case some of the stock takes a notion to leave this way. I'll be quick about it."

Peter and Effie Gilbert were evidently among the last few families reluctant to end the social hour, for there was no sign of them or their kids at their wagon. Clint quickly tied one end of his rope to the seat of their wagon, then tied it to the tailgate of Tyson's. Concerned then that the horses might not see the rope and stumble over the wagon tongue, which was lying on the ground, he said to Ruby, "I need to ask you something." Before she had a chance to respond, she was interrupted.

"You don't need to ask my wife nothin'," Ralph growled from his bed under the wagon. "Any questions you got on your mind, you'd best ask me."

"Well, all right," Clint replied. "I'll ask you, then. Have you got a couple of old rags or something I could tie on this rope, so the horses can see it?"

Flushed with embarrassment by her husband's insinuating remarks, Ruby quickly answered Clint. "Yes, I think I do. I'll find some and tie 'em on your rope. Won't be no trouble a-tall."

"Thank you, ma'am," Clint said. "I 'preciate it. Sorry I woke you up, Tyson." He walked back to the front of their wagon where Biscuit was standing waiting. She walked back behind him, trying to decide if she should apologize for her husband's attitude, or if it was best not to say anything. Feeling her embarrassment, he said softly, "If it wouldn't be too much trouble, could you save that rope for me, if you hitch up in the mornin' before I come get it?"

"No trouble," she assured him. She stood there for a

moment, watching him ride off toward Clayton Scofield's wagon, until she heard Ralph summon her.

Still under the wagon, Tyson was up on one elbow when he said, "Bring me a dipper of water." She went to the water bucket, dipped out some water, and took it to him. He gulped the dipperful down and held the dipper toward her, but when she took hold of it, he didn't let go. Instead, he jerked hard on it. "Maybe you wanna tell me what you two was whisperin' about over yonder."

"He said he'd like to have his rope back," she answered, impatiently.

"Is that so? I expect that ain't all he'd like to have, is it? Ain't it kinda funny he's worried about the gap by our wagon. I don't ever see him worryin' about any other gaps."

"Oh, for goodness sakes, Ralph, it's because we've got the only gap behind our wagon big enough to drive a stagecoach through!" She lost her composure for that moment, and she immediately feared it might cost her.

Lucky for her, he was too lazy to get out of bed, so she escaped with a warning. "You'd best watch your mouth. You're fixin' to get another black eye to match that one. Besides, that gap ain't no fault of mine. He needs to be talkin' to Gilbert about it. He's the one who didn't pull his wagon up close enough." He paused to release a belch, brought on by his gulping of the water. "I reckon it's because Effie Gilbert's a little too old and dumpy to suit Buchanan's taste."

Ruby cringed in response to his remark. At least Effie wasn't there to overhear the insult. She thought about Clint Buchanan again and wished he would not come around anymore. It never failed to set Ralph off on one of his jealous illusions. She wished he would not come around for other reasons, too, the primary one being an example between a decent man and the man she married out of desperation to escape an abusive family.

As for the young man Ruby was thinking about, his thoughts were of compassion for a young woman who had to put up with a husband like the man she married. And he wondered why God wasted breath on a man like Ralph Tyson. He felt really sorry for the woman.

Ruby busied herself with some sewing until she heard the heavy snoring from under the wagon that told her Ralph was fully in the clutches of deep slumber. Only then did she put her sewing away and go to bed herself. Being as careful as she could manage, so as not to wake him, she crawled into the blanket beside him, wishing they had a tent, like most of the others had. All the camp was quiet now, and soon she drifted off to sleep, unaware of the three Lakota raiders lying flat behind a low rise, barely twelve yards from where she was sleeping.

"They have tied ropes across our gate," Pony Walks whispered. "How will we get the horses out now?"

"Stay here," Lame Horse replied. "I will go to the wagon and see if I can take it down. It can't be too strong because they want to drive the wagons in the morning." He rose to his feet and hurried cautiously to the rear of the wagon where the rope was attached to the tailgate. He paused when he looked down and saw the man and woman sleeping almost at his feet. The impulse to kill them both struck him at once, but he decided they might cry out. He examined the rope and determined it was a temporary barrier. He easily untied the knot and laid the rope down on the ground, took another look at the sleeping couple, and hurried back to his friends. "The gate is open. There is a man and a woman asleep under the back of the wagon. If I tried to kill them, I was afraid I would make noise and alert the camp."

"Should we go in and herd the horses on foot?" Wounded Buffalo wondered. "Or should we ride in and stampede the herd through the gate?" They had discussed their plan of attack while they were waiting for the camp to go to sleep and had not decided which was best for them. A silent, stealthy raid, where they entered the enclosure and quietly led several horses through the gap, hoping that more of the horses would follow, was favored by Wounded Buffalo. Lame Horse was more in favor of riding their ponies into the circle, getting behind the herd of horses and herding them all through the gap, making plenty of noise and shooting anyone who attempted to stop them.

Pony Walks made the decision for them. "If we ride into that camp, shooting and yelling, we can move the whole herd through the gate. The white men may try to come after us, but we will be on our horses, and they will be on foot."

"Pony Walks is right," Lame Horse said. "We will surprise them, and it will take time for them to know what is happening. By then, it will be too late. We will be out of the circle and away."

So, with Lame Horse leading, the three Lakota Sioux warriors walked their ponies through the gap between the two wagons in single file. The horses' hooves treading silently within six feet of the sleeping man and woman. Once they were clear of the wagon, they continued on toward the horses gathered in the center of the circle. Using hand signals to communicate with each other, they circled around behind the settlers' horses.

"What the hell . . . ?" Ron Settle started when he saw three riders positioning themselves on one side of the horse herd. From his guard post at the easternmost part of the circle, he strained to see who the riders were. After a moment, he realized he was looking at three Indians and they were about to steal the horses. He raised his rifle and aimed at the one closest to him. Lame Horse raised his hand in the air, preparing to give the signal to start the stampede, but a shot from Ron's rifle started it before he could. Lame Horse keeled over on his horse's neck, the bullet in his side. Unaware of what had actually happened, Wounded Buffalo and Pony Walks fired their rifles in the air and released their war cries, pushing the horses toward the gap in the wagons.

Alert now as well, Tim Blake saw what was happening and took a quick shot at the galloping horse thieves but missed. He reloaded his rifle and ran to close the distance between him and the herd. It was obvious what the Indians planned to do. They were driving the entire herd toward the gap between Tyson and Gilbert, and there was no way to stop them. When the frightened horses reached the gap, they suddenly turned on each other in a seeming chaos just before gaining the freedom of the gap. The herd split, half turning to race around the wall of wagons in one direction, the other half going the other way. Blake and Settle both saw the reason for the confusion then. Clint Buchanan, on Biscuit, was anchored in the gap, firing his six-gun in the air and yelling at the horses, effectively turning them away from the gap.

In the midst of the confusion, none were more at a loss than Wounded Buffalo and Pony Walks. When the horses scattered, they realized what had happened and saw that Lame Horse was dead. With no thoughts of surrender, they both raced toward the man they knew was Rides Ahead. Both fired shots at him but missed. With no other choice, Clint dropped his empty six-shooter in his holster and pulled the Henry rifle from his saddle scabbard. Taking dead aim, he knocked Wounded Buffalo off his horse. Then he cranked in a fresh cartridge and dispensed with Pony Walks, seconds before the young brave reached the wagons.

Clint continued to sit there between the two wagons for a minute, watching the two bodies on the ground to make sure they didn't move. Both Tim and Ron arrived then and pronounced them both dead. "Tyson," Clint called out. "Are you and Ruby all right?"

A voice came from the front end of the wagon, where they had crawled during the chaos. "Yeah, we're all right."

"Good," Clint said. "I wanna tie this rope back up now. Is that all right with you?" He wanted to make a point of getting Ralph's permission.

"Yeah, it's all right."

Before he replaced the rope barrier, he walked Biscuit around to the rear of the Gilberts' wagon. "Mr. Gilbert, you and your family okay?"

"Yeah, Clint, I reckon so, just scared the bejeebers outta us, though," Peter answered. "We've got all heads accounted for."

By this time, a sizable crowd began to emerge from their hiding places. Among the first to reach Clint was

Scofield. He walked around to take a look at all three corpses before coming to talk to his nephew. "I'm gonna pay closer attention to you the next time you tell me you've just got a feelin'." He looked around him. "They rode right inside the circle and was gonna drive the whole herd out that gap."

"That's a fact," Clint allowed. "Only it backfired on 'em. Ron was the one that messed up their plan. He knocked the first one down. And after that, it was just a big stampede."

"Good work," Scofield said. "All three of ya." He looked down at Pony Walks. "Sioux?"

"Yep," Clint said, "Lakota Sioux."

"Good work," Scofield repeated. "We'da been in a helluva fix if these three Injuns had run off with all our horses."

"Well, they damn-near did," Ron said. "And they would have if Clint hadn't been settin' there in that gap to turn 'em back." He looked at Clint then and asked, "When did you ride over there and get in that gap? I never saw you ride across the circle."

"I was outside the circle and I was just lucky to see the three of 'em when they rode through the gap," Clint answered. "One of 'em sneaked up to the wagon on foot first and untied that rope I had up there. Then they all three just walked their ponies through nice and easy."

"What were you doin' outside the wagons that late at night?" Tim asked.

Scofield answered for him. "He just had a feelin'." Clint shrugged, then Scofield continued. "I hope everybody standin' here will learn a little lesson from this shindig. And the next time we make camp and circle the wagons, we get 'em hooked up right and don't leave no more gaps the size of this one here." He looked around at the gathered souls and his gaze lit on Peter Gilbert for a few moments, causing Gilbert to look a little sheepish. "I reckon we oughta bury these three Injuns, since there'll be other folks campin' here." Several of the men volunteered. "The rest of you best get back to your beds, if you can still sleep. We'll be pullin' out in the mornin'." Just to be doubly sure, he asked Clint, "There ain't no more of 'em out there, is there?"

"Nope. Just those three," Clint answered.

Chapter 10

With a new-found sense of potential danger, the emigrants moved out the following morning after their first encounter with the hostile Sioux. Though only three horse thieves, they were a fierce-looking breed to those who came to take a close look at the bodies before they were taken away to be buried. The sobering fact on everybody's mind was, if Clint Buchanan had not been there to plug up their escape route, the three Indians might have run off with all the horses. On the other hand, there was quite a lot of discussion about Blake and Settle's description of the young scout astride his horse, six-gun blazing in defiance of the Sioux warriors. It effectively dispelled any thoughts that anyone might have harbored that Clint had a job simply because he was Scofield's nephew.

After a few more days on the trail, the tiring numbness of the daily routine returned to put the fear of Indians farther back in their minds, however. The trail beside the North Platte they had been following since Fort Laramie, continued to become harder as they progressed up the high prairie toward the Continental Divide. After a little over a week and a half since leaving the camp at Register Cliff, they said good-bye to the brackish water of the North Platte at a point that had been named The Parting of the Ways. There, they picked up the Sweetwater River, which they would follow to South Pass. On the Sweetwater, the train came to another prominent marker on their journey, Independence Rock. They arrived at the rock at noontime, which afforded time for everyone to look at the giant mountain of granite in the middle of the grassy prairie while the horses were rested and the noon meal was prepared. "Why do they call it Independence Rock?" twelve-year-old Johnny Zachary asked his father.

"I've heard different stories," his father said. "Some say it's because when you get to Independence Rock, you're finally free of travelin' the Platte Valley. Clayton Scofield says they call it that because it's halfway to where we're goin'. And if you reach Independence Rock by the fourth of July, you'll make Oregon before the snow closes up the mountain passes at the other end."

"Is it the fourth of July yet?" Johnny asked.

"Nope, it's still June," his father replied. "We started plenty early enough."

Ten-year-old Mary stared at the many names and dates carved into the rock. "Do you have to put your name on it?"

Her mother answered her. "No, child. This is just like

Register Cliff. Folks just wanna carve their names, so everybody can see they were here."

"Why?" Mary wondered aloud.

"'Cause they ain't got enough sense to know nobody cares if they were here," Marcy said. "They don't know better'n to mess up Mother Nature's work."

Mary pointed to her father several feet away, busy recording the Zachary passing on the rock. "Then, why is Papa doin' that?"

"I just told you why," Marcy snapped. "Now, let's get back to the wagon. It'll be time to pull outta here soon." She turned around to look at the wagons and was prompted to remind her husband. "You'd best be hitchin' the horses up, John. There goes Clint, already headin' out." She remained there a moment to watch the young horseman lope away from the parked wagons.

"We've still got a little time," John assured her. "I expect Clint's gone on ahead to check the river crossings. Scofield said we'll have to cross this river nine or ten times before we get to South Pass, which is about one hundred miles from here. But because we've got to cross back and forth across the river so many times, we might be ten days or more, dependin' on how high the river is at the crossin's."

"I declare," Marcy exclaimed, "that doesn't sound like it'll be much fun, does it?"

"Just part of the journey," John responded, making an attempt to sound unconcerned. "He does it every trip back and forth, so he oughta know what he's doin'."

"Who's that?" Marcy asked.

John turned to see who she was referring to. "Damned if I know," he replied when he saw a stranger riding a bay horse toward the circle of wagons. From where they were standing by the rock, the rider looked to be a young man. He was leading a sorrel packhorse. "Now, where do you suppose he came from?" John wondered aloud. "Come on, kids," he called to Mary and Johnny. "Let's go back to the wagon."

When they got back to the wagons, the stranger was approaching a group of emigrants gabbing by one of the fires that had been used for cooking dinner. The group included Lonnie and Susie James and Pat and Ginny Shephard. John and Marcy walked over to join them, since any stranger was a source of news. They stepped up their pace, so they could get there when the young man pulled his horse to a stop and dismounted. "Well, howdy, young fellow," Lonnie greeted him. "Where'd you come from? You on your way to Oregon all by yourself?" He laughed, so they would know he was joking.

The young man smiled and nodded to each lady. "You might say that," he said, "at least till I caught up with you folks. I've been tryin' to catch up with somebody I think is on this wagon train."

Lonnie found that fascinating. "Where'd you start out from?"

"Independence, same as you folks," he said. "I thought I'd catch you at Fort Laramie, but you moved along faster'n I figured."

"Well, you caught us," Pat Shephard said. "Who you lookin' for?"

"Mildred Wallace," he answered.

"Mildred Wallace," Ginny Shephard repeated. "Nobody on this train by that name."

"There's a Fancy Wallace," Lonnie reminded her.

"Close enough," the stranger said. "Which wagon's hers?"

Susie started to raise her hand to point, but Lonnie caught her arm before she could point Fancy's wagon out. "Does Fancy know you?" No one on the train had really gotten close to Fancy and it was her attitude that ensured it. But there was a sense of loyalty on the part of the members who had made it this far on the trail together. Along with that was an obligation to protect a fellow traveler. "What's your name?"

"Oh, I think she'll know me," he answered. "My name's Billy Wallace."

"Oh, hell, you're kin?" Pat Shephard exclaimed. He turned and pointed to Fancy's wagon. "Yonder it is! Does she know you're comin'?"

"She oughta know," Billy answered. "Much obliged." He tipped his hat to the women and led his horses toward Fancy's wagon.

"Mildred," Susie commented. "I reckon Fancy is just a name she gave herself." She watched the young man riding across the pasture. "He walks with a swagger kinda like Fancy does, doesn't he? You think he's Fancy's husband?"

"More like a play toy," Ginny remarked. "He's too young to be her husband."

"His name's Wallace," Pat reminded them. "Least, he says it is."

Ginny grinned and looked at Susie. "Gives us something to talk about."

"We best quit talking and hitch up," John Zachary said. "We've got a ways to go today."

While the little group dispersed to prepare to start out

on the second half of the day's march, Billy Wallace pulled up to Fancy's wagon. He didn't dismount at once, his curiosity having been triggered by the sight of a brute of a man who had just led a team of horses up to the wagon. When there was no indication the man had even noticed him, Billy continued to sit there in the saddle while the man started hitching the horses up. "Howdy," Billy finally spoke, and when it appeared the man was still blind to him, Billy asked, "Is this Fancy Wallace's wagon?" Lemuel turned his head only partially toward him, seeming to look at him out of the corner of his eye. Then he nodded in answer to Billy's question. Finally concluding that Lemuel was touched in the head, Billy dismounted and asked, "Where is she?" Lemuel stared at him for a long moment before pointing at the wagon. "She's in the wagon?" Again, his question was answered with a nod. "Right," Billy said. "You're a regular talkin' fool, ain't you?" When Lemuel made no reply, Billy walked to the rear of the wagon, pulled the canvas cover apart, and asked, "Mama, you in there?"

"Don't call me that!" Fancy came back at once. She had been peeking at him when he was questioning Lemuel and feared she recognized him. Because of that, she had tried to stay as still as she could, hoping he would think she was not there.

"Whaddaya want me to call you? Mildred?" Billy asked.

"Call me Fancy, just like everybody else does," she said, not at all pleased with the sudden drop-in. "Billy, what the hell are you doin' here?"

"Fancy, huh? Is that what you're still callin' yourself these days? I figured, after Dodge City, you'd be callin' yourself by your real name."

"Keep your voice down," she barked. "Lemuel will hear you."

"Lemuel? Is that that buffalo's name who's hitchin' up your horses? You weren't too particular when you hooked up with him, were you? He don't look like he's got good sense. You'll be lucky if he don't hitch 'em up backward." He chuckled over his remark. "Maybe he'll figure it out when he starts to drive 'em and they're both lookin' at him."

"Lemuel don't drive my horses. I drive 'em, myself. And I ain't hooked up with him. He just works for me. I asked you what the hell you're doin' followin' me. Who's after you? Is it a posse or just one man? I don't want you bringin' your trouble to this peaceful train of settlers."

"There ain't no posse after me," Billy replied. "I left that posse when I left Kansas. And you oughta know, if it was just one man after me, why, hell, I'd let him catch up and settle his grits for him in good fashion. Nope, Fancy, dear, you got it all wrong. I came lookin' for you, just like any good son wants to look after his mama. Ain't you gonna invite me inside your wagon? Maybe offer me a drink of likker? I've been ridin' a long way to catch up with you."

"No," she blurted. "There ain't no room in here for anybody but me and my possibles, and there ain't no likker."

"How 'bout ol' Lemuel? You got room in there for him?"

"Hell, no. Lemuel's like everybody else. He stays outside. And if he's got my horses hitched up, I'm fixin' to get on the driver's seat and drive 'em outta here. So whaddaya want here, Billy?"

"Kinda hurts my feelin's when you have to ask me why I come to find you," he said. "I came to help you. When I heard about somebody shootin' that feller you were hooked up with in the Fancy Pantz Saloon there in Dodge City, I knew you'd need somebody to help you. But then I was almost took sick with grief when I heard you was missin', too. And the saloon burnt nearly to the ground. They found the safe, but it was empty. I don't blame you for wantin' to get away. They said that partner of yours was shot in the back of the head. The person that did that lowdown job mighta been after you next. You were smart to get as far away from Dodge City as you can." He paused to give her a wide grin. "Now, here's what I figure, you're on your way to Oregon country to build you a new saloon. And you're gonna need a smart young business partner to help you, one with a fast gun to handle any trouble that a woman saloon owner might need help with. That's what families oughta be all about, ain't it? To help one another out, and that's the reason I came to find you, Mother, dearest, to help you build that saloon."

She just stared at him for a long couple of seconds, ignoring his sarcasm and cursing the luck that enabled him to find her. He was the image of his father come back to haunt her, a man she had been married to for a total of twelve years, off and on. The father was never home for more than a week or two at a time, and the times he was gone were the best times of her marriage. The last time he came home, he said, "This time, I'm home to stay." He made her life a living hell for three weeks, and then one night he sent her to town to buy him another bottle of whiskey. She never came back. Twelve-year-old Billy seemed to have more in common with his father than with her, so she had no regrets about leaving the boy with his father. She worked the cattle towns for a couple of years after that, doing whatever she had to in order to live. Then she met Raymond Pantz, an Englishman who had aspirations about building a saloon in Dodge City. He had the money from his inheritance but hadn't the first notion about running a saloon. He wanted to hire someone to do it for him, but she persuaded him to let her manage it. She convinced him that they should have a name that would attract customers and that his name was a natural. She started calling herself Fancy and they named their business the Fancy Pantz Saloon.

The saloon was a success, right from the start, and grew to be a lucrative investment for Raymond, due entirely to her natural ability to operate a saloon. In exchange for a decent salary, he got her management skills, plus attention to his sexual needs, which were quite frequent. Accustomed to years of having to do whatever was necessary to survive, Fancy was content to remain in that role until Dolly Hammond arrived in Dodge with a troop of actors. Raymond became so enamored with her that he was soon sending her expensive gifts, and once Dolly found that he was a wealthy saloon owner, she decided to drain as much of that wealth as she could. With the end of his calls upon her body, Fancy realized there had never been any real affection for her. She also realized that he was spending great sums of the saloon's profits on the enchanting Miss Dolly, while she received a pittance in comparison. At that point in her life, her choice was a simple one.

Now, when she had been convinced she was in the

clear, the reality of her past had appeared in the form of her only child, grown into a man. She knew him only by reputation. This was the first actual reunion since he was twelve, but the little she had heard involved gambling and guns with a recent report of bank robbery. "Back up, I'm comin' out," she told him. He backed away to give her room. When she was on the ground, the two of them took a couple of minutes to look at each other. "You look a lot like your pa," she commented.

"You don't look a whole lot different from the last time I saw you," he said, "except you've got some gray in your hair."

"I don't have to go far to know who to thank for that," Fancy commented.

They were interrupted then when Scofield rode out in the middle of the wagons on his black Morgan and yelled, "All right! Get 'em hitched up. We're pullin' outta here in ten minutes!"

She found herself in an awkward position. It was a free country. She couldn't tell him he couldn't ride the Oregon Trail. Maybe she could tell him he couldn't ride along with the wagons, but she was sure, if she did, he would simply ride along in sight of the train. "You know you're on your own here, don't you? I ain't in no position to take you in, even if I wanted to." He just smiled and nodded in response. "But I expect you'd best go talk to Clayton Scofield and let him know, if you're plannin' on ridin' with us. He's the wagon master, the man who runs this train. Whatever he says is the law while you're on this train."

"Hell, he don't own this road," was Billy's initial reaction.

"See," Fancy responded at once, "that's the reason you ain't got no business ridin' along with us. He don't own the road, but he damn-sure owns this wagon train till we get to Oregon. And that's what everybody on this train has agreed to."

"All right, all right!" Billy replied. "I'll go talk to him, but it don't make no difference what he says. I'm goin' to Oregon with you. I know you cleaned that safe out in the Fancy Pantz and you're gonna build another saloon with it. I ain't askin' for nothin' but a chance to help you run it. You walked out and left me when I wasn't but twelve years old, so you owe me that."

"I don't owe you crap. Let's get that straight right now. I don't owe anybody anything. I don't know nothin' about who shot Raymond Pantz and emptied his safe. So you're makin' a poor bet, if you're thinkin' I'm gonna support your sorry ass. It took all the money I'd saved just to buy this outfit. I'll be scratchin' around for money just like everybody else when I get to Oregon."

"I do declare, Mama . . . Excuse me, I mean, Fancy. If I didn't know you as good as I do, I mighta swallowed all that." The cocky grin returned to his face. "Yes, ma'am, I'll be ridin' to Oregon country to look after my dear ol' mama."

She stared at him in angry frustration for a long moment. "It ain't none of my affair what you do. You better go talk to Clayton Scofield." She shifted her gaze toward the horses then. Lemuel was still standing there holding one of them by the bridle, waiting for Fancy to climb up in the driver's seat. She turned on her heel, marched to the front of the wagon, and climbed up. "All right, Lemuel, I got 'em." He backed away and took his usual place beside the wagon, watching Billy anxiously as he got on his horse and rode up to Scofield's wagon.

"Mr. Scofield," Billy called out when he pulled up beside Scofield's wagon. "Have a word?"

"What can I do for you?" Scofield asked, well aware that Billy had been back at Fancy's wagon, talking to her.

"My name's Billy Wallace. I've been tryin' to catch up with your train." He gave Spud Williams, who was sitting in the driver's seat, a nod. Spud returned it.

"Wallace," Scofield repeated. "You any kin to Fancy?"

"She's my mother," Billy said, knowing Fancy didn't want him to tell anyone that.

"Your mother?" Scofield was genuinely surprised to hear that. "Did she know you were comin' after her?"

"No, sir," Billy replied with a grin. "She didn't have no idea a-tall."

"Well, I'll be . . ." Scofield started. "I reckon she was surprised to see you."

"She was tickled to death," Billy said. "She said I'd best come tell you about it and see if it's all right to ride along with the wagon train."

"Why 'course it is," Scofield said at once, "you bein' her son and all. Glad to have you. This road ain't just for wagons, anyway. Anybody's got a right to ride on it."

"That's what I told Mama," Billy said. "Anyway, I thought I'd come look for her 'cause I knew she'd need some help gettin' herself set up in Oregon."

"Well, I know she'll appreciate that," Scofield said. "I've known your mama for a few years, back when I used to pass through Dodge City on occasion. She was runnin' a saloon in partnership with some Englishman, name of Pantz. I sure was surprised when she showed up in Independence with a wagon ready to head for Oregon. She never said nothin' a-tall about havin' a son. She got any more young'uns she don't like to talk about?"

"Nope," Billy answered with a chuckle for Scofield's attempt at humor. "I'm the only one. I reckon she musta been so disappointed with her first attempt at makin' young'uns that she figured she just wasn't good at it." They both chuckled at that, but only Billy knew that it was more than likely his mother's precise feeling on the subject. "I'll be takin' care of all my needs, myself," Billy went on, painting a picture of a devoted son. "I don't want Mama to use up her supplies tryin' to take care of me. I wouldn'ta come if I had to make her supplies run short. Besides, I expect she's already feedin' that feller with her—that Lemuel feller."

Scofield was impressed with the young man's attitude, and he didn't want Billy to get the wrong picture of Lemuel Blue's relationship with his mother. "Your mama, bein' a lady, she needed somebody to do the heavy liftin' for her, somebody to take care of the horses and the wagon. So that's what Lemuel does for her. He sleeps under her wagon, so it gives her a little feelin' of protection, too."

"Is he a little tetched in the head?" Billy asked.

Scofield snorted a short chuckle. "I don't know. I ain't sure if he is, or if maybe he's smarter'n the rest of us and that's the reason he don't wanna talk to us. Whatever, the fact is, he don't cause your mama no trouble, and he keeps her wagon ready to roll." He paused to take a look at his pocket watch. "It's time to get 'em rollin'. Welcome to the train." He pulled the dented-up bugle up to his lips and blew one screeching blast back toward the wagons.

"Wagons Ho!" he shouted and gave his horses a slap with the reins.

Billy backed his horse out of the way of the wagons lining up behind Scofield's and waited until Fancy's wagon came by. He pulled his horse alongside her wagon and rode in step with her horses. "I just had a fine talk with your wagon master. He's tickled to hear I came to help you on your trip to Oregon. Said for me to make myself at home. So I'll be here to make sure you're all right."

"You might as well get it into your head, Billy," Fancy responded. "I don't work with no partners in my business. And that don't matter if they popped outta my belly or not. I've learned my lesson about friends and family in business. It don't work. I can't stop you from ridin' along on this drive, but you're on your own. We get to Oregon City, you go your way and I'll go mine, just like it was yesterday. The sooner you understand that, the better off you'll be."

"I hear what you're sayin'," Billy replied, a wide smile etched across his face. "But it's a long way to Oregon City. You might change your mind by the time we get out there." He wheeled his horse away and rode farther up the line of wagons, closer to the leaders, to avoid the dust already being kicked up.

Scofield looked back at the young man on the bay, riding at an angle from the trail Scofield's wagon followed. He had accepted the stranger's story, although he found it hard to believe Fancy Wallace had a son. He would wait to see what Fancy had to say about Billy's unexpected arrival. His instincts told him there was something about Billy Wallace that caused him to be cautious. One thing he noticed, even with Billy sitting in the saddle, was the low-riding holster, strapped to his leg by a rawhide cord. Scofield wasn't close enough to get a good look at the handgun riding in the holster, but it looked like a Colt .45. The holster was a favorite among gunfighters and men who sought to make a name for themselves by the speed of their drawing and firing. There was no one on his wagon train who fancied himself a fast gun, as far as he knew. And there was no place for such a man on this train of families, striking out to find land to homestead. "I don't know . . ." he mumbled to his team of horses. "We'll just have to see how this plays out with Fancy."

Scofield led his wagons on a well-defined road adjacent to the dark water of the Sweetwater with no sign of his scout for several miles. Then at a point where the river took a sharp turn through a thick grove of trees, Clint suddenly appeared in the trail ahead. He sat waiting for Scofield to catch up to him. "You're gonna have to cross over here, Uncle Clayton," Clint told him. "The place we crossed over last time got washed out. There musta been a real storm 'cause half of that bank looked like it caved in. But you can cross right here. The bank ain't too steep on either side right here, and the water ain't too deep, didn't come up to Biscuit's belly. So I think we can drive the wagons across."

"How's the bottom feel?" Scofield asked. He was picturing massive hunks of riverbank breaking off and being moved downstream by the tide to settle at this new crossing point suggested by Clint.

Knowing what his uncle was thinking, Clint answered. "It feels pretty solid under Biscuit's hooves. He didn't sink at all, and I think the wagons might pack it down a little more, but not enough to float 'em." He grinned and japed, "I reckon you can test it right now and see if your wagon sinks, and if it does, I'll fix the other wagons to float across."

"Ha!" Scofield snorted. "You better be right. Tell Moody to hold up till Spud pulls out on the other side." Spud turned his horses toward the water and headed across, trusting Clint's recommendation, following Scofield on his horse. Clint signaled Walt Moody to stop. He was first in line behind the lead wagon that day.

"Wait for a signal from Scofield before you start across," Clint told him. Then noticing that Emmett Braxton was driving the wagon behind Moody's, he rode back and pulled up beside it. "I came back to see if Lou Ann is gonna swim across this one, like she did when we crossed the Kansas River," he joked. "The water ain't deep enough to be over her head, anyway."

Emmett and Sarah both chuckled in response. "No," Sarah said, "the young'uns and I all climbed in the wagon till we get across."

Clint asked Emmett then, "Who's the fellow ridin' with a packhorse?"

"I don't know for sure," Emmett answered. "He came ridin' into camp just before we pulled out wantin' to know which wagon was Fancy's. John Zachary said he told 'em his name was Billy Wallace. He rode up and talked to Scofield before we pulled out, and evidently, he's gonna ride along with us. That's all we know about him."

Clint wondered why his uncle hadn't mentioned it just now. He nodded to Braxton and started to pull away but stopped when he saw Lou Ann's little face pop up behind her parents in the wagon seat. He pointed a finger at her and teased, "There's that little swimmer. Don't you jump outta the wagon this time."

She giggled and responded, "I didn't jump out last time. I fell out."

"Oh, well, don't fall out this time."

"I wanna go across with you and Biscuit," she said.

Sarah started to tell her that Clint couldn't be bothered with seven-year-old little girls, but Clint interrupted her. "You might get your feet wet, if you ride over on Biscuit," he told her.

"I don't care," Lou Ann said and giggled at the thought.

"All right," Clint said, "it's up to your mama, then."

"Clint, you don't have time to fool with our young'uns," Sarah quickly responded.

"It's no bother on my part," he told her. "There's nothin' I have to do on the crossin' but watch, so Lou Ann can help me do that." He winked at the eager little girl. "Right, Lou Ann?" She nodded vigorously. Back to Sarah then, he said, "I'll wait till you're makin' the crossin' and we'll ride over at the same time. Then, if she doesn't fall in the river, I'll give her back to you." Lou Ann didn't wait for her mother's okay but wiggled up from behind the seat and climbed over her father's lap in her excitement to climb on behind Clint. He pulled Biscuit up close beside the wagon, so he could reach out and take her off the wagon. He sat her in the saddle in front of him, so he could hold onto her, then he pulled away from the wagon and rode back to the edge of the river.

Scofield's wagon was on the other side and Walt Moody's wagon was almost halfway across, so Clint waved Emmett and Sarah on. Scofield yelled back to tell him that the bottom was good, just like he said it was.

"You ready?" Clint asked his young passenger, and she said she was. He urged Biscuit, and the big Palouse started across. Clint raised his feet up in the stirrups, so that only the heels of his moccasins got wet before Biscuit started up the other bank. They waited for her father to drive across, then when her mother and brothers got out of the wagon to walk again, Lou Ann was lowered gently to the ground to join them.

"Oh, yeah," Sarah remarked to Emmett, "she's gonna marry him. We've lost our daughter."

Emmett and Sarah weren't the only interested spectators of Lou Ann's crossing of the river. Another spectator, this one on horseback, too, found the young man wearing a buckskin shirt and riding a Palouse horse interesting. He appeared to be quite the hero. Billy guessed he might be a scout for Scofield. As he was always inclined to do when encountering a man who appeared to be comfortable in his skin, Billy angled his horse to ride closer to the wagons approaching the river. He was curious to see how the buckskin-clad scout was armed. He could see a rifle butt sticking up from the saddle sling, but he was more interested in his sidearm. He was curious to see what kind of weapon he carried, but also how he wore his holster. "Wasn't as much trouble as you figured, was it?" he called out.

Clint and Scofield both turned to see who said it, not having noticed Billy riding up to join them. "We wasn't expectin' any trouble, but this ain't the usual crossin', so we just thought we'd test the bottom here," Scofield responded. "But we ain't got half the wagons across yet. And you never know. Clint, here, tested the bottom and said it would hold, so that's why we just waved 'em on."

He nodded toward Billy and said to Clint, "This is Billy Wallace, Fancy's son. He up and surprised her at the noonin' today."

"Clint Buchanan," he said and nodded. "Pleased to meet you. I reckon your mama was glad to see you."

"Yeah, I figured she was hopin' I'd show up before she got to Oregon, so I can get that saloon up for her." He was satisfied to see that Buchanan carried a Colt Navy revolver in a plain cowhand holster. *Nothing to worry about on that score,* he thought as he smiled at Clint.

Chapter 11

When the last wagon crossed over the river, there were not many hours left before it would be time to go into camp for the night. Since the horses weren't very tired, having spent much of the afternoon just waiting at the river, Scofield proposed to drive an extra hour. "Ride on ahead and find us a good spot to camp," he told Clint. "It don't seem worth it, I reckon, one measly hour saved when you think about how many hours we've got ahead of us to get to Oregon City." Clint merely shrugged his shoulders, rather than state his opinion. "It's the principle of the thing," Scofield stated.

"You're the boss," Clint said. "I can't say as I know much about the principle of it."

"Well, I don't either," Scofield replied, "but it won't hurt to have supper one hour later."

"Reckon not," Clint said as he climbed on Biscuit and

turned the gelding upriver. They were not going to make decent time on the Sweetwater River, anyway. The river, with its snakelike course, ran directly west and was the best course to South Pass. If there had been no heavy spring storms to cause flooding, the river crossings would be no problem at all, even though he counted nine crossings when traveling the road the last time. At one point, where the valley narrowed down quite a bit, they would cross the river three times within a distance of one or two miles. He knew that Scofield was concerned about the time it would take them to travel the one hundred or so miles to South Pass. The attempt to steal the horses by the three Sioux warriors told him there were Sioux in the Sweetwater Valley, probably hunting buffalo. That was enough to make him cautious. If those three would-be horse thieves were part of a larger party of Sioux, then Scofield could probably count on a visit from more raiders, this time with scalps in mind.

Always alert when he rode out ahead of the wagons, Clint did his best to keep his senses especially sharp in this winding river valley. Scofield was wary of the possibility of an attack on the train after the attempt by the Sioux raiders, even though they were traveling closer to Shoshone hunting grounds now. There had been very little trouble from the Sioux or the Cheyenne for the last couple of trips across the high plains. But it was important to put as much distance as possible between the wagon train and the camp at Independence Rock before the rest of that Sioux hunting party showed up to look for their three missing warriors. The train was traveling a river valley that offered little concealment. It was a land of high grasses but no trees except those lining the winding river.

Thinking he had gone about as far as Scofield had in mind for the day's travel, Clint selected a spot where there was a broad gap in the trees, allowing easy access to the water for man and beast. Looking far ahead, he got a glimpse of Split Rock, another landmark on the Oregon Trail. It was actually a large granite mountain with a deep cleft in the top that looked like a gunsight. Although he could see it from where he was, the wagon train wouldn't reach it for several days. He started to nudge Biscuit to start over closer to the river's edge but stopped when a movement in the trees on the other side of the open gap caught his eye. *Deer?* He thought but then made out the head of a horse through the leaves of some tall bushes. *If they are hostile, they must not have rifles,* he thought, *'cause I ain't been shot.* He thought about turning around and heading back toward the wagons, as casually as possible, so as not to let them know he saw them. He had an idea they may be no more than two or three, and if they thought he hadn't seen them, they might leave before the wagons arrived. They were no doubt familiar with the white man's wagon trains, knew they carried many guns, so they were not likely planning on attacking them. Then he heard someone behind him.

At first, thinking he had ridden into an ambush, he wheeled Biscuit around, drawing his rifle out of his saddle sling as he turned. "Whoa!" Billy Wallace blurted. "Don't shoot! I didn't mean to spook you." He rode on up beside Clint and stopped. "Whatcha lookin' at?" Billy asked. "You looked like you was lookin' at somethin' in the bushes over yonder." Clint didn't answer right away. He was still wondering why Fancy Wallace's son was riding up ahead of the wagons. Then he told himself there was no reason Billy couldn't ride ahead of the wagons.

He didn't have time to speculate further on the matter because Billy interrupted his thoughts. "Injuns! That's what you was lookin' at."

Clint looked back toward the river to see what had caught Billy's eye. Two Lakota hunters came out of the trees along the water's edge, leading their ponies. Clint turned back to face them and held up his hand, making the peace sign. As the two Indians continued toward them, Clint said aside to Billy, "Most likely huntin' for deer. If we're lucky, we'll just pass the time of day and they'll move on. Shouldn't be any trouble."

"No trouble?" Billy responded. "Hell, they're Injuns. Ain't but one way to deal with Injuns." Before Clint could stop him, Billy whipped out his six-gun and shot one of the Indians in the chest. The other hunter turned and ran, but Billy was quick enough to put a round in his back. Both executions happened within a span of only a few seconds. Equally as surprised as the two victims, Clint could not react in time to stop the senseless killing. But when Billy turned back to look at him, a smug smile of satisfaction upon his face, Clint could only react in contempt. His rifle already in hand, he swung it like a club to land beside Billy's head, knocking him out of his saddle. Clint came off Biscuit at once to make sure he got to Billy's gun first. Billy had dropped it before he hit the ground and Clint picked it up before Billy could gather himself to his knees. "What the hell?" Billy gasped, shaking his head, still trying to figure out what happened.

"You damn fool," Clint swore. "They came in peace! You mighta just brought a full load of hell down on us."

Still trying to clear his head after having his brain rattled around inside his skull, Billy struggled to defend his actions. "There ain't but two of 'em. They ain't gonna bother nobody now."

"Why the hell did you ride out here in front of the wagons, anyway?" Clint fumed over the insensibility of the young gunslinger's actions. "Yeah, there ain't but two of 'em, and it looks like they were hopin' to run up on a deer. If they got one, I reckon they woulda took it back to their village where who knows how many more warriors are camped. 'Course, that ain't gonna happen now since you're so handy with this pistol. Reckon the rest of the warriors in their camp will wonder why these two didn't come back?" He wasn't sure his sarcasm was getting his message across or not. Billy still looked to be rattled. He put his hand on the side of his head to feel his injury. When he brought it back down again, it was covered with blood. The sight of it seemed to unnerve him even further.

"We're gonna have to get these bodies outta sight before a war party shows up to see what the shots were about," Clint thought aloud. He was troubling over the fact that he had picked this spot to make camp. It would be close to six o'clock by the time Scofield showed up, an hour past the usual quitting time. His uncle was going to have a decision to make, push on farther, or go ahead and make camp and prepare for some warriors looking for the two dead men. Regardless, he had to get rid of the bodies. "Get up from there and help me load these two on their horses," he said to Billy.

"Pick 'em up, yourself, you damn Injun lover," Billy spat back, seeming to gain some of his cockiness back. "You and your damn Injun shirt and your Injun shoes. The only good Injun is a dead Injun and there's two good ones layin' there. Leave 'em there, and if any more of 'em show up, maybe they'll get the message."

Clint just stood there staring at the insolent young man for what seemed a long moment, his contempt for his attitude beyond control. Finally, he said, "Just get back on your horse and get on back to the wagons. I'll clean up your mess by myself. Tell Scofield to keep his eyes open for Lakota scouts. We might have some company tonight."

"As soon as you gimme back my gun," Billy responded.

"You'll get it back when we make camp tonight," Clint told him.

Regaining much of his arrogance now, Billy managed a painful smile. "What if I run into some more Injuns on the way back to the wagons?"

"Then I reckon you'll be in the same fix as these two poor devils were," Clint answered.

Billy climbed up on his horse, a painful smirk still in place as he made eye-to-eye contact with Clint. "This little shindig here ain't over between us, Buchanan, not by a long shot. You'll answer to me for that cowardly blow you gave me. We'll see how tough you are when you're standin' face-to-face with me, Injun lover." Clint didn't reply to the challenge. Instead, he walked behind Billy's horse and slapped it on the rump, causing the bay to jump and gallop away.

Chapter 12

Left with the job of hiding the evidence of Billy Wallace's reckless murders, Clint got to it right away, concerned that some of their tribesmen might have heard the shots and were on their way to investigate. The two unfortunate hunters were not big men, but they were still a problem to load on their horses, because the horses were leery of the white man and wouldn't hold still to accept their burdens. In desperation, he finally gave up on them and loaded the bodies on his horse, then led Biscuit into a thick clump of trees some thirty-five or forty yards downstream. He had no tools to dig a grave with, so he looked for a place to dump them where they might not be found so easily. The best he could find was a thick clump of gooseberry bushes, so he unloaded them and dragged the bodies up under the bushes. Sorry, he thought, that's the best I can do right now. When the wagons catch up with me, maybe I'll come back with a shovel.

His bigger concern was the two horses. It wouldn't be wise to leave them to run around loose, waiting for a Lakota scouting party to happen upon them. When he rode Biscuit out of the group of trees where he had left the bodies, he saw both Indian ponies down beside the river, drinking. Thinking it might be a chance to catch both at the same time, he guided Biscuit over between them. Evidently, they weren't as shy of his horse as they had been of him when he had approached them on foot, for he reached down and took the reins of the one closest to him. The horse followed dutifully when Clint moved Biscuit closer to the other horse. When he had the reins of both Indian ponies, he took them into the trees to wait for the wagons and the horse herd to catch up to him. While he waited, he nudged Biscuit into a lope and moved farther along the trail, thinking it might be better not to camp at the scene of Billy's executions. He rode about a mile when he found a place he thought would do, so he turned around and went back to his original choice to wait for Scofield.

In a short time, he saw the wagons approaching, so he rode back to pull up beside Scofield in the lead wagon. "What the hell was Fancy's boy talkin' about? Trouble with some Injuns?"

Before he answered, Clint looked back at the wagons coming on behind Scofield's. He saw Billy riding beside Fancy's wagon, so he asked Scofield, "What did he tell you?"

"He said he saved your life. Said there was a couple of Lakota Sioux warriors sneakin' up on you, but he shot 'em before they could jump you. Is that a fact? Did you run into some more Indians?"

"Yeah, I came up on two hunters here, but that's as close to Billy's story as I can get. Did he tell you how he got hit in the head, or how I happen to have his gun?" He pulled Billy's six-gun out of his belt and held it up for Scofield to see.

"He said you went kinda crazy on him and hit him in the head. Said he figured you musta had a pretty bad scare when the Injuns came after you and you didn't know what you was doin'."

"I went crazy, all right," Clint remarked. He went on to tell Scofield what had actually happened. He concluded by saying, "Their bodies are hid under some gooseberry bushes over yonder." He pointed downstream. "Their horses are tied in that clump of trees yonder. I figured we might hide 'em in our horse herd." He shrugged then and confessed, "This gap in the trees is where I'd picked to camp, but with all that happened here, I figured it'd be best to move on upriver a-ways. Whaddaya think?" When Scofield agreed, Clint said, "There's another spot almost as good about a mile farther on."

"We're late makin' camp, anyway. Another mile ain't gonna make much difference," Scofield answered. Back to the subject of Billy Wallace, he made a comment. "I knew there was somethin' cockeyed about that boy when he came to tell me who he was. And Fancy didn't seem like she was tickled to see him show up. What you tell me he did with them two Sioux hunters is just plum loco. I can't have nobody like that ridin' with this train."

"'Course, that's dependin' on whether you believe my version of what happened or his version," Clint said.

"Ha," Scofield grunted. "There ain't no doubt about which one I believe."

"He's wantin' to call me out to settle this business between him and me. He didn't care much for that lump I put on the side of his head."

"You shoulda shot him, just like a dog that's gone mad," Scofield said. "I expect I'd better step in if he's thinkin' about callin' you out. I can't have nothin' like that goin' on in my train."

"Just let me take care of it," Clint insisted. "There's no use for you to get into it with him."

"Don't be a fool, Clint. Look at the way he wears that quick-draw holster, and that gun of his you're holdin', with a shorter barrel, so it don't snag on the holster. I think you ain't the first man he's faced in the middle of the street. How many times have you practiced a quick-draw with that pistol you're wearin'? That's what I thought," he said when Clint just smiled in answer.

"Well, let me set your mind at ease about that," Clint said then. "I ain't plannin' to lose my life so everybody can see how fast Billy can draw this weapon." He paused for a moment, then commented on a possibly bigger problem. "I know you're thinkin' the same as I am. Those two hunters mean there's a village or at least a bigger huntin' party somewhere around here."

"You're right about that," Scofield agreed. "If we're lucky, it's a village north of here in the Wind River Mountains, and these two came down from there for just a couple of days hunt. Might give us time to get on up the Sweetwater a little farther." He shrugged his shoulders and concluded, "Ain't much we can do but play the cards we're dealt. Come on and show me the spot you picked to camp."

* * *

When they reached the place Clint had in mind, Scofield pulled his wagon up and signaled Buck Carrey in the wagon behind him. Buck pulled his wagon alongside, Lonnie James drove his wagon off the right side of Buck's, and the train moved into position in line until the circle was formed. The teams were unhitched from the wagons and herded to the water with the extra horses and the milk cows. It was an exercise they were highly efficient in by this time in their long journey. No one took much notice when Clint released two unshod horses to water and graze with the others. When the camp was settled, the search for firewood and buffalo chips began while the women prepared to cook supper. Scofield snagged Skeeter Braxton and sent him to fetch his father and Mr. Zachary. "You stay, too," Scofield told Clint, and in a few minutes' time, John Zachary and Emmett Braxton walked up to Scofield's wagon.

"You wanna talk to us?" Zachary asked.

"What's the matter?" Braxton japed. "Were we kickin' up too much dust?"

Scofield gave him a weak smile for his attempt at humor. "No, but there's somethin' I'd like to talk to you about. I know it said on that paper you signed back in Independence that I was judge and jury on any crimes that happen on this trip." That captured their attention right away.

John didn't wait for more before he asked, "Does this have something to do with Billy Wallace?"

"Why do you ask that?" Scofield asked.

"I don't know. It just looked like something was wrong. I was drivin' right behind Fancy Wallace's wagon today, and her son Billy was ridin' all around her for a while. Then I reckon he got tired of hangin' around her wagon 'cause he rode on up ahead of the column and he was gone a long time. Then all of a sudden, he was back, and he rode up beside her wagon for a long spell, and it looked like they were arguing about something. I asked Marcy if she could hear what they were fussin' about, but she couldn't hear 'em, either. Billy looked like he was pretty hot about something. Then when he turned his horse away from the wagon, I could see what looked like a bloody lump on the side of his head. Is that what you wanna talk about?"

"That's part of it," Scofield answered. "I'll let Clint, here, tell you how Billy got that lump, seein' as how he's the one who gave it to him." He nodded for Clint to begin. Then he watched the reactions of the two captains he had named for this journey. Judging by the look of alarm he read in each of their faces, he surmised that they saw it as a despicable act, as well, so he told them why he sought their advice. "I'll tell you the truth," he started. "I've acted like a judge on these journeys before. And it ain't never been no problem to make a rulin' on stealin' or wife-beatin', or botherin' somebody else's wife. I usually use my whip for that. And I did order one hangin' for a murder. We faced two wagons and made the gallows out of the wagon tongues. I didn't have no problem with that. But I'd like to have your opinion about what we oughta do about what Billy did. He didn't bother anybody on this wagon train. Matter of fact, he ain't even officially on this train. And he wasn't with the train when he shot those two Injuns. But what he done just ain't right under God's eyes, and I feel like he's gotta pay for what he did. I just ain't sure I've got the right to punish him."

"I see what you mean," Emmett said and looked at

John, not sure what to do, either. "What do you think, John?"

"I think Scofield's right. Billy oughta have to pay for that act of murder, even if they were just Indians." He thought for a minute, then declared, "I understand what you're worried about when you say Billy ain't even a part of this wagon train. But what he did is liable to bring down a band of wild Indians on this train and endanger all our lives. So in that respect, he's liable to the wagon train and everybody on it."

"I can't help feelin' bad for Fancy," Scofield had to say. "And I don't know what we oughta be thinkin' about as punishment. Sure, we're gonna tell him he can't ride with us after what he done, but oughtn't it be more than that?"

"I think so," Emmett said. "He took two lives for no reason at all. If they were white men, he'd pay with his own life."

"We'll damn-sure feel that way when the village they came from finds out they're dead and they come after us," John said. "We'll all be payin' for the sin he committed. We oughta tie him to a tree and ride off and leave him for the Indians to deal with. I'll bet they'll know what to do with him."

"Well, I appreciate all your help talkin' this problem over," Scofield said. "I'm gonna arrest Billy and chain him to my wagon when he shows up around here again. We'll give him a trial tomorrow at the noontime stop. I wanna move away from here in the mornin' in case some Sioux scouts come lookin' around. I'm gonna go talk to Fancy and tell her why we've got to try him. That ain't gonna be no fun a-tall, but she's got a right to know what I'm gonna do to her son and why." John and Emmett nodded their understanding and let him know that they agreed with his decision. "Me and Clint will be watchin' out for Billy, to take him under arrest when he comes back to camp. If we need some help, can we count on you?" They both volunteered immediately. "Good," Scofield continued. "Maybe we'll enlist Lonnie James, too."

"We'll talk to Lonnie for you," John said. "He'll be glad to help." Then they returned to their wagons, not envious of Scofield's visit to Fancy Wallace.

Back at his wagon, Scofield was warning Clint to keep a watchful eye out all evening. Billy was nowhere to be seen at the supper hour, but Scofield was concerned about the threat and the challenge Billy had left Clint with. "You might say you ain't gonna face him if he calls you out, but that yellow dog will more likely try to shoot you in the back."

Clint shrugged and replied, "I've got his gun." He held Billy's pistol up.

"He's got a rifle," Scofield countered. "You mind where you set your back tonight."

"I will," Clint declared. "When you gonna go talk to Fancy?"

"Right now," his uncle said.

"Want me to go with you?"

"No, ain't no use for both of us to have to go tell her we're fixin' to hang her son. You go somewhere and set down with your back against a wagon."

Fancy was in the process of building her small cook fire, after having paid Skeeter Braxton one peppermint stick for two buckets of buffalo chips, when Scofield approached. "Clayton," she acknowledged and got to her feet to receive him. "What's on your mind?" She was the only person on the wagon train who ever addressed Scofield by his first name.

"Billy," Scofield answered.

She couldn't say she was surprised, after Billy showed up at her wagon earlier with a bloody knot on his head and complaining about Clint Buchanan. "Before you get started, I'll tell you the same thing I told Billy when he came bellyaching to me about Buchanan. I don't give a damn about any bad blood between those two young boys. What Billy does is his own business. It ain't got nothin' to do with me. He's on his own. I sure as hell didn't invite him to come on this wagon train. So, if you've got a problem with Billy, take it up with him."

"It's a little more serious than a fight between two young men," Scofield said. "I'm fixin' to make some heavy charges against Billy in a regular trial. And I expect the result of it will be a hangin'." Then he told her what had actually happened. And it was obvious from her reaction that she had heard nothing of his unwarranted attack on the two Sioux hunters. "That's why I thought I owed it to you to let you know what we're dealin' with before I arrest Billy." She made no vocal reply for several long moments, and her face appeared ashen and expressionless. He guessed what she might be thinking, so he said, "I know it don't seem like a crime to kill an Injun, but what he's done is liable to bring us all under attack." He continued to study her reaction, then added, "They weren't hostile in the first place. Clint said they made the peace sign and just came up to talk."

When Fancy finally spoke again, it was in a calm tone of finality. "I 'preciate you feelin' like you need to talk to me about this, but you coulda saved yourself the trouble.

Like I said, I ain't got nothin' to do with anything Billy does. I told him that. Givin' birth to him weren't my choice and not knockin' him in the head as soon as he came out was my biggest mistake. So any business you've got with Billy is between you and him. I don't care one way or the other. It would be fittin' if you had his pa here to hang with him."

Scofield was not sure what he should say to her after hearing her position on the trial and punishment of her only son. "Well," he finally blurted, "thought I oughta at least tell you what was goin' on." He turned to leave, then paused to say, "We might not have to do anything about it, anyhow, 'cause it looks like he's run off." *Maybe he's got to thinking about the possibility of paying for what he's done,* Scofield thought. "He might be gone for good," he speculated aloud.

"Maybe," she said while thinking, *Yeah, but he didn't take his packhorse and he still wants to call Clint Buchanan out, so he can show off how fast he is with a gun.*

Scofield nodded to Lemuel Blue, who was just coming back from taking care of Fancy's horses. "Lemuel," he muttered.

"Mr. Scofield," Lemuel responded respectfully while keeping his eyes focused on his feet.

After leaving Fancy, Scofield returned to his wagon to find not only Clint, but John, Emmett, and Lonnie waiting for him. "We thought we'd let you know we'll all be extra alert tonight. As soon as Billy Wallace shows up again, we're all ready to take him prisoner," John said.

"Still no sign of him yet," Lonnie declared. "What did Fancy say about what we're plannin' to do?"

Scofield shook his head in wonder. "Not what you'd expect," he answered, then told them what her reaction had been. "I wanna keep an eye out for any sign of Injuns sneakin' around tonight. I hope they won't be lookin' for those two hunters till tomorrow. I'd like to be gone by the time they show up. We ain't even got to Split Rock yet. We've got a ways to go before we get to South Pass."

"I expect Buck and Doc and some of the boys will start tunin' up their instruments after supper," Emmett wondered. "You think we oughta tell 'em to hold off on that tonight, since we're on the lookout for Injuns and Billy Wallace, too?"

Scofield paused to think about that for a minute before deciding. "No, I don't want all the folks to get upset thinkin' about an Injun attack. It's better to let 'em think everything is runnin' normal. I think the time we have to worry about an attack is gonna be late, after everybody's gone to bed, anyway. We're gonna double up on our guards tonight and make sure nobody slips into camp like them three horse thieves back at Register Cliff. I plan to stay awake all night tonight." He paused then and looked around at the faces of his security team. "Anybody got any suggestions or a better idea?" Nobody did, so they broke up and went to eat supper.

When the dishes were cleared away, the usual social hour began with no sign of Billy or Indians. By the time the music and the dancing was finished for the evening, and the folks began to drift away to their beds, Scofield was hoping maybe all the precautions were for naught. "Druther be ready and nothin' happens, than not ready and somethin' happens," he said. Although his captains volunteered to stay awake all night, also, he decided it unnecessary. They finally decided to stay with double guards until the usual changing of the guard at midnight, and then just post the regular two guards for the final four hours. That's what they did and the evening remained quiet long after everyone else went to bed. At midnight, Tim Blake and Pat Shephard reported for guard duty as they were scheduled on Scofield's guard roster.

"That's just what I thought," Billy Wallace muttered to himself, as he watched the small group of men standing around the dying campfire. From the low swale between the river and the circle of wagons, he had lain on his stomach for two hours, waiting for a chance to sneak into the camp. "That bunch of hotshots were settin' around that fire half the night waitin' to jump me when I came back." *I reckon they've finally decided I ain't comin' back to this two-bit wagon train,* he thought. It seemed pretty obvious to him. Fancy had told Scofield about all that money she took out of the safe in the Fancy Pantz Saloon, and that he had come back and demanded half of it after he shot those two Indians. At first, he was going to call Clint Buchanan out in front of the whole party of emigrants. But after the big argument with his mother over a share of that money, she promised him that no amount of threats would cause her to give in to his demands. Even when he said he would tell them all that she murdered her partner to steal his money, she had still held firm. He had been tempted to shut her mouth permanently and take her wagon apart board by board until he found that money. But it was early in the evening with too many people to come to her aid. He had been forced to curse her and run before the wagons went into camp.

Now, he felt his patience and determination had paid off. The camp was asleep. Scofield and his three men were finally going back to their wagons, and the camp was left in the hands of just two sleepy-looking wagon drivers. After watching them for a few minutes, he decided they intended to split up and walk around the circle of wagons in opposite directions. *That's right, you dumb farmers,* he thought. *Walk around like you're guarding everybody. I'll just wait right here until you pass Fancy's wagon, then I'll pay my mama a little visit.* Since Fancy was one person alone, he knew that she made her bed in the back of the wagon, instead of pitching a tent like the wagons hauling whole families. That would make his job easier. With his skinning knife pressed tightly against her throat, she might even be able to reach her fortune without moving.

The guards were starting on their rounds now, so he flattened himself behind the swale and watched while Pat Shephard walked past Fancy's wagon. He rose carefully to his feet, and with his rifle in hand, he crept silently up to the wagon. He stopped at the tailgate to listen. There was no sound from inside the wagon. Satisfied, he looked under the wagon to spot Lemuel Blue, rolled up in a quilt under the front of the wagon. Billy almost laughed at the occasional snore that pushed past Lemuel's lips. It occurred to Billy that the dull-witted handyman probably slept almost under the front axle because Fancy didn't want his snoring right under her bed. *Time to get to business,* he told himself and raised up to cut the cords that held the rear curtain in place.

Once he cut the cords, he pulled the canvas apart to reveal his mother sleeping peacefully right there in the back of the wagon. He placed a wooden box used as a step behind the wagon and stood on it, so he could easily reach into the wagon with both hands. After taking one more look at the unconscious figure asleep under the wagon, he laid his rifle down and stepped back up on the box. He reached in with one hand and clamped it tightly over Fancy's mouth, waking her with a start. Before she had a chance to struggle, he pressed the point of his knife against her neck and whispered to her. "You make a sound and I'll push this knife right through your throat. If you wanna live to see the sun come up, you better do exactly what I tell you to do. I gave you a chance to split that money with me, but you were too greedy to share it with your own son. So now, I've come to take it all. And I'll bet you've got it close by you when you sleep. Ain't that right?" She tried to nod. Her eyes wide with fright, she could barely move. "You're wastin' time," he said and pressed the knife point hard enough to draw blood. "The sooner you give me that money, the sooner . . ." That was as far as he got before he felt the razor-sharp blade drawn quickly across his throat, opening a wide gap in his windpipe. The shock of knowing he was a dead man caused him to freeze, helpless, as he was dragged away from the tailgate and thrown on the ground. His eyes recorded the image of the brute-like Lemuel smiling down at him while he tried in vain to breathe.

Fancy climbed out of the wagon and bent low over her dying son. "You shoulda stayed gone when you left here earlier," she whispered to him. Then she looked up at Lemuel, who was standing beside Billy, the smile still on his face. "You done a good job. Is that guard still at the other end of the circle?"

"Yes, ma'am," Lemuel answered.

"Hurry then," she instructed. "Carry Billy outta here before that other guard shows up. Hide him somewhere where nobody ain't likely to find him before we move outta here in the mornin'." Lemuel, still grinning down at Billy, nodded to let her know he understood. "And see if you can find that horse he's ridin'. Ain't no sense in losin' a good horse. If you mind where those two guards are, you oughta be able to lead that horse back between the wagons and let it go to the other horses."

"What about the saddle?" Lemuel asked.

She paused only briefly to consider that. "Just leave it on. That'll let everybody know the horse oughta belong to me, if Billy don't show up anywhere, and his packhorse, too." She nodded her head, satisfied with that decision. "You can have anything you find on Billy for your trouble—anything in his saddlebags, too."

"Yes, ma'am. Thank you, ma'am," Lemuel replied, gratefully.

"Watch for the guards," she reminded him, "and don't let anybody see you. This will be a secret just you and I know." That seemed to greatly please the simple being. It might not be so important to cover up her involvement in Billy's death, since it was plain and simple that he was killed while trying to attack her in her wagon. But the fact that it was her own son who had been killed was not something she wanted to be associated with. And the way he had been killed, in an effort to keep it quiet, instead of shooting him, made it even harder to explain. It looked almost as if it was a planned murder and never mind the fact that he had a knife to her throat. These were the thoughts swirling in her brain as she watched Lemuel lift her son effortlessly and drop him across his shoulder.

Then after another look to make sure the guards weren't near, he disappeared into the darkness.

With a tired sigh, she took a handkerchief and dabbed the tiny scratch on her neck where Billy's knife had pricked her. Satisfied that it was no longer bleeding, she stuffed the handkerchief back inside her nightgown and attempted to go back to sleep. She found that she could not, however, after the rude awakening she had just suffered. She had not been prepared for Billy's appearance at her doorstep after so many years absent. She felt no sorrow for the killing of her son, for she had always regarded him as an unwanted affliction, the same as cholera or pneumonia—or his father, for that matter. She should be pleased that the issue with Billy was done with as quickly as it was, for it could have been a great deal messier had not Lemuel been on the scene. She almost smirked when she thought about Billy's evident disregard for Lemuel. It cost him his life.

The thought of Lemuel now caused her to wonder if she could count on the simple-minded brute to keep his mouth shut about Billy. She felt there was no doubt that his childish brain was pleased to share a secret with her. And he would not intentionally tell that secret, but how far could she trust him when it came to accidentally giving it away? Was it going to become necessary to eliminate Lemuel? She recalled how she had hired him on the spur of the moment. The right rear wheel of the wagon she had just bought began to wobble dangerously on her way back from the stable. When she stopped to look at the problem, there were several men standing around on the street in front of the saloon, and they came to offer her assistance. As it turned out, the problem was not serious, just one of simple neglect. The large square cast iron nut that held the wheel on tightly had not been tightened down to seat the hub properly. "I've got the wrench to tighten it with in my wagon," one of the men offered. "But I ain't got a wagon jack, and you're gonna have to jack it up to take the weight off while you tighten that wheel down."

"He's right, ma'am," one of the other men said. "You need to go back to the stable and get John to bring his wagon jack down here."

None of them offered to go get the jack for her, so she started to walk back, but stopped when a young brute of a man walked over to her wagon. Without saying a word, he took hold of the right corner of the wagon box and lifted the wheel up off the ground. "There you go!" The man who had spoken first exclaimed, "I'll get my wrench." He ran to his wagon and returned with the wrench especially formed to fit the square nut. With Lemuel still holding the wheel off the ground, the man tightened the left-hand threaded nut tight enough to seat the wheel firmly.

She shook her head slowly as she recalled the day she met Lemuel Blue. *And the wagon had a load of supplies I had just bought for this journey,* she thought. When she had offered to pay him, he had shyly thanked her and said, "Just enough to buy me some supper would be good."

Thinking how handy a man like that could be, since she was starting out alone on a wagon train, she questioned him about his family, and it turned out he had none. She quickly realized his brain had not developed at the same rate that his body had. He had been abandoned as a child, and as a young adult, he found work wherever he could, and begged for food when he had to. After taking him to a small dining room for supper, she decided to take a risk on him. "How'd you like a full-time job, workin' for me?"

With his head still bowed, humbly, he had responded. "I don't know how to do nothin'."

"You just have to do what I tell you to do, just like you did today when you picked that wagon up. You ever work with horses?" He said that he had, so she continued. "I'm headin' for Oregon country. You wanna go with me?"

"Yes, ma'am," he said at once.

The relationship had worked out fine until Billy showed up. Lemuel had taken care of that problem for her. But it had brought this new problem. How much could she trust Lemuel to keep his mouth shut?

After only a few hours' sleep, Scofield was ready to blow his bugle at four o'clock the next morning. He was happy to see he had spent some sleepless hours needlessly and the night had passed peacefully, with no appearance of vengeful Sioux warriors. As far as Billy Wallace was concerned, it might be too soon to tell if he would ever come back into camp or not. He would just have to wait and see. So, while Clint and Spud went to drive the horses down to the river with the other men in the train, Scofield started to rebuild a fire to cook some breakfast.

"We're gonna need to do some huntin' pretty soon and get us some fresh meat," Scofield announced to Clint when his young nephew came back to the wagon. "We're fixin' to run outta the buffalo range between here and South Pass where there won't be nothin' for 'em to feed on. I was hopin' we'd see buffalo somewhere along the

Sweetwater. I expect everybody would be tickled to halt a day to butcher a mess of buffalo meat." From the expression on Clint's face, Scofield could see that his scout wasn't really paying attention to his comments about hunting. "What's on your mind?" he finally asked.

"When we drove the horses down to the water, Billy's horse was in the herd with his sorrel," Clint said.

That captured Scofield's attention. "You sure it was Billy's?"

"Pretty sure," Clint responded. "It looked like that bay of his and it still had Billy's saddle on him." Scofield looked as if he was about to ask, so Clint answered first. "Nope, there wasn't any sign of Billy, just the horse. And even Billy's got enough sense to take the saddle off his horse. If it was Indians, they sure wouldn'ta let that horse get away. You reckon he got thrown and the horse ran off and left him? Maybe the horse came on back here and Billy will show up on foot."

Scofield shook his head. "I doubt that horse woulda come back here on his own and come inside the circle of wagons. I expect I'd best go see if Fancy knows anything about it. Hell, Billy might be sleepin' under his mama's wagon with Lemuel. Maybe Fancy softened up on him. But I'll give her time to eat a little breakfast first. I need some coffee, myself."

Chapter 13

Scofield left Clint and Spud to clean up the breakfast dishes and the frying pan while he went to talk to Fancy Wallace. "You keep your eyes open," he said to Clint in parting. "If Billy is in camp somewhere, he's still lookin' to settle up with you for that knot you put on his head."

"I reckon he wants his pistol back," Clint replied, just remembering that he still had it.

"He's still got his rifle," Scofield called back over his shoulder as he walked down the line of wagons. When he came to Fancy's wagon, he met her just coming back from the river carrying her coffeepot and breakfast dishes. "Mornin', Fancy," he greeted her.

"Mornin', Clayton," Fancy returned. "You lookin' for me?"

"No, I'm lookin' for Billy and I'm wonderin' if you've seen him since I talked to you last night," he replied.

"You got a memory that ain't worth a damn, ain't you?" Fancy replied. "Like I told you last night, I ain't got nothin' to do with Billy. I don't expect to hear anything from him anymore. If he's got hisself in trouble again, it ain't got nothin' to do with me." He told her then about the horse showing up with the other horses this morning and the fact that the saddle was still on him, all without any sign of Billy, himself. Fancy said that they should all be glad that Billy was gone. "Once and for all, Clayton, I don't wanna hear nothin' more about Billy."

"Well, one last thing," Scofield said. "If Billy don't show up before we move out, there's the matter of a bay horse, a sorrel packhorse, and a good saddle that used to belong to him. Since you ain't interested in anything that has something to do with Billy, I reckon I've got room in my wagon to throw that saddle in, and the two horses can just go with the extra horses."

It gave her pause, and he made a mental note of that, but she had taken such a hard line in distancing herself from Billy and anything related to him, that she felt she couldn't afford to soften her stance. "I don't feel any right to claim anything of his, no more'n I would of anybody else's in this wagon train."

"Just wanted to be sure," Scofield said and turned to leave. When he did, he caught Lemuel Blue staring at him intensely. "Lemuel," he greeted him. "You gettin' those horses hitched up, ready to go? We'll be pullin' outta here in thirty minutes."

As soon as he spoke, Lemuel dropped his head to its usual position when in the presence of other adults and he studied his feet while managing to reply, "Yes, sir, Mr. Scofield." He immediately went around to the other side of the wagon until the wagon master had left. Then he came back to finish hitching up the horses to find Fancy still staring after Scofield. "He don't know we got a secret. Does he, Miss Fancy?"

She turned around and looked at him. "No, he don't, and it's a secret we'll never tell anybody. Right, Lemuel?" He nodded happily. She climbed up into the wagon and refolded the small blanket she used to cushion the hard seat. In a few minutes, she heard a long blast from Scofield's offensive bugle, followed by his customary call of, "Wagons Ho!" Once again, they were underway to follow the winding Sweetwater River. Fancy held her horses back until it was her time in line for the day's march. Then she popped the reins to start her team in the parade. Standing on the other side of the wagon, Lemuel remained for a few moments after she pulled out. He took his foot and brushed some loose dirt over the few bloodstains he saw on the ground before he walked after the wagon.

They had not traveled a mile before Lemuel's three young friends caught up with Fancy's wagon and elected to walk with him. Johnny Zachary, Skeeter Braxton, and Sammy James managed to slip ahead of their parents' wagons for an opportunity to hear stories about the wild Indians who were always watching the white emigrants. Lemuel told them that the deadly Sioux liked to sneak into the wagons at night when everyone was asleep. He would describe how the warriors killed by silently slitting their victims' throats. He demonstrated on Sammy, using his finger as the knife blade, and drawing it swiftly across the youngster's throat. "It happens so quick, he don't even know he's gettin' his throat cut till it's sliced wide open and it just makes a gurglin' sound when he tries to say somethin'." He grinned when he saw the expressions on their young faces.

"I don't believe they do that," Skeeter said. "They just try to steal the horses, like them three they killed tryin' to steal ours."

"Yeah," Sammy said, "you're just makin' that stuff up."

"Is that so?" Lemuel replied. "You just remember that when you wake up one night and feel somethin' on your throat." When all three made skeptical faces in response, he snapped, "Git your little asses away from here. You been told to leave me alone, anyway."

"Why ain't you got a gun in that holster?" Skeeter asked. "Where'd you get it, anyway? You ain't never wore it before. Whaddaya wearin' an empty holster for?"

"I ain't got a handgun," Lemuel said. "I found the belt and there weren't no gun in it. You don't have to tote a gun just 'cause you got a holster." That was as far as the conversation progressed because it was interrupted by Fancy Wallace at that point.

She had paid no attention to the idle ramblings between her mentally challenged hired man and the three young boys who seemed fascinated by him. But the mention of a belt and holster broke through the monotony of her aimless thoughts and she realized what the youngsters were questioning Lemuel about. "Lemuel!" she suddenly called. "I need you up here."

"Yessum," Lemuel answered obediently and hurried up to walk beside the driver's seat of the wagon.

Fancy looked over at him in horror to see that he was indeed wearing Billy's gun belt. Although she never paid much attention to the simple man's appearance, she was sure she would have noticed the gun belt, had he been wearing it when they started out that morning. Looking toward the three youngsters, she said, "You boys run along now. Lemuel's got work to do." Never thinking to disregard any order the stern-faced woman might decree, they immediately stopped walking and let the wagon proceed ahead. When she felt she was out of earshot of the three young boys, she exclaimed, "Lemuel, you damn fool, take that belt off!" He immediately unbuckled the gun belt and removed it, spurred along by her deep furrowed eyebrows, a look he had learned to associate with a mood of displeasure. "Throw it in the back of the wagon!"

He almost stumbled in his haste to obey her command. After he put the gun belt in the back of her wagon, he hurried to catch up with her again. Confused, he sought to apologize. "I'm sorry, Miss Fancy, I thought you said I could have anythin' I found on you know who."

"I did, Lemuel," she replied calmly now, knowing she had to explain to an undeveloped brain. "But think about it, if folks see you wearin' a new belt, they're gonna wonder where you got it. There ain't no stores out here. And when there ain't no gun in that holster, don't you think they're gonna remember that Billy wore a gun belt like that? And last time anybody saw him, his holster was empty, too. Whaddaya reckon they'll think, if they see you walkin' around with that belt on?"

Lemuel continued to look confused for a second, but then his eyes lit up and a wide grin of understanding spread across his wide face. "That's right," he uttered, almost in a whisper. "They might think it's Billy's."

"And then they might guess our secret," Fancy said. "And we don't want anybody to find out what you did to Billy. Right?"

"Right," Lemuel answered. "I reckon I just weren't thinkin' about that. I'm awful sorry."

"That's all right, long as you check with me before you sport anything else you got offa Billy. Did you take any of his clothes?"

"No, ma'am. I tried 'em on, but they was all too small for me. So I left 'em with Billy."

"Good," Fancy said. "You did the right thing. You can wear your gun belt when we get out to Oregon." She smiled in answer to his wide grin for her remark, realizing the simple brain in the oversized brute was even more childish than she had at first suspected. The question in her mind now was, should he be dealt with in the same fashion as was Raymond Pantz and her son, Billy? The more she thought about it, the more convinced she became that it would be best to guarantee Lemuel's silence when she and her wagon were transported safely to Oregon City. But she needed him on the trip out there, so she decided to gamble on the odds he wouldn't make any further blunders before they reached their destination. *It's too bad,* she thought, *the simple child just doesn't know any better*. And that made it different from the assassinations of Pantz and Billy. Lemuel was devoted to her.

With the noon hour approaching, Clint waited in a crook of the river that offered good grass and easy access to the water. In a short while, the wagons caught up to him and went into a circle formation, even though there had been no sign of any Indian activity. The women began the preparation of the noon meal as soon as cook fires were started. After eating, many of the emigrants participated in their usual visiting with friends while the horses were resting. Clint and his uncle were sitting by the fire at Scofield's wagon, drinking the coffee left in the pot, when Emmett Braxton and his son, Skeeter, came up to join them. "Emmett," Scofield greeted him. "Might be a little coffee left in that pot."

"No," Braxton responded, "thank you just the same. I brought Skeeter over to tell you what he and Johnny Zachary were talkin' about at the noonin'. You know how those boys love to pester Fancy Wallace's hired man." He hesitated then. "Well, you tell Mr. Scofield what you told me and John . . ."

Looking as if he had been caught stealing dried apples out of the barrel, Skeeter looked first at Clint, then at the wagon master, who were both smiling at him expectantly. "I told 'em Lemuel had on a new belt."

"Tell 'em what you said, son," Emmett pressed him. "You said it was a gun belt with cartridges in it, right?" Skeeter nodded rapidly. "And it had a holster." Skeeter nodded again. "And what else did you say about it?"

"He didn't have no gun in his holster," Skeeter said.

Braxton turned back toward the two men whose smiles had now frozen in place. "Lemuel Blue, walkin' around this mornin' wearin' a gun belt and holster with no gun in the holster. When the boys asked him where he got it, Lemuel said he found it." Satisfied that he had generated the response he wanted, he paused to see what Scofield would do about it.

"Did he tell you where he found the holster and belt?" Scofield asked the boy.

"No, sir," Skeeter answered.

"Did he say he saw Billy Wallace?" Clint asked.

Skeeter shook his head. "He didn't say nothin' about

seein' anyone. Just said he found the belt. He mighta told us later, but Miss Fancy called him to come do somethin' for her and told us to git. She made him take that belt off."

"What are you thinkin', Emmett?" Scofield asked. "You thinkin' Lemuel killed Billy Wallace?"

"I don't know what to think," Emmett answered honestly.

"What about you, Clint?" Scofield asked his nephew. "What do you think? You think Lemuel mighta done for Billy?"

"Not if they were standin' face-to-face," Clint replied. "Question is when and where? We sat on that camp damn-near all night and there wasn't anybody comin' or goin'. If Lemuel found that belt, like he says, it woulda had to be this mornin'. And that means it woulda had to be close by our camp. We can ask Lemuel where he found it, but we ain't come that far from that camp. So, I could ride back there and look for Billy, maybe pick up some tracks that would tell me where he'd been. That might be better than just takin' Lemuel's word for it."

"I ain't got no reason to suspect Lemuel of killin' anybody," Scofield said. "Maybe if somebody was hurtin' Fancy, he'd try to defend her. More than likely, he just found Billy's gun belt somewhere, like he told those boys."

"It mighta been Injuns that got him," Skeeter piped up. "Lemuel says they sneak up on you at night and cut your throat, so you can't holler or nothin'."

Scofield looked down at the boy and nodded. Thinking further, he said, "And Billy just mighta left that holster and belt in Fancy's wagon, since he didn't have a pistol to tote in it. Clint, why don't you go on back, like you said, and look around that campsite to see if you can find any sign that Billy's body is layin' around there somewhere. His horse got back here, somehow, and that is a mystery. I'd like to see if you find anything before I go see Fancy and Lemuel again." He reached down and ruffled Skeeter's hair. "Skeeter may be right, the Injuns mighta done for him."

"I'll see what I can find," Clint said, "soon as I rinse out this cup and saddle Biscuit." He left to get started while Scofield was telling Braxton to refrain from discussing the affair with the other emigrants until they knew a little more about what had actually happened.

It was a short ride back down the river. Due to the necessity of making another river crossing, the wagon train had only traveled about eight miles before stopping for the noon break. As he rode back along the road just traveled, Clint tried to recreate a picture in his mind of the way the camp had been set up. And he thought he could pretty-well guess where Fancy's wagon had been parked in the circle. He remembered that it was on the north side, closest to the river, and he believed it was the fourth wagon behind Scofield's. When he reached the campground, he went down the line next to the river, counting off each wagon by the marks left in the dirt by their wheels.

He dismounted and closely examined the ground around the parking spot of Fancy's wagon. There were multiple footprints around the area that would have been the back of the wagon. Many of them were quite large and he figured those had to have belonged to Lemuel, but he also found other boot prints as well from a smaller size but not small enough to belong to Fancy. He allowed that they could belong to Billy, or someone else, one of the guards, maybe. He noticed a patch of ground right about where the tailgate might have been, that had been raked back and forth, possibly with someone's foot. He took his moccasin and gently brushed the loose dirt but could see nothing to explain the disturbance of the dirt. The sign that caught his eye and stimulated his interest, however, were another set of Lemuel's footprints. The difference from the others was the depth of the imprints in the soft sandy soil, which indicated to Clint that Lemuel was carrying a heavy load. The prints led straight away from the wagon, toward the river. Clint followed, feeling pretty sure he was following a man toting a body.

When he reached the riverbank, he saw that the tracks led downstream toward the trees where everyone in the wagon train went to bathe or answer nature's calls. By general agreement, the ladies visited the closest area of dense vegetation, while the men walked farther down. It was no longer easy to follow the tracks, but he figured Lemuel would have carried his load well beyond the usual spots frequented by the men. Clint walked farther down to search the thickets along the banks, counting on Lemuel's simple mind to ensure the disposal spot for Billy's body would not be that hard to find. He was certain now that it was Lemuel he was following, and he was carrying Billy's body.

As he suspected, Billy was not hard to find. The body was lying, facedown, in a shallow gully. Billy had been stripped down to his underwear and his clothes were lying all around on the ground; his jacket hanging on the limb of a gooseberry bush, his boots yards apart, as if they had been thrown. Probably in frustration, Clint thought, since they were far too small for Lemuel's huge feet.

Even the hat was left to lie on the ground. Clint remembered the cocky angle at which Billy had worn it. Since there were no bullet holes in the back of Billy's underwear, Clint turned the body over. He thought immediately of what Skeeter had said, for he saw the ragged gap sliced through Billy's windpipe. *That's the way the Indians do it, according to Lemuel,* he thought. There wasn't much doubt left in Clint's mind concerning who killed Billy. But he could only speculate on what caused Lemuel to do it. If Billy had been threatening to do harm to Fancy, and Lemuel stopped him, there would have been no need to carry the body down the river to hide it. And he would have most likely shot Billy, instead of cutting his throat. That suggested that Lemuel had sneaked up behind Billy to do the job—like the Indians would have done it—according to what he told Skeeter and the other boys.

There were still pieces of the puzzle that he couldn't fit for certain, but as far as what happened to Billy, that question had been answered. He decided he would go back and tell Scofield what he did know for sure and let him figure out what he should do about it. He took one more look at the body. He had no tools with him to dig a proper grave, and he didn't think Billy deserved the effort it would take to scratch out a grave with his bare hands. "So, I reckon I'm just gonna leave you for the buzzards, just like Lemuel did."

Chapter 14

He caught up with the wagon train some three miles beyond the spot where he had left it at noontime. They were in the midst of yet another river crossing of the snakelike river they followed. He found Scofield standing on the other side of the shallow crossing, watching Lonnie James drive his wagon across the axle-deep water. "Ain't no trouble when they all ain't no deeper'n this'un," he said to Clint when he rode Biscuit across to join him. "What did you find out?"

"I found Billy," Clint answered. Then he told his uncle about following what he figured to be Lemuel's footprints to the body, the evidence of trying on Billy's clothes, and the way Billy was killed. "Still ain't no way to tell how Billy really came to get his throat cut. Nobody but Fancy and Lemuel know what happened."

"If it had to be done to keep Billy from killin' one of

them, why did they try to cover it up?" Scofield wondered aloud. When Clint said he had wondered the same thing, Scofield confessed his indecision about what he should do about it. "I feel, as wagon master, I should hold a trial to decide who's guilty of what. Trouble is, Billy Wallace wasn't a member of this party, so he oughta be treated like an outlaw or an Injun who attacks the train. Maybe we really need to be pinnin' a medal on Lemuel for savin' Fancy's life. Hell, I don't know. Reckon they'd tell us the truth?"

Clint realized that his uncle really was at an impasse with the right and wrong of the situation. He knew Scofield wanted to be fair in any decisions or judgments he made regarding the people in his care. "Look, Uncle Clayton, why don't you have a quiet hearing with Fancy and Lemuel, and don't have a regular trial, so nobody else knows what's goin' on? To make it seem more official, you could include your captains in the hearing, since Braxton and Zachary already know about it, anyway. But nobody else, just those people, then if you think you don't need to punish anybody, just let it go and nothin' more need be said about it."

Scofield thought that over for a minute or two before responding. "You might be right. That might be the best way to handle it. That damn brainless gunslinger son of hers oughta been shot for riskin' this whole wagon train. We were damn lucky to get away from there before some more Injuns came lookin' for 'em. But weren't none of that Fancy's fault or Lemuel's neither." He nodded his head as if to signify he'd made a decision. "I'll call a meetin' with Fancy and Lemuel tonight after supper, and have Braxton and Zachary come, too. Both of them have already crossed over to this side of the river. I'll go tell 'em now before they get a chance to talk to anybody else about it." He started to leave but paused to say, "I want you at that meetin', too, since you found the body. Go up to my wagon and tell Spud to pull on ahead about forty yards, so the rest of the wagons can come out of the water in line of travel."

Leaving the crossing, the train moved along, still with the image of Split Rock before them to let them know they were still traveling west toward the Continental Divide. At five o'clock, they went into camp as usual. Clint helped Spud gather some extra wood for his cook fire, since Scofield had scheduled his meeting after supper. While Spud made biscuits for supper, Scofield walked over to Fancy's wagon. She was busy fixing supper for Lemuel and herself. "Clayton," she greeted him in her usual way when she saw his shadow fall across her fire. She turned around to squint up at him.

"How'd you know it was me?"

"Nobody else has got a shadow that big, but Lemuel and maybe Lonnie James," she replied. "And I can see Lemuel over there with the horses, and Lonnie James ain't gonna set foot around my wagon, unless he's got his wife with him. What can I do for you?"

Her answer forced a chuckle out of Scofield. "I just came to invite you to a little meetin' at my wagon after supper, you and Lemuel, both."

Immediately wary when Lemuel was invited along with her, she got to her feet and faced him. "What kind of meeting? What's it about?"

"Like I said, it's a small meetin'," Scofield tried to assure her. "It ain't nobody's business but yours and mine, so the only people that'll know about it will be me and you and Lemuel. And I've asked John Zachary and Emmett Braxton to attend, too, just to be sure you're treated square."

"For the love of . . ." She started, clearly agitated. "That sounds like a damn trial to me. This is some more crap about Billy, ain't it? I've told you once and for all, I ain't got nothin' to do with Billy. I've said my piece on it, and I ain't sayin' no more. So you go ahead and have your little meetin'. I won't be there! Lemuel, neither!"

Her reaction to his polite invitation was not entirely unexpected, so he remained patient, and when she finished her rebuke, he calmly advised her. "I had planned to have a sensible discussion on this business with you and Lemuel and your son, Billy. I want it to be private, so that it's just between us. The purpose is to clear it up for good. I'm invitin' you and Lemuel to come so we can be done with it. But make no mistake, if you don't come, I've got chains in my wagon and I'll drag you in chains to the meetin'." He paused for a moment while they locked eyes and exchanged smoldering glares. "It'll be kinda hard to keep it from the rest of the wagons, if we have to do it that way."

She continued to fume for a long moment. It was not her style to cower before any man since the day she walked out on Billy's father. But now, she had a lot to lose—too much to risk starting out on the rest of the journey on her own, with no one but Lemuel. She couldn't forget how easily Lemuel slit Billy's throat with nothing to gain but a belt. "All right," she finally said, her voice calm now. "I'll come to your damn meeting, after I've finished supper."

"Good," Scofield said. "I'm sure you'll be glad you did, then we can get on to Oregon."

Fancy and Lemuel showed up for the meeting, although not until they were late enough to cause Scofield to wonder if he should break out his chains. The reason they were late was because Fancy waited until the fiddle and the banjo tuned up in the middle of the circle. She figured she and Lemuel would be less likely noticed on their way to the wagon master's wagon. She walked up to the fire and looked around at everyone sitting there. Then she announced, "Well, here I am."

"I 'preciate it, Fancy," Scofield said. "I'll tell you what we know, then you can tell me what you know, and we'll see what it adds up to. All right?" She shrugged in answer, still defensive. "Billy's horse showed up in our herd last night without Billy. Clint, there, went back to that campground when we stopped for noonin' today. He found where Lemuel carried Billy's body away from your wagon, down the river to a gully where he dumped Billy. Billy had his throat cut. That's all we know for sure." He looked over at Lemuel when the simple man started to fidget as if he was thinking about running. "Just set still there, Lemuel. This ain't no hangin' party." Back to Fancy then, he said, "Now tell us what you know."

"What I know is simple," she replied. "Billy came to my wagon last night, late. Woke me up with a knife to my throat." She pulled her collar away to show him a scab where the knife had cut her. "He said he was fixin' to kill me because I don't have a bunch of money he thought I had. If Lemuel hadn'ta woke up and heard him, I'd be dead right now, and that's what I know."

Scofield looked at Lemuel, still fidgeting. "How come you slipped up behind him and slit his throat, instead of just shootin' him?"

"I didn't have no gun," Lemuel answered. "The guns are in the wagon with Miss Fancy. I had a knife."

"What you're both sayin' is Lemuel killed Billy to save your life, Fancy. So why the hell did you think you had to sneak his body off and hide it?" John Zachary asked.

Fancy was ready with an answer. "Because Billy was my son. Would you want everybody to know you killed your own son, whether he deserved it or not?"

Zachary and Braxton exchanged glances and shrugged in response to her answer. "I think I can understand that," Zachary said to Scofield. "It is an unfortunate position to be in. I reckon I don't blame her for wantin' to cover it up."

"Sounds to me like a simple case of self-defense," Braxton offered. "I don't think there was any doubt that Billy just brought trouble for Fancy and he damn near brought the Indians down on the rest of us. If you brought me and John here to act like a jury, my decision would be to say, 'good riddance' and forget about it. What do you say, John?" John quickly agreed.

"Well, as judge and jury on anything happenin' on this wagon train, I have to make the final decision," Scofield said. "So, I reckon I agree with John and Emmett and that'll be the last I wanna hear about it. You understand that, Lemuel?"

Lemuel was not quite sure. He looked to Fancy for help. "He means you ain't done nothin' wrong. Just go on about your business like before," she told him, then looked back at Scofield. "That's right, ain't it, Clayton?"

"Yes, ma'am," Scofield answered. "And there ain't no use in anybody but the six of us here knowin' what happened to Billy. He just left and never came back."

Early the next morning, Scofield was startled to the point where he almost thought he didn't have enough breath to blow his wakeup call. As far as he could see, there were nothing but dark lumps on both sides of the river. He was at a loss for only a few seconds, however, before he realized what he was seeing in the darkness. During the night, a herd of buffalo had moved into the river. He had been despairing to Clint about the lack of buffalo sightings when normally he could count on seeing thousands of the beasts. Now, at last, they showed up, and just before the wagon train traveled out of the buffalos' normal grazing country. He blew his bugle, louder than usual, then when he saw Clint stirring, he yelled to him. "Grab your rifle! We've got buffalo!" That's all it took to bring Clint scrambling out of his blankets. "We ain't even gotta go chase 'em, they came to us!"

Only those dark humps close by reacted to Scofield's bugle blast, and they merely got up and moved slowly back toward the river. In a few minutes, the rest of the camp came alive, so Scofield hurried out into the middle of the circle to caution everyone. "Buffalo!" he shouted. "We'll stay right where we are today while we take some fresh meat. I don't need but three of you to get your rifles out, Tim Blake, Ron Settle, Walt Moody. With me and Clint, that'll be enough to get all the meat we can handle. And there ain't no use killin' more'n we need. We'll kill enough for fresh meat for everybody and some more to smoke. Be careful you don't shoot each other or your horses. You men that I called out, get your rifles and meet me and Clint at my wagon. The rest of you men keep the horses and the cows inside the circle. Them buffalo are already in the river. They'll be on the move soon as the shootin' starts, so we need to hit 'em while they're steppin' on our toes."

The hunt couldn't have been much easier, since the buffalo were passing all around them. By the time the sun made an appearance, Clint counted fourteen of the massive beasts on the ground and Scofield was yelling for all shooters to stop. "That's more'n enough to give every wagon some fresh meat and leaves plenty to smoke."

With the killing over, the real work began as almost all hands turned out to skin and butcher the carcasses. The breakfast for the day was fresh roasted buffalo and smoking racks were devised over many fires to smoke-cure strips of the meat for other days. It was hard work, but it was a joyous endeavor since everybody had come to believe there would be no buffalo meat for this party on the Oregon Trail. There were no complaints about losing a day's travel, and on the day following, they started out again with cheerful determination. "There ain't nothin' like fresh meat to cure everybody's bellyachin'," Scofield told Clint while they ate their breakfast of fresh-roasted buffalo meat.

* * *

The days that followed saw the wagon train continue along the Sweetwater River, passing Split Rock and points that had been named by those passing before them—like Three Crossings and Ice Water Slough—until they finally reached the end of the Sweetwater and passed over the Continental Divide at South Pass. In almost shocking contrast to the winding Sweetwater River Valley, the emigrants gazed out across a broad open saddle of prairie and sagebrush with the Wind River Mountain Range to the north and the Great Divide Basin to the south. Thirty-five miles wide and almost flat, it was not an inviting sight to travelers already weary at this point in their journey. Clint was accustomed to seeing his uncle making the rounds to the individual wagons upon reaching South Pass. Upon reaching this wide expanse of flat, treeless prairie, Scofield felt it necessary to encourage the families and promise this stretch of their journey would not be as difficult as it first appeared. He counted a great deal on the banjo and fiddle and the several guitars to help keep the morale up. A major disappointment to both Clint and his uncle had been the shortage of buffalo in the Sweetwater Valley. Now, they had passed out of the buffalo's natural range, so there would be no more feasts on fresh buffalo for this wagon train. At least they were able to have one good hunt. Scofield liked to give thanks for other blessings that had been realized, however. There had been one incident with Sioux horse thieves, but that was the only threat they suffered. And there had been no cases of cholera. So many wagon trains had been hit by cholera and, so far, his train had escaped that dreaded sickness.

About a day's travel west of South Pass brought the train to a point in the sagebrush prairie where there was a fork in the road. It had been given the name of *The Parting of the Ways*. It was marked as such by a stone marker, on which had been carved two arrows, one pointing left, the other pointing right. Scofield explained to his charges that this was the beginning of the Sublette Cutoff on the right, a shortcut that saved about seventy miles travel. The left arrow pointed toward the continuation of the original trail, which led to Fort Bridger. "Which one are we takin'?" Pat Shephard asked.

"We'll follow the road to Fort Bridger," Scofield answered him.

"Why is that, if the other way saves us about seventy miles?" Peter Gilbert asked.

"'Cause, if you take the cutoff, you've gotta cross about fifty miles of desert," Scofield replied. "Fifty miles, and there ain't no water, and there ain't no grass. The way we're goin', there's water and grass. It ain't as good as we'd like it, but it's a sight better than what you'll find on the cutoff, and there's at least willow wood for fires. And when we get to Fort Bridger, you'll be able to restock any supplies you're runnin' short on and get any repairs you need on the wagons. You could save some time on the cutoff, but you run a risk of losin' some stock. And it's a helluva walk across that desert when you ain't got any water. We're in good shape as far as the progress we've made. If nothin' really bad happens, we've got plenty of time to get past the Blue Mountains before snow falls."

"You've convinced me," Lonnie James volunteered. He walked over to stand in front of the stone marker and looked out across the wide, flat prairie. "I don't see nothin' out there I'd wanna feed my horse." There were no votes to take the shortcut, even if Scofield had intended to give them a choice. At seven o'clock the next morning, the wagons started out toward Little Sandy Creek, a healthy creek running south through the sandy sagebrush plain. It was an easy crossing, barely slowing the wagon train down, since the creek was only about ten feet wide and two feet deep. In the days after that crossing, they followed Big Sandy Creek to its confluence with the Green River. The Green, wide, deep, and swift, was usually at high water this time of year, making it an even more treacherous crossing. According to Scofield, he had seen as many as five ferries operating on the river a few years back, when traffic on the trail was at its peak. Even on the day they reached it, there were two ferries competing for their business. This was not news to the emigrants, for they had been told before leaving Independence that there would be some tolls they should be prepared to pay.

The Green River crossing presented a surprise encounter with one, Cal Nixon, however. They noticed his lone wagon on the other side of the river with his team of horses tied to it, but not in harness. When the first of their wagons were loaded on the ferries, Clint noticed the man when he jumped out of the wagon to watch the crossing. Clint didn't give it much thought, even though it was just the one wagon. He figured he might have something to do with one of the ferry boats going back and forth across the river. When the last of the wagons rolled off the ferry and pulled up on the south bank of the river, Scofield and Clint led the train to a much-used campground, deciding to camp there for the night. While the men went about the usual routine of caring for the stock and cutting wood for the fires, the women began preparing supper. It was then that the man in the lone wagon came to call.

"Evenin'," he said when he walked up to Clint while

he was pulling the saddle off Biscuit. "I couldn't help admirin' that horse. That's one of those horses bred by the Nez Perce isn't it?"

"Evenin'," Clint returned. "That's right. Biscuit's a Palouse."

The stranger chuckled. "Biscuit, huh. I'll bet there's a story behind that name."

"You'd be right about that," Clint replied but didn't offer to tell it. "Is that your wagon over there?" He took a casual look at the man as he pulled the saddle blanket off the Palouse gelding and decided he looked more like a professional gambler than anything else he could think of. He noticed a handgun, worn high on his left side with the butt facing forward. *Cross-hand draw,* Clint thought.

"My name's Cal Nixon," the stranger said. "That big fellow you've been talkin' to, is he the wagon master?"

"Clint Buchanan," he answered. "Yep, he's the wagon master. His name's Clayton Scofield. You wanna talk to him?"

"Yeah, I do. I'd like to see if I can't hook up with you folks, at least as far as Fort Bridger, anyway."

"Is that your wagon over yonder on the bank?" Clint repeated the question, even though he saw him get out of it before.

"That's right and that's where it's gonna stay, unless you've got an extra axle you wanna sell me."

"You got a broke axle?" Clint asked. "That's a sorry piece of luck. You got a family in the wagon?"

"No, there ain't nobody but me. I don't have any family. Like you folks, I'm just tryin' to get out to Oregon country. But I drove my wagon off the ferry boat, pulled all the way up on the bank and the axle just broke right in two." He nodded toward his wagon. "And it just sat down right there. Wouldn't move another foot."

"Were you headin' to Oregon by yourself?" Clint asked, somewhat surprised.

"Well, not originally. I was with a wagon train that started out at Council Bluffs, thirteen wagons. When we got to The Parting of the Ways, the other twelve wagons took the cutoff. But from what I'd heard about it, I didn't wanna go that way. So, I told 'em I'd just go by myself." He chuckled. "I hope I don't run into 'em out in Oregon, so I won't have to confess what happened to me. Hell, one of the reasons I left 'em was because there were thirteen of us and that was bound to be bad luck." He and Clint both laughed at that. "I musta brought the bad luck with me. Anyway, I decided I'd wait till another wagon train came this way and maybe go on with them. I'll just pack what I can on one of my horses and ride the other one. There ain't nothin' I can do to fix the wagon."

"Have you got a saddle?" Clint asked, thinking about Billy Wallace's saddle in Scofield's wagon.

"Yeah, I've got my saddle in the wagon," Cal said.

"Come on and we'll go talk to Scofield," Clint said. "I'm sure he'd be glad to have you tag along with us."

The wagon master was helping himself to a cup of coffee when Clint and Cal approached. He glanced up and gave Cal a quick looking-over. "Howdy," he offered.

"This is Cal Nixon," Clint said. "That's his wagon settin' over yonder on the bank with a broke axle. He'd like to go along with us to Fort Bridger." Scofield extended his hand and they shook. "You want some coffee, Cal?" Clint asked, but Cal declined, saying he must have downed a barrel of it while he was watching their wagons cross the river. Clint left Cal to repeat the story he had told him while he went to pour himself a cup. He returned in time to hear Scofield's response.

"Why, sure," the wagon master said, "you're welcome to tag along with us." He paused to grin. "Unless you druther wait for a Mormon train. There's one behind us, but I don't know how far behind—maybe no more'n three or four days."

"I might have too many sins to travel with a Mormon train," Cal japed. "I believe I'd better go with you boys. I paid a fee when I started out from Council Bluffs with that other train. Do I owe you anything to travel with you? I'd be glad to go on your guard roster, like everybody else, and help out on any crossings or Indian attacks."

"I 'preciate your offer to help out, but I don't see as how I oughta charge you anything to ride along with us. We wouldn't wanna leave you out here on the prairie alone. You'll be packin' all your supplies on your horses. So we won't be goin' to any extra bother on your account. Did you fix your supper yet?" Cal said that he had not, so Scofield offered some strips of smoked buffalo. "After supper, a lot of the folks will be crankin' up some music, so you can join us and get to meet some of 'em."

"'Preciate your hospitality," Cal responded. "I'll surely do that, and thanks for the meat." He shook both Clint's and Scofield's hands again. "I'll go on back to my wagon and take care of my horses, and I'll see you after supper."

"Reckon what he's plannin' to do when he gets to Oregon?" Clint mused as he and his uncle stood there watching Cal when he walked away. "He don't look like a farmer or a cattleman."

"No, he don't," Scofield replied. "He looks more like he belongs in Fancy Wallace's line of work. I reckon we'll find out."

When Doc and Buck limbered up their instruments and began the evening's entertainment, the word had already begun to spread among a small portion of the members of the train. When Cal Nixon arrived to watch the dancing, he was greeted with more than stares and gaping mouths. He had already met several people by the time Scofield walked over to officially introduce him as a new member of the train. Cal was well received by everyone he met, especially the women, since he was well-mannered and polite. The fact was that he was a tall, handsome man, who was well groomed, even in light of the circumstances he found himself. Driving a wagon. And with a broken axle. He had a quick smile below his neatly trimmed mustache, causing Sarah Braxton to comment to Marcy Zachary, "I wonder how many marriages he's put a strain on." He was the cause of many similar remarks and speculations, but none so surprising as that which came from Fancy Wallace.

As a rule, Fancy was not a regular attendee to the evening entertainment hour, but on this night, she decided to join the gathering in the middle of the circle of wagons out of sheer boredom. Realizing this was an unusual occurrence for Fancy, Marcy spoke to her when she walked over to those gathered near the fire. "You comin' to meet the new member to our wagon train, Fancy?"

"We've got a new member?" Fancy responded. "I wondered why everybody was crowdin' up over there. What's his name?"

"I've already forgotten," Marcy confessed. "Scofield introduced him, but I guess I wasn't paying attention when he said his name." *I was too busy admiring his good looks,* she thought to herself.

Not particularly interested in meeting some new emigrant, Fancy decided she was ready to return to her wagon. She started to turn to leave but stopped when something changed her mind. Without any explanation to Marcy for her turnabout, she walked over to the gathering around the new arrival. She stood at the edge of the group of people, watching, until some of those in front of her parted and he saw her. Not certain, he didn't say anything until she spoke. "Hello, Cal. Been a pretty good while since I saw you."

"Well, I'll be damned," he exclaimed. "Fancy Wallace! If I was given a hundred chances to guess who I'd run into on the banks of the Green River, I still wouldn't have guessed Fancy Wallace. What are you doin' here?"

"Looks like about the same thing you are," Fancy answered, "goin' to Oregon." She favored him with a smile that was closer to a smirk and added, "Or maybe you're headin' to California and the gold claims."

"Well, I'll just say I won't rule that out. It's been a while since I last set foot in Dodge City, seein' as how your fellow citizens were so fired up about wantin' to hang me." He lowered his voice, so those standing closest to them couldn't hear. "That lyin' snake was cheatin', I don't care if he was the postmaster's son. Then his next mistake was thinkin' he was fast with a gun when I called him on it. And the folks wanted to hang me because I showed him that he wasn't fast a-tall. So, I figured I'd make myself scarce around Dodge City." He shrugged and smiled, like it was all in a day's work. "But I heard about the fire in the Fancy Pantz Saloon and your partner gettin' killed. I reckon that had to hit you pretty hard. Heard Pantz was shot in the back of the head. Did the killer rob the place, or was he just out to finish Pantz?"

"He robbed the place, took every penny that was in the safe," she said.

"Damn," Cal swore, "that is awful tough news, lose your partner and all your operatin' cash, too."

"Yes, it was, but I wasn't really his partner. Folks just thought I was. I ran the business for him, but he just paid me the same as he paid Jack, the bartender, and the cook." She paused to allow for his expression of surprise before continuing. "It didn't cost me much to live, so I saved almost everything he paid me. It was enough to buy this wagon and my horses and some supplies."

"Did they catch Pantz's killer?" Cal asked.

"No, at least they hadn't caught him when I left there," she said.

He nodded thoughtfully. *Right,* he told himself, *and they ain't likely to because she's standing right here telling me about it.* He never doubted for a minute that Fancy Wallace had the nerve to destroy anyone who crossed her. "What you gonna do when you get out to Oregon?" Cal asked.

"Don't know," she answered. "Have to wait and see what I find. Maybe I'll find somebody who needs help runnin' a saloon. Maybe, one day, I can have my own saloon. How 'bout you? You gonna still try to make a livin' with a deck of cards?"

"Maybe, if I can't find something better. That's about all I'm qualified to do." The problem he feared he might have to face in Oregon was a lack of gambling potential compared to the eastern states. "Damned if we ain't two fish outta water, ain't we?" Their private conversation was interrupted then when Scofield walked over to join them.

"I declare," Scofield started, "it's unusual to see you out here at the entertainment hour, Fancy. I see you've met Cal." He turned to Cal and said, "You don't know how rare it is to see Fancy out here with the singers and the dancers."

"I knew Cal before," Fancy informed him. "He used to come into the saloon from time to time when he was in Dodge."

"Well, I'll be . . ." Scofield exclaimed. "How's that for a small world? Cal's got a broke axle. Did he tell ya?" Fancy nodded. Scofield turned toward Cal then. "I came over to ask you if you want Lonnie James and some of the other boys to take a look at that axle. Might be, we could rig up a tree limb or somethin' to support that axle enough to get it to Fort Bridger. And I expect they can fix you up with a new one there."

Cal was surprised, but he was quick to refuse. "No, sir, I thank you kindly for the offer, but I don't want the dog-gone wagon. I didn't pay much for it 'cause it was pretty beat up when I bought it. This ain't the first trouble I've had with it, so I'm sick of messin' with it. I've got my horses and my packs. I'd a whole lot rather sit in the saddle the rest of the way, so I'm just gonna leave that wagon where it is. I'll go ahead and sleep there tonight, but when we leave in the mornin', I'll be on horseback. Thank you just the same."

Scofield found his refusal curious. It was an odd attitude for someone on a wagon train, but he had to allow for the possibility that a man like Cal just naturally traveled light. He didn't need a wagon, so Scofield was surprised that he bought one in the first place. *More likely he won it in a card game,* he thought. He left the two of them to talk about old times. They obviously knew each other pretty well.

Chapter 15

Leaving the treacherous Green River crossing early the next morning, the wagon train followed a distinct trail left by countless wagons before them. It led in a generally southwest direction as they headed for Fort Bridger. It took four days and part of a fifth day before they reached the former fur-trading post on Black's Fork of the Green River. Consisting of a few crude log buildings, surrounded by a picket wall, plastered with dried mud, the post was now a critical stop for emigrants on the Oregon Trail. For Fort Bridger provided a source for depleted supplies as well as repairs for those wagons in need of them. The fort, now operated by the army, showed ample evidence of the Mormon uprising against the Union in what was known as the Utah War. Much of the original fort that Jim Bridger built had been burned to the ground. For the few people in Clayton Scofield's wagon train who even knew about the short war, Scofield had assured them that it had all been settled a couple of years before the present day. There were several wagons needing the blacksmith's attention, but since they arrived early in the day, Scofield felt they could get that finished and be ready to start again in the morning. It would still allow for a good rest for people and horses.

For Cal Nixon, Fort Bridger offered an opportunity to find a card game. He would have preferred a higher-stakes game, but in lieu of that, he was not opposed to relieving some of the soldiers of their army pay. Once he had set up the small tent that he brought from his wagon and turned his horses out with the others in the center of the train, he walked over to the sutler's store. It wasn't necessary to go inside the store, for he almost bumped into a young soldier on his way out. "Pardon me, soldier, I just rode in with that wagon train. Where can a fellow get a drink of whiskey on the post?"

"You can't get one on the post," the soldier answered. "You have to go to Shorty's." He motioned for Cal to follow him and walked out in the road in front of the building and pointed toward the river. "'Bout a quarter of a mile past your wagons down the river."

"Much obliged," Cal said. "If I see you down there this evening, I'll buy you a drink."

"Much obliged," the soldier said, "but I've gotta pull guard duty tonight, so I don't reckon I'll be down at Shorty's." Cal told him he'd like to buy him a drink, anyway, and gave him two bits to pay for one the next time he did visit Shorty's.

Cal figured wherever whiskey was sold, that would be the place to find a game of cards. Because he preferred to play in the evening when the whiskey flowed more freely, he went back to the wagons. He had been invited to eat supper with Fancy Wallace. He had insisted that he should not eat up her food, but she said she had restocked on everything as soon as they got there. "Just don't get the idea that I'm gonna take you to feed every night," she had said. "This is just a welcome to the gang supper. I've already got one oversized child to feed. If I take on another one, it'll be more trouble than I need to mess with." He had laughed when she said it, knowing she was referring to Lemuel. Then he had joked that he'd been with the wagon train since the Green River Crossing and it took her long enough to do what was properly polite.

When suppertime came, the cookfires were glowing and Lemuel was adding wood to Fancy's. He immediately dropped his gaze down to the piece of limb he was poking up the fire with. "You need a hand with some more wood for that fire?" Cal asked. Lemuel didn't answer, he just shook his head, still looking down.

"Be careful you don't get him started," Fancy joked as she came from the back of the wagon. "He'll talk your head off."

"Maybe he's just a little smarter than the rest of us," Cal said. "Maybe the rest of us oughta take a lesson from him. If you ain't got nothin' important to say, it's better to just keep shut. Ain't that right, Lemuel?" Lemuel didn't respond.

"Well, that fire's ready for my fryin' pan now," Fancy said. "So, if you're thinkin' about havin' coffee with this meat, you'd best go get some water in that coffeepot."

Lemuel started to get up from the fire to do Fancy's bidding, but Cal jumped to the coffeepot first. "Here, let me get the water, you're busy already." He strode down to the edge of the river. Lemuel looked out from under his bowed head at Fancy then, his eyes questioning.

"It's still your job, Lemuel," she told him. "He's just tryin' to be polite because I'm lettin' him eat with us." He raised his head to look at her, and it struck her that she saw the same forlorn look in his eyes that she noticed when Billy showed up at her wagon. She had made it very plain to him that she was hiring him to do the work she didn't care to do on the trip. And she emphasized the fact that the job ended when they reached Oregon City. She wondered again how big a problem it was going to be when the journey was done. *I reckon I'll deal with it when the time comes,* she thought.

It was not a meal indicative of her name, but Fancy served one that was filling. She fried up bacon with some of the smoked buffalo she had left and mixed it up with some soup beans and pan-baked some cornbread to hold it down. There were no complaints from her guests. "I'm gonna walk down the river a-ways," Cal announced after they finished eating. "There's supposed to be a place called Shorty's down about a quarter of a mile where a man can get a drink of whiskey. You want me to bring a bottle back for you?" She declined, as did Lemuel, his gesture no more than a headshake. Cal thanked her for her hospitality and bade them both a good night.

Shorty's turned out to be pretty much what Cal expected, a small log structure with a porch on the front. There was a small barn in back, a smokehouse, and an outhouse. There were a couple of horses tied at the hitching rail, which caused him to think Shorty's business might not all be from the soldiers at the fort. He walked into a bar room that looked to be half full, most of them soldiers. But there were a couple of tables where cards were being dealt. One of them was occupied by four soldiers, but the other table looked to be all civilian. That one sparked Cal's interest, so he decided to watch it for a while before asking to join them. With that decision made, he walked over to the bar and found a spot to slide in. An extremely tall, gangly man with a bushy white beard moved down the bar to serve him. "Howdy," the bartender greeted him. "You come in with that wagon train?"

"Let me guess," Cal responded as he looked up at the tall beanpole of a man, "you've gotta be Shorty."

"That's a fact," Shorty grinned in reply. "What gave it away?" He was quite accustomed to remarks made about his height, and it appeared not to bother him. "What's your pleasure?"

"Rye whiskey, if you've got it, corn if you don't," Cal said. He watched Shorty pour his shot, then knocked it back, tapped the empty glass on the bar, and asked for another. "Looks like you do a pretty good business here, Shorty. I expected to see nothing but soldiers. I wouldn'ta thought there were many civilians around here."

"I reckon that's the nice part about being the only saloon in this part of the country," Shorty crowed. "Some of my customers take a long ride to come see me. And it's always a little extra busy whenever a wagon train comes through." He paused to grin, then said, "Unless it's a Mormon train. But I've already done a little business with some of your folks. Matter of fact, that feller down at the other end of the bar, he's one of your people, ain't he?"

Cal looked toward the end of the bar, at the man Shorty indicated, but he didn't recall seeing him before. "He might be, but I just joined this wagon train a few days ago, back at the Sandy Creek-Green River confluence, so I don't know half the people I'm travelin' with. Do you remember his name?"

"No," Shorty hesitated, trying to recall. "Ralph somethin', I think." He lowered his voice and said, "He was tossin' down one shot after another, but then his money ran out, I reckon. Tell you the truth, I was thinkin' about tellin' him it was time for him to go home, but he ain't botherin' nobody right now."

Eager to change the subject, since he didn't care to get involved with some fool's drinking problem, Cal asked, "Who are the fellows playin' cards near the four soldiers?"

"Two of 'em, I know," Shorty replied. "Feller wearin' the Derby is Red Cannon. The one settin' across from him is Jack Simmons. The other two fellers are strangers, just rode in today. I think they drove a small herd of horses in and sold 'em to the army. They've been playin' cards since four o'clock."

"Which one's the big winner?" Cal asked.

"I don't think any one of 'em is cleanin' up. Looks like everybody's winnin' a few hands now and then, so ain't nobody made any complaints."

"Well, that sounds like a gentleman's game," Cal decided. "I think I'll ask 'em if they'll let me sit in for a few hands." Shorty shrugged and poured him another shot when he signaled for it. "Wish me luck," Cal said and walked over to the table. "Excuse me, gentlemen. Is this a closed game, or have you got room for one more?"

His enquiry generated a pause in the game while all

four players stared openly at him. After a long moment when no one answered his question, finally the man wearing the Derby, Red Cannon, responded. "Well, now, that depends. We've got a friendly little game goin' here. You got the look of a man who might make his livin' at the card table."

Cal chuckled good-naturedly. "Now, I don't know if I should take that as a compliment or be offended. The fact of the matter is, I was hopin' to pass a little time playing cards and you fellows looked like you felt the same way. If you're concerned that I might be lookin' to cheat you outta your money, I would remind you that that's your deck of cards I'd be playin' with. And if you prefer, I'll skip my turn to deal when it comes around to me. We'll all just play the cards we're dealt and hope to be lucky."

"Damn, mister, you're better at speechifyin' than Red," Jack Simmons said. "Pull you up a chair and set down and we'll see if we can't relieve you of whatever money you're totin'. You can just take your regular turn with the deal, and if we catch you cheatin', we'll shootcha." He extended his hand. "Jack Simmons," he declared.

"Cal Nixon," he replied and took his hand.

"That's Red Cannon," Simmons went on to introduce the others. "And these two fellers are Ace and Slack. So far, they ain't give any last names, but I wouldn't remember 'em, if they did. They're just passin' through Fort Bridger, anyway, most likely runnin' from the law somewhere." They all laughed at Jack's remark, with only Ace and Slack aware of the accuracy of it.

Cal had barely settled into a chair and placed a modest sum of money before him when he felt a tap on his shoulder. He looked around to find the man Shorty had said was Ralph Something from the wagon train. "Howdy, partner," Tyson slurred drunkenly. "You're the new feller that joined up with the wagon train at Green River, ain'tcha?" Cal looked up at him and nodded. That was enough to encourage Tyson to continue. "I ain't had a chance to welcome you to the train, and I'd like to buy you a drink of likker. But I seem to have run outta cash. So, how 'bout you lend me some money and I'll buy the drinks and pay you back when we go back to camp?"

"Looks to me like you've had all the whiskey you need already," Cal replied. "We'll just say you made the offer and let it go at that, and I'll turn my attention back to poker. I think these boys want me to keep all my money right here on the table."

"Hell, man, just one little drink," Tyson complained. "I ain't askin' you to buy a whole bottle."

Cal hesitated for just a moment, then decided to see if he could get rid of Tyson peacefully. "Here," he said, picked up a couple of coins, and held them out toward Tyson. "Go to the bar and spend this. Don't come back here to bother us. I'm busy here. Fair enough?"

He continued to hold the coins until Tyson, unable to refuse, repeated, "Fair enough," and held out his hand. Cal released the coins to drop into Tyson's hand.

Red and Jack made no attempt to hide their annoyance for the interruption in their card game. Annoyed as well, the two strangers said nothing, but being naturally cautious, at one point in the negotiations between Cal and Tyson, they exchanged questioning glances. It was enough to prompt Ace Pittard to ask, "Just what is your line of work, Cal? You say you ain't no professional gambler. And you sure don't look like a farmer, lookin' to settle a homestead out in Oregon country. You got a family back at that wagon train camp?"

"Nope, no family," Cal answered, oblivious of any suspicions directed toward him, other than the possible gambling profession. "Matter of fact, I don't even have a wagon."

"So, you ain't got no real reason to go out to Oregon except just to see what's out there?" Slack questioned as he shuffled the cards and prepared to deal.

"More or less," Cal said. "I never been to that part of the country. Thought it was time I took a look at it."

"It's a mighty long way to chase a man to collect a damn bounty," Ace announced, as his partner started to deal the hand.

"I expect it would be. Depends on how much the bounty is." Cal allowed, more interested in the cards he was being dealt, until it suddenly struck him funny when he realized the reason behind the two's inane questions. "You think I'm a bounty hunter?" He didn't wait for an answer and laughed outright. "How much are you worth? What did you do? You didn't kill anybody, did you? 'Cause I don't like to play cards with killers." He remembered then. "Shorty said you drove some horses in with you to sell to the army, so I reckon you're just horse thieves and that's all right, I play cards with horse thieves all the time."

"Mister, you got it mixed up in your head about what's funny and what ain't," Ace said and got up from his chair. Standing almost over Cal, he stated, "I don't stand for no man to call me a horse thief. So, let's get that straight right now, unless you're ready to back it up with that damn gun you got on backwards."

Suddenly, the harmless laughter faded away, replaced by an air of tension that descended over the table. "Just slow down there, partner," Cal responded, his voice calm and serious now. "You don't wanna go there. There ain't no need to get upset about a little harmless jokin'. I won't call you a horse thief, since you're a little touchy about it. All right?" Ace didn't reply at once but remained standing over Cal, his face flushed with anger. Against his better judgment, Cal couldn't resist one more joke, since it was obvious that he had struck a nerve. "We'll just call Slack a horse thief."

He found that humor did nothing to defuse the situation. "Damn you! You think I'm japin' with you!" Ace roared, totally intent upon shooting Cal down. "Stand and face me, or I swear, I'll shoot you settin' there in that chair!"

The altercation was loud enough now to attract the attention of everyone in the saloon and particularly Shorty. He came rushing over to the table, making his way through the spectators who turned from the bar to watch what was turning into a gunfight. "Hold on here, men, I don't want no gunfights inside my business. If you two are hell-bent on tryin' to shoot each other, do it outside."

Cal, still sitting at the table, said to Shorty, "I've got no intention of participatin' in a gunfight with this gentleman, here. I didn't go to insult him. I was just tryin' to do a little funnin'. Thought it might loosen us all up some. I admit I mighta made a mistake and I apologize to Mr. Ace, here, if I upset him."

"Well, that seems fair enough to me," Shorty said. "That's mighty sportin' of you, Cal. That oughta settle it, right, Ace?"

"The only thing it settles is that he's a yeller dog with his mouth where his ass oughta be," Ace replied. "When he admits that, then it'll be settled."

The expression on Cal's face changed from one of

frank apology to something more akin to serious amusement. He smiled and said, "Whether I'm a yellow dog or not, I ain't admittin' it to you. But I am willin' to set you straight on one thing. I'm not a bounty hunter and I never heard of you or Slack, there. So it doesn't make any sense for you to get yourself shot over something you've made up in your head. All I want from you and Slack is some of that money in front of you on the table, and I intend to get it fair and square. So sit down and let's play poker."

Ace was struck dumb for a few moments, not sure if he was being insulted by Cal's unexpected statement or not. But he was damn-sure that Cal was trying to manipulate him. Suddenly, he realized the entire bar room had gone silent, watching him, and he was the only one of the card players who was on his feet. Cal's flippant response to his challenge made him think he was not being taken seriously by the glib stranger. He could feel all eyes upon him as he stood there alone, his demand for satisfaction totally ignored, and he feared he was being made a fool of. Even Slack, his partner, seemed puzzled by his actions. "By God, I warned you," he spat at Cal and reached for the pistol he wore.

Ace's pistol never cleared his holster before he was doubled over by Cal's shot, startling all the onlookers. When Ace dropped to the floor, all eyes shifted back to Cal, who was holding his .44, already cocked, on Ace's partner. Slack very wisely held his hands up, palms facing Cal, and said, "I got no part in this. I don't know what set him off like that. He's been kinda touchy lately, a little off his feed. You don't think we're really horse thieves, do ya?"

"Mister, I don't care whether you are or whether

you're not. It ain't got nothin' to do with me," Cal said. "We're done, right?"

"We're done," Slack answered and picked Ace's money up off the table. "I'll take care of Ace. I'll take him home." Then he picked up his own money.

"Whoa!" Cal said. "You ain't leavin' the game, are you? Hell, we can still play some poker. We can tote Ace out to the front porch, till you're ready to go. I'll help you carry him."

"Thank you just the same," the bewildered Slack replied, "but I've got a long ride to take Ace home. So I'd best get started right away."

"Why don't you just bury him?" Cal asked.

"No, I think I owe it to Ace and his family to take his body home, so they'll know for sure he'll have a grave near home," Slack insisted.

"Where's home?" Red Cannon asked.

"Colorado Territory," Slack said.

"That is a helluva ride," Red remarked. "He's liable to get pretty ripe before you get there."

"That's why I reckon I'd best get started as soon as I can," Slack replied. "I'll go back to our camp and wrap him up in his blanket and tie him on as best I can."

"Well, least I can do is help you carry him outta here and get him on his horse," Cal volunteered. "I'm awful sorry I had to shoot him, but he didn't give me any choice. I was hopin' we could play us some poker."

"Ain't no hard feelin's," Slack assured him. "Ace always did have a kinda hot temper."

Just to be sure, Cal took hold of Ace's boots, but not until Slack had his hands occupied with Ace's shoulders. They lifted the body up and carried it out the door. Once it was settled firmly across the saddle, Cal stood back and watched until Slack rode off, leading Ace's horse. He was frankly somewhat surprised by Slack's reaction to the shooting of his partner. He figured he must have some feelings for Ace, or he wouldn't go to the trouble to transport his body back to his family. As far as Slack was concerned, he was not looking forward to the long trip with a decomposing body. But there was a two-hundred-dollar reward for Ace Pittard, dead or alive, in Colorado Territory, and he needed the body for proof. He counted himself lucky that he was never identified as one of the men who participated in that bank holdup.

While Cal was outside, watching Slack ride away, there was a lively discussion among the spectators of the shooting. "I swear," Jack Simmons insisted, "I never saw him reach for that gun, and I was lookin' right at him."

"I was lookin' at the feller he shot—saw him reach for his gun—then he was bending over, shot, before I had time to turn my head to look at the feller that shot him," Shorty said. Several of his customers were reenacting the face-off as they remembered it, making the cross-body motion Cal made to draw his weapon and marveling at how clumsy it felt. The soldiers seemed especially fascinated by the speed with which the seemingly carefree man reacted. The discussions ended abruptly when Cal walked back in the door.

"We can still play some three-handed games," Cal exclaimed when he saw that there was no money left on the table but his. "You boys ain't quittin', are you?"

"We was about ready to quit when you came in," Red lied.

"Damn, I hate it that I came in and broke up the card

game," Cal said. He looked around at the other men standing there. "Maybe somebody else would like to get a game goin'." There was no interest from anyone, so he picked up his money and walked over to Red and Jack. "Shorty said you two were regular customers, so I wanna apologize for breakin' up your game. I sure as hell didn't have that in mind when I came in here." They assured him that there were no hard feelings, and they were getting ready to go back to their camp for the night, anyway. "Least I can do is buy you a drink before you go," Cal offered.

"Well, I reckon a little shot to warm the belly would be pretty good," Jack responded. "It's a pretty chilly night out there." They walked over to the bar and Shorty put out three clean glasses and started to pour.

Cal glanced down toward the end of the bar and saw Ralph Tyson supporting himself with one arm on the bar, an empty glass before him. He was watching Shorty pour the three drinks with eyes that reminded Cal of a dog begging for food. "He already spent that four bits I gave him?" Cal asked Shorty. Shorty said that he had. "You sure he's with the wagon train?"

"I'm pretty sure," Shorty answered.

"All right then, pour him one, too, and I'll see if I can help him back to the wagons, 'cause I ain't so sure he can find 'em on his own." Shorty moved down the bar to Tyson and filled his shot glass. Watching Tyson's reaction, Cal was prompted to say, "I swear, if he had a tail, he'd be waggin' it."

When Shorty moved back to Cal and the two regulars, Tyson moved up the bar to join them. "Doggone it, mister, you're all right," he slurred. "I done forgot your name, but I know you're that new feller on the wagon train."

"That's right," Cal said. "You remember how to get back to the camp?"

"Hell, yeah," Tyson answered. "I ain't drunk."

"Well, if you ain't, I'd like to see you when you are," Cal said. "I'll tell you what, I'm headin' back right now. You can walk back with me. Whaddaya say?"

"I don't mind if I do, partner," Tyson said. "You might need to stock up on whiskey, a bottle or two, anyway. We never know when we'll get to another place to buy some."

Cal bade a good night to Red and Jack and apologized again for breaking up their card game. By this time, the two, who ran a sawmill on the river, had decided that Cal was a pretty standup fellow, who just happened to be fast with a gun. On the quiet, they wished him good luck getting Tyson back to the camp. Moments later, they found it was wasted effort to whisper, for Cal turned back toward Tyson just in time to see him sink to the floor like a wilting weed. He proceeded to lie there, totally unconscious, a contented smile spread wide across his face. "He's passed out," Jack informed them quite unnecessarily.

"Well, ain't that a fine mess," Red commented. "Now, what are you gonna do with him? Leave him here till he wakes up?"

"Oh, no," Shorty exclaimed at once, "on the porch, maybe, but not in here. He's drank so much he might not wake up till mornin'. Let's see if we can wake him up." He went over to a bucket sitting on a shelf against the wall, came back with a dipper full of water, and emptied it on Tyson's face. The unconscious man mumbled and licked his lips, trying to drink it. Shorty repeated the process. This time Cal grabbed a handful of Tyson's hair, so he got the full dipper in his face. Tyson was oblivious to the water, seeming to go into a deeper sleep.

Cal stood back and looked at the problem he had unwisely stepped into. "He ain't gonna wake up till mornin'," he mused. He looked at Shorty to explain, "I can't leave him on your porch tonight. That wagon train is pullin' outta here at seven o'clock in the mornin'. He's gonna have to get up at four to water and feed his horses, hitch 'em up, get his breakfast, all before seven. Hell, he ain't that big, I'll just have to carry him back."

It was at this point that the U.S. Army stepped up to serve the civilian population. The four soldiers, who had been playing cards at the other table, had been interested spectators to the demonstration of a fast-gun face-off. They were now watching, with great interest, the efforts to bring Ralph Tyson to life. Rising to the moment, one of the young men stepped forward. "Don't mean to stick my nose in your business, but if you need a hand, me and my pals, here, are headin' back to the fort right now. We pass right close to that pasture where your wagons are parked. Wouldn't be no trouble a-tall to carry this feller for ya."

"Soldier," Cal exclaimed, laughing, "that sure would help me and this fellow, too. I gotta say, this is one time when we was saved by the cavalry."

"Well, sir, we ain't cavalry, but it looks to me like what you need is foot soldiers, anyway."

The four soldiers picked up Tyson and carried him like a board with one man at each corner. His head being unsupported, hung down, but Tyson was too drunk to be aware of it. Cal was sure the effects of it would appear after he had sobered up. Shorty's was less than a quarter of a mile from the wagon camp and the music from the entertainment hour could be clearly heard from the saloon. Cal wanted to get Tyson back before the entertainment period broke up and everybody went to bed. He could have carried the smallish Tyson himself, but it would have been a tiring job along the rough river path, so he had gladly accepted the soldiers' offer of assistance. When they reached the closest point to the camp, Cal had them drop Tyson across his shoulder. Once the body was settled to Cal's satisfaction, he thanked the soldiers and wished them all well. Then he walked inside the circle of wagons and headed for the folks gathered at the big fire.

The music stopped when he walked up to the center of the singing and dancing and dumped Tyson on the ground. "Sorry to interrupt the party," he asked, "but does anybody know where this belongs?" He pointed to the body at his feet.

"Good Lord," Pat Shephard exclaimed, "Ralph Tyson! Is he dead?"

"Nope," Cal answered, "dead drunk."

His words were followed by many groans of pity, but they were all for Ruby Tyson. "Poor Ruby," Marcy Zachary remarked. "At least, she didn't have to see him carried home and dumped like a sack of potatoes in front of everybody."

"I apologize for that," Cal was quick to respond to her remark. "I guess it was a little bit rude to dump him like a sack of potatoes, but I don't know the man, or which wagon is his." He looked around him then at the folks gathered there. "If his wife is here, I'm sorry I had to bring him home this way."

"You don't have to worry about that," Sarah Braxton spoke up. "Ruby doesn't ever come out to the entertainment hour." She pointed at the man still lying there unconscious. "And that's the reason why." She turned to her close friend, Marcy, and muttered, "He ain't worth as much as a sack of potatoes."

Clint and his uncle, coming from inspecting the horses, wondered why the music suddenly stopped and everybody had gathered around something on the ground. They arrived at the gathering in time to hear Sarah's aside to Marcy. When Scofield learned that the *something* on the ground was Ralph Tyson, his anger immediately flared up in his veins. "Who brought him back?"

"I did," Cal responded. "He was down the river at Shorty's and Shorty told me he was from the wagon train. He was passed out, so I figured I'd best bring him back here. I didn't know who he was, or where he belonged, or I'da took him to his wagon."

Scofield made an effort to control his temper when he saw who it was. "Well, I reckon I oughta thank you for bringin' him back to camp, so we don't waste half our mornin' lookin' for him tomorrow. I'm sorry you had to fool with him. Clint and I'll carry him to his wagon." He motioned to Clint, and the two of them picked him up and started toward Tyson's wagon.

Following them with his eyes, Cal was barely able to make out the tiny figure waiting by the wagon. He couldn't help a feeling of compassion for a woman married to a man like Ralph Tyson, unaware as he was of Tyson's past history since just joining the wagon train. His thoughts were interrupted then when someone tapped him on the shoulder. "If you'll slip outta that jacket for a little while, I'll clean the back of it while we're this close to the river."

"What?" Cal responded, confused.

He turned around to see little Susie James standing in front of her bear-sized husband, a wide grin on his face, as his wife held out her hand for the jacket. "Looks like Tyson decided to decorate the back of your jacket when you was totin' him over your shoulder," Lonnie said.

Chapter 16

After Scofield's bugle blast the next morning, the camp came alive with the usual chores of preparation for the day's drive. On this particular morning, however, Ruby Tyson discovered the compassion for her situation from her fellow travelers. Clint Buchanan was the first to show up at her wagon to see if her husband was preparing his mules for the day. They had been watered and grazed with the horses until time to hitch them to the wagon, so that was no problem. When Clint arrived, Ruby was struggling in vain to rouse the still drunken Ralph from his blankets. Scofield showed up a few minutes later, took one look at the half-conscious man, and told Clint to grab Tyson's boots. The two of them dragged him out from under the wagon and carried him down to the edge of the river where they started swinging him back and forth. At the count of three, they released him to fly as far out in the river as they could throw him.

For a few long moments, Clint feared they had drowned him, but finally, he came sputtering up to the surface and began flailing in the water frantically. "I can't swim!" he cried out.

"Then drown," Scofield roared back. He turned to walk back up the bank, pausing only to tell Clint to come on. "We need to get his mules hitched up to his wagon."

Clint followed, but he wasn't at all sure if Tyson could make it back to the bank on his own. "You think I oughta go back and help him outta the river?"

"Nah, he'll make it. How'd you learn to swim?" Scofield asked.

"My pa threw me out of a canoe on the Laramie River," Clint answered, "and paddled the canoe on across."

"And you damn-sure taught yourself to swim, I reckon. Tyson might be too ornery to learn to swim. Be better for everybody if he don't, that sorry piece of crap. But ain't no use to worry about him. Useless clods like him always show up."

When they got back to the wagon, they found Cal Nixon helping Emmett Braxton hitch Tyson's mules up, with Ruby insisting she could do it and that they should take care of their chores. "I'm sure Ralph will be ready to take care of everything," she said, grateful for the voluntary help, but fearful that Ralph was going to be angry when he sobered up. When she saw Clint and Scofield coming back, she looked to see if Ralph was following. Not seeing him, she asked, "Is Ralph coming?"

"He stayed back at the river to clean up a little," Scofield said. "He'll be along." He fully intended to stick with that story, even if Tyson did manage to drown himself trying to get out. "Don't fret about him, he'll be along directly. Now you go ahead and get your breakfast cooked. If Ralph ain't able to drive his mules, we'll get you somebody to drive 'em for you."

"I'd be glad to drive 'em," Cal volunteered, "since I ain't got a wagon of my own anymore."

"You're very kind, sir, but I couldn't ask you to do that," Ruby replied timidly. "Ralph's been sick like this before, and he usually manages."

"Wouldn't be any trouble at all, ma'am. We'll just wait and see if your husband's up to it. Then we can decide."

"I expect I'd best go down to the river and see if he's all right," she said then.

"I'll go for you, Ruby," Scofield said. "He may need some help." Clint started to go with him, but Scofield stopped him. "You stay here and see that she has plenty of wood or anything else she needs." Immediately concerned, Clint started to object, but Scofield said, "I ain't gonna drown him, but I hope to hell he's already drowned himself." He turned and marched down to the river like a man who was just about fed up.

When he reached the riverbank again, he was somewhat disappointed to see Tyson staggering toward the grassy bank in knee deep water. Scofield stopped to watch him climb up the bank, only to plop down on his behind on the grass and sit there. "If you're through cleanin' up, you'd best get your hind end back to help Ruby get ready to move outta here."

Although he had not heard Scofield come up behind him, Tyson was too hungover to be startled. "How the hell did I wind up in the river?" He asked the question with no memory of his flying launching.

"Maybe it'll come back to you, if whiskey ain't already fried your brain so bad you ain't ever gonna remember. Damn you, Tyson, you got a fine little woman up there tryin' to pack up your wagon, and cookin' breakfast for your sorry ass at the same time. Right now, because you ain't man enough to handle a drink of likker, some of the other men are hitchin' up your mules and helpin' Ruby get ready to roll."

Scofield's dressing down lit a fire that was always just a spark away from flaring up to full flame. "Who's helpin' Ruby? There's gonna be hell to pay for the hound dog I catch sniffin' around my wife! I'll bet it's that damn nephew of your'n, ain't it? Him and his, 'Is ever'thin' all right, Ruby?' I don't stand for no pussy-footin' around my wife."

Scofield just looked at him in disgust for a few moments before Tyson started to struggle to his feet. He managed to get up on his hands and knees before having to pause to vomit somc of thc rivcr water he had swallowed. Scofield offered no help, determined to let Tyson pay the full price for his indiscretions. Finally, he offered some incentive. "Ruby's got you some coffee made and I expect somethin' to eat with it by now. I'll tell her you're on your way." He turned then and started back toward the wagons. "We'll be pullin' out of here at seven, just like always. That's about half an hour from now," he called back over his shoulder. He didn't look back again, but he could hear the grunting and swearing accompanying the miserable man's efforts to make it to his feet and get back to his wagon. The hint of a smile spread slowly across Scofield's face.

"Is Ralph all right?" Ruby asked as soon as Scofield came back to the wagon.

"Yep, he's on his way," he told her. "You all ready, except for your breakfast cleanup?"

"Yes, thanks to all the help I got from everybody," she replied, still looking toward the river anxiously. "I'd better go see about Ralph," she decided.

"Don't worry about him," Scofield insisted. "He'll be along. He's just got the mornin'-after sickness. I ain't sure he'll be able to drive the mules, but Cal, there, said he'd be glad to drive 'em, if Ralph ain't up to it."

Plainly concerned, Ruby said, "I don't know how Ralph would feel about somebody else drivin' his wagon. Maybe I oughta try, just so he don't get upset."

"Has he ever let you drive 'em?" Clint asked, since he had never seen her driving the wagon.

"No, he always drives 'em, but I think I can do it," Ruby insisted. "Fancy Wallace drives hers, so I oughta be able to take care of ours."

Scofield exchanged glances with Clint, both men comparing the stern, no-nonsense image of Fancy with the mouse-like shyness of Ruby. "We'll wait and see what kinda shape your husband is in when I give the signal to move out. If he ain't settin' up there in that driver's seat, ready to roll, we'll take Cal up on his offer." With that his final say on the matter, Scofield left to see about making sure the rest of the wagon train was ready to depart.

When Scofield had gone and Emmett returned to his wagon, Cal left them to load the packs on his horses. With only Clint left with Ruby, she openly confessed her fears to him, since she had come to trust him and count him as her friend. "Clint, I don't know what Ralph's gonna do if Mr. Scofield tells him he can't drive the wagon. He's gonna be as mad as a wet hen."

Clint couldn't help thinking what an apt comparison that was to Ralph in his present state, but he chose not to express the thought. "I know you're worried, but Scofield ain't gonna stick anybody on your wagon seat if Ralph's ready to drive." He shrugged. "And if he ain't ready to drive, he oughta want somebody to drive for him. So maybe you can get some coffee in him and a piece of cornbread or something, and he'll be ready to go."

They both turned toward the river then when they heard Tyson complain. "I swear, I mighta knowed," he ranted. "I ain't gone half an hour and I find Mr. Clint Buchanan sniffin' around my wife again. What the hell do you want, Buchanan?"

"Ralph!" Ruby cried out, ashamed. "You've got no call to talk to Clint that way. If it wasn't for Clint and some of the men from other wagons, we might get left behind when the others pull out."

"The hell you say," Tyson blurted. "They sure as hell better not leave us behind."

Determined not to get into an argument with the belligerent drunk, for fear he might cause trouble for Ruby, Clint asked, "You feel like drivin' your mules this mornin'?"

"Hell, yes, I can drive my mules," Tyson boasted. "I better not catch anybody tryin' to drive 'em." He lunged toward the small fire. "Get me some coffee," he snapped at Ruby. "I got me a headache."

She went at once to do his bidding. "You'd best eat some of this cornbread, too. I know you ain't had no food since yesterday at noon." She took a piece of the cornbread out of the pan where it had been warming and put it on a plate for him. "When you went to the river to wash up, why didn't you take your clothes off? You're soakin' wet."

"I didn't go to the river to wash up," Tyson said. "I fell in the river. I ain't figured out how yet, 'cause my mule weren't there with me." Ruby looked at once to Clint, who shrugged in return. There was no doubt that she knew the answer.

Clint could have told him he didn't ride one of his mules to Shorty's that night, he walked. But he decided the more confused Tyson was, the less chance he might take out his frustrations on his wife. "Well, looks like you're all set," he said to Ralph. "I'll be goin' now to see what's waiting for us up ahead." He nodded to Ruby and headed back to Scofield's wagon where Biscuit was saddled and waiting.

"Yeah, Buchanan," Tyson called after him when he was sure Clint was out of earshot, "I'll holler for you, if I need any help."

Tyson gutted it out until noon that first day, although Ruby thought a couple of times that he was sitting, asleep, with the reins in his hands. Fortunately, the road was not that difficult, as Scofield led them on a northwest course, and the mules simply followed the wagon in front of them. They had not traveled ten miles when they came to the first of several crossings that lay ahead of them. Walking beside him, Ruby called to him several times to alert him to the fact that they were approaching a crossing. When her summons failed to get his attention, she picked up some small pebbles and began to throw them at him. Finally, when one of her tosses struck him on his neck, he jolted awake. Startled, he looked around him to see what had plagued him. When he met her eyes, he growled, "What's the matter with you?"

"Nothin'," she answered, "but we're slowin' down for a stream crossin' that looks like a pretty wide one."

"Hell, I know it. I got eyes," he grumbled.

Yes, but they were closed, she thought. To him, she said, "I expect it's not too long before the noonin'. Maybe it would be a good idea if you took a little nap then."

"I don't need no nap," he replied at once. "I could drive these mules all day long without no rest. Ain't many men could do that, but your husband can. Tell that to young Mr. Clint Buchanan."

She bit her tongue, wanting to tell him how wrong he was about Clint, but every time she did, it usually earned her a new bruise or welt. Most of the time, they were located on her body in a spot where they were hidden beneath her clothes. He had been careful in this, ever since her last black eye and Scofield had promised to "beat the hell out of him" if he saw any more marks on her. Because of this, her face was almost healed completely, and it was the first time she remembered it being that way for quite some time.

Ruby was correct in her prediction that Scofield would call the nooning as soon as the last wagon was across the creek. There was good grass there and wood to build fires, so the horses were unhitched and allowed to graze by the creek. Ruby was happy to see her husband lie down after the noon meal and go to sleep. It afforded her the opportunity to enjoy the rest of her coffee in peace. The only problem was when the rest period was over, Ralph was once again dead to the world, resisting Ruby's efforts to rouse him. She finally sought out Clint to tell him of her predicament. “You’re the only one I can tell,” she said in apology. “But I’m afraid if I tell Mr. Scofield, he might throw him in the creek to wake him up. And Ralph’s other clothes aren’t dry yet from this mornin’.”

“Well, we’ll just be quiet about this and we won’t even tell Uncle Clayton what we’re up to,” Clint said. “I have to scout on up ahead, or I’d drive ’em myself, but I’ll get ’em hitched up and ready. Don’t you worry yourself about it no more. I’ll take care of it.”

“If you hitch ’em up, I’ll try to drive ’em,” she said. “It sure looks like I’m gonna have to learn some time.”

“Maybe,” he said, “but not today. Now, you go on and get yourself ready to go.” He left her to return to her wagon and her sleeping husband, while he went to get help from Cal Nixon. As he figured, Cal was more than happy to help the little lady out, so he tied his horses to Tyson’s wagon after he and Clint decided Tyson was again dead to the world. They helped Ruby clear a place for him in the back of the wagon, then they picked the body up and loaded it in the wagon. A short time after that, Scofield blasted his signal to move and Cal hopped up in the driver’s seat. “You’re a good man, Cal,” Clint said.

“So are you,” Cal returned.

The next few days were uneventful as the wagons continued on a northwest track. Although he was mad as hell to wake up once again not knowing where he was, or how he got there, Ralph Tyson knew he had no one to blame but himself. Consequently, he took over the reins of his mules after most of the afternoon riding in the back of his wagon, with little show of suspicion and no expression of gratitude to Cal. He saw fit to warn Ruby, however, of the punishment she could expect if he caught her flaunting herself in front of Cal. He made no threats of violence against Cal, however. His overall memory of the previous night was foggy, to say the least. But one thing stuck in his mind that happened just before he passed out in Shorty's saloon—the lightning-fast reaction that sent Ace Pittard to hell. It might be a different story with Clint Buchanan. The young scout showed no indications of being a fast-draw gunslinger.

Most of a week had passed since they had rolled out of Fort Bridger to find themselves at a crossing of the Thomas Fork of the Bear River. Turning west from Thomas Fork, it was only a few miles from there that the wagon train would face their first real test for the horses pulling their wagons. On the trail markers, it was called simply, Big Hill. It was necessary to climb over a steep spur of the Eastern Sheep Creek Hills in order to descend into the Bear River Valley. The hills were steep and treacherous. Scofield assured them that he had led parties over the hills before. It was a tough and dangerous crossing, but it had to be done. There was no way to go around, and as difficult as it seemed, it was the best place to cross over into the Bear River Valley. He cautioned everyone to make sure everything was tied down securely in their wagons, and for safety sake, anyone who could walk, should.

They started the climb at seven in the morning with Spud driving Scofield's wagon up the narrow, winding ruts. The other wagons followed along behind him, until reaching one part of the trail so steep that they had to hitch another team on to pull each wagon up. It took most of the morning to get the last of the wagons on top, only to find the most dangerous part to wagons and animals was the long steep descent into the valley. The wheels on the wagons were tied firm to keep them from rolling, and ropes were used to help lower the wagons down the steepest parts. The wagons ended up sliding all the way to the bottom, but the crossing was accomplished with no loss of life or severe damage to any of the wagons. In total, the crossing took over six hours, and with no opportunity to stop for the customary noon meal and rest, it seemed even longer. Scofield called for a halt for the night after traveling another five miles along the level Bear River Valley.

"This place looks like the Garden of Eden on this side of those damn hills," John Zachary remarked. It was a contrast to the many days of traveling the treeless, sagebrush prairies, to suddenly find themselves in a valley with trees, grass, flowers, and berry bushes.

"I'm glad that's behind us," Marcy commented. "When Emmett's wagon slid sideways, I thought it was gonna double back on his horses. I'll bet he was sayin' his prayers for all he was worth." She picked up the coffeepot from the edge of her fire and poured him another cup. "I noticed Fancy didn't try to drive her wagon down that mountain. She drove it up to the top, though. I reckon we oughta give her credit for that. You'da thought her man, Lemuel, woulda drove those horses down that slippery trail, instead of gettin' Cal Nixon to do it."

"You sure seem to care a lot about what Fancy Wallace is doin'," John commented. "I'm just damn glad our wagon didn't come down on top of my head."

"I don't care what she's doin'," Marcy insisted. "I just wonder how well she knew Cal before. Musta been pretty well 'cause she invited him to set up his tent right beside her wagon. Wonder what Lemuel thought about that?"

John paused to give her a look. "Now, what in the world

would Lemuel have to think about it, one way or the other? Lemuel's just Fancy's hired hand."

"She might say he's just a hired hand, but he killed Fancy's son. Had to sneak up behind him and slit his throat. Fancy's son!" She repeated it to emphasize the cruelty of the act. "And Fancy ain't shed the first tear for his death."

"How do you know that?" John responded. "You don't know if she did or not. Fancy don't let anybody know what she's thinkin' anytime. Besides, Lemuel had to stop Billy 'cause he was fixin' to kill Fancy."

"Right, that's what she said, all right."

"Emmett and I went to Scofield's wagon when he talked to Fancy and Lemuel about that night. Clint Buchanan was there, too, and Scofield laid it out on the table about Clint findin' Billy's body. We came away from that meetin' pretty much convinced that it all happened just like Fancy said it did. There wasn't any reason to think otherwise. You and Sarah and Susie need something better to do than make up nonsense about Fancy."

"You men, you think you know so much about women. But you ain't got the first little clue about what goes on in a woman's mind."

"You're startin' to give me a headache," John complained, ready to change the conversation. "Where's the young'uns? Did they eat?"

"Yes, they ate. Mary's playin' with her doll in the back of the wagon. I don't know where Johnny is. Off someplace with Skeeter and Sammy, I s'pose."

Marcy was right when she said the three young boys were off someplace together. She would have been upset with Johnny and his friends if she had known they were paying Lemuel Blue a visit after all three boys had been warned not to go near the slow-witted hired man. To begin with, their young minds had been intrigued by the mysterious servant of the mysterious woman who was Fancy Wallace. When their parents issued strict orders to avoid Lemuel, that really perked their interest. And when Skeeter overheard his father tell his mother that Lemuel killed Fancy's son, he became irresistible to the young adventurers. When they spotted him down by the river, on his way back from answering a call from nature, they took advantage of the opportunity to see what he had to say about crossing Big Hill. "Hey, Lemuel, where you been?" Skeeter called out.

"Down the river to take a squat," Lemuel replied. "I thought your mama told you to keep away from me. She'll dust your behind for ya, if she catches you talkin' to big ol' bad Lemuel."

"She can't see us down here at the river," Skeeter said.

"How come you didn't drive Miss Fancy's wagon down that hill after she got too scared to do it, herself?" Johnny asked him.

"Ain't my job to drive her wagon," Lemuel replied. "I coulda done it as good as Cal Nixon did, but it ain't my job."

"Yeah," Skeeter teased, "your job is to cut wood and hitch the horses, while Fancy sips her coffee with Cal Nixon. Ain't that right, Lemuel?"

"That's what you think," Lemuel came back right away. "My job is to take care of more important things that you don't even know about."

"Like killin' Billy Wallace?" Skeeter asked in hopes of getting him to tell them about it.

"Who told you I killed Billy Wallace?" Lemuel demanded. "Wasn't nobody supposed to say anythin' about that."

"I heard my mama and papa talkin' about it," Skeeter answered. "Papa said you killed Fancy's son with a knife."

Lemuel was too vain about his murderous act not to want to gloat about it, knowing he could impress these young boys. "It woulda been easier to just shoot Billy," he said and then he grinned slyly. "But I killed him Injun style." He pulled the skinning knife he wore and held it up in front of his face, testing its edge with his thumb. "Billy was bent over Miss Fancy's bed, holdin' a knife to her throat, talkin' about all the money he knew she had. He told her he wanted his share of that money. Anybody coulda stabbed him in the back, but I sneaked right up behind him and slit his throat, ear to ear, Injun style." He made the motion on an imaginary victim, his eyes that always shied away from an adult's gaze, now gleaming with the evil thrill of the memory. "Billy didn't even know what happened till he staggered backward and tried to holler." Lemuel chuckled as he recalled the scene to his mind. "He couldn't make a sound." Lost in the evil thrill of the killing, he was oblivious of the three pairs of wide-open eyes staring at him for a few moments. Thinking then of the trouble he may have bought for himself, should any of the three repeat his words to their parents, he said, "Now you know what my job is. But you can't tell nobody else 'cause Mr. Scofield said don't nobody else need to know." He couldn't resist putting something else in their minds for them to think about. "He might have to get me to come after you, like I did with Billy . . . Injun style."

"Well, I ain't gonna tell nobody," Skeeter said.

"Me, either," Sammy declared at once.

"Me, neither," Johnny was quick to join them.

"That's good," Lemuel said. "'Cause I don't wanna have to come slippin' around tonight doin' my business. I don't never sleep. I have to keep my eye on what's goin' on in this camp when everybody else is asleep. I don't need no sleep."

Lemuel left an image in the boys' minds that interfered with their natural desire to fall asleep for the next couple of nights. At the midday stop on the third day after leaving Big Hill, they had the nooning at a place well-known to the Indians for its hundreds of natural carbonated springs. Like their mothers and their fathers, the boys took great delight in the hot carbonated water. Since there was also plenty of fresh water and grass for the horses, Scofield was persuaded to remain there for the rest of the day. Marcy and Sarah were the first to take advantage of the opportunity to wash their clothes in the hot water. Due to the difficulty of having hot water the rest of the time on the trail, this was an opportunity too good to pass up. The nooning took on the semblance of a holiday.

Chapter 17

"I figured you'd show up when it got around toward suppertime," Scofield japed when Clint pulled Biscuit up at his wagon and dismounted. "Ain't you gonna jump in the hot spring and take a bath like the rest of 'em?"

"I kinda thought you might be takin' a bath," Clint replied with a chuckle for the thought.

"Not me," Scofield stated. "It ain't good for you to take too many baths, especially in the wintertime. Washes off all your skin's protection and that soda water in them springs will take it off quicker'n washin' in the creek." He waited for that piece of wisdom to sink in, then asked, "So where you been?"

"You pay me to scout, so I've been scoutin'," Clint joked. "I took a little look around, since we're campin' here tonight."

"Good idea," Scofield said. "Find anything?"

"I found right many tracks from Indian ponies, both east and west of this place. Most of 'em were old tracks, but there are a few that are still pretty fresh. I doubt they were made since we got here, but they were as fresh as this mornin' sometime."

"Sounds like the Injuns are checkin' on their sacred springs right regular," Scofield speculated. "Maybe we'd best circle the wagons tonight. Might be some more Injuns lookin' to run off our horses."

"I think it'd be a good idea," Clint said. "Wouldn't be a bad idea to keep a sharp eye when we start out in the mornin', too. You never can tell."

Scofield knew what he was referring to. This country was the land of the Shoshone Indians. They had almost always been friendly with the white man, often times trading furs for fresh meat with the emigrants on the wagon trains. But with all the settlers moving into the Shoshone's usual hunting ground, Chief Pocatello had begun trying to discourage the emigrant trains from passing through the Shoshone range. In recent months, there had been reports of attacks on the smaller wagon trains. With twenty-seven wagons, Scofield was not overly worried about an attack. It would take a sizable war party to attack his train, but you could never tell what kind of mood the Indians might be in. With that thought in mind, he unconsciously took a look around him. From where he and Clint stood, he could see garbage and debris left behind by countless wagons before them. It was hard not to sympathize with the Shoshone. On the other hand, he had no choice but to defend himself if he was attacked. "Yeah, you're right," he said to Clint. "I'd better tell my captains to have their folks keep their guns handy when we start out in the mornin' and tell everybody walkin' to stay close to the wagons."

"When you gonna bring us some fresh meat?" Spud asked Clint when he came back to the wagon with some wood to build his cookfire.

"When I see some," Clint answered. "I ain't seen nothin' but tracks ever since we had the buffalo come lookin' for us. I can kill one of Tyson's mules for you, if you want."

"That wouldn't be much better'n this bacon I'm fixin' to fry for our supper," Spud said. "That buffalo was pretty good, even smoked, but I've got a cravin' for some antelope, or if there ain't no antelope, some deer meat."

"Well, hell, Spud, why didn't you say so?" Clint japed. "When I think of all the antelope I had to shoo outta the trail today just so we could get by. If I had only known."

Spud slowly shook his head in mock disgust. "I reckon I shoulda brought my big shovel with me on this trip, so I could shovel some of this manure you're spreadin' around."

"All right," Clint said. "I'll get outta your way." Back at Scofield then, he asked, "Want me to tell Zachary and Braxton you wanna see 'em before supper?"

"Yeah, we'd best circle the wagons up before they start to build their supper fires," Scofield said.

Clint found John Zachary and Emmett Braxton sitting on a large rock, watching the children splashing about in the springs. Seeing Clint coming their way, leading his horse, Zachary declared, "I swear, Buchanan, a little bit of this would make a man too lazy to go any farther."

Braxton laughed and commented, "Spoken by the man who wanted to stop and build his cabin back in Ash Hollow."

Clint laughed. "That is a pretty little valley. I wouldn't mind buildin' a place there, myself, if there was some way to keep other folks out."

"I can't see you ever settlin' down in one place," Zachary said. "You were bit by the wanderin' bug when you were born."

"He better get over that wanderlust," Braxton joked, "if he's still plannin' on marryin' my daughter." He pointed his finger at Clint and declared, "You ain't got but eight years before Lou Ann will be fifteen."

"You're just gonna have to let Lou Ann and me work that out," Clint replied. "I'm glad to see you're both in good spirits 'cause Scofield told me to tell you he wants to talk to you before the women start up their fires. He's gonna have you tell your folks to circle the wagons, so we can keep the livestock inside tonight."

"Why is that?" Zachary wanted to know. "You've been scoutin' the river ahead. Did you see sign of Indians?"

"Not on the trail ahead of us," Clint said, "but there is sign that the Shoshone have been watchin' this spring. Maybe not since we got here, but Scofield thinks it'd be a good idea to be ready in case some do show up."

"I reckon we'd best go talk to him," Braxton said, then yelled to his wife. "Sarah, keep your eye on the kids. I gotta go see Scofield. Come on, John." They got up from the rock and headed for Scofield's wagon. Clint led Biscuit over to graze with the other horses close by the creek.

The night passed uneventfully. Clint could only guess that it was in some part because of the extra sentries Scofield had posted. Clint was one of three who stayed alert all night, Scofield and Cal Nixon were the other two. Such was the faith that Scofield had in Clint's "feelings." They decided that the size of the wagon train must have discouraged thoughts of attacking the circled wagons. To confirm his suspicions, Clint pointed out numerous footprints that told them Shoshone scouts had come in very close during the night. No doubt the presence of extra sentries had made an impression on the would-be raiders.

When the wagon train started out after breakfast, Scofield directed Clint to stay within sight of the train, as they followed the Bear River west until it turned back to the southwest on its way to Salt Lake. From that point, they began a journey up the Portneuf River Valley toward the Snake River and Fort Hall. It was not easy for the travelers to enjoy the beauty of the Portneuf Valley with the possibility of Indians watching them. By the time of the nooning that first day after leaving the springs, there was an easing in general of the tension built up the night before. "Well, it was all based on another one of Clint Buchanan's feelin's," Walt Moody remarked during the noon rest. "He had a feelin' there was Injuns watchin' us. Might be that ol' Clint just got hold of some side meat that's turned." The group gathered to visit around Walt's fire enjoyed a good laugh over the comment. But there were second thoughts on the matter when Clint signaled Scofield to call his attention to a string of eight Shoshone warriors on a ridge to the west, watching the wagons as they prepared their noontime meal.

"Whaddaya think, Scofield?" John Zachary asked after it became obvious to everyone that the savages seemed intent upon letting the emigrants know they were watching them. "Are they gonna attack this train?"

"I don't know," Scofield replied. "They might just be tryin' to intimidate us, to let us know they don't want us to stop and settle on their huntin' ground. But if there ain't but eight of 'em, I don't know why they'd bother." During the last couple of years, the Shoshone had been nothing but friendly. He truly hoped they weren't going to be like the Sioux and the Cheyenne now. "What do you think, Clint?" he asked when his nephew walked over to join them. "You think those eight warriors we see over on that ridge are the whole party? Or are there about a hundred more of 'em hidin' behind that ridge?"

"I don't know, Uncle Clayton, but I think I'll go up there and ask 'em," Clint said. "That way we'll know for sure."

"Right," Walt replied. "Hell, I'll go with you."

"Better get you a horse to ride, then," Clint said, turned around, and headed back to Scofield's wagon where his horse was tied.

His statement was good for another round of chuckles, even under the watchful eyes of the Shoshone warriors. And the conversation soon reverted back to the speculation upon the intent of the eight Indians. A few moments later, Emmett Braxton, murmured, "What in the world . . . ?" Then he blurted, "Where is he goin'?" Everyone turned to see what he was talking about and saw Clint crossing the river between them and the ridge.

"He's goin' to ask them damn Injuns what they're up to!" Emmett exclaimed.

"He'll get himself killed!" Doc Meadows blurted. He turned at once to ask Scofield, "What's he gonna do?"

"Don't ask me," Scofield replied at once. "I'm still tryin' to figure that boy out."

Cal Nixon, who came to the discussion late, but in time to see what they were looking at, bellowed, "He's ridin' straight at 'em! We better go help him!"

"Hold on!" Scofield stopped him. "That boy always knows what he's doin'."

"Yeah, but this might be that one time," Emmett said, "and I've gotta explain this to my daughter." Under the circumstances, nobody laughed as all eyes were trained on the lone white scout riding toward the ridge to the west.

"He's lost his mind," Doc declared. "Whaddaya think we oughta do, Scofield?"

"Oughta do?" Scofield echoed. "What the hell is there to do? He knows what he's doin'." If they could see what was going on in his mind, they'd all be alarmed. Like them, he thought his nephew had taken leave of his senses.

Clint held the Palouse gelding to a steady lope when he left the river and headed straight toward the eight warriors, who, like the white men behind him, were undecided as to his intentions. When he reached the foot of the hill, Clint reined Biscuit back to a walk. Then drew his Henry rifle from the saddle sling and held it in both hands above his head and continued up the hill toward the warriors. "He has the gun that shoots many times," Stone Horse said. "He comes to fight."

"No," Red Wing disagreed. "He holds it in the sign of peace. He comes to talk. I think he wants us to know he is not afraid. Hold your ponies still. Let us show him no fear." He took his single-shot rifle in both hands in the same manner that Clint held his Henry and held it over his head. "I will go talk to him." He gave his horse a nudge with his heels and started down the slope to meet

Clint. When he pulled up about halfway down the hill, he stopped and sat waiting for Clint to get there. Watching Clint closely, Red Wing let his rifle drop to rest across his thighs when he saw Clint return his rifle to his saddle sling.

"We come in peace," Clint began, talking in the Crow tongue because he figured it a greater chance the Indian might know that language better than English. "My Absaroka name is Crawls Through Fire and I am guiding these people to lands many moons from this valley. We only stop in the land of the mighty Shoshone to rest our horses and feed our families." He wasn't sure if that would placate the Indians or not, but he figured the appearance of the eight warriors was simply to let the emigrants know this was Shoshone country—and settlers weren't welcome. "I come to tell you this, so you will know we mean no disrespect to our Shoshone friends."

The Shoshone warrior nodded, seeming to be satisfied by the Crow scout's respectful attitude. This, even though the scout looked more like a white man than a Crow. "I am called Red Wing," he said. "It is good that you tell us what you are doing in our land. I will go back to our village and tell our chief, War Bonnet, what you have told me. Go in peace," he said, making the peace sign.

"Go in peace," Clint returned, also making the peace sign. He turned then and went back down the hill. When he reached the bottom, he glanced back, and they were gone. Turning his head back toward the river, he was startled by a small explosion of rustling leaves and branches. Startled as well, Biscuit jumped to the side as three frightened antelope bolted from a thicket not thirty feet from where Clint was about to ford the river. Without taking time for conscious thought, he grabbed his rifle and downed the rearmost of the three in flight. That was all he had time for because they disappeared into the trees again before he could crank in another cartridge.

He wheeled Biscuit back from the riverbank and rode over to collect his gift. "That's sure a good sign," he told the unfortunate antelope, a healthy-looking doe. "Not so much for you, but sure a welcome change in the grub Spud's been cookin'." After he put the doe out of her suffering, he hauled her up across his saddle. Then he stepped up to sit behind her and crossed back to the camp on the other side of the river. He carried his prize straight to Scofield's wagon and confronted a curious Spud Williams, who had heard the rifle shot and was staring out toward the river. "Well, you said you had a cravin' for antelope, so here you go." He pushed the carcass off to land at Spud's feet, then wheeled Biscuit toward Walt Moody's wagon, hoping to catch Scofield before he came running.

"What the hell were you doin'?" Scofield exclaimed when he ran out to meet Clint. "What did you say to those Injuns?"

"I just went up there and told 'em we weren't fixin' to start buildin' cabins here by the river, we're just stoppin' to eat and rest our horses. They were all right with it. One came down and talked to me, said his name was Red Wing. I don't think we've got anything to worry about from that bunch. They seemed peaceful enough. The main thing is I got an antelope."

"Yeah, I saw you had somethin' across your saddle," Scofield said. "An antelope, huh?"

"That's right," Clint japed. "Well, you know, Spud said he had a cravin' for antelope, and I hate to disappoint him. We'll have meat to share. I'm just sorry I couldn't get enough for the whole wagon train."

"I'll go back and tell Walt and the others that it looks like we might make it on in to Fort Hall without an Injun attack, thanks to you makin' your peace talks with those warriors. Then I expect we'd best help Spud get that antelope ready for roastin'."

Below the crest of the ridge west of the river, the party of Shoshone warriors stopped when they heard the rifle shot down near the river. Naturally curious as to the cause, Stone Horse decided it in their best interest to find out, so he volunteered. "I'll go back to the top of the hill and see if it is anything for us to worry about." They waited while he worked his way along the top of the hill. In a short time, he returned to report. "You were right," he said to Red Wing. "It was the Crow who looks like a white man who fired the shot."

"What was he shooting at?" Red Wing asked.

"He killed one of the antelope we have been tracking all the way to the river," Stone Horse answered. "And the other two disappeared into the trees up the river."

"I knew the antelope had found a place to hide in the bushes on the bank of the river," Red Wing declared. He had convinced the other seven members of the hunting party of that fact. Since four of them had rifles, their plan was to wait the antelope out until the wagon train moved away again. Then the antelope would come out of the bushes and they would be waiting to shoot all three of them at the same time. "We would have had three antelope to take back to the village. Now, thanks to the white man, he has one, and we have none."

"Maybe we can go back down the river where we

started this morning," Crooked Stick suggested. "Maybe some of the rest of the antelope herd will come back there before dark."

"I think we would be better off without the white man in our country," Red Wing said, disgusted.

Chapter 18

Twelve days after leaving Fort Bridger, Clayton Scofield led his wagon train into camp beside Fort Hall. The fort, originally built as a fur-trading post on the Snake River, was now occupied by the army, their purpose being to protect emigrants traveling the Oregon and California Trails. The fort was a welcome stop for Scofield's train with more than a few of the wagons in need of some repair, much of which was caused by the hair-raising descent down Big Hill. Fortunately, none of the repairs were as serious as the broken axle Cal Nixon had suffered upon crossing the Green River.

The one exception to the appreciation for the chance to restock supplies that were getting low, was Ruby Tyson. She knew that Ralph would immediately go in search of medicine to treat his sickness. She knew that their financial state, modest to begin with, had already suffered enough to send it reeling. And this with so many miles left before them, she could not help but suffer feelings of desperation. Desperation called for desperate actions on her part, and her only weapon was deceit. She had tried to talk to Ralph about the need to save as much of their money as they possibly could, but he refused to discuss finances with her. His usual response to her plea was, "You just let me worry about the money. That ain't none of your business, anyway."

But she had to worry about it. There were needed supplies that were running low. There were tolls to be paid at river crossings ahead of them. And they needed every cent they could get their hands on to pay for their land and to build a house, if they ever did reach Oregon. But at the rate her husband continued to dig into the money in the iron cash box with the heavy padlock on it, they were destined to arrive in Oregon destitute, with money enough to build nothing more than a lean-to. So, to guard against this, she had taken steps to save some of their money. It started after the drunken episode at Fort Kearny. Since Ralph usually succeeded in drinking himself into an unconscious state, it was easy for her to steal the key to the padlock and open the cash box. Counting out a sum she thought he might not notice was gone, she began her own savings cache in her sewing basket. As she suspected, he wasn't aware of the shortfall, not being sure how much he had taken, himself.

When she realized that he couldn't remember how much, or even when, he had struck their fortune, she repeated the practice at Fort Laramie, then again at Fort Bridger. Now, at Fort Hall, she decided to make another withdrawal while Ralph was taking the mules to water with the other men and their horses. He had conveniently left the padlock key in the pocket of his jacket, which he left hanging on the tailgate of the wagon. As soon as the animals were taken care of, she was sure the men would be going to the fort to do their trading and arrange for any repairs. So, she didn't waste any time counting out her usual payment and depositing it with what she had already saved and packed it away in her sewing basket.

When Ralph returned to the wagon, she was fanning her kindling to a blaze, in the process of starting her supper fire. He went straight to the wagon and climbed in it, so she announced, "I'll be puttin' supper on to cook. You ain't fixin' to go anywhere, are you?"

He didn't answer her, but she could hear him fumbling around with the iron box inside the wagon. She heard him mumbling a few swear words and she wondered if he was counting the money left in the box. That was, in fact, what he had been doing, for in a few minutes, he called out. "Have you been into my box?"

She quickly moved to the side of the wagon. "You'd best keep your voice down, lest you want ever'body in the wagon train to know about your iron money box."

He glared at her and repeated, "Have you been in my box?"

"No," she lied, "I ain't been in your box. You're the only one with a key. Ain't nobody been in it but you. Why?"

"'Cause there ought to be more in here than there is."

She could see that he was truly confused, and while he was, she sought to take advantage of it. "I expect it's hard to keep track of how much you're spendin' after you've had a lot to drink. Maybe you've been buyin' a few rounds for some of the men you're drinkin' with."

"I ain't bought nobody no damn drinks," he insisted, knowing it was not in his nature to do so.

"I'm glad to see you're keepin' an eye on the money we've got to start out our new life with in Oregon," she said, hoping to play on his sense of responsibility. "We sure can't afford to waste any more of our money."

He didn't say anything more for a long few moments, obviously worried with himself for not realizing how much money he had spent. He stared at her as if trying to think of somc way he could blame her for it. He wrestled with his conscience for only a few minutes before he said to himself, *to hell with it, I need a drink.* He took only a few dollars, telling himself he would only have a couple of drinks. Then he hesitated before locking the box again. *Might better take a little extra, just in case something comes up I ain't planned on,* he told himself. They were staying at the fort an extra day to allow for repairs on the wagons, so he would get any supplies he needed tomorrow. Right now, he needed to find out where the nearest bar was. Fort Hall was an army post, so there was a hog ranch somewhere not too far away. He climbed down out of the wagon. "I'll be back for supper," he told her. "I'm gonna take a look at what they've got in this fort—gimme an idea if we need anythin' tomorrow."

"Flour, cornmeal, sugar, coffee, and some dried beans," Ruby called out at once. "That's what we're runnin' out of. We're gonna be travelin' some rough country followin' the Snake River from here. That's what Clint said."

"Oh, is that what Clint Buchanan says?" Ralph responded at once. "When was he tellin' you all this?"

"He wasn't tellin' me," Ruby replied. "He was talkin' to about five of us when we went to get wood for the fire.

When are you gonna realize that Clint ain't never been nothin' but polite to all the women on this train?"

"He's a sneaky dog, just waitin' for a chance to catch somebody when they ain't lookin'," Ralph charged. "You better hope you ain't the one I catch him with." He turned then and headed for the fort gate. "I'll be back directly," he said in parting.

Take your time, she thought. *Tomorrow morning will be soon enough.*

"You goin' over to the fort before supper?" Scofield asked his nephew when Clint didn't take his saddle off Biscuit.

"Yeah, I figured I'd take a little ride over there," Clint replied. "Biscuit needs new shoes and I'm gonna see if I can catch Ned Blanchard before he goes to supper. Maybe he'll do 'em this evenin'. I expect he'll be pretty busy tomorrow."

"How 'bout pickin' me up some smokin' tobacco at the store there," Scofield said. "Then I won't have to go over there till tomorrow. I'm slap-out of tobacco."

"You can pay me when I get back," Clint said when Scofield started digging in his pocket for some money. He stepped up into the saddle then and wheeled Biscuit toward the picket walls of the fort, a little over one hundred yards away.

"Clint Buchanan," Ned called out in greeting when he saw the young scout ride up to his forge. "So that's Scofield's train that just pulled in. How you doin', partner?"

"Howdy, Ned," Clint returned the greeting as he stepped

down. "Can't complain. Thought I'd bring Biscuit over to pay you a visit. I think he's wantin' to go shoppin' for some new shoes, so I figured I'd come here first thing. I expect there'll be some more of our folks comin' to see you."

"Good," Ned commented, "always glad to have the business. Have you got any problems with Biscuit?"

"No, it's just time to get new shoes," Clint said. "He could actually go a little longer before he needs 'em bad, but I'd rather you go ahead and shoe him."

"Well, I 'preciate that," Ned responded. "Tell you what, I'll take care of him before I go to supper. How's that?"

"That was what I was hopin' you'd say. That's why I wanted to be the first one to see you."

Ned responded with a little chuckle. "Well, you ain't the first one that got here offa your train. There was one fellow that beat you. Wasn't fifteen minutes ago."

"Is that right?" Clint replied. "Who was it?"

"I didn't get his name. He didn't want anything from me, anyway. He just wanted me to point the way to the closest place to get a drink of likker." Ned paused to chuckle for the humor of the incident. "Now there's a fellow who knows what's important and what ain't."

"Ralph Tyson," Clint muttered with disgust.

"Was that his name?" Ned asked, when he saw that Clint wasn't laughing with him.

"I'd bet on it," Clint answered, with no way to know for sure. "We've already had some problems with this fellow's drinkin', and the one I feel sorry for the most is the little woman who had the bad luck to marry him." He shrugged in a gesture of indifference, even though he was anything but. "Where'd you send him, Lucky's?"

"Yep. I figured he was desperate enough to drink that rotgut Ike Ennis calls whiskey. And Lucky's is the closest place, anyway." Judging from Clint's reaction, Ned figured it was of some concern to the young scout. "I'm sorry I told him where to go," he apologized.

"It's no fault of yours," Clint replied. "You didn't have any way of knowing who Ralph Tyson was. I 'preciate you shoein' my horse right away," he said in an effort to switch the conversation away from Ralph Tyson. He was afraid he was not going to be able to rid his mind of the matter, however. With enough experience now to know what to expect when Tyson was able to find a bottle, he could not help his feelings of compassion for Ruby. No matter how this evening turned out for Tyson, it would most likely guarantee hell for his unfortunate wife. *It ain't none of my business,* he immediately told himself, but he knew that wouldn't allow him to put it out of his mind. The poor little woman did not deserve the fate that had been handed to her. She was such a fragile flower. It seemed an outright sin for her to have to live with Ralph Tyson. He shook his head, trying to clear those thoughts out of his mind. "I'll be back in about half an hour," he said to Ned then. "I'm gonna pick up some tobacco for Scofield."

"Shouldn't take me but about an hour to shoe your horse," Ned said, "since he ain't got no problems with his hooves."

Clint walked over to the sutler's store to get Scofield's tobacco, but his mind was still working on Ralph Tyson. He wondered who was going to bring him back to camp tonight. Last time, it was Cal Nixon. Maybe he should tell Cal he might find a card game at Lucky's, and tell him, "Bring Tyson with you when you come back." Like himself, he knew that Cal had a lot of compassion for Ruby. Maybe Tyson will meet with some bad luck at Lucky's and solve everybody's problem with him. Lucky's was a pretty rough place to go for an evening's entertainment. A man named Ike Ennis built it on the Snake River, as close to Fort Hall as the army would permit, which was not quite a mile. He sold whiskey and some food, and there were three soiled doves in residence the last time Clint had been there. Ennis called his business Lucky's River Club. When Clint had asked Scofield why Ike had named it Lucky's, Scofield had replied, "'Cause you're lucky if that rotgut he sells don't kill ya. And you're lucky if one of his customers don't stab you in the back and take your wallet. And if you visit with one of his ladies, you're lucky if you don't come down with a problem when you go to the outhouse."

"And last, but not least," Clint added on his own, "you're lucky if you don't carry it home and pass it on to your wife." He suddenly felt overcome with disgust for Ralph Tyson. He decided to go to talk to Ruby as soon as his horse was finished, to at least warn her of the possibility of harm from her husband. That seemed to be his habit, to take out his frustrations on his defenseless wife. *None of your business!* The phrase kept popping up in his mind. But he was unable to let it go.

He passed a little bit of time just looking around at the merchandise in the store after he bought his uncle's tobacco. Seeing nothing he needed, he went back to the blacksmith's shop when Ned was just starting to work on the last hoof. Another quarter of an hour passed before Biscuit was ready to go. Clint paid Ned and rode back to the camp where the cookfires were already glowing. Instead of going straight to Scofield's wagon, he rode over to Tyson's, where he found Ruby preparing to cook a pot of beans that she had soaked in the wagon since morning. When she looked back to see who had ridden up behind her, she stood up to greet him. "Evenin', Clint. Are you lookin' for Ralph? He ain't here right now, but he said he'd be back for supper."

"Yes, ma'am," he replied. "I know where he is, and I'd be surprised if he shows up for supper." He saw the immediate sign of alarm in her face, so he quickly explained that he didn't know for sure, but he figured it was a pretty accurate assumption. At that point, he decided he'd already opened the subject, so he might as well tell her what he had learned from Ned Blanchard. After telling her of Ralph's asking for directions to the closest saloon, he told her that he knew she would be worried about her husband. "I don't blame you if you tell me it ain't none of my business, but I thought you oughta know. And to tell you the truth, it's you I'm worried about, or I wouldn't stick my nose in your business at all."

"Clint, I appreciate everything you've done for me, and I know you put up with a lot of sarcastic remarks from Ralph. I wanna thank you for just lettin' 'em roll off your back. He thinks every man that says good mornin' to me is thinkin' sinful thoughts. But if it wasn't for you and Cal, I don't know where Ralph would be today." She paused to think about it, then added, "And I appreciate Mr. Scofield for not sendin' Ralph and me back right after that incident at Fort Kearny. I know he was thinkin' about it."

"Are you sure you've got a place waitin' for you out in the Willamette Valley?" Clint asked. He knew Ralph claimed his brother would welcome him and Ruby, but he doubted that Ralph even knew how to find his brother.

"I'm not sure what we'll find when we get out there," Ruby told him. "But I know what we're leavin' behind in Missouri, and it'll be better than that."

Clint could only shake his head, concerned for Tyson's young wife. On the spur of the moment, he said, "I wanna give you something." He opened his saddlebag, reached in, and pulled out something wrapped in a cloth. Then he unrolled the cloth to reveal a Colt handgun. "This used to belong to Billy Wallace. I don't know if you have a pistol, but I think you oughta have one to protect yourself if you ever have to."

She was shocked. "You think I should have a pistol to protect myself from my husband?"

He shook his head. "I think you should have a pistol to protect yourself from anyone who threatens to harm you." He held the weapon out to her. She looked at it in horror for a couple of minutes, but he continued to hold it out. "Here," he said, "take it. It has five cartridges in it, but it's settin' on an empty chamber, so it won't go off on accident. And I have a few more cartridges I can give you. It's a lot easier to handle in a tight spot, where a shotgun would be awkward." Finally, she took the pistol in her hands, and when he asked if she had ever fired one, she said that she had, once before she was married. He showed her how to load it and how to prepare it for firing. "Well, I hope I ain't upset you too much. You might as well go ahead and cook those beans." He turned to step up in the saddle. "If Ralph ain't back by dark, I'll ride down to Lucky's to look for him, if you want me to. Just let me know."

"Thank you, Clint. You're a good friend."

* * *

"Ruby," Marcy Zachary called out to her when the usually timid young woman approached a group of her fellow emigrants sitting together to watch some of the men showing off their special dance steps. "Come on over here and sit by me, honey." Ruby hesitated, then doing her best to avoid the curious eyes of all those who turned to stare at her, she made her way over to Marcy. "Sit yourself down and watch our menfolk makin' fools outta themselves." She patted the bench beside her where her two children had been sitting moments before. "I'm tickled to see you come out to the social hour. It'll do you good to visit your neighbors. You might find out we ain't so bad after all." She favored Ruby with a warm smile, but was aware of the shy, uncertain expression on her face. So, she asked, "What is it, honey?"

"I'm lookin' for Clint," Ruby said, apologetically, "but I didn't see him out here anywhere." She didn't want to admit that she was too shy to go to Scofield's wagon to look for Clint.

"Clint?" Marcy responded. "He's right over there near the fire, talkin' to Tim Blake and several others." She pointed to a small group of men on the other side of a communal fire. With a pretty good idea that Ruby's business with Clint had to have something to do with Ralph, she was not surprised by the girl's reluctance to approach him. She volunteered, "You want me to go get him for you?" When Ruby insisted that she couldn't ask her to do that, Marcy said, "Come on, I'll go with you." Ignoring Ruby's feeble protests, she took her hand and led her from the small gathering. "Wait here," Marcy instructed when they were a dozen yards short of the fire.

Then she continued on to approach Clint. There was a pause in the conversation when she walked up to Clint and took his arm. "Come on," she said, "somebody needs to talk to you." She pulled him after her to the surprise of the men talking there.

"Marcy, what the hell?" John Zachary reacted.

"None of your business, John," Marcy replied and kept walking. When Clint realized who had summoned him, he was immediately concerned. And when they got to her, Marcy said, "Here he is, honey. When you're done with whatever you need to say, you can come back and sit on the bench beside me, if you want to." Then she walked away to leave them alone.

"Ralph ain't come back?" Clint asked Ruby, knowing the answer beforehand.

"No," Ruby said. "I'm sorry to bother you with my problems, but I don't know what else to do. I'm afraid of what might have happened to him."

"It's good you came to tell me. That's what I wanted you to do. I'll go see if I can find him, and if I can, I'll bring him home. You go on back to your wagon, unless you wanna go sit with Marcy and the others, like she said."

"I can't do that," she replied. "I'll go back to my wagon."

"All right, as soon as I saddle my horse, I'm on my way. Don't you worry, he's most likely just gone to sleep somewhere." He found himself thinking she would be a hell of a lot better off if the drunken lowlife she was married to had finally succeeded in drowning himself in whiskey. But if that happened, he knew Ruby would be in a desperate situation. She needed someone to take care of her.

These were the thoughts that took control of his mind as he saddled Biscuit. He turned when he heard a footstep behind him to discover Cal Nixon approaching. "Couldn't help noticin' back there when Marcy dragged you away from the fire, that Ruby was waitin' for you. Now you're saddlin' your horse. All that adds up to Ralph Tyson. And since you don't need your horse to ride across to Tyson's wagon, I'm thinkin' he must be somewhere else, and you're goin' to look for him. Is that about the size of it?"

Clint couldn't help smiling. "Yep, that's about the size of it."

"You got any idea where to start lookin'?"

"I do," Clint replied. "There's a rough hog ranch about a mile from here called Lucky's. I think that's where he'll be, if nobody's thrown him in the river yet."

"You say that Lucky's is a rough place, do ya? Well, I expect in that case, it wouldn't hurt to have a little help to ride along with you. Whaddaya say?"

"I'd say it wouldn't hurt at all," Clint said with a little chuckle. "I'll wait here while you go saddle a horse. Biscuit don't like to tote double."

"Mine's already saddled," Cal replied. "I was about to go find myself a card game."

Clint had been to Lucky's a couple of times before, so he knew the way to the two-story log hog ranch, built on a steep bluff beside the Snake River. Even if he hadn't, it wouldn't be difficult to find because of the well-worn path beaten out through the trees by the soldiers stationed at Fort Hall. The final section of the trail was a steep path about forty yards long, leading to the clearing where the building sat. It was already dark when they approached the hitching rail before the porch, but the building was lit up like a lantern. When they dismounted and stepped up on the porch, they paused a second when Cal nodded toward the one mule tied at the rail. Clint nodded in agreement, then paused to take a look at a soldier sprawled on the porch floor, dead to the world. Taking care not to open the screen door wide enough to jam it open on the soldier's fingers, they went inside the noisy establishment. They both scanned the room, searching for Tyson's familiar drunken face. It was at that point that Cal asked, "What are we gonna do if we find him? Tell him mama says it's time to come home?"

"We'll see what kinda shape he's in," Clint replied, strictly speculating, because he wasn't sure, himself. "If he's like we usually find him, he'll be unconscious, so we'll just haul his ass back on his mule and dump him for poor Ruby to deal with. First, we gotta find him, so we might as well start with the bar."

They walked across the room to the bar, hardly unnoticed, since they were two tall, strapping young men who were obviously not soldiers. The three women working the room paused to look them over, thinking there might be an opportunity to work for higher than army pay for a change. The one wearing the morning coat and a six-gun with the handle facing forward, looked to be a little more refined than his friend, who wore a buckskin shirt and moccasins, and was carrying a Henry rifle. "You like 'em house-broke, or wild and wooly?" Sally Switch asked Pudding Reilly as both doves sidled up to the bar to eavesdrop on the conversation with Ike Ennis.

"I'll take either one of those gents for a tumble or marriage, whatever they want," Pudding replied. They moved up closer to Cal's elbow. He favored them with a smile while Clint engaged the bartender.

"What's your pleasure, gentlemen?" Ike asked. "I've

got anything you want, rye, corn, brandy and it all comes outta the same bottle. You just call it what you want."

"Maybe you can tell me about a fellow we're lookin' for," Clint started. "I know he came here a little earlier this evenin', but I don't see him in here anywhere."

With an immediate show of caution, Ike asked, "You fellers lawmen?"

"No," Clint said. "We're with a wagon train that just pulled into Fort Hall. The fellow we're lookin' for owns one of the wagons and he ain't good for much of anything when he gets to drinkin'. His name's Ralph Tyson."

"Ralph," Sally piped up. "You're right about that. He ain't good for nothin' but talkin' big when he's drunk."

Cal and Clint both turned to face the women. "You were with him?" Cal asked.

"I was with myself," Sally answered. "I don't know who he was with. We was both in my room, if that's what you're askin'."

"Is he still in your room?" Clint asked.

"Hell, no!" Sally fairly grunted. "I had a couple of the boys from the fort haul that big-talkin' loser outta there. He was out cold. I went through his pockets and the deadhead didn't even have any money to pay me. I coulda been downstairs workin'."

"You said he was passed out," Clint pressed. "Where did they take him? He didn't leave, did he? 'Cause his mule's still tied at the hitching rail."

"I don't know." Sally shrugged, not really caring. "Out on the porch, or log-rollin', I don't know, and I don't care. What about you boys? You got any money?"

Clint ignored the question and turned back to Ike, who seemed as disinterested as Sally and Pudding now. "Log-rollin'? What is she talkin' about, log-rollin'?"

Ike shrugged then. "That's somethin' I ain't got nothin' to do with. That's somethin' some of the customers come up with. You see, I remember your man, Ralph, now. He drank till he ran outta money and ran his mouth the whole time after that."

"He told me he had some more money hid in his boot," Sally reminded Ike.

"Yeah," Ike went on. "Well, when you get some blowhard who can't hold his likker and gets to botherin' everybody, a bunch of 'em will pick him up and take him log-rollin'. That's what happened to Ralph after they carried him outta Sally's room. They took him log-rollin'."

"Damn it, man, what are you talkin' about?" Cal demanded.

"It ain't nothin' much," Ike explained. "They just take 'em out on the back porch and drop 'em over on the ground and let 'em sleep it off back there."

"Damn," Cal swore. "You mean he's just layin' in the back yard somewhere?"

"If he ain't woke up and left, I reckon," Ike said. "Hey, you boys come on back in after you find him," he yelled after they both turned and headed for the front door. "Ain't no use passin' up a chance to wet your whistle with some good corn whiskey."

Out the door they hurried, stepping over the customer still lying in front of the door. "He must be one of their good customers," Cal remarked, "to rate sleepin' it off on the porch." They went down the steps and went around the side of the building, almost stumbling before they realized how steep the bluff was. When they got to the rear of the saloon, they saw the back porch. Due to the severe slope of the ground, it was fully twenty feet above the ground. It struck them at once where the term "log-rolling" came from. "Those sorry buzzards, they drop drunks off the porch to land on that steep bluff and the poor devils hit the ground and roll like a log down toward the river. They most likely bet on 'em to see if they'll make it all the way into the river."

"Let's see if we can find Ralph," Clint said. "I hope to hell he didn't make it to the river. I don't wanna have to go back and tell Ruby that. It seems like every time we bring him home, he's soakin' wet."

Walking across the dark, steeply sloped yard, being careful not to stumble and involuntarily enter the log-rolling contest, they searched for any sign of a sleeping Ralph Tyson. "Shoulda brought a damn lantern," Cal complained. "I'm afraid that jasper rolled all the way off the edge of the bluff, and if he wound up in that river, he's dead."

"Yonder," Clint said and pointed to a dim outline of a small structure in the blackness of the night. It was located more in line with the other side of the saloon, so they both focused their eyes on the object for a few moments before Clint remarked, "It's an outhouse."

"Funny place to build an outhouse," Cal commented. "Mighta been the only place to put one, though." It occurred to them that the barn and a couple of smokehouses were built up on the flat top of the bluff, beside the saloon. They both started over to that side of the back yard.

"What the hell?" Clint blurted when he suddenly ran into a rope about hip high. He was about to warn Cal to watch his step when he realized what it was. "They got a rope nailed to the trees to hang onto to go down to the outhouse."

"Nah," Cal uttered, thinking Clint was wrong. But when he thought about the two of them worrying about falling off the back yard, he reconsidered. "I reckon it is a damn good idea." They followed the rope line down to the outhouse and that was where they found Tyson.

He was lying crossways in front of the door of the privy, after having been dropped from the porch and evidently rolling down, only to be stopped up against the door. "Saved by the outhouse," Clint announced.

"Maybe, maybe not," Cal remarked. He reached down, and taking hold of Tyson's shoulder, rolled him over on his back. "It's Tyson, all right." Then he shook him. "Tyson, wake up!" He repeated the attempt several times with no response from the body. He looked back up at Clint and said, "He's dead. It's too bad he didn't make it to the river." He rose to his feet again while they both thought about the news they had to deliver to Ruby. "I swear, Clint, I ain't so sure this is bad news for Ruby. Might be the best thing that ever happened to her, but I don't know if she'll see it that way." Clint just shook his head, uncertain. "I can't believe she felt anything for this piece of dung," Cal went on, "every time I think about the way he treated her . . ."

"I expect the only reason she hangs onto him is because she can't take that wagon out to Oregon by herself," Clint replied. "She needs help. She ain't no Fancy Wallace." He thought about it a moment, then said, "and even Fancy hired her somebody to do the man's work for her." He paused a moment before continuing. "Too bad there ain't some man on the wagon train who ain't got a wagon, himself."

"Now, wait a minute," Cal at once responded. "I'll sure as hell drive those mules of his the rest of the way out there. I already told her I would, if Tyson couldn't, but that deal ends as soon as we get to Oregon City."

"I knew you had the right kinda blood in your veins," Clint japed. "Just like a knight in shinin' armor. But whaddaya think we oughta do about Tyson's body? Think we oughta take him back to the camp and bury him for her? Be a lot easier to let the sorry rascal roll on into the river and be done with it."

"It might be a whole lot easier on her, if she didn't have to see him like this," Cal suggested. "The river might be the best thing for him."

"I agree," Clint said. "We'll tell her we buried him, so she won't think he might still be alive somewhere." Cal nodded in agreement. They dragged the body away from the outhouse to be sure it had a clear path all the way to the edge of the bluff. "I'm pretty sure he was wearin' his gun, but he ain't got it on now. I doubt there was much of anything else he had of value with him. We'd best inquire about the gun belt inside." They gave him a good push to start him down the slope again. Just to be sure they waited until they heard the splash when he hit the water before returning to the saloon.

Chapter 19

"Did you find the feller you was lookin' for?" Ike asked when they walked back inside. The noise level in the saloon lowered considerably, as most of the customers seemed interested in what the answer might be.

"As a matter of fact, we did," Cal answered him. Ike looked genuinely surprised. "He got caught on your outhouse down the slope. He didn't have his gun belt on, so we'll just get that from you to take back to his widow. That way, she'll know for sure he's dead. Then we'll be on our way without askin' how he happened to be dead."

"Now, wait a minute, you ain't thinkin' anybody in here had anythin' to do with that, do ya? 'Cause he just passed out as peaceful as you please. Too much whiskey probably killed him. I've seen it before. So I'd advise you two to walk on outta here while you can, unless you're wantin' to try log-rollin', yourself." He nodded to a smirking man watching from the end of the bar, who upon Ike's signal, dropped his hand to rest on the handle of his six-gun.

"I wouldn't advise you to draw that weapon, friend," Cal threatened. "I'm not really in a mood to suffer fools right now. Who's got Tyson's gun?" He looked back at Ike for an answer. Seeing that as an opportunity, the smirking man drew his gun, only to take two steps backward, a result of the impact of Cal's bullet against his chest. He collapsed at the foot of the wall, his .44 not halfway out of his holster. Looking extremely impatiently at Ike, Cal said, "Now, I told you I ain't got the time to play games with you people. I can tell my partner over there is gettin' restless, too. If we don't get that gun pretty quick, he's gonna start thinnin' this crowd out. That Henry rifle he's totin' ain't got no conscience at all. The sooner we get that gun and holster, the sooner you gentlemen can get back to your drinkin'."

"Give him the gun, Benny," Ike directed a large man behind the bar, wearing a bartender's apron.

Benny reached under the bar and produced the gun and holster. He placed them on the bar and Cal took them with his free hand, knowing Clint would be more efficient using both his hands with the Henry. "Now, you see how easy that was," Cal said. "Too bad about that fellow against the wall over there. I told him not to try it, but some fools just gotta go for it. Hope he wasn't none of your kin." He and Clint backed slowly toward the door.

"Just get on outta here," Ike said. "And none of us had anything to do with that jasper's dyin'. We was just unlucky that he picked my place to die."

"Maybe you oughta change the name of this place to Unlucky's," Cal said as they reached the door. Outside, they almost knocked the drunk down who had been passed out in front of the door.

"Hey, partner," he said, grabbing Clint by the arm. "Can you buy a feller a drink? I need one bad."

Clint forcefully freed his arm. "Next time I'm in here," he told him. "I'm kinda in a hurry right now. Or you can tell Ike to put it on my bill." He left the dazed drunk even more confused as he and Cal wasted little time preparing to leave.

"If you'll cover the door with that rifle of yours, I'll pick up Tyson's mule," Cal exclaimed and ran to the hitching rail while Clint climbed into the saddle and held his rifle trained on the front door, further confusing the unsteady drunk on the porch. In a matter of seconds, Cal was on his horse and they were away, galloping up the path to the trail back to Fort Hall.

Behind them, the rattled individual, who desperately needed a drink of the hair of the dog that bit him, was left wondering if the man carrying the rifle really did have a bill open at the bar. Maybe Ike would believe he had been offered a drink on the man's bill. "Worth a try," he blurted and reached for the doorknob just as a crowd of curious spectators bolted out to see which way they went, flattening the unfortunate drunk once more. As for the man whose mule was trailing behind Cal's horse, his body had been accepted by the wide, swift-moving, and dangerous waters of the Snake River, but not entirely. It was as if the mighty river operated its own purgatory, for Tyson's body was caught, bobbing up and down behind a rock, right under the bluff behind Lucky's, its fate uncertain.

* * *

The after-supper social hour was still in full swing when Clint and Cal rode back into the circle of wagons. Sitting with a group of the emigrants, listening to Buck Carrey pick the banjo, Clayton Scofield noticed the two riders when they entered the circle and headed toward the horse herd. He also noticed the mule Cal was leading, carrying an empty saddle. Fearing the worst, he turned to look toward Tyson's wagon and saw the shadowy figure of Ruby Tyson by the tailgate of the wagon. He had to assume that she had seen the empty saddle on Tyson's mule as well. *I'd best go see if I can help out,* he thought and quietly got up from the stool he had been sitting on. "There's somethin' I've got to go see about," he told Lonnie James, who he had been sitting beside. "I'll be back later." He started toward his wagon when he saw Clint and Cal heading that way with their saddles. He reached the wagon a few steps ahead of them and stood waiting. "Bad news?" he asked.

"Depends on how you look at it, I reckon," Cal answered. "Tyson's dead. We ain't lookin' forward to takin' the news to Ruby."

"Reckon not," Scofield said. "I figured I'd go with you to help any way I can, but I imagine she already knows. She saw you come in just now. When you two saddled up and rode outta here, I figured it had to have somethin' to do with Tyson." He paused to look directly at Clint. "I woulda appreciated it, if you'da told me what you were fixin' to do before you rode off. Then I mighta had some idea where to look for you, if you didn't come back. All right? Now tell me what happened to Tyson."

They told him how they had found Tyson back of Lucky's saloon, rolled up against the outhouse door. "I don't know," Clint answered when Scofield asked how he died. "He didn't have any gunshot wounds. We didn't see any blood on him at all."

"The fellow that owns that place, Ike somebody," Cal offered, "said he just plain drank himself to death. But I don't know how the hell you can do that, unless you try to swallow the bottle."

"He made it upstairs with one of the whores, but she said he couldn't do nothin' when he got up there," Clint said. "And he passed out and never woke up when they carried him outta there. Ike claims they didn't know he was dead when they dropped him off the porch. Thought he'd wake up sometime and leave."

They paused and waited while Scofield was thinking about everything they had told him. After a few minutes, he shook his head and said, "I reckon there ain't no way you could know if it all happened the way Ike Ennis said it did or not. So what's done is done and we need to go tell poor Ruby her husband's dead."

"Whaddaya think we oughta tell her about his body?" Clint asked. "We decided it'd be easier on Ruby if we told her we buried him, instead of bringin' him back here. I kinda hate to tell her we threw his sorry ass in the river."

"Best stay with the buried story," Scofield agreed at once. The three of them walked around the circle until they came to Ruby's wagon.

She stepped away from the shadows when she saw them approaching and walked forward to meet them. "He wouldn't come back with you?" She asked the question because she hesitated to ask what she knew in her heart.

Scofield said it for her. "No, Ruby, he ain't comin' back. Ralph's dead. I feel awful bad havin' to tell you that, but there wasn't nothin' anybody could do to help him.

Near as anybody could tell, he musta had cholera or somethin' like that, and the whiskey musta made it worse." Then an idea struck him, so he embellished his story. "They have to be real careful about cholera 'cause it's so easy to catch. So, they put him in the ground right away." He glanced at Clint and nodded. "They gave him a right proper burial. You can feel comforted by that and we're real sorry about Ralph's passin'. Clint and Cal brought his gun and holster back to give you. There wasn't anything else of value on him."

She couldn't say anything for a few minutes, but her fear and dismay were plainly written upon her face. A feeling of helplessness overcame her when she pictured herself alone, trying to drive her mules from there to Oregon City. Guessing that to be what was causing her anxiety, and not mourning for the loss of her no-account husband, Cal stepped forward to make a proposal. "Ruby Tyson, I hereby offer my services as your mule handler and general handyman from here to wherever you decide to go in Oregon."

Ruby was surprised, to say the very least, and struck with guilt at the same time for the giant feeling of general relief his offer brought her. It far outweighed her emotions over the loss of her husband. She realized at that moment that she had been expecting the arrival of the night when Ralph failed to come home for all of the few years they had been married. And now, with Cal's generous offer, she could rejoice in the knowledge that she was at last free of Ralph Tyson. Furthermore, she felt confident that, should anything happen to Cal, Clint would be there to help her. Even with those thoughts swirling inside her head, she thought it best not to show her true feelings, lest the other women might think her shameful.

She smiled politely and quietly replied, "I accept your offer. Please accept my deepest gratitude for your kindness." She looked at Clint and added, "All of you, thank you for your concern for me."

Scofield was convinced he could see the lifting of her spirit right in the middle of the notice of her husband's death. He was even moved to joke. "Me and Clint are witnesses to the contract between you and Cal. We'll be ready to come down hard on him, if he don't live up to his end of it." He gave her a wink then and said, "You can even call him Lemuel, if you want to."

"And I'll call you Miss Ruby," Cal quipped.

She smiled at them, not offended by their irreverence considering the situation. "I expect I'd best clean out some of Ralph's old things, so I can make some room for Cal to put his things in the wagon."

"Right," Scofield replied. "We'll go and let you get busy. I'd like to say one thing to you, if you don't mind." She paused and waited for him to speak. "You're still a young woman, Ruby. I'd like to see you look at this as the next step in your life. And this time, I hope you take a step that leads to a good life. At your young age, you've already found out how bad life can be if you take the wrong step. I'm hopin' to see you come out to the social hour after supper every night. Let everybody know how pretty and bright you really are. Whaddaya say?"

She smiled and said, "Maybe I will. I've always wanted to, but Ralph wouldn't allow it."

Scofield bit his lower lip when he thought about the times he had threatened her husband if he saw any more marks on her from his abuse. He guessed it was fortunate that it never came to that. It might have been bad for business. "Well, let's go, boys. She's got some things she's wantin' to do."

"I'll bring my tent and my bedroll over and sleep by your wagon tonight," Cal told her. "I can move my possibles in the wagon tomorrow. Is that all right with you?"

"It's all right anytime you want to," she answered.

When they left her wagon, they started walking toward the gathering around the dancers. "I swear, I feel like dancin' myself tonight," Cal remarked.

Scofield stopped. "I feel like celebratin' tonight, too. I think tonight's events call for a good drink of rye whiskey. And I just happen to know where I might find a bottle of it."

"You talkin' about that one that's hid under those rags in the toolbox under the wagon seat?" Clint asked.

"Damn!" Scofield swore. "You knew about that?"

"Yeah," Clint answered. "Spud told me about it. He found it when he was lookin' for a hacksaw one day."

"Damn," Scofield swore again. "Well, I'll offer you a drink, if there's any left. We need to celebrate Tyson's funeral."

The weather had been cool, but fair on the last couple of days before they had reached Fort Hall. But on the day after Tyson's death, a front moved in from the southwest, bringing rain. It was not a welcome change, especially for those folks who needed repairs on their wagons. And, in spite of doing plenty of it, complaining didn't seem to influence the rain at all. But, even with the poor conditions, the wagons were on schedule to roll the following morning at seven o'clock. They started out on a road that followed the Snake River, running on the south side of that river for a distance of about one hundred and eighty miles to Three Island Crossing, where they would cross over to the north side for better grass and water, and generally better traveling conditions. In all that distance between Fort Hall and Three Island Crossing, there were only one or two places to cross the river, for most of the way the river was running deep in a canyon, or otherwise inaccessible. Scofield preferred to deal with Three Island Crossing, even with the potential hazards there.

Luckily, the rain had ended during the night, so when they started out toward American Falls in the morning, the sky offered a promise of sunshine. The rain on the previous day had no doubt caused the river to rise. But there was no need to worry about high water at the crossing, for they wouldn't reach Three Islands for about eleven or twelve days. As Scofield said, "This time of year, ain't no tellin' what that crossin' will look like. Maybe it'll be froze over and we'll just walk across." Of more concern at this point was the Raft River crossing, which they would reach in about three days. On some occasions, it would be flooded because of the many beaver dams on that river and it would be necessary to build rafts to carry the wagons across. That was how it came to be called the Raft River. If they were lucky, the river might be low enough to drive across, in spite of the recent rain.

Whenever the road ran close enough to get a view of it, then it was easy to see that the Snake River had indeed risen during the night. One indicator no one on the train chanced to notice might have had an unsettling effect upon the observer. But no one had the opportunity to notice the bobbing and rolling corpse being carried along with the swift current. During the night, the river had risen just enough to dislodge the body trapped against a rock near the riverbank some distance upstream, behind Lucky's River House. Some on the wagon train might have found it ironic had they known that Ralph Tyson was heading to Three Island Crossing ahead of them.

As far as the widow Tyson was concerned, there was an attempt on her part, for the sake of propriety, to make some show of mourning. Ruby had a black dress in her trunk, as well as a black shawl. She tried to present a proper picture of a grieving widow. But should anyone look closely, they would have noticed a glowing radiance in the widow's face that was not there before. Those who knew her best—Clint, Cal, Scofield, and possibly Marcy—noticed it and rejoiced in the justice of it. Cal moved his spartan-like belongings into her wagon and combined his food supplies with hers. She did the cooking for both of them, as well as the other wifely chores like sewing and washing his clothes whenever the opportunity was there. As for anything of a more personal nature was concerned, there was nothing to indicate that Cal had moved in lock, stock, and barrel. On the other hand, he now pitched his tent right up beside the wagon, so there was always a mystery for the rest of the folks to speculate upon. As for Marcy Zachary, she sincerely hoped there was something of a deeper nature going on between the two young people. Ruby had certainly earned a shot at life without the misery she had endured with Ralph. And Cal seemed basically decent. Marcy decided that the next thing for her to concentrate on was to bring Ruby out of her defensive shell. She started on that endeavor the first night the wagon train was back on its way, when she literally dragged Ruby out to the social hour. By the time they reached the Raft River, Ruby was making sure the supper dishes were washed in time, so Marcy wouldn't have to come looking for her. And the black dress and shawl were back in the trunk.

"Whaddaya think?" Scofield asked Clint.

"Seems okay to me," Clint answered. Both men were sitting on their horses in the middle of the river. Scofield turned his horse downstream and walked him a few yards before turning him to face Clint again. "It feels pretty solid to me," Clint said, "all the way to the bank."

"Yeah, that's what I think," Scofield said. "I don't think we'll have any trouble. As early as it is, we might as well take 'em across today and camp on the other side tonight."

Several of the men, led by John Zachary and Emmett Braxton, walked up to the bank of the river. "What's the word, Scofield?" Zachary called to him, "we gonna have to raft 'em?"

"No," Scofield yelled back, loud enough for them all to hear. "Clint thinks you can drive 'em across, so that's what we'll do, and if anybody loses a wagon, you can talk to him."

They all knew he was japing his nephew, so Zachary asked again. "We buildin' rafts?"

"I don't think we'll need 'em," Scofield said. "We'll drive on across tonight, in case it takes a notion to rain before mornin'." He motioned to his cook. "Show 'em, Spud."

Spud nodded, climbed back up on the wagon and started his horses across. The group of spectators grew right away as the other drivers came to watch. The water came up to the bottom of the wagon box before it went down again as Spud approached the other side. He pulled on up the bank for a good distance, then crawled back inside the wagon to check for water. In a few minutes, he stuck his head out the back of the wagon and yelled, "Dry as a bone!"

The next in line was Cal, driving Ruby's wagon. He didn't hesitate and urged the mules into the river. Like Spud, he crossed with no problems except for a small amount of water that managed to seep into the wagon box. Ruby went to work on it immediately with some rags to soak the water up. She apologized to Cal, since it was his bedding that caught the worst of it. She confessed then that Ralph had neglected to use the wax Scofield had given them to seal the cracks, although he had told Scofield that he did. Once the wagon was across and parked in the beginning of the circle, Ruby rigged up her clothesline and hung Cal's bedding to dry. The rest of the wagons crossed over without incident, and the camp was set up for the night.

Perhaps due to the ease of the river crossing, with no requirement to raft their wagons across, there seemed to be a more jovial mood at the social hour than usual. Even Fancy Wallace decided to join the people watching the dancing and listening to the picking and singing. Lemuel continued to watch from his bedroll under Fancy's wagon, however. "We got Ruby paired up with Cal," Sarah Braxton whispered to Marcy Zachary as they watched Fancy nodding her head in time with the music. "I wonder if we can get Lemuel Blue out from under Fancy's wagon."

"Ha," Marcy exclaimed, then lowered her voice to a whisper. "I'll let you work on that. I'm still workin' on Ruby and Cal."

The session broke up a little later than usual, due to the

easy mood of the travelers. The Zacharys, the Braxtons, and the Jameses remained a while after Buck and Doc had put away their instruments to talk about everything that had happened on this journey. "And we've got a long way to go yet," Susie James commented. "I'm still askin' myself if we're doin' the right thing."

Never one to pass up a chance to jape his wife, Lonnie answered her. "Why, sure we are, honey. If you hadn't come, you'd still be back in Missouri, and I'd be way out in Oregon with nobody to cook for me."

"I ain't so sure that would be a bad thing," Susie answered in kind.

"Well, I reckon it's time for me to get to bed," Emmett declared. "I don't wanna stay here and watch a good marriage break up."

They all followed his lead, knowing Scofield would be blasting away on his bugle early in the morning. They drifted off to their wagons. No one noticed that Cal Nixon's bedding was still hanging on the line to dry beside Ruby's wagon.

Chapter 20

After leaving the crossing at Raft River, the days that followed took them past Twin Falls, Cauldron Linn Rapids, and Shoshone Falls, but the spot that most of the emigrants were looking forward to reach was Salmon Falls. Scofield had told them stories about the thousands of salmon that went over the falls and guaranteed them that there would be Indians catching the fish, and would likely be looking to trade them for whatever the emigrants had to trade. The timing of their arrival at the falls came conveniently at noon time, and there were in excess of fifty or so Shoshone and Bannack fishermen reaping the harvest of salmon. They all came running with their strings of salmon when they saw the wagons pull into sight. The covered wagons were no real surprise to the Indians at the falls because they had been scouting the train's progress for the past several days. The trading began as soon as the horses were unhitched.

"Well, I declare," Ruby uttered when Cal unloaded the packs from his horses. "So, this is why you packed that stuff on your horses."

He grinned at her and replied, "Guilty. Clint told me about this place, but I didn't wanna say anything to you about it at the time. I wasn't really sure how you would feel about it." When he had moved his belongings into her wagon, Ruby had removed all of Ralph's possessions, clothing and personal items, as well as his favorite cup. Her desire was to rid her life of anything that reminded her of her late husband. And her intent was to simply abandon it beside the trail, like so many emigrants had done before them. It was pure coincidence that Clint had recently told him about Salmon Falls when Cal was complaining about a need for something to eat instead of salt pork for a change. It struck him when he and Ruby emptied the wagon that Ralph's things were means for bartering. So, he packed them on his two horses, planning to exchange them for fish. He thought the subject a little too awkward to tell her of his intent.

"Well, now that you know what I had in mind, I hope you don't think ill of me," he said. "I mean, not havin' any respect for the death of your husband and all."

"I could never think ill of you, Cal," she said. "I wouldn't expect you to have any respect for Ralph. I know I didn't, and I'm the one who made the mistake of marryin' him. I was too desperate to get out of the house of my childhood. But I found out I didn't know what desperate was until I married Ralph. He was just like my father, only worse. I reckon now, since you've taken over my wagon, and things happened between us, you must think I'm a pretty loose woman. I know I don't deserve any respect from anybody, but I don't care. These last few days, since we left Fort Hall, have been the happiest days of my entire life. So, I'll just thank you for that and tell you that I think you're a fine gentleman." Finished with her statement, she fairly beamed with happiness. Then she thought of one thing more she should say. "And I don't hold any bonds on you, Cal. Our agreement runs only as far as the Willamette Valley. I expect you to move on, once you get me there."

Fairly astonished by her open confession, Cal was at a loss when it came to a response. After a long pause, he finally thought to address her declaration. "I 'preciate what you're sayin', but I was kinda hopin' we'd give it a longer try. That is, if you are interested. I was afraid Ralph Tyson had scared you off marriage for good."

She was not sure she could believe what she was hearing. "Cal, are you talkin' about gettin' married?"

"What?" He stammered, realizing he had referred to marriage, a word that had always seemed repulsive to him before. It was the first time she had ever seen him at a loss for words. "I don't know," he started, then hesitated again to think about it for a second. "Hell, I reckon I am, but you might be against it. So you might wanna give it a tryout before you take a chance on hookin' up with another loser. Then if it don't look like it's gonna work out for you, you can just say so. I won't hold it against you. Whaddaya think?"

Having hung his head while he made his confession, he looked up when she failed to reply right away. He found her gazing at him, a broad smile on her face, still saying nothing until finally she said, "Cal," but continued to stare.

His emotions seeming to come back under control again, he was suddenly aware of a sound behind him like a footfall. He spun around then to confront an elderly Indian man. He held up a string of what looked to be about fifteen salmon. "You trade for fish?" the Indian asked and pointed toward Ralph's two shirts that Cal had laid on the ground.

Feeling every bit the fool for letting an Indian walk right up to his back without his knowing it, Cal laughed, embarrassed. "You bet I will," he blurted, and when the Indian looked puzzled by his response, he said, "Yes, I trade shirt for fish."

The Indian smiled and nodded, then he held out the string of salmon to Cal. Cal took them and handed them to Ruby when she held out her hand. "They're heavy," he said when he passed them over. "Lotta good eatin' there." She gave him a happy grin. He turned back to the old Indian, who appeared to be having trouble deciding which of the two shirts to pick. Cal reached down and picked up the two shirts and held them out to the Indian. "Here," he said, "take 'em both. That's a fair trade for that many salmon." They smiled at each other and the Indian continued to nod his head over and over, until he turned and went back to his friends by the falls. "Good trade," Cal said when he turned back around to face a beaming Ruby. "He's happy, I'm happy, you're happy. We're all happy, right?" She nodded rapidly, just like the old Indian had. Feeling in control again, he asked, "Now about that thing we were talking about before we were interrupted, you wanna give it a try?"

"I do," she said and nodded again.

They were to find that their trading day was not over, for the old man took the spoils of his trading back to show his friends. As a consequence, Cal and Ruby were swamped with Shoshone men and boys bringing their catches to display until Cal had nothing more to trade. The other wagons were busy trading for salmon, too, but not at the pace Cal and Ruby set. The trading resulted in a delay of half a day on the trail to Three Island Crossing. The second half of this day was spent cleaning fish, roasting more than enough to enjoy for supper, and smoking great quantities to be eaten later. Everyone was too busy to attend a social hour that night, because Scofield told them they could not waste any more time at the falls. The bugle would blow at four in the morning.

When Clint and his uncle determined it was time they turned in for the night, Clint had a question for him. "I was wonderin' about something," he said. "You bein' the wagon master of this outfit, have you got the authority to marry two people?"

Scofield paused to give it a thought. "Well, I take the part of a judge. I can hang a man. I don't see why I couldn't officially marry somebody. Why?"

"Nothin'," Clint replied. "I've just got a notion that you might be called upon to tie the knot for two of our people."

"Cal and Ruby?" Scofield asked.

"Looks that way to me," Clint said. "He sure don't hang around with the boys as much as he used to."

"Yeah, I noticed that. Hell, they could just jump over a broom together," Scofield said. "But maybe it would be a little more official if I said some words over 'em."

The journey to Three Island Crossing took only a little over two more days. They arrived close to midday, so

Scofield decided to stop for the nooning before attempting to cross over to the north side of the Snake. The crossing, as its name implied, was a section where three small islands had formed in the river. This reduced the job of crossing the wide and treacherous river to four shorter crossings. Scofield planned to drive the wagons across, since the river had gone down after the rain had luckily stayed away after that one full wet day. It was still a dangerous undertaking, however, because of the swift current and the hidden holes in the river bottom that had the potential to overturn a wagon or entangle a team of horses. Every year, there were drownings at this crossing. Scofield had been lucky that none of these drownings had occurred on any of his trains. He was counting on the crossing being no more difficult than the Raft River crossing, just that it would take about four times as long. What he had not counted on was a raiding party of twelve Ute warriors.

Wounded Bear, the Ute war party chief watched the wagons as they pulled up close to the bank of the river, forming a circle before they began building small fires to cook over. Crawling up beside him at the edge of the ridge, Crow Killer commented, "They are too many. They will all have guns."

Breaks His Leg, lying on the other side of Wounded Bear, spoke, seemingly puzzled. "They look like they are going to camp there."

"It doesn't matter," Crow Killer said. "They are too many. Every man in those wagons will have a gun and the wagon to hide behind."

"I think they are going to cross the river," Wounded Bear said. "They didn't unhitch their horses from the wagons. They just want to eat first. We have ridden this far to raid the Shoshone and we have found something better, the white man. He will have guns and bullets. We will make big medicine." Crow Killer started to repeat his warning, but Wounded Bear interrupted. "You are right when you say they are too many. But we don't have to fight them all. We will wait. When they start driving their wagons across, we will wait until there is only one wagon left on this side—maybe two. Then we will attack that wagon. The rest of the white men will try to come back to help their brothers, but twelve of us can keep them from coming back across the water while we take what we want."

Crow Killer thought about that for a few moments, creating a picture of it in his mind. The white men would be helpless to defend their wagon. "I think that is a good plan." He looked at Breaks His Leg. "Wounded Bear is right. The white men cannot cross the water without getting shot. Let's go back and tell the others." They backed away from the edge, then went back down the slope where the other warriors were tending the horses. Wounded Bear's plan was met with enthusiasm, for they had come a long way from their village in Utah Territory with hopes of raiding a Shoshone village. When they reached the Snake River Valley, the village was no longer there. And then luck brought them to this river crossing just as they were preparing to go back to their village. The only thing to do now was wait. And while they did that, they took the opportunity to check their weapons again. Five of their number carried rifles, all five were Harpers Ferry Model 1855 percussion rifle-muskets. The rest of the party were armed with bows. There was a good chance that the settlers in the wagons had more modern rifles, perhaps even the repeating rifles like the carbines the soldiers carried.

As Wounded Bear had predicted, the fires were put out and the wagons prepared to move again. Soon, the first wagon entered the river and made its way carefully across the short expanse of water to the first of the three islands. The accomplishment was worthy of a chorus of hearty cheers as the second wagon followed. Some trouble occurred when Fancy Wallace's wagon left the second of the three islands and found a deep hole that swallowed one of the rear wheels and almost flipped the wagon. Lemuel was driving her wagon and did a credible job of managing the horses to keep the wagon upright. The wagons that followed gave his path a wide shoulder and were able to avoid the problem. From his vantage point on the ridge, Wounded Bear watched the crossing. He had told his warriors how they would attack and then how they would defend against any of the white men who tried to come back. Ready to strike, they awaited his signal.

Finally, there were only two wagons left to enter the river, Walt Moody's and Tim Blake's. Wounded Bear decided to attack both of them. His signal was one long war cry, and his warriors, already creeping up toward the top of the ridge, responded at once, sweeping over the top of the ridge and down the other side. Startled, Tim stood up to try to see around the wagon cover, only to be met by a hail of arrows and rifle balls ripping the canvas cover. The dull thud of a Ute arrow in his chest knocked him back down on the wagon seat while he fumbled for his revolver. In the other wagon, Walt did not hesitate, slapped his horses hard and drove them into the water. Yelling for Ellie to stay down, he got down behind the seat and continued to flail his horses with the reins as rifle balls snapped around him. Lonnie James, in the wagon ahead of Walt's, and already safely on the first island, reacted at once. He grabbed his rifle and started firing at the warriors on the riverbank.

Angry that the one wagon got away, Wounded Bear grabbed the bridle of one of Tim's horses to hold them. With the Ute arrow protruding from his chest, Tim managed to draw his pistol. And when a second arrow struck him, he pulled the trigger, putting a bullet in Wounded Bear's chest. Several of the warriors reached up and dragged Tim off the driver's seat and, in an act of anger and defiance, one of them took his scalp, held it up for the white men to see, and screamed a bloody war cry. He and two of the other Utes took cover behind the wagon then as Lonnie tried to zero in on them.

"They killed Tim!" Lonnie blurted when Clint and Scofield crossed back from the other side to join the fight. "He killed one of 'em, and I got one. I count about eight or ten more."

Clint didn't wait to get any instructions. He ran down to a gully near the edge of the water and started thinning out the raiders. The Ute warriors seemed surprised by the sudden firepower coming their way in rapid fire from Clint's Henry rifle. Before they realized how vulnerable they were, he had knocked three of them down, chasing the rest behind the wagon with the others. "Any sign of Amy?" Scofield asked Lonnie. Lonnie just shook his head. Scofield looked back into the wagon to see Susie and twelve-year-old Sammy lying as flat as they could on the floor of the wagon box. "I reckon you'd best get your family on across this river," he said to Lonnie.

"What are you gonna use for cover, if I move the wagon?" Lonnie asked.

"I'll find something," Scofield said, "jump in that gully with Clint, maybe. You get Susie and the boy to safety. I don't wanna take a chance on them gettin' hit with a lucky shot."

"All right," Lonnie said, "but let me throw a few shots over there to keep 'em behind that wagon while you run for cover." He snorted half a laugh. "You're as big as I am. You'd be an easy target to hit."

"Fire away," Scofield said, and when Lonnie did, he ran to the gully and jumped in beside Clint. Lonnie drove his wagon into the river, leaving the two of them to look across the small section of the Snake River at probably six or seven savages. "Have you seen any sign of Amy?" Scofield asked Clint.

"No, I ain't," Clint answered, "and I'm real worried about that. I wish we could get over there."

"I know what you're feelin'," Scofield told him. "I'm feelin' the same thing. But there ain't no way for us to cross that stretch of water without them seein' us. It'd be like shootin' ducks settin' on a pond. Least you ain't heard no screams, have you?" Clint shook his head, so Scofield said, "I don't think they'll hurt her. She's young and pretty—too valuable alive. They can sell her to the Mexicans or Spaniards for a slave."

"You're thinkin' they must be Utes, right?" Clint asked. "They were most likely up in this part of the territory to try to raid a Shoshone village. They never did get along very well with the Shoshone." He was about to ask his uncle if he had any good ideas about what the two of them should do about this apparent standoff when they heard the scream.

Moments before that, Breaks His Leg was asking Crow Killer virtually the same question Clint just asked Scofield. With Wounded Bear dead, there could be no plainer sign that the plan had been a bad idea. "Bad, bad, sign," Crow Killer said. "We must take what we want from this wagon and leave." Reaching around in the back of the wagon, he suddenly felt a shoe. Realizing at once that it held a foot, he took hold of it and yanked it toward the tailgate. Amy screamed. When he pulled her out from under a pile of blankets she had tried to hide under, she was holding a shotgun, but Crow Killer was quick enough to knock the barrel aside before she could aim it at him. He jerked the gun from her hand and handed it to one of the warriors behind him. "Maybe this raid has given us something of value, after all," he spoke in his native tongue. In English, he said. "You not be bad, I don't kill."

Too frightened to scream again, and not sure what had happened to her husband, she could only stare at the savage faces, all staring back at her. Finally, she cried out, "Tim!" Not understanding, the Indians looked at each other, puzzled. "Tim!" She cried out again.

This time, the warrior who had scalped Tim guessed that she was calling her husband's name. He grinned as he held the scalp up for her to see, and said, "Tim."

Certain that she was witnessing her moment of death next, Amy became faint, her body lifeless. Crow Killer unlatched the tailgate and dragged her out of the wagon to land on the ground behind it. "Hold her!" he ordered while he thought over the situation they found themselves in. "We cannot stay here," he told the others. "The white devil has the gun that shoots many times without reloading. We must back away from here to the ridge and our horses."

"I will get his weapons," Running Fox said and scrambled up into the wagon. He pulled and shoved everything he could back toward the tailgate in the packed wagon box to clear a path to the driver's seat. By the time he worked his way back to the tailgate, the others had picked through the couple's belongings, taking what they wanted and leaving the rest on the ground.

"What about the horses?" Breaks His Leg asked Crow Killer, who was tying a rope around Amy's neck. "They are two good horses. I don't want to leave them."

"Do you want them bad enough to go around there and unhitch them while those white devils shoot at you?" Crow Killer asked.

Breaks His Leg thought about that possibility, then a much simpler solution occurred to him. "I won't unhitch them. I will drive the wagon. I will back the wagon to the foot of the ridge, then I will unhitch them and that will be too far for them to shoot at me."

Crow Killer nodded as he thought the plan over. "We could use the wagon as cover for all of us," he saw at once. "You have never driven a wagon. Do you think you can make their horses back the wagon?"

"I've seen the white man do it. If he can do it, I can do it." They looked at each other and nodded agreement, so Breaks His Leg didn't hesitate. He crawled into the wagon and made his way up to the driver's seat. Seeing the reins lying across the foot board, he reached under the seat and took them back behind the seat. Then, trying to imitate commands he had heard the white man use, he called out to the horses and pulled back hard on the reins. To Crow Killer's amazement, the wagon began to back up slowly, causing those using it for cover to scramble backward as well, to keep from being run over.

"They're takin' the whole damn wagon," Scofield blurted, finding it hard to believe they would want to bother with it.

"I think they're just usin' it for cover till they can get to that ridge behind 'em," Clint said. "I expect they're gonna try to take the horses, though. Then maybe we'll get a clear shot at 'em again, especially if they try to unhitch 'em before they climb that ridge. My guess is the base of that ridge ain't over a hundred and fifty yards from here. That's well within the range of this Henry."

Clint's speculation turned out to be accurate, for just before reaching the foot of the slope, Breaks His Leg stopped the wagon. No longer having it for cover, the rest of the raiding party scurried up the slope as fast as they could manage. Taking the opportunity presented to them, Scofield and Clint threw shot after shot at the slope, killing three before they could reach the top of the ridge. They could not risk a shot at Crow Killer, for he labored up the slope with Amy draped on his back, holding her arms around his neck. "I'll be comin' after you, Amy," Clint murmured under his breath, then turned his attention to the two horses still hitched to the wagon.

Breaks His Leg made use of the distraction created by his friends when they ran up the slope. Down on the ground, he crawled along beside the wagon to get to the horses. Using the horses as cover, he quickly slipped around between them. Then he cut all the traces hooking them to the wagon until he could free them of chains and collars. When they were completely free of all connection to the wagon, he held both horses by the bridle. Clint watched him as he walked the horses off the wagon tongue, staying between them for protection. All his concentration now on the warrior leading Tim's horses, Clint laid the front sight of his rifle on the horse's head blocking his view of the Indian and kept it there, knowing the Indian was going to have to turn the horses to go uphill. When Scofield glanced over at Clint, he knew what he was counting on, so he said nothing so as not to distract him. Clint waited patiently, knowing he would have no more than a second or two. The horses began to turn now to climb up the slope. Clint took a breath and held it as the horse he had taken aim on turned off his line of fire and the Ute's head came into his view. Finally, for one brief moment, the Indian was directly on his line of sight, between the two horses' heads. To be certain, Clint dropped his sight to the broader target of Breaks His Leg's back. He didn't remember squeezing the trigger, only aware that the warrior dropped, and the two horses bolted away from the slope.

"Helluva shot," Scofield stated, almost reverently.

"I've gotta go after 'em," Clint stated matter-of-factly. "We can't leave her in their hands."

"I know," Scofield replied. "We'll get a posse together."

"I don't think that's a good idea," Clint said right away. "That'll take too much time. My horse is right here. I need to get up there and see which way they headed while there's still plenty of light to track 'em." He looked back over his shoulder. "Walt's just gotten to the second island. You need to take care of your people. They're gonna be shook up pretty good. And I don't think anybody's gonna feel too easy about campin' here tonight, so you'd best move 'em on up the trail."

"I can't let you go after those Indians by yourself," Scofield protested, even as Clint climbed out of the gully and headed for his horse.

"We've got a better chance, if I go by myself," Clint insisted. "It'll be easier for me to stay outta sight when I need to."

Scofield knew he was right. He would have a better chance to sneak her away from them if he were alone. The appearance of a posse coming after them might cause the Indians to kill the woman, so as not to be hampered by her in their flight. And he knew Clint was as much at home in the woods as any Indian. "Dag-nab-it, boy, you watch yourself."

"I will," he said as he climbed up into the saddle, then paused a second. "And, Uncle Clayton, don't wait around for me. This might take some time. I'll catch up with you as long as you stay on the usual trail." He gave his horse a touch with his heels. "Come on, Biscuit, let's go swimmin' again."

Scofield stood there, watching him until Biscuit climbed up the bank and loped off toward the ridge. He had a bad feeling about letting his nephew ride off alone to deal with savages already enraged by the loss of the lives they had suffered. But he knew Clint was right when he reminded him that his first responsibility was toward the people who trusted him with their lives. And now, he had already lost one of them, and possibly two. He looked behind him then when he heard Lonnie and Ron Settle coming to help. "Clint's gone after 'em," he told them. "I wanna pick up Tim's body and bury him on the other side. At least, I want him to have gotten to the other side of the Snake."

Chapter 21

Having no desire to ride over the top of that ridge to be greeted by a volley of gunfire from all three Indians, Clint came out of the saddle a dozen yards from the top. He dropped Biscuit's reins to the ground and continued up the slope in a crouch until just before the crest. Then he dropped to the ground and inched his way up to a position to see the backside of the ridge. There was no ambush waiting for him, the Ute warriors had fled. He hurried back to his horse and rode over the top and down into the ravine where the Utes had left their horses before. There was no question as to which way they ran, for the soft soil of the ravine was plowed up from hoofprints. Thanks to the fact that they took the horses the dead had ridden, there were plenty of tracks to follow and too many to hide. He had to respect the fact that the three were now better armed than they were when they were firing flintlock rifles at Scofield and him back in the gully. For now, they were in possession of Tim's weapons, a Pennsylvania percussion rifle, a double-barrel shotgun, and a Colt single-action revolver.

Judging from the tracks, he could tell the Utes were not sparing their horses, so he was not apt to catch up with them right away. At any rate, he was not sure it would be wise to catch up too soon, in broad daylight. He didn't want to end up in a long-range shootout. His chances for success in rescuing Amy were much better after dark when they had gone into camp. It was not an easy thing, thinking she might be subjected to any amount of unpleasantness or pain. But he had to plan his attack based on a reasonable possibility of bringing her back with him. He checked his pursuit, judging as best as he could that he was keeping pace with the Indians.

The chase continued throughout the afternoon, causing him to apologize to Biscuit, and wondering if the Indians would ever rest their horses. They continued on until the sun dropped below the horizon. Thinking he would just have to let them gain on him, he came out of the saddle and started walking to spare the exhausted horse. His walk was not to be very long, however, for soon after he dismounted, he saw a small stream, predominately bordered by willow trees and scrubby bushes. He stopped at once. There was no sign of the Indians or the horses they were leading. He was convinced that the Utes had to stop to rest their horses, or they would soon be walking. It was just a question of whether they went upstream or down since he felt sure they were not straight ahead. At that point, it was fairly simple to see they had chosen to go upstream, so now it was a question of how far. It was also the point where it was important to continue on with great caution, lest he was spotted.

He did not go far before he heard their horses up ahead of him, so he decided to leave Biscuit right where he was and continue on foot, working his way carefully through the willows and banks of berry bushes until he saw the smoke of a fire. Inching his way forward now, he crept from one bush to the next until, at last, he had a clear look at the camp. As he had figured, there were three of them, but he didn't see Amy until one of the men got up from the fire and went to take a look at his captive. She was tied to a tree on the other side of the narrow stream, her head hanging down, so that her chin looked to be resting on her breast. He could not tell if she was conscious until Crow Killer grabbed a handful of her hair, jerked her head back, and yelled something at her. Clint could see her whole body flinch. Crow Killer shoved her head back down forcefully, still ranting something. Clint knew enough of the Ute language to catch a few words, but he could not understand everything the belligerent warrior hurled at Amy. One statement he did hear clearly was when the warrior pounded himself on his chest and declared that he was Crow Killer, a great warrior. He turned then and went back to the fire with his two companions. *Maybe I should have shot him while I had a clear shot,* he thought, but he was still of the opinion he needed to first free Amy.

Clint knew how terrified Amy had to be, likely almost out of her mind knowing they had killed Tim and having no idea what they planned to do with her. He wished he could tell her that the horrible images she may have formed of what they had in mind for her might not happen right away. There was a good chance that they were so devastated by the massacre of most of their raiding party, along with the shame of their defeat, that they would not be thinking of using her for their pleasure. He hoped he was right in his thinking. At any rate, he felt it best to wait for the Indians to settle down for the night before he made any attempt to get to her.

"It is bad that we had to leave the bodies of the others behind," Running Fox lamented as he and the other two survivors ate the sowbelly they had taken from the wagon.

"It was bad medicine that Wounded Bear made to begin with," Crow Killer said. "I do not say this to blame him. I, too, thought it was a good plan to attack the wagons at the river. But I think the white man's medicine was stronger at the river. At least they did not capture our horses, and we have the woman to sell."

"That will not make up for the warriors we left behind us," Running Fox insisted. "We should go back and kill those white men."

"I don't think we could kill all of them before they killed us," Crow Killer chided. "They are too many, and they all have better guns than we do. They had the guns that shoot many times without reloading. Those guns make one man like ten. I cannot tell another man what he should do. But for myself, I will rest my horse tonight and return to the village two days from now to honor the brave warriors who did not return."

"What of the woman?" Crippled Beaver asked.

"I will sell her to the Comancheros," Crow Killer replied. "She is young and fair. She should bring a good price. There were no children with the wagon, so I will tell them she has not known a man. That should increase the price the Comancheros can ask for her."

"Maybe she has given birth before, but the child died," Crippled Beaver suggested.

"I will look at the woman, to see for myself if she has given birth or not," Crow Killer said. Then with a mischievous smile, he said, "After I have satisfied myself that she has not carried a child, perhaps you and Running Fox may want to satisfy yourselves."

"That is the only fair way to test the woman," Running Fox commented, a smile of anticipation creeping across his face.

"Hah," Crippled Beaver snorted in contempt. "You talk of testing the woman's virtue. She was the wife of the man we just killed." He held the scalp up to remind them. "So, I think we already know she is not a maiden. We'd better worry about the other white men who might come to avenge her husband's death. I don't want to lie with the white woman, anyway. I have heard that white women are dirty and never bathe."

"I'll bet your wife told you that," Crow Killer said, and he and Running Fox laughed. "You must do what your mind tells you to do. As for me, I will go now and judge this woman we intend to sell to our friends, the Comancheros." He rose to his feet and headed for the patch of willows on the other side of the stream where he had tied the white woman.

Straining in an effort to free her hands from around the tree behind her back, Amy pulled and pulled until the skin broke and she felt the blood trickle down into her hands. It was no use. Crow Killer had bound her too securely to give her any chance of escape. She had to pause in her struggle when tears of frustration streamed down her face. With no other option, she took a deep breath and prepared to strain against her bonds once again, but she stopped short when she heard someone coming through the stand of berry bushes between her and the stream. *Maybe he's not coming to hurt me,* she prayed. *He could be coming to bring me some food or water.* But when he walked through the willows toward her, she could see it was the same one who had cursed her before, and he was not carrying any food or water with him.

"Please let me go," she pleaded when he approached her, not even sure he could understand her words. "I have done you no harm."

"Many Ute warrior dead, you must pay," Crow Killer said. So he knew some English.

"You killed my husband!" Amy cried out. "Isn't that enough?"

"I say what's enough," he said, walked up to the tree, and dropped to his knees, facing her. "You have babies?" He grabbed both her ankles.

"No, I don't have babies," she cried. "Let go of me!"

She tried to kick him, but his grip was too strong on her ankles. Her frustration amused him. "Now, I think I will see if you are able to have babies." Helpless in his grasp, she knew there was nothing she could do to stop him. She started to sob uncontrollably and clinched her eyes tightly closed in a desperate attempt to shut it all out. Then she thought she felt his grip on her ankles relax and he uttered a labored grunt. Thinking she was hallucinating, or perhaps dead, she opened her eyes to see her assailant struggling for his life, a rope knotted around his throat so tightly that he could not breathe or speak. He clawed frantically at the hands drawing the rope tighter and tighter but was unable to free himself. She opened her eyes wide in disbelief, recognizing the rugged features of Clint Buchanan.

Feeling the last breaths of his life leaving his body, Crow Killer could not prevent himself from being bent over until his face was crushed against the ground. His assassin held his face close to his ear and whispered, "Die, Crow Killer. Know that it is I, Crawls Through Fire, a Crow warrior who sends you to hell."

When Crow Killer stopped struggling and relaxed in death, Clint dragged him away from the stunned woman, so she could not see him. Then, as a precaution, he drew his knife and cut the Indian's throat. He cleaned his knife on Crow Killer's shirt, then went back and cut the rope tying Amy's hands together.

"Clint! Clint!" Still reeling in a state of shock, that was all she could say for the moment.

He put his forefinger to his lips to signal her to be quiet as he reached down to help her to her feet. "I'm goin' to take you back to the wagon train," he told her. "But first, I've got to make sure his two friends don't come after us. All right?" She nodded rapidly, although she wasn't really sure what he was going to do. "Come," he said, took her by the elbow, and led the still-trembling woman back down the stream a dozen yards to a thick clump of willows. "I'm gonna leave you here for just a little while till I make sure you're safe. If you hear gunshots, don't worry, they'll be comin' from me. Understand?" Again, she nodded her head rapidly. He could see that she was still dazed by the sudden reversal of circumstances. "I'll take care of you," he tried to reassure her. "Just sit here and wait a little while." Again, she nodded, fearful that she might never see him again when he disappeared into the darkness of the little stream.

He would have preferred to take Amy and run, but he was sure the two Ute warriors still sitting by the fire would come after them. And there was still the issue of exhausted horses, both Biscuit and theirs. The only safe way was to eliminate the other two warriors and he was sure he could take one of them out while they were still sitting by the fire, and possibly both. But if he wasn't able to fire the second shot before the other one rolled into the darkness, it might turn into a drawn-out game of hide and seek. And for Amy's sake, he hoped to avoid that. Maybe it would be better to let them come to him, he thought when he returned to the tree where Amy had been tied. A sudden voice from the campfire made his decision for him.

"Crow Killer!" Running Fox called out. "Have you finished testing the woman?" There was no reply from the willows across the stream, so he yelled again, laughing, "Maybe you need some help." Still there was no answer from Crow Killer for a long time. "Crow Killer," he called out again, concerned now, lest the woman had somehow hidden a knife on herself somewhere. "Something must be wrong," he said to Crippled Beaver. "I'm going to see why he doesn't answer."

Concerned now as well, Crippled Beaver said, "I'll go with you." They hurried into the darkness across the stream. Approaching the clump of willows, they could see a figure seated at the base of the largest willow, just as Crow Killer had left her. But when they came closer, they discovered too late that it was not the woman. It was one of the white devils from the river crossing, with a Henry rifle in one hand and a single-action Navy Colt in the other. They both discharged, almost at the same time, striking both warriors in the chest. A dozen yards downstream, Amy Blake bolted upright, shocked by the report of the two shots. Frozen then with uncertainty once more, she listened for sounds that might tell her more. But the only sounds that reached her were the sounds of the horses left to graze and water, restless because of the gunshots. And then she almost sobbed in relief when she heard him call. "Amy, you're safe now. They're all gone. You can come out now." He appeared then, as she was struggling to her feet. Still a little shaky, she almost stumbled until he caught her arm. "You all right?" he asked.

"I think so," she said. "I'm sorry I'm such a weak soul. Tim would be ashamed of me. I always told him I was a tough woman. Look at me, shaking like a leaf. They killed my husband!" she suddenly sobbed. "I don't know what I'm going to do now. Tim was my whole world."

"Don't try to hold it back," he said. "Let it all come out. You've been through a helluva lot more than most folks could stand. You are a tough woman. There ain't nobody but you and me here now. Those Indians are dead. So, we're gonna wait here for a little while to let the horses rest. Then we'll head back north to catch Scofield and the others on the north side of the Snake. I reckon those are the cards fate dealt us, so we'll play 'em. All right?" She nodded, gaining back some control of her emotions. "I expect you might be a little bit hungry, too," he said. "I'll see what I can find to eat."

"You're a good man, Clint Buchanan. Thank you for coming to get me. Thank you for risking your life to save mine. I know in my heart that Tim is thanking you somewhere, too."

"He was a mighty good man," Clint replied. "I'll always remember how him and Ron Settle were the ones who helped me keep those three Sioux horse thieves from stealin' all our horses at Register Cliff." Eager then to get her mind off the loss of her husband, he said, "Come on, let's get you over there by the fire. It's too cold to sit out here in the willows. If I'da been thinkin' straight, I'da brought my coffeepot with me, or at least brought some coffee to boil in a pot. I might throw a fit if I have to go too long without coffee," he joked.

"I know they took food from our wagon," Amy said.

"We'll look through their packs and see what we can find. I expect they were livin' off the land, whatever they could find to hunt. We might be doin' the same thing on our way to meet the wagon train."

Once he got her settled by the fire with a couple of slices of sowbelly the Indians had taken from her wagon, he apologized again for having no coffee, then he went to look at the horses grazing along the stream bed. That was another decision to make, whether to try to herd all the horses back with him, or just set them free. He felt no urge to try to herd that many horses. Some of them looked to be old and in rough shape. He decided to select a good horse for Amy and take a couple more for packhorses, and set the rest of the bunch free. He picked out a gentle paint mare for Amy and took the best of the Indian saddles that were on three of the horses for her comfort. After taking the best two horses in order after that to be used as packhorses, he stripped the remaining horses of their bridles. They were all rope bridles, anyway.

While she was eating her bacon, he went back across the stream to move the bodies back away from the water, hopefully far enough away so there was no chance Amy might stumble upon them, if she went downstream to take care of nature's business. Back at the campfire, she was thinking about the necessity of attending to that problem fairly soon, but she didn't want to leave the fire before he returned, afraid she might accidentally bump into him. Things inside her were bad enough as it was, without the possibility of an embarrassing encounter while doing what her nervous bowels were suggesting. Then she heard the shot. It came from the direction he had gone in. There was just the one shot, nothing more, but it was enough to set her mind spinning out possible causes. Luckily, it was not a great amount of time after the shot when he appeared, leading his horse and three of the Indian ponies.

"Thank goodness," she sighed. "I heard the shot. Was one of those Indians still alive?"

"No, they were all dead when I dragged 'em away from the stream, but he wasn't." He reached back and pulled a raccoon off one of the Indian ponies. "I found him nosin' around the bodies, so I figured I'd invite him for breakfast, or supper, if you're wantin' somethin' besides that sowbelly." She looked a little uncertain, staring at the hairy creature, so he said, "I take it you ain't ever ate raccoon before. It's pretty good eatin', especially when it's the only thing on the menu. I'll go ahead and skin it and butcher it and we'll roast some on the fire. You might not want any other kind of meat but raccoon after you've tried it." He was trying his best to keep her spirits up and her mind from dwelling on the loss of her husband, but he was afraid his next suggestion was going to disappoint her. "Listen, Amy, I know you wanna get back to the wagons as soon as you can. So do I, but it's already goin' on hard dark, and I'm thinkin' we'd best stay right here tonight and start out early in the mornin'. That road goes a long ways away from the Snake and it doesn't see the river again until we cross it for the last time at Fort Boise." He could tell by her puzzled expression that he was only complicating his point.

"Whatever you think is best, Clint," she declared. "I trust you completely."

"What I'm tryin' to explain is we'll catch the wagons quicker if we turn around and go right back the way we came, back to Three Island Crossin', and cross over the Snake, follow the road away from the river."

She couldn't help smiling at him. "Clint, I'm sure you wanna get back as fast as you can. Just set me on a horse and I'll follow you." She could have told him that, after the loss of her husband, she couldn't care less about what route they took to overtake the wagon train. As long as she was no longer a captive of the Indians, she felt she was indifferent to what happened tomorrow or the day after tomorrow.

She had been surprised by the roasted raccoon Clint prepared. It was not likely to become one of her favorites, but she found it was really not bad at all. She ate enough to make her belly feel full and ready for sleep. Unfortunately, the only bedding they had was the blankets they found among the Indians' belongings. In her mind, all Indians were savages, never bathing or washing their bedclothes. In this particular case, Clint had to concede to her that this Ute war party had evidently traveled far and had given little preference to cleanliness. Conducting a sniffing test, he tested each blanket and selected a blanket for her that he deemed least offensive. She reacted to it as if it conveyed smallpox. Before the night was over, however, and she felt the chill in her bones, she gratefully pulled the blanket tightly around her. Helped in great part by her exhaustion, she managed to fall asleep.

Morning found her stiff and groggy, desperate for a cup of coffee, of which there was none. Clint was already up and had revived the fire. Thinking it best to give her something to eat before they started back, he speared some more strips of the raccoon to roast over the fire. "Ain't nothin' that'll start your day off better than some fresh hot 'coon strips," he japed.

"If you say so," she japed back. "I'm not especially particular this mornin', anyway."

"Well, it'll be a little something to put in your belly till we stop to rest the horses. And that'll be when we get back to the crossin'. We'll start out as soon as you're ready to ride your new paint pony."

"Give me a few moments to take a little walk down the stream a-ways and splash some water on my face, and I'll be ready to go," she said. She was true to her word, taking very little time to be ready. He could see that she was making an effort to disguise it, but she was unable to create any enthusiasm for her return to the wagon train. The chilly morning was too appropriate for the cold feeling of the loss of her loved one. He set a pace for the horses that was slightly less than the pace they had maintained when they rode in the opposite direction the day before. When they rode away from the stream, most of the horses they left behind followed for a while before eventually wandering off in other directions. Under other circumstances, he might have gone to the trouble to try to drive them, but he didn't think they were worth the extra effort it would take.

Chapter 22

It was past noon when they crossed back over the ridge just before reaching the Snake again, and Clint intended to give the horses a good rest before committing them to the crossing of the three islands in the river. The first thing he noticed when they got back was that Tim and Amy's wagon was gone. Evidently, they had caught Tim's horses, and someone must have supplied some new harnessing to hitch them up again. He recalled that the Indian who tried to steal the horses had hacked the old harness up in his attempt to free them from the wagon. Reading the sorrow in Amy's eyes, as she stared at the spot on the bank where their wagon had sat, waiting their turn to cross over, Clint helped her down off the paint. "You wanna build a fire while I take care of the horses?" he asked, thinking to give her something to do to get her mind off her loss.

Since there was not much left of the small raccoon after breakfast, their noon meal was more of the sowbelly the Utes had taken from the wagon. Amy bemoaned the fact that there was so much more the Indians could have taken, like flour, sugar, cornmeal, even some dried apples in a small barrel. If they had taken something other than what they could roast over a fire, she could have mixed up a simple meal. Not to be denied, however, Clint rigged up a fishing line and dropped it in the river with a small piece of the pork fat for bait. When he was successful in catching the first fish, he was encouraged to try it again. When he caught two more, he deemed that enough to supplement their sowbelly dinner.

After he figured the horses were rested and fed enough, Clint asked Amy, "Are you ready to go for a little swim?"

She consciously inched over a little closer to the fire before she replied. "I suppose, but I'm not looking forward to it."

"When I crossed it yesterday, it was not real deep," he told her. "I was able to stay in the saddle all the way across. Biscuit didn't have to swim but a little way and that was between the second and the third island. I only got wet a little above my knees. You might be able to pull your feet up behind you and maybe that little mare will get you across without gettin' you too wet." He grinned at her. "When you get across, you can wrap up real good in your blanket." She made a face in response to his remark. "You better be careful to keep that blanket outta the water, though," he went on.

"I need to soak it in the river with some strong lye soap," she remarked. "When do you think we'll catch up with the wagons?"

"With us on horseback, I'm hopin' we'll catch 'em

tonight. And since they took your wagon, you won't have to sleep with your new blanket anymore."

"That's right," she said. "I guess I'd better keep an eye out, too, to make sure I don't see any of my things on the side of the road anywhere." She gave him a painful smile. "Well, let's go swimmin'."

He was pleased to find the river crossing as easy as he had told her it would be, although they did not get across completely free of issues. He encountered some reluctance from the two packhorses, causing Biscuit to have to pull them across over a good part of it. He ended up with wet pants above his knees again. Amy tried his suggestion to pull her feet up behind her. She managed to keep her feet dry, but ended up with her knees wet, too.

Once they were on the north side of the Snake, Amy could readily see the reason for crossing. It reminded her of the day they crossed over Big Hill, into the Bear River Valley, leaving the endless sagebrush prairie to find a valley lush with trees and flowers. Now, it was the same when they left the south side of the Snake and entered the lush Boise River Valley. It was easy traveling, as well, and the wagons should be making good time. Consequently, Clint maintained a steady pace and figured to push the horses a little farther than usual, if he was to catch the wagons by suppertime. More than likely it would be after supper but before the usual social hour.

As the afternoon wore on, Amy began to fret. She didn't voice her concerns to Clint, but she wondered who might be driving her wagon, and if they took it with the thought that it was now an abandoned wagon. Trying to decide who might be in a position to take her wagon, her thoughts lit on Fancy Wallace. Fancy drove her own wagon, but she could have Lemuel drive her wagon. But surely she knew that Clint had gone after her. Maybe she was counting on the Indians killing her or, at the least, losing Clint. The thought of it made her angry and determined. That was her wagon, and Fancy was dead wrong if she thought she was going to claim it. So lost in her determination, she suddenly realized that Clint had said something. "What?" she asked.

"I said, what are you thinkin' about?" Clint replied. "You got an expression on your face like somebody's kickin' your favorite hound dog."

Embarrassed to be caught with ill thoughts, she relaxed and smiled. "Sorry, my mind was somewhere else. What did you say to me?"

"I was just gonna tell you that it's five o'clock by my pocket watch, and if I remember correctly, there's a nice little creek a couple of miles farther up this road. If we're catchin' up like I hope, they might be camped there for the night." When he saw the look of excitement that statement immediately brought to her face, he wondered now if he shouldn't have made it. She was clearly going to be disappointed if the wagons were not there. "'Course, they could be movin' faster than I figured," he hedged his prediction. "But there ain't another good campin' spot for about six or seven miles past this one," he said, again in support of his knowledge of the trail. He was also counting on some time lost by the wagons when they had to rerig Amy's wagon and catch her horses.

They continued on in silence with Clint thinking he should have kept his mouth shut, instead of getting her hopes up, then having her disappointed if he was wrong and with Amy worrying about who she might have an issue with over her wagon. In a few minutes, they came to a point where the road turned sharply to avoid a wooded knoll. It was a familiar sight to Clint and he breathed a sigh of relief when they rounded the curve to find a circle of wagons in place. He turned to Amy and announced, "I believe we're in time for supper."

Pat Shephard was the first one in the camp to spot the two riders leading packhorses, entering the circle of wagons. He paused on his way to his wagon, a load of firewood in his arms, to see if he could identify them. He at once recognized them and shouted out as loud as he could yell, "They're back! Clint's back! And he's got Amy!" He yelled it over and over again until everyone came running from their wagons to see. Scofield, on his horse at the bottom of the circle, turned the Morgan gelding around so he could see them. He grinned and nudged his horse to lope toward them. It was only a matter of seconds before the four horses and their two riders were engulfed in a crowd of smiling faces. Amy was at once besieged by a forest of the women's outstretched hands, seeking to help her off her horse to console her. The men gathered around Clint, waiting for the story.

Scofield, still on his horse, pushed through until he was beside Clint. Still grinning, he asked simply, "Trouble?"

"Some," Clint answered and dismounted.

Amy seemed beside herself, overwhelmed by the reception she received. Every way she turned she was met with a smiling face. Even Fancy Wallace was there to greet her. "We've been worried sick about you," Marcy Zachary said. "But everything's all right now. You're back." She turned to look at Clint, then added, "Thanks to Clint Buchanan."

"Yes, I owe my life to Clint," Amy said. "I am so

grateful to you all for welcoming me back. I only wish Tim could be here to see how wonderful you people are."

"Well, I'll bet he would be, if he could walk," Fancy said, causing Amy's face to frown at such an insensitive remark, even for Fancy Wallace. She was about to tell her as much when she was interrupted by Sarah Braxton.

"He's liable to try, if you don't go over there pretty quick," she said. "He can probably hear what's goin' on out here."

Suddenly, everything went black in Amy's mind and her knees started to give way, and she would have collapsed if Clint had not caught her in time. Horrified, the crowd of women around her pulled back to give her room. Marcy's painful face asked for an explanation. "We thought Tim was dead," Clint told her, stunned almost as much as Amy. "I reckon that shocked her pretty hard. She's been grievin' herself sick over it ever since those Utes grabbed her at the crossin'. Where is he?"

Marcy pointed. "Yonder in his wagon. He's laid up in the back of it in pretty bad shape, but he ain't dead."

"You hear that, Amy?" Clint asked. "Tim's alive. You understand? Tim ain't dead." He wasn't sure he was getting through to her, but her eyes began to flicker, and finally she opened them.

"What happened?" she asked, confused. Clint looked at Marcy for help.

"You fainted, honey," Marcy said. She took Amy's hands in hers. "What you heard is the truth. Your husband did not die. I'm going to take you to see him right now. Can you walk, or do you need someone to carry you?"

Almost fully awake now, Amy looked to Clint, whom she had come to trust among all others. He nodded to confirm what Marcy said. "I can walk," Amy said to Marcy.

Clint was as confused as Amy. When the women all gathered around Amy to support her while they walked her to the wagon, Clint looked to Scofield for answers to his questions. "I saw Tim's body on that bank with two arrows in him," he said, "and that one damn Indian took his scalp."

"That's a fact," Scofield said. "I was right beside you and saw the same thing. But after you went after them Injuns, we went to pick up Tim's body and damned if he weren't still alive. He had two arrows in him, all right, but luck was with him, I reckon. The one in his chest mighta broke a bone, but it didn't get his heart. The other arrow was more in his side. Fancy Wallace did the doctorin'—got the arrows out of him and stopped the bleedin'."

"Fancy?" Clint exclaimed, surprised.

"Yeah, she done him up real good, bandaged him up and got him restin' now."

"But he got scalped," Clint protested. "I know I didn't imagine that."

"He got scalped, all right," Scofield maintained, "but that Injun didn't have much time to do a good job of it before Lonnie opened up on him with his rifle. So the Injun didn't get a very big scalp." He smiled again. "You'll see when you go to see him. Fancy fixed up some kinda poultice and made a patch on top of his head. You need to go see him pretty soon. I know he'll wanna thank you for goin' after Amy."

"Fancy, huh?" Clint was still thinking about that. "How come she done the doctorin'? I'da never thought she'd know much about takin' care of a wound." He shook his head, amazed, then commented, “And she knew how to doctor his head where they lifted his scalp?”

“Yeah, ain’t that somethin’?” Scofield replied. “She said she doctored a lot of gunshot wounds when she was runnin’ that saloon. And fixin’ Tim’s scalped head wasn’t much different than patchin’ up a skull that got laid bare with a whiskey bottle.”

“Who drove his wagon here?” Clint next wondered.

“Doc Meadows’ boy, Ben,” Scofield answered. “He didn’t have no trouble handlin’ those horses a-tall. ’Course, he’s fifteen years old, he oughta be able to handle a team of horses.”

“Reckon so,” Clint said, and looked at Spud, who had joined the welcoming committee by then. “You got any coffee left in your pot? I swear, I’m sufferin’ for some.”

“If I ain’t, I’ll make some,” Spud said. “Matter of fact, I’ve got some biscuits left. I made the usual number, even though you weren’t here for supper.”

“I reckon I oughta go see Tim first,” Clint said, “and I oughta take care of these horses.”

“Why don’t you go see Tim?” Scofield suggested. “I’ll take care of your horses and Spud can make us a fresh pot of coffee while we’re doin’ that. Then I wanna hear the whole story about you and them Ute raiders.”

All three agreed, so they split up to do the chores. Clint took the small sacks from the packhorses with him when he was ready to go to visit Tim. Everything in them had been taken from Tim’s wagon. The women who had escorted Amy to her wagon were gathered around the open tailgate that served as Tim Blake’s hospital bed. When Clint walked up, they all smiled at him, including Amy, who was holding a cup of coffee in one hand while the other one held Tim’s hand. He stared hard with raised eyebrows at the cup, then shook his head, causing her to laugh. "Who did she ask to see first?" he asked Tim. "You or the coffeepot?"

Tim chuckled gamely, although it appeared to cause him pain. He was bandaged around his chest with another around his waist. And the poultice Fancy had plastered on the top of his head was held in place with a ribbon tied under his chin. "Fancy said it oughta heal, but there likely won't be no hair growin' there again."

"I told him it'll probably just look like an extra-wide part in his hair," Amy said. "It'll make him look distinguished."

"It'll make me look different from everybody else. That's for damn sure," Tim said and extended his free hand toward Clint. "I wanna thank you for what you done, Clint. It looks like I was lucky enough to pull through this thing. But if you hadn't brought Amy back, I wouldn't have wanted to live." Clint grasped his hand and they shook. "I owe you, and I ain't gonna forget it," Tim said.

"I expect you'da done the same thing for me, if things had been turned around the other way," Clint said, modestly. "The main thing is we didn't lose anybody at that river crossin'." He turned to grin at Amy. "And that's what Mr. Scofield would tell ya. I'll leave you in the hands of all these capable women now, and I'll see you later." He left then to meet Scofield and Spud for some much-anticipated coffee and biscuits.

After the near-tragic event at the Three Island Crossing, and the rescue of Amy Blake, things returned to a more normal pace. The wagon train pushed on west along the Boise River Valley toward old Fort Boise and the crossing of the Snake River at that point. It would be their last crossing of the Snake. Spirits were generally high among the travelers due to the improved driving conditions with plenty of grass, water, and wood for fires. But there was also the feeling that they were getting closer to the completion of this long journey they had so blithely taken on, back on the first of April. As for Clayton Scofield, they were not as far along as he would have liked. The wagon train arrived in this valley after the first week in August, and they were still a week short of Fort Boise. He still had six hundred miles or so to go before reaching Oregon City. There was plenty of time left before worrying about the Blue Mountains—unless they were hit with one of the freak early snowstorms that had been known to blanket the slopes with snow. No sense worrying about it unless you see signs of it happening, he told himself. In the meantime, young Ben Meadows seemed downright excited about driving Tim Blake's wagon for him.

It was anyone's guess how long it would take Tim to recover to the point where he could drive his horses again. Amy was content to walk along beside the wagon where she could keep an eye on her husband. By the time the emigrants reached the Snake again at Fort Boise, at its confluence with the Owyhee River, however, Tim insisted he was fit enough to drive his horses. Ben was relieved of his driving job and sent back to his family with Tim and Amy's expressions of appreciation. Typically a wagon ford, the Snake was not in a receptive mood on the morning of the crossing, however, so the entire train elected to pay the native ferry operators to ferry their wagons across on their bullboats while the rest of the livestock swam across. It was not a total surprise to the emigrants because Scofield had advised them of the various possible tolls in the information packet he had given everyone before leaving Independence. It was, however, the last toll they anticipated before reaching the Columbia River, where the plan was to pay to drive their wagons on the Barlow Road instead of paying the enormous fee to ship their wagons down the Columbia by boat.

After crossing the Snake, the emigrants moved on, crossing the Malheur River, on to Farewell Bend, where they said good-bye to the Snake, as it turned sharply north. From that point, they traveled for five hard days up the Burnt River, through shoulder-tall sagebrush, heading for Flagstaff Hill and the valley beyond it.

"You what?" Scofield responded, not sure he had heard Cal correctly. "You wanna climb up on that hill and get married?"

"I told you Ruby and I want to make it legal, and you said you could marry us."

"That's true," Scofield replied. "I did say I'd try to say somethin' in my official capacity as wagon master. I told you, though, I don't know if that'll be any more official than just jumpin' over a broom. I'd be plum happy to do it, but whaddaya wanna climb up on that hill for? That ain't gonna make it any more legal." He shot a sideways glance at Clint, who was grinning like a dog eating yellow jackets. "Did you put that idea in his head?"

"I ain't got no say in this," Clint quickly declared.

Scofield took a quick look at the steep face of the hill now behind them. One of the earlier pioneers on this trail had named it Flagstaff Hill. It was a fairly tall hill, and he had no desire to climb up it with the belly-full of supper he was toting. "How 'bout you bring Ruby out to the social hour and I'll marry you right here where everybody else can see it. Then you and her can climb up on that hill and jump over a broom together."

"That ain't gonna do," Cal replied. "This is somethin' Ruby got in her mind. When she got that first little peek at the Blue Mountains, she said she'd bet you could really see 'em from the top of that hill. She said that's where we oughta exchange our vows, where we could get a clear view of where our future was waitin', on the other side of those mountains." He looked at Scofield and grinned while he shook his head. "There ain't no way I can tell her that kinda stuff ain't important."

"Hell, Uncle Clayton," Clint interjected, "you don't have to walk up that hill. We can jump on a couple of horses and ride up the hill."

"Yeah, Uncle Clayton," Cal said, mocking Clint. "We can ride up the hill." He stood there a few moments longer, grinning. "Whaddaya say? You wanna let the little lady have her weddin' up on the hill? It ain't a helluva lot she's askin'."

"Oh, hell, all right," Scofield gave in. "Is she ready now?"

"Yep," Cal answered. "I told her it'd take about ten minutes to talk you into it, and she said that was long enough for her to get ready."

"I'll go get the horses," Clint volunteered. "You need a saddle?" he asked Scofield, but Scofield said no, not just to ride up the hill.

And Cal said his horse was tied at his wagon. "Ruby will ride up with me."

"Let's get it done, then," Clint sang out. "Let's get ol'

Cal hogtied for the rest of his natural-born days." He left to fetch his and Scofield's horses. On his way back to the wagon, he led the horses by the small group of emigrants who were already gathered to enjoy the singing and dancing.

"Where you goin', Clint?" Emmett Braxton called out.

"Been invited to a weddin'," Clint answered.

Overhearing, Lonnie James declared, "Cal and Ruby, right?"

"That's a fact," Clint replied. "Scofield's gonna marry 'em up on top of the hill, right now in a few minutes."

"Hot damn!" Lonnie exclaimed. "I just made twenty dollars!" He looked over at John Zachary. "I told you they wouldn't be able to put it off much longer. And when Clint told us about Flagstaff Hill being the next trail marker, I knew this was a sure-fire bet. I'm goin' to the weddin'." He looked around for his wife. "Susie! You wanna go to Cal and Ruby's weddin'?"

That was all it took to generate an enthusiastic wedding crowd, for almost everybody wanted to attend the ceremony. Zachary had to remind Peter Gilbert and Buck Carrey that they were on guard duty that night, and somebody had to stay to watch the camp. In no time at all, a parade of people was marching up Flagstaff Hill. There was music, but only Doc Meadows with his fiddle. He delivered a lively version of *Here Comes the Bride,* and Scofield managed to sound very official while saying little more than confessing that he wasn't sure what to say. When he ran out of words, he pronounced them man and wife. Everybody cheered. Off to the west, they could see the clear outlines of the Blue Mountains, causing most of them to marvel over the fact that the mountains did appear to be blue. In discussing the ceremony afterward, there was general agreement, especially among the women, that Ruby seemed to be radiant. And they prayed that Cal would be the husband Ruby deserved. Beaming almost as proudly as Ruby, Marcy Zachary almost clucked her satisfaction for the transformation she could now see in the frightened and abused little girl who set out from Independence. She looked around and discovered Sarah Braxton waiting to catch her eye. Sarah grinned and nodded. "If we'da had a little advance notice, we mighta cooked up a wedding feast," she said.

"If we had a bottle, we could drink a toast to Mr. and Mrs. Nixon," Walt Moody said. When his suggestion was met with a deep frown from Ellie Moody, he realized he might have stuck his foot squarely in his mouth. He truly hoped he had not offended Ruby with a recollection of her first husband.

Ruby set him at ease with a big smile and said, "I might drink to that, myself, and I don't even drink."

"You best watch out, Cal, you're gonna be walkin' the straight and narrow from now on," Lonnie warned.

"Don't I know it," Cal came back. "I'm already watchin' my P's and Q's."

Chapter 23

The trail dropped down into Ladd Canyon and the Grande Ronde Valley after leaving Flagstaff Hill and a few easy days of travel were a relief after the rough days before. They followed the river west, with the view of the Blue Mountains always before them to remind them that there were some tests yet to come before they reached the Willamette Valley. For the present, however, the emigrants were inclined to enjoy the trek up the valley. It was anybody's guess, however, as to the probable cause of Lemuel Blue's sudden inspiration. The peaceful valley, the recent marriage of Cal and Ruby, the fact that everybody could now see an end to their journey in sight—any of these might have turned Lemuel's simple mind toward things he hadn't thought of before. But the spark that lit the fuse was provided by Skeeter Braxton one chilly evening by the Grande Ronde River.

"You better not let your mamas see you over here talkin' to me," a grinning Lemuel teased when the three young boys sneaked over to visit him under Fancy Wallace's wagon. It was a rare chance to talk to the mysterious hired man, since Fancy did not typically attend the social hour. When they had spotted her, sitting near the fire, talking to Johnny's mother, they decided to take advantage of it and go see if they could pay Lemuel a visit.

"They're all settin' over by the fire, watchin' the dancin' with the rest of the grownups," Johnny Zachary said.

"How come you don't never go watch the dancin'?" Skeeter asked, genuinely curious. "You're a grownup, ain't you? Won't they let you go?"

"I don't know," Lemuel said. "I just never thought about goin' over there with the rest of 'em. They all look at me kinda funny, anyway. I'd go if I took a notion. Can't nobody tell me I can't go. I go where I damn please."

"Maybe they're just scared of you because you killed Billy Wallace with a knife," Skeeter suggested.

"Yeah," Sammy James crowed, "like an Injun sneaks up on 'em and slits their throats." He pretended his finger was a knife and made a slashing gesture across his throat.

Lemuel looked at him and giggled nervously, seeming tense and fidgety, his hands moving involuntarily with Sammy's as he went through the motions, his teeth clamped shut so tightly until his neck seemed about to explode under the pressure.

Skeeter looked at Johnny and winked. It was obvious that Lemuel was getting cranked up. It was a game they played on the slow-witted man and it seemed like it took less and less to get him worked up to give them a reenactment of the killing of Billy Wallace. Each time, there seemed to be a little more detail than the last telling. "Tell us how you sneaked up on Billy Wallace again," Sammy said.

"I've done told you that three or four times," Lemuel replied, but he grinned with delight when he remembered the night. He drew his skinning knife and felt the edge on the blade with his thumb, as if that brought his mind back to the moment when he awoke and saw Billy reaching over the tailgate of the wagon. "I moved so quiet, an Injun couldn'ta heard me. Miss Fancy didn't hear me, either. She didn't have nothin' on but her nightgown and the way the moon was shinin', I could see she didn't have nothin' else on. He shouldn'ta been lookin' at his mama like that, so I reached under his neck and sliced his throat wide open." He demonstrated with an imaginary victim.

"Ugh!" Skeeter grunted. "Didn't she get mad at you for killin' her son?"

"Shoot, no," Lemuel replied. "She said I done her a big favor and told me to go hide his body. Said it'd be our secret, just mine and hers." He paused for a moment after he said that. "But now, you boys know the secret, too. So, you can't tell it to nobody, else I might have to come sneak up on you one night."

"You didn't go up on Flagstaff Hill to see Cal Nixon and Ruby Tyson get married, didja?" Skeeter asked. Lemuel just shook his head, so Skeeter continued, eager to see if he could get him started on something else. "Miss Fancy ain't got no husband. Why don't you and her get married? You're already doin' the husband's chores."

"Except drive the wagon," Sammy pointed out. "If you and her was married, maybe she'd let you drive the wagon."

"I could drive the wagon, if I wanted to," Lemuel declared.

"She let Cal Nixon drive the wagon down Big Hill, when she was afraid she couldn't hold it, slidin' down that slope," Johnny reminded him. "If you hadda been her husband, I'll bet she'da had you drive it down."

"She mighta been mad at you 'cause you ain't ever asked her to marry you," Skeeter commented.

Lemuel didn't respond right away. Instead, he thought about the idea. After a few moments, he did speak, but when he did, it was to warn them. "Yeah, and now you better get your little behinds away from here 'cause here comes Miss Fancy, back from the dancin'." They took his word for it and immediately scurried off behind the line of wagons.

"What is it, Lemuel?" She could tell that something was on his mind, for he was standing beside the wagon, waiting for her.

"I was wantin' to talk to you before you got in the wagon and closed up," Lemuel responded.

"What do you wanna talk about?"

Still not sure of himself, but determined to proceed, he cleared his throat and turned his head to spit. "I think when we start up in the mornin', I oughta drive the wagon."

His statement took her by surprise, so she paused to give him a good looking over. Seeing nothing but the usual simple expression on his face, she responded. "You think you oughta drive the wagon. Why do you think that? I always drive my wagon."

"'Cause the man oughta drive the horses," he answered.

"So, you think you wanna sit up there on the wagon

seat and drive the horses, and I should walk the rest of the way to Oregon City. Lemuel, who have you been talkin' to?"

"I ain't been talkin' to nobody," he insisted. "But look at all the other wagons. The man drives the wagon and the woman walks or rides sometimes."

Impatient over wasting her time with the simple thoughts rolling around in Lemuel's empty head, yet curious to find out where they came from, she tried to talk to him. "Lemuel, all those other wagons are carrying families, with a mother and a father, or a husband and wife. This is my wagon, and I hired you to do the jobs you do for me. We're not married." *God forbid,* she thought to herself.

"That's the other thing," he said. "I think we oughta get married, like Cal and Ruby did."

His statement was almost too much for her to believe, and she had to pause and step back to gather her senses. Her natural character would have blasted him with a tornado of swearing and insults to his very being for suggesting such a ridiculous mating. But to her credit, she remained calm, determined to make allowances for his profound stupidity. "Lemuel, that is not a good idea at all. Our relationship is strictly business. It wouldn't work, anyway, because I'm old enough to be your mother. It would be like marryin' your mother for you. Do you think that would be a good thing?"

"My mama's dead," Lemuel replied, while he scratched his head and thought about what Fancy said. After a long moment, he said, "You don't look all that bad for an old woman."

That signaled the end of her patience. "Well, it ain't gonna happen, so get those crazy thoughts outta your head. And I don't wanna hear no more about drivin' my horses or gettin' married. A husband is the last thing I need. You just do your job, and we'll get along just fine."

"You ain't mad at me, are you?" Lemuel asked.

"No, just don't let your brain go off half-cocked like that again. Crawl back on your bed under the wagon and don't be thinkin' any more of those crazy thoughts." She paused a second to watch him crawl back under the wagon. *Just like a damn dog,* she thought, *crawling back in his bed with his tail between his legs.* Then another thought struck her. *It might be the best thing for him and me, if I put him down as soon as we reach the Willamette Valley before he takes a notion to tell everybody out there about Billy.* She was planning to build a fine new saloon, and she couldn't afford to take a chance on Lemuel telling folks about her part in the death of her own son. With those thoughts coming to worry her some, she climbed up into the wagon and closed the canvas cover. She removed the .44 she always wore and got into her nightgown. Still thinking about the crazy conversation she had just had with Lemuel, she pulled the gun and holster close beside her.

The days that followed finally brought the wagons to start a climb up the east slope of the Blue Mountains, traveling over a rough and winding road, to a place called Emigrant Springs where they made camp among the tall trees. Scofield thought it best to call a halt where there was good water from the nearby springs and plenty of wood for their fires. It was a little earlier than the usual five o'clock stopping time, but he wanted his people to rest before moving on to Crawford's Hill. That was the name a rugged and often dangerous seven-mile pass had been given by the trappers. The pass would end at Emigrant Hill and a long winding descent into the Umatilla Valley. Scofield's concern was the weather. The mountain pass they faced was difficult and dangerous in fair weather, and to make matters worse, there were heavy clouds hovering close over the mountains on this night in late September. "I don't like the look of them clouds," Scofield confessed to Clint as they pulled the saddles off their horses. "They look like snow clouds. If this was October or November, I'd bet everything I had that it would snow before mornin'."

"I was thinkin' the same thing," Clint declared. "But it's too doggoned early in the year for snow, even in Oregon Territory. From the looks of that trail up to this point, they've had a pretty good spell of bad weather." The train had been delayed several times to remove fallen trees from the road in order to make it up to the spring. The even rougher part of the trail was yet to come before they reached Emigrant Hill. Steep and winding like a waiting snake, the narrow trail bed of rocks and shale could be a slippery passage for the iron rims on the wagon wheels—even if it was only a light dusting of snow. "Let's just hope we're wrong about that snow," Clint said.

"I ain't never been wrong about the weather," his uncle replied. "That's what scares me the most. There's plenty of wood for fires. I'd like it better if there was a little more grass." This was by far the first real forested country they had passed through since leaving Independence.

"I'll saddle Biscuit up again before it gets dark and take a little ride up that pass to see what kinda shape the road's in," Clint volunteered.

"That's a good idea," Scofield replied, seconds before he was going to request it.

"What's a good idea?" Cal Nixon asked, walking up behind them.

"Slippin' off from the missus for a little rest when you ain't been married no longer than you have," Scofield japed. "Ain't that right, Clint?"

"Don't ask me," Clint answered quickly. "I ain't never been faced with that problem."

"How is Mrs. Nixon these lazy fall days?" Scofield asked, still enjoying the teasing.

"She seems to be fairly happy, since she was able to hogtie the man so many ladies were out to get," Cal replied at once, ready to give as good as he got. After all three ante-upped the required chuckle, Cal asked a serious question. "We're stoppin' kinda early today, I notice. Is the road ahead any worse than what we've been ridin' on today?"

"For a fact," Scofield answered, "and there ain't no campin' spots as good as this one till we get clear of these mountains." He paused when he saw John Zachary and Emmett Braxton approaching them. "I was just tellin' Cal what we've got ahead of us in the mornin'," he said loud enough for them to hear. "We're gonna be climbin' up a pass that ain't nothin' but hard road all the way to the other side. There ain't no good places to stop and there won't be any water for about seven miles, unless there's some little run-off streams from the weather they've had a couple of days before this. I'm hopin' we'll get through the pass in half a day. It might take longer, depends again on the weather. At the end of the pass, we'll come out on the crest of a high hill. It's called Emigrant Hill, and you'll see the valley way down below you. And there's water and grass waiting for you, but you'll have a steep road down that hill that twists and turns like a snake. You don't watch yourself, your wagon's gonna wanna turn upside down on some of them curves." He studied their faces to make sure they were understanding the task that the pass and the hill presented. Then he said, "Other than that, it'll be like takin' candy from a baby." It was good for an uncertain chuckle.

His message seemed to convey the serious concern he intended, for his two captains expressed the need to talk to all the wagons they were responsible to. They would emphasize the necessity to make sure everything was tied down and ready to take on the pass. Both John and Emmett left at once to pass the word along before supper. Clint decided to go ahead and put Biscuit's saddle back on him and ride on up the trail while there was still daylight. He told Spud and Scofield that he would eat when he got back. "I won't be goin' very far up that trail," he said, "because I don't wanna be ridin' back down it after dark."

When he rode out, he caught a movement out of the corner of his eye, and he turned to see Ruby waving at him. He waved back. It pleased him to see her obviously happy. She had traveled an emotional road to this point every bit as rough as the trail the wagons now followed—maybe rougher. He was happy for Cal, too, but knowing Cal's background, he wondered if he was going to live up to his vows to Ruby. "Ain't nothin' we can do about that," he said to Biscuit and rode out of the camp.

As he anticipated, there was quite a bit of storm debris on the rocky road, most of it of little concern, pine cones and small limbs covered large areas of the narrow road, but the wagons should roll right over that. About a mile up the trail, he encountered the first obstacle that required attention. A small pine had been uprooted and now lay across the road. "You didn't know I was gonna put you to work, didja?" He stepped down from the saddle and gave Biscuit a pat on the neck. "You thought we were just goin' for a little evenin' ride." He took his rope from the saddle and tied one end of it around the roots of the tree. The other end he tied around Biscuit's withers and looped the end around his saddle horn. Then he took a look around to see where he could haul the tree to get it out of the way. He picked a deep gully beside the road and led the horse up into it far enough to get most of the pine clear of the road. He untied the rope and returned it to the saddle, then went back in the road to move the top branches of the tree out of the way by hand. Even then, there was just barely enough room for a wagon to pass. He had to wonder if this was going to be the routine every mile or so. If that were the case, he wasn't sure they'd get to Emigrant Hill in half a day, as Scofield hoped. As he had told Scofield, he didn't go but about half a mile farther before deciding to turn back. The sun was already settling down, and once it dropped below the mountains it would be like The Man Upstairs blowing out the candle that lit the road he was riding. And he didn't fancy Biscuit tiptoeing down the trail he had just ridden up. When he returned to the camp, he told Scofield and Spud that it appeared the trail was going to be as rough as they expected.

Scofield shrugged and commented, "I don't know why we'd expect it to be any better than it was the last time we was here. I don't reckon the Shoshones had a crew of road builders up here to improve it for the wagon trains."

* * *

The next morning, while Biscuit was grazing with the other horses, Clint decided to go ahead and saddle him and take him to water. Then he rode back to the wagon where he found Scofield and Spud staring up at the low-hanging clouds. "Don't look much different from yesterday, does it?" Scofield asked. When Clint gave nothing more than a shrug in reply, his uncle asked, "You fixin' to leave? Ain't you gonna eat any breakfast?"

"I thought it wouldn't hurt if I took a look up that trail a little farther than I got last night," Clint answered. "I'd appreciate it, if you'd save me a couple of biscuits with a slice of bacon in each one," he said to Spud. To Scofield, he called out, "I'll see you up the road a few miles." He turned the Palouse gelding toward the trail that led through the pass and started out again. He soon caught up to the point where he had turned around the night before, and as he passed on by, the trail steepened and took the first of a series of snake-like curves. It appeared that the heavy clouds were resting on the tops of the tall trees on each side of the trail. He couldn't help thinking, *If something punches a hole in those clouds, it might wash the whole wagon train down the mountain.*

He continued on until he figured he was about halfway through the pass before he came to another blockage in the trail. He became immediately alert because this roadblock would not be as simple to move as the one he had pulled off the road last night. This one had the look of human involvement, for it was not one, but two trees, both of them bigger than the small tree Biscuit had dragged in the gully. He looked around him quickly, expecting to see an Indian war party emerge from the forested slopes on either side of the trail. But all was quiet. And he told himself, *the wind in a storm might have done this, laid two trees across each other, but it would be a sure-enough miracle of nature*. He pulled his rifle from the saddle sling and dismounted, thinking he made too tempting a target sitting on his horse. Leaving Biscuit where he was, he climbed up into the trees above the trail, ready to fire at the first sign of an Indian. There was no sign of anyone as he worked his way along the slope, so he climbed a little higher until he could see the top of the mountain above him. He spotted what appeared to be an ideal spot for snipers. A naturally formed swale about three-quarters of the way to the top ran parallel to the road below. If there was going to be an ambush, that was the spot, but there was no sign of an ambush waiting for the wagon train. So, he made his way back down to the road and started up the slope on the other side. He was met with the same results as before, but there was no swale. There was no sign of an ambush on that side either. It made no sense to him. The roadblock was put there for a reason. *Unless it wasn't,* he thought. It might have been the work of mother nature. But the trees were pulled over and uprooted, one fell to the south, the other fell to the north. It would have had to have been a cyclone or a tornado to fell two trees in opposite directions. "Lord, I wish you wouldn't confuse me with things like this," he complained directly to God, as he often did. *I'll go back and tell Scofield what I've found and let him decide what he wants to do,* he thought.

At the top of the slope on the north side of the pass, Nez Perce war chief, Faces the Wind, lay still beside a laurel bush. He watched the white scout as he looked the roadblock over. When Clint had started up the slope,

Faces the Wind had told his warriors to withdraw from the summit of the hill and drop back down the slope, leaving him alone to watch the white man. If the scout discovered their presence, he would tell the wagons not to come. As tempting as it was to shoot the scout, that would be foolish, for his people needed the weapons and supplies the wagons carried. He was relieved when the scout decided there was no one on the hill and turned around. He couldn't help thinking the scout must be of better-than-average intelligence, judging by the Palouse horse he rode—a horse bred by his people, the Nez Perce, near the Palouse River. *I think it is only right that the horse should come home to its people,* he thought. He rose to his feet, turned around, and made the sound of a hawk. In a few seconds, the warriors emerged from the trees on the back of the slope.

"The scout was suspicious," Faces the Wind said when the other warriors climbed back over the crest of the hill. "It was good you went back with the horses. He would have seen you at the top of the hill."

Chapter 24

When Clint returned to the camp, the people were preparing to leave, breakfast was finished, and teams were being hitched up to the wagons. He rode straight to Scofield, who was already in the saddle and was riding his Morgan gelding around the circle of wagons, urging everyone to get ready to roll. "Whatchu doin' back here?" Scofield asked when Clint rode up to him. He had expected to catch up to him on the trail ahead somewhere.

"I need to tell you what I found up there in the pass," Clint said. He told him then what he had found in the trail and what it appeared to be to him. "But I went up both sides of that road, high enough to see the top and I didn't see a livin' soul, nor a footprint."

"And you don't think it coulda been done in a storm?" Scofield asked.

"Well, I don't say that it couldn'ta been, but it just looked too much to me like some raidin' party set 'em up to hem up a wagon train. Those two trees were more than Biscuit and me could move. It'll take a couple of men and a crosscut saw before we can throw that stuff out of the way. It just seems to me to be a mighty odd coincidence for a storm to have uprooted two trees and happened to drop 'em right in the middle of the trail. So, I thought I'd try to catch you before you had all the wagons drivin' up that trail 'cause there ain't no room to turn around."

Scofield hesitated a moment while he gave it some thought. To go around was not an easy choice. It might take a week, if they could find a way. "Seems like, if it was an ambush, they woulda been settin' up on the sides of that slope waiting for us to show up," he finally offered. "Or it coulda been set up for somebody else and already over with."

"There wasn't any sign of it," Clint insisted.

Scofield clearly did not want to try to find another way. "Hell, I didn't drive all the way up here to these springs, just to turn around and go back. We'll drive these wagons right on up that trail till we get to that roadblock. I'll tell Lonnie and Ron to bring a saw and we'll clear those trees outta the way. I'll tell every wagon to have their guns loaded and ready, in case that feelin' of yours is right. That's gonna have to be a good-sized war party to take on twenty-seven wagons. Hell, you and I can give any raidin' party all the lead they can handle."

"If you say so," Clint responded.

"Good," Scofield said, taking another look up at the clouds. "We need to get through that pass and down into the valley before that cuts loose. You can ride around the other side of the circle and tell 'em to have their guns ready and the women and children in the wagons till we get past that block." Clint wheeled his horse toward the other side of the circled wagons to spread the word. By the time the message was delivered to everyone, there were some mighty sober and tense emigrants in the wagons that trailed out of the circle and struck the road through the pass. Clint felt it appropriate that the two best targets, in the event it was an ambush, were himself and his uncle, who would be leading the wagons into the trap.

They rode up the pass with their rifles out and ready to fire. Behind them, they could hear the wagons rumbling over the rough rocky roadbed and the drivers encouraging their horses. Both Clint and Scofield constantly searched the slopes beside the trail, both hoping Clint's intuition was false. Scofield looked over at Clint and nodded when they passed the small tree he had removed from the road.

Approximately three miles farther up the trail, Faces the Wind rose to his feet when he saw Yellow Horse approaching on the wagon road. "They are coming," Yellow Horse called out when he dismounted and led his pony up the slope to the low swale three-quarters of the way to the top of the hill. When he reached the swale, he told Faces the Wind that the wagon train was making its way slowly along the trail but should reach the ambush before very long. Hearing his report, the warriors closest to Faces the Wind passed it along to the others spread out along the swale, and the news was met with low grunts and nods of excitement for the battle to follow. Although there had been treaties with the white men and their government, there were still many Nez Perce who didn't recognize the treaties as valid. Faces the Wind and his village were among those who resented the encroachment of the white man on ground that had been Nez Perce territory for many years. There would be horses as well as guns, ammunition, clothes, blankets, kitchen utensils, pots and pans, and much more in the wagons. And there would be scalps to be taken and maybe women or children to capture. Yellow Horse led his pony up over the top of the hill and down to the ravine where the other horses were tied. Then he came back over the hill and found a place to shoot from in the swale. Their ambush ready, all that remained to do was wait for the white men to draw their slow-moving targets before them.

Still a couple of miles short of the trap, a worrisome thought kept pestering Clint as he and Scofield rode ahead of the wagons. Finally, it succeeded in getting the best of him and he could not rid his mind of it. "Damn it, Uncle Clayton," he blurted, "I ain't ever seen a more perfect spot for an ambush. It might as well have a big sign nailed on one of those trees, 'Warnin', this is an ambush.' I've got a feelin' about this thing."

"I figured you must," Scofield replied. "But if we can get to work clearin' those two trees out of the way, maybe we won't be stopped but a few minutes. If your feelin' is right, we still oughta be able to throw more lead at the Indians than they can fire at us."

"Well, how 'bout if we assume I'm right," Clint persisted. "It wouldn't hurt nothin' if I'm wrong, but it might make a helluva difference if I'm right."

"Whaddaya got in mind?" Scofield asked. Thinking of past experiences with Clint's "feelings," he thought it best to hear what Clint had to say. Clint explained then what he would like to do. Scofield listened and could really find no reason to try to talk him out of it. He said, "As long as you make sure she's all right with it. She might not like the idea a-tall."

Clint reined Biscuit to a halt right away and remained there as Scofield and the wagons rolled on past him. He waited there until Cal and Ruby's wagon caught up to him, then he rode Biscuit in pace alongside the wagon. "What's up, Clint?" Cal asked.

"I told you about the roadblock up ahead before we started," Clint said. "If it's all right with you, I'll tie my horse onto your wagon. I'm gonna go the rest of the way to that roadblock on foot and I'll pick him up on the other side of it."

Cal took a questioning look at Ruby on the seat beside him before asking, "Why are you gonna do that, Clint?"

"I've just got a feelin' that I need to work around the back of that hill over the roadblock to make sure there ain't a reception party waitin' in a little swale above the trail," Clint said. "I didn't see any sign of one when I was on that slope earlier, but that don't mean there ain't one now."

"That sure makes sense to me," Cal said at once. "I wasn't too crazy about the idea of all our wagons settin' dead still on this narrow little rut while we were tryin' to saw our way past that trap in the first place. But you don't know how many you might find up there, if there is an ambush. You're gonna need some help."

"That's what I figured," Clint replied. "That's why I promised Scofield I would ask."

"Hell, you know you don't have to ask," Cal responded. "I doubt if there's a better shot than I am on this train, and I know there ain't nobody faster."

"I ain't askin' you," Clint said. "I'm askin' her." When

both Ruby and Cal looked puzzled over that, he explained. "Sure, I was hopin' you could help me, 'cause we don't know how many there might be waitin' to ambush this train. But you two bein' newlyweds and all, Ruby might not want you takin' any chances with me. So, I'm askin' her." He looked directly at Ruby then. "You rather he didn't take any chances with me and stay here to protect you?"

When Cal started to speak again, Ruby quickly reached over and placed a finger on his lips to quiet him. Looking back at Clint, she asked, "Will you take care of him?"

"I will," he answered. "I'll do everything in my power to bring him back to you."

"All right, he can go and help you," Ruby said. "You two be careful and look after each other."

"Well, in all my born . . . If that ain't the . . ." Cal sputtered, totally astonished.

"Do you know how far back Doc's wagon is?" Clint asked. "I'll see if he'll let Ben drive your mules again."

Again, before Cal could answer, Ruby reached for the reins. "I can drive these poky ol' mules. You two be careful, I can't afford to lose either one of you."

"You heard the little woman," Cal said, as he climbed over the seat and picked up his rifle and gun belt, while talking to Ruby as he hurried along. "Here's the shotgun and shells right beside the seat if you need 'em. If any shootin' starts, get down behind the seat to drive the mules." He gave her a quick kiss, then went out the back of the wagon.

As soon as Cal hit the ground, Clint stepped down from the saddle, and while keeping pace with the moving wagon, tied Biscuit's reins to the tailgate. Then he pulled his Henry rifle from the saddle sling before he stepped aside and let the wagon roll on. "Come on," he said to Cal and started out on a line toward the back of a high hill, explaining to Cal while he hurried along. "The road takes a wide curve around this hill we're headin' for. We oughta be able to get to the back of the one next to it before the wagons get to that roadblock."

Climbing the steep slope at a half-trot, they made their way up through heavily forested terrain of the first hill, working steadily toward the summit. Once they rounded the first hill, they came to a smaller one, and Clint stopped short when he discovered the Indian horses tied in the trees of a ravine below the summit of the smaller hill. He held up his hand to stop Cal behind him. "This is the hill," he said softly. "There are their horses." They approached much more cautiously then, looking for someone left to watch the horses. It didn't take long to determine that no one was left to guard them. He quickly gave Cal a picture of what they would be facing. "Over the top of that hill, about a quarter of the way down, there's a shallow swale, and right now, I'm guessin' there's"—he paused to count the horses—"about fifteen warriors with real bad intentions layin' in that swale." *I hope Uncle Clayton did what I told him to,* he thought. He had cautioned Scofield to dismount before he rode up to those two trees lying across the road, and to take cover behind the horses or the wagon.

"Why don't we untie those horses before we go up the hill," Cal suggested. "Give these boys something else to think about."

"Sounds like a good idea to me," Clint said. So, they went into the ravine and untied all the horses before turning their attention to the riders. As a result, they were a little later arriving at the top of the hill than they would have liked, for they heard the first rifle shots a few moments before reaching the summit. Hurrying now, they climbed up to see all fifteen warriors firing down at the wagons, totally unaware of the chain lightning about to be unleashed upon them from behind. Both men, firing repeating rifles, cut down on the bushwhackers unmercifully. The warriors didn't know where the deadly fire was coming from right away, and some of them scrambled back out of the swale, making themselves even easier targets. The first ones lucky enough to scramble out and dive over the crest of the hill, saw their horses scattering and cried out the alarm.

Faces the Wind suddenly realized where the killing fire was coming from, rolled out over the front of the swale and came up on one knee to level his rifle at Cal, who was firing down toward the end of the swale. Acting without having to think, Clint knocked the war chief down before he could pull the trigger. The shot, right behind him, caused Cal to spin around, his six-shooter in hand to see Clint cranking another cartridge into the chamber. "I promised Ruby," Clint said. Before Cal could think of a come-back, they both flinched when a rifle ball snapped off a pine limb between them. They both realized then that the shot came from the wagon train below and they became aware of more rifle balls hitting the trees.

Clint looked down the back of the hill behind them to see the survivors of their attack running after their horses. "I counted six!" he yelled to Cal. "How many did you count?"

"I counted six, too," Cal confirmed.

Clint turned back toward the road and yelled, "Hold your fire! It's all over!" He and Cal both had to repeat the order a couple more times before the shooting stopped. When it finally did, Clint turned again to keep an eye on the surviving warriors as they chased their horses. They were sometimes easy targets, but he chose not to kill any more. It seemed wrong to kill so many in what amounted to a massacre with their element of surprise and their repeating rifles. He had to remind himself that the nine dead warriors had been lying in wait to slaughter the innocent people in the wagon train. "What are you lookin' so serious about?" The question from Cal startled him, and he had to bring his thoughts back to the business at hand.

He walked over beyond the swale to look at Faces the Wind's body. "Nez Perce," he said, surprised. "They're not Bannock or Shoshone."

"I thought the government had a treaty with the Nez Perce," Cal said.

"I reckon nobody told these fellows," Clint replied. He turned then when he heard Scofield and several others coming up the slope to view the aftermath.

"I reckon I'm just always gonna have to give in to them damn feelin's of yours," Scofield remarked. "How many were there?" When Clint said there were fifteen total, Scofield counted the dead. "You killed nine of 'em." He rolled one of the bodies over. "Nez Perce," he said, surprised.

"That's what Clint said," Cal felt the need to comment.

"I expect he might be the one they call Faces the Wind," Scofield said. "They were talkin' about him at The Dalles last year." He turned to look back down the slope at the men working to clear the road of the two trees. "Ought not take 'em long to move that outta the way. Probably be a good idea if you stay up here till we're ready to roll, so you can keep an eye on those Injuns," he said to Clint. "I doubt they'll be back for more of what you and Cal was servin'." He turned toward Buck Carrey and Walt Moody, who had climbed up to the swale with him. "I expect it'd be a good idea for us to collect their rifles and ammunition. No sense in leaving 'em here for some other Injuns to shoot at us."

It took Lonnie James and Ron Settle more than an hour to saw the two trees forming the roadblock into sections that could be dragged up the slopes on either side of the road. Then with no more sign of the crippled Nez Perce bushwhacking party, the wagons were set to continue through the pass, known as Crawford's Hill. At the end of the pass, they reached the western slopes of the Blue Mountains at what was known to Scofield and Clint as Emigrant Hill, which presented more concerns for the emigrants. Climbing for several days to get to this point, now the challenge facing them was the descent down the steep face of the hill to reach the valley below. To add to the risk, the clouds Scofield had been watching since the day before decided to release a steady, cold rain upon them. Scofield warned his people that they were going to have to be on their toes and stay alert. The road leading down into the Umatilla Valley was steep with many a winding curve as it descended two thousand feet to reach the valley floor. "And friends," he warned, "on some of them curves, your wagon is gonna wanna flip over on its side. So, I recommend the women and young'uns stay clear of the wagons and walk down."

The winding roads down Emigrant Hill were as dangerous as Scofield warned, with the rain making the sharp turns in the road slick as well. However, by heeding his advice to be cautious, no wagons or animals were damaged, even though all wagons experienced some sliding on the now-slippery roads. Only one wagon failed to keep all four wheels down on the first really sharp curve after leaving the top of the hill. Fancy Wallace failed to give the turn the proper respect and ended up with her wagon sitting against the side of the road, perched on two wheels. She was fortunate that the bank was high on that side of the road and consequently held the wagon before it could turn on its side. Fancy was properly mortified, having turned down an offer from one of the men to drive her wagon down for her. She refused other offers to drive her wagon down after it was righted by the men, determined to prove her capability. She was aware of Lemuel's silent gloating, although she pretended not to notice him. Then she drove her wagon to the bottom of the hill with no more mishaps.

When the wagons behind Fancy's were stopped while they waited for hers to be up-righted, Clint reined his horse to a stop beside Cal and Ruby. "Don't you wish you were still drivin'?" he asked Ruby. "You could show Fancy she ain't the only woman who can drive a team of horses."

"No, thanks," she replied. "I'm just as happy walking down this hill. And by the way, I never got the chance to thank you for takin' care of Cal for me."

"Why, I told you, I'd bring him back." Clint laughed. "Tell you the truth, we were pretty much takin' care of each other. Weren't we, Cal?"

"I reckon so," Cal said, "especially that one time when that buck rolled out of the front of that swale and was gettin' ready to cut down on me." He chuckled when he thought about it now. "This big ol' Injun had his rifle on me, gettin' ready to shoot me in the back. I didn't even know he was there till Clint blew a hole in him. I reckon I musta jumped when I heard the shot right behind me. I looked at Clint and he just said, 'I promised Ruby.'" He chuckled again and shook his head. "Uh-oh," he said then, "we're fixin' to move. You'd best get down now, honey, in case I ain't as good a driver as Fancy." They could see Sarah Braxton getting off the wagon in front of them, a large sheet of canvas over her head against the rain. "You need something like that to put over your head," Cal said. "You shoulda got something outta that trunk while we were waiting for the wagons to start moving again."

"I'll just stay in the wagon," Ruby said.

"No," Cal replied. "Scofield's right about that. If I turn this wagon over, you could get hurt bad. Ride down the hill with Clint, then find you a tree to get under. Okay, Clint?"

"Sure, I'll give you a ride. Hop on behind me." He pulled Biscuit up close beside the wagon seat and Ruby hopped over behind him. "We'll see you down at the bottom," Clint said to Cal and pulled away from the wagon. "Hold on, Ruby, and don't tell Lou Ann Braxton about this." He rode a little way from the road and pulled Biscuit to a stop. "Here, let me fix you a rain shelter." He unbuttoned his jacket and opened it. "Hold my coat tail over your head."

She lifted the tail of his jacket and crawled under. With her arms around him, she pulled herself up tightly against his back in an effort to give him some benefit from the jacket as well. With her cheek pressed tightly between his shoulder blades, she held herself snug against his back. It suddenly struck her that she was as content as she had ever been in her entire life. The road to this small taste of Eden had been a rough and painful one, but she almost felt as if she owed Ralph Tyson her heartfelt thanks for his part in bringing her to meet two young men who genuinely wanted to make her happy. *The good Lord knows I love both of them, one as my husband and the other like a brother.*

Clint dropped Ruby off under a large tree where many of the women and children had gathered to await the circling of the wagons. She was immediately summoned by Marcy Zachary who was sheltering some of the children under a large canvas flap. "Come in here," Marcy called to Ruby. "You're not much bigger than some of these young'uns." Blushing, Ruby eagerly accepted the invitation.

Clint headed for Scofield's wagon, which Spud had parked in position for the circle to be formed over near a small creek. When Clint got to the wagon, Spud was trying to coax a fire to burn while cursing the rain at the same time. "Damn rain," he swore. "There ain't no dry wood anywhere along this creek. I've damn-nigh used every bit of the dry tinder I had in my bag. And it'll start up, but it won't catch up enough to burn this wet kindlin'."

Clint dismounted, then pulled his saddle off Biscuit and set the big Palouse gelding free to join the other horses at the creek. After he stowed his saddle under the wagon, he said, "Hand me the ax and I'll find you some tinder. There's a dead pine over yonder that's been broke off about eight or ten feet high. I'll see if there ain't some dry tinder in it."

Spud handed the ax to him and Clint walked over to

the dead tree. It looked to be just what he needed. It had been rotting for quite some time, and most of the bark had dropped off and was lying on the ground thoroughly soaked. Clint went to work with the ax and chopped down the standing ten-foot section of the trunk. As he anticipated, the trunk and stump were rotted clear through. But the rain hadn't penetrated through to the center portion, leaving a generous supply of dry, rotten tinder, that should get Spud's fire going. It was easily broken up in his hands, and Spud blended it in with his dry grass and wood chips, and pretty soon he had a fire going that could burn the wet firewood. Then Clint went back to work with the ax on the length of trunk he had chopped down. He split it open and cleaned out the dry part and used it to refill Spud's tinder bag. He would be needing it when they made camp for the night. What with the fight with the Nez Perce, the hard drive through the pass, then the hazardous descent down Emigrant Hill, Clint had to remind himself that this stop was for the nooning, and not for the night. There was still half a day's travel to make today.

Chapter 25

In the days that followed, there seemed to be a new sense of excitement among the folks in the wagons. Scofield said he had seen it before after passing the Blue Mountains. He believed the travelers were confident at this stage in the trek to the point where they truly believed they were going to make it. Clint couldn't say if that was the reason or not, but he agreed with his uncle that there seemed to be a general upbeat in the morale of the company. However, he allowed that it could be solely because the weather seemed to have improved. At least the rain had stopped. Before long, however, they wished for the rain's return, for they found the Columbia Plateau to be a land dry and dusty. Water was scarce, there was no wood for fires, and no grass for their animals. In fact, there seemed to be no sign of life at all in the vast tableland, with the exception of an occasional juniper tree as they rode along. They crossed the Umatilla River with a minimum of trouble and drove on to an easy river crossing of the John Day River. After crossing the John Day, the trail turned in a more northwest direction, and after another day and a half's drive, the emigrants found themselves looking down at their first sighting of the Columbia River from the top of a hill. Clint and Scofield sat on their horses, watching the wagons coming up to them.

The first wagon was Scofield's, as usual, and he called out to Spud. "Lead 'em on down to the river, Spud. We'll make camp there by the river and everybody can get set up for supper." The trail would continue along beside the river from here till they reached the Deschutes River crossing. Spud followed the trail down off the high tableland, as the other wagons came along behind him. In short order, the people walking caught up to Scofield and Clint and stopped to gaze down at what so many of them anticipated as a view of the promised land. Weary and footsore and feeling half-starved, their disappointment upon seeing the dry, dusty landscape around the Columbia almost oozed from their pores.

One of those who stopped to stare at it, Marcy Zachary, was inspired to confess. "I do declare, there were times on this journey when I doubted I'd ever lay eyes on the Columbia River."

Walking with her, Sarah Braxton remarked, "Shoot, I doubted it when we crossed the Kansas River. I was ready to turn around then." They both laughed. "We weren't sure you knew the way to Oregon City," she japed to Scofield, doing her best not to reflect her disappointment.

"I didn't," Scofield joked in return. "But Clint said

he'd been there before and all you had to do was follow the road signs. How am I doin'?"

"We ain't there yet," Clint felt it his responsibility to remind them. "So don't let this place disappoint you. When we get to the Willamette Valley, then you'll wanna celebrate."

"Clint's right," Scofield said. "We'll be followin' along beside the river tomorrow, but we've got one more difficult crossin' before we get to The Dalles, and that's the Deschutes River. We'll be makin' that crossin' tomorrow."

When all twenty-seven wagons were down to the river level, Scofield led them no farther than two miles before he signaled a stop for the noon meal. While the horses were resting, he called everyone together to tell them what lay ahead for them. "A couple of miles from here, we're gonna strike the Deschutes River. The crossin's at the mouth of the river where it joins the Columbia, and it's about a hundred and fifty yards across. It's a pretty tricky crossin', especially when the water's high. There are three different ways to try to cross the river. You can float the wagons across and swim the horses. If we cross that way, you're gonna have to get rid of everything you don't have to have to live, unless you wanna take a chance on losin' the whole load. Or you can pay the ferryboat man ten dollars a wagon, plus twenty-five cents apiece for your family."

He was interrupted then by Doc Meadows. "Dad-blame-it, Scofield, I don't remember seein' anything in that letter you sent me about any ferryboat toll for crossin' that river. What was the name of it?"

"The Deschutes," Scofield answered. "I never said

nothin' about payin' a toll to cross this river 'cause it ain't the way I plan to cross. And since I'm plannin' on crossin' another way, I'll pay for it. But if you don't wanna take a chance with me, I wanted you to know you had other options—but you'll have to pay, if you don't wanna cross with the rest of us."

"Why didn't you say something about this damn river before?" Fancy Wallace asked. "According to my letter, there ought not be but one more toll we agreed to pay and that's a toll road to go around Mount Hood."

"And there ain't gonna be another one after the Barlow Road toll," Scofield responded. "I didn't say anything about the Deschutes River because I wanted to wait to see if the river was high. And lookin' at the Columbia, I can see that it ain't, so we'll be drivin' 'em across."

"How were you plannin' to get us across if the river was high?" Fancy asked.

"Well, I'da had to float the wagons across and swim the horses," Scofield replied. "And you'd be leavin' a lot of stuff on the bank, after you've hauled it all the way across the country. Now, I'll say it again, if you hadn't wanted to do that, you'da been free to pay for the ferry."

"I see what you mean," Fancy said. "I reckon I'll be goin' with you." There was a general murmur of agreement from the rest, since they had all learned to trust Scofield over the past months.

"Another thing I wanna tell you," Scofield continued. "When we get near that river, you're gonna see more Indians than you've seen anywhere since we left Salmon Falls. Don't shoot at 'em. They're just like the Shoshone and Bannock we bought all the salmon from, back on the Snake. They're friendly with the whites and they'll help us get across the river. They'll trade fish for anything you got to trade, too. One in particular, I'll be lookin' for. His name's Jim Two Hooks. He'll lead our wagons across. That river is wide, with an island in the middle of it. The current is swift and there's a lot of big rocks on the bottom, and the crossin' is crooked. I've used Jim before. He knows exactly how that crossin' runs, so I'll send Clint on ahead to find him."

No one had any questions after Scofield's briefing, so he told them to enjoy the rest of the nooning. There was some enthusiasm generated already for the prospect of more salmon. Cal gave Ruby's hand a little squeeze. When she looked at him and smiled, he winked and said, "Maybe I shoulda hung onto some of Ralph's things."

Clint guided Biscuit along a narrow trail to an Indian village close to the Columbia where the river flowed over towering waterfalls, named Celilo Falls. It was a large village and he attracted the gaze of many of the inhabitants as he rode past, leading a paint gelding on a lead rope. When he came to a shack with a small corral behind it, he pulled up before the front door. Before he stepped down, the door opened and a squat man with long gray hair walked out to meet him. "Buchanan," he said in greeting.

"Jim," Clint returned.

Jim Two Hooks walked out as Clint stepped down from the saddle. Clint offered his hand and they shook. "We got word that a wagon train was coming this way. Scofield is with you?"

"Yes, my uncle is bringing another wagon train. He sent me to ask for your help again when we cross the river," Clint said.

Jim nodded, his eyes were on the paint pony, however. He walked around the horse, looking it over. When he got back to Clint, he commented, "That is a fine-looking paint pony."

"Scofield wants to know if you will lead our wagons across the river in exchange for the gift of this pony." Jim didn't respond right away, but Clint detected a glint in his eye that told him that was what the Indian had hoped.

"How many wagons do you have this time?" Jim asked. Clint told him there were twenty-seven. Jim was definitely interested then. For a horse, especially one in as good a shape as this one appeared to be, he thought there might be one hundred or more. "Yes, I will help you. When will you be ready to cross?"

"The wagons should reach the river in about two hours."

"I'll wait for you there," Jim said and took the lead rope from Clint.

Jim Two Hooks was waiting on the bank of the river when Clint and Scofield led the wagons up to the crossing. He and Scofield exchanged greetings, and Jim expressed his appreciation for the generous gift Scofield gave him to guide them. "You're wet," Scofield pointed to Jim's trousers. "Have you been across already?"

"Yes, I wanted to see how deep the water is, and I want to make sure no big rocks moved on crossing." He glanced back at the wagons behind them. "You make good crossing. I show you the way. Water come up to horse's belly, no higher. I show." He jumped on his horse, an older bay horse, and entered the water. Clint and Scofield watched him until he climbed out of the water on the opposite side. Then he turned around and came back. "Okay?" he asked.

"Okay," Scofield answered and waved Spud forward. When Cal came next behind Spud, Scofield yelled, "Stay right behind him, Cal. You go where he goes. When you get across, drive on up to the top of that bluff. That's where we'll camp."

"I gotcha," Cal yelled back and drove his mules into the water. And so, the crossing began, slowly but surely, relying on Jim Two Hooks' knowledge of the actual path of the crossing on the river bottom. The wagons waiting their turn, meanwhile, were swarmed with Indians with fish to trade. By the time the last wagon crossed over, and the rest of the free horses swam across with the help of some of the Indian boys, most of the afternoon was gone. They set up their camp there on the western bluff of the Deschutes. The horses too weary to continue already, had to strain to pull the wagons up the steep climb to the top of the bluff. Jim Two Hooks thanked Scofield again for the gift of the paint pony, and Scofield gave him two dollars to buy some tobacco. He went away happy with the two dollars and anxious to work with the paint pony that had once belonged to a young Sioux hunter on the Sweetwater River.

There had not been a real social hour ever since the wagon train had left Emigrant Hill. The journey across the Umatilla Valley had sapped the interest for most of the travelers. But tired as everybody was, there was a general mood of relief after successfully crossing the Deschutes with everything intact. So that night, the musicians were back on key and some felt like singing. After all, they had reached the end of the Oregon Trail—not officially, for the true end was about ten or twelve miles away at a little settlement called The Dalles. They were still many days away from their destination, Oregon City.

But they had driven to the end of the original road. Before 1846, travelers on the road had no choice when they reached The Dalles. Because of the high mountains and sheer cliffs along the river, the only way to continue on to Oregon City was to break the wagons down and go down the turbulent Columbia by boat. A dangerous trip with many tragedies, it was also expensive. But in 1845, Sam Barlow, leader of a wagon train, arrived in The Dalles to find it crowded with people stranded there, waiting to have their wagons floated down the river by barge. He determined to find a way around Mount Hood, which led to the building of the Barlow Road. Scofield knew Sam Barlow and trusted he knew what he was doing. For that reason, Scofield had been one of the first to travel the rugged road, even though it was at a cost of five dollars a wagon toll. "It was a sight cheaper than payin' to ship 'em down the river," he maintained.

"Amen to that," John Zachary declared. "We need to have something left to buy seed with."

"At least I didn't have to throw that plow in the back of my wagon in the river back yonder," Emmett Braxton stated. "Wouldn't that'a been somethin', after hauling it all the way from Missouri?"

"Where's the little woman?" Fancy asked when Cal walked up to join her where she sat, listening to the music.

"She's doin' something back in the wagon," Cal answered. "She's always cleanin' or shinin' something. I expect she'll be out here before long." Fancy unfolded part of the gutta percha bed pad she was using as a seat for him to sit on. "Much obliged," he said and sat down next to her. "I swear, if it gets any colder, I might wanna sit in the fire." He peered up at the dark cloudy sky. "We might see some weather if it stays cold like this."

"You must be gettin' thin-skinned in your old age," she teased. "It ain't even winter yet, unless somebody tore a page outta my calendar when I wasn't lookin'."

"Shoot," Cal replied. "It doesn't have to be winter up around these mountains to have a damn snowstorm. They like to call 'em summer snows, but they ain't no different from winter snows. Snow is snow, and accordin' to what Clint told me, we've got close to a hundred miles to go before we get to Oregon City. And most of that is goin' around that big mountain we've been lookin' at for the last few days."

Fancy was aware of a negative attitude surrounding Cal, which was unusual. Cal was almost always in a positive mood. It seemed especially apparent at this particular time, when everyone else was upbeat and looking forward to the end of their journey. "What's eatin' on you, Cal? I've known you for a long time, and nothing ever got you worried about anything. Has Ruby been mixin' sand in with your beans or something? Or has married life already got you thinkin' about the old days?" She couldn't resist adding, "I remember some of your old days, myself."

"Oh, no," Cal quickly responded, just then realizing how he might have sounded. "There ain't a thing Ruby ever does that's wrong." He thought to himself then, *Maybe that's what's bothering me.* To Fancy, he said, "I reckon my whole life up to now has been in your business, and I can't get myself excited yet about raisin' corn and taters."

"You'll have Ruby there to help you," Fancy reminded.

"And that little gal ain't ever known nothin' but hard work."

"Yeah, that's right," he said with little enthusiasm. "We'll work the soil together."

Nothing more was said for a few minutes while the whining sounds from Doc's fiddle filled the void. Fancy studied Cal's face as he stared into the fire, and she told herself that a proper person would not say what she was about to say. But she had never been accused of being proper, so she proceeded. "Cal, I know you better than anybody else on this wagon train, maybe a little better than you know yourself. I know you well enough to be sure you married Ruby with the intentions of takin' care of her for the rest of her life. If I had it on, I'd tip my hat to you for that. I also know you weren't cut out to be a homesteader, and I was surprised when you hooked up with her. It's a helluva lot different dealin' with a shovel than it is dealin' cards. And there ain't much call for a fast gun just to shoot a hog in the head. So I'm gonna tell you something I ain't told anybody else. I'm plannin' to build a saloon out here as soon as I decide on the spot to build it. I've got the money to build it, and I'm gonna need a man like you to help me run it. I'm just tellin' you this in case you decide to make some changes. You can bring Ruby with you. That's up to you. I ain't sayin' get rid of her. She's a fine little girl who's had a rough life. I'm just thinkin' you and I would make a good business team."

He shook his head as if trying to shake his brain back in order. From the first time he heard about the killing of Raymond Pantz, he was sure that Fancy was the one who shot him in the back of the head. She confirmed it when she said she had the money to build the saloon. And he knew she wasn't worried that he might tell, because she knew that he had been a gun for hire back in Kansas. He looked away from the fire to lock eyes with her. "Damn, Fancy, I don't know. That's a mighty tempting offer, and God knows, I ain't cut out to be a farmer." He was about to say more, but they saw Ruby coming to join them.

"You just think it over," Fancy said hurriedly. "We've got some time before we get to Oregon City." She turned to greet Ruby then. "It's a good thing you showed up. Your husband ain't been doin' nothin' but complainin' about the cold."

"I'll try to keep him warm," Ruby said with a cheerful smile for Fancy. She sat down and cuddled up close to Cal. After half an hour of small talk between Fancy and Ruby, and silence from Cal, Ruby announced that she was going to go fix their bed for the night. "You comin', hon?"

"You go ahead, I'll be along in a minute," Cal told her.

"You've been thinkin' about what I said, haven't you?" Fancy asked as soon as Ruby left.

"Yeah, I have," he answered. "And I reckon you know me pretty well. I'm bound to let her down sooner or later. Might as well do it now before she starts talkin' about havin' kids. But I don't wanna tell her till after I get her and her wagon to Oregon City, all right?"

"Whatever you say, partner," Fancy replied with a satisfied smile.

Chapter 26

The wagon train rolled into their first Euro-American settlement in Oregon when they reached The Dalles the next day. They were surprised to find houses and cultivated fields as well as a trading post, all a result of the Methodist mission established in 1838. The stop there was very brief, however, only long enough to give the emigrants a chance to buy any supplies they might be desperate to have before setting out on the last leg of their journey. They left The Dalles, heading south toward the Tygn Valley on the Barlow Road before stopping for the night. The next morning, they continued on for half a day before the road turned to the west, crossing several healthy creeks and the White River. They climbed northwest over the foothills on steep and rough trails, some hills so steep that double teams of horses were required to climb them. Of concern to all was a worsening of the weather and the dread that they might be caught on these treacherous trails by a late-summer snow.

They found it impossible to make decent distances for each day's travel, arriving about halfway to Oregon City after six days of rugged travel. At the end of that sixth day, the weary travelers found themselves at the most dangerous segment of the trip, Laurel Hill. Here, they were faced with a descent down a hill so steep that it would require ropes to lower the wagons. It was too late in the day to start such a long and difficult descent, so Scofield ordered a stop for the day. There was no room to circle wagons, so they just sat where they were on the trail. If there was a positive to the situation, it was the fact that wood and water was no problem. The negative, however was the light dusting of snow that had now begun to fall. Scofield and Clint walked back to the middle of the line of twenty-seven wagons, calling for the men to gather to talk over what they were going to do. Several of the men had already walked forward to see what was waiting for them in the morning. One of them, Peter Gilbert, was the first to ask, "Scofield, what are you plannin' to do tomorrow? There ain't no more trail. We're stopped at a cliff."

"Looks that way, don't it, Peter?" Scofield replied. "The trail's there, all right, it just looks like it's gone in the dark. But that's what I wanna talk about. There ain't no other way to get down to Sandy Creek." He glanced up at the snow still falling, then continued. "We have to go down this hill, and it ain't gonna be easy in this weather. Hell, it ain't easy in any kind of weather. Even when it's dry, that hill's too steep to drive down, so we're gonna have to lower the wagons down on ropes."

"Are you talkin' about with the horses hitched up?"

Walt Moody wanted to know. As soon as he asked, there were several vocal responses in the negative.

"It's been tried before, but I heard about one fellow that tried it and the wagon ended up sideways and cripplin' one of his horses, and that was in dry weather," Scofield said. "So I'm sayin' we oughta play it safe, unhitch the horses and lower the wagons with another rope on the tongue to keep it from turnin' sideways."

"Sounds crazy to me," John Zachary commented, "but damned if I know any better way."

"That's the way we've done it before, and it ain't been easy. Anybody got a better idea?" Scofield asked.

"Yeah," Lonnie James japed, "let's turn around and go back to The Dalles and float 'em down the river."

"That'd be a good idea, but we ain't got room to turn around," Buck Carrey offered.

"Sounds to me like there ain't nobody with any better idea," Scofield said. "So eat your supper and get some sleep. Tomorrow's gonna be a workin' day."

They awoke the following morning to discover the ground was covered by a three-inch blanket of snow. Fires were immediately rekindled, and the coffeepots set to boil. Not much time was devoted to breakfast, since everyone was anxious to see how the snow was going to affect their situation. The men gathered around a fire Spud built at the edge of the incline to discuss their possibilities. "You still thinkin' about lowerin' the wagons down this hill?" Emmett asked Scofield, as he stared at the snow-covered trail.

"I sure am," Scofield answered him. "I don't see as how we've got any other choice. Bad as it was, it's gonna be worse now with that snow on it. But we can't stay here stuck on this hill all winter. We've got to move, and we might as well go forward. If you're thinkin' we might oughta go back to The Dalles and wait the winter out, maybe you need to think about the road leadin' up to here. It ain't in no better shape than the road we're settin' on right here. We get down this hill and the road ain't near that bad on into Oregon City."

"Whatever it takes," Fancy Wallace spoke up as she came up to join the men, "let's get started with it. I sure as hell don't wanna sit here all winter."

"I reckon you heard the boss, boys," Cal said and winked at Fancy. "How we gonna do this, Scofield?"

Scofield explained what he had in mind, and they soon realized it was going to take all of them to perform the operation. So, they began, one wagon at a time, driven up to the edge and turned around. Then the horses were unhitched, and the owner led them down the steep hill while three ropes were tied to the wagon, one on each side of the front axle, and one on the wagon tongue. Then with Scofield manning a rope winched around one tree, Lonnie winching one around another, and Clint controlling the tongue with the third, each wagon was slowly lowered to the bottom. When it was down, the team was hitched up again and driven up the trail, while the procedure started on the next wagon. "There's gotta be a better way," John Zachary remarked as he watched the first wagon lowered down the hill, but no one suggested any. The slow and exhausting work continued, hampered by the worsening of the steep trail with the sliding descent of each wagon.

When it was time for Lonnie's wagon, Fancy sent Lemuel to take Lonnie's place lowering one of the ropes, since Lemuel was almost as big as Lonnie. Lonnie took a few moments to make sure Lemuel understood how to use the tree for leverage before he unhitched his horses and tied the ropes around his axle and wagon tongue. Then he led his team of horses down to wait at the bottom of the hill.

Clint's job was to keep the front wheels straight, guiding the wagon with the tongue, if he had to. The slushy snow made that job harder and harder as the day wore on. And by the end of the day, they had managed to slide only fifteen of the twenty-seven wagons safely down to the trail below. So, they went into camp that night with over half of the wagons down on the trail at the bottom of the hill, and the rest still sitting on top.

The next morning found the slush frozen and foreboding, but the first wagon was lowered without a great deal of trouble, which served to heighten morale. Pat Shephard hitched his horses back up and drove it away to join the others waiting on the Sandy Creek trail. Cal Nixon was the next in line with Ruby's wagon. "All right, boys, you need to be on your toes with this one," he joked. "We don't want nothin' broke and not a dish cracked. Ruby told me to tell you that." They all laughed at the thought of timid little Ruby saying anything of the sort. Cal unhitched the mules and led them down the hill. Ruby watched from the top of the hill with the other women and children.

Watching the wagon as it slid slowly down, Lonnie was climbing back up the hill with the intention of relieving Lemuel of his job with the rope. Suddenly, something caught his eye that stopped him in his tracks. "Look out!" he yelled. "It's gonna break!" No one knew what he meant as he ran the rest of the way up the hill. "It's fixin' to break!" He yelled at the top of his voice because he could see the rope on Lemuel's side was starting to splay, right in the middle, plain enough for everyone to see now. One who could not see from where he waited below, Cal tried to determine what the yelling was about. He climbed partway up the slope again to a higher spot to look. At that moment, Lemuel's rope snapped in two. Scofield managed to quickly tie-off his rope to keep the wagon from dropping down the slippery road, but it caused the rear end of the wagon to whip around sideways to roll over on its side.

"Damn!" Scofield swore. "That coulda been really bad. You all right, Clint?"

"Yeah, I'm all right," Clint answered. "I just got my fanny wet when that wagon tongue threw me about five feet down the hill." Then when he didn't see him, he yelled, "You all right, Cal?" Cal didn't answer. Clint called out again, and again there was no answer.

They found him under the wagon. His chest had been crushed from the weight of the heavy wagon. He had apparently walked right into the path of the careening wagon. When Ruby was given the dreadful news, she dropped to her knees, sobbing. Marcy and Sarah came to her at once, but there was nothing that could be said to console her. When she was able to get to her feet again, she looked around, searching for her one true friend. When she saw him standing there, obviously hurting for her sorrow, she went to him and sobbed in his arms. It seemed an awkward moment to most of the folks standing around, but Marcy understood the young girl's feelings. From the beginning, Clint had been a friend to Ruby, long before Cal joined the train at Green River. She had learned to trust Clint, so it was natural that she would go to him in her time of grief. So, Marcy gave her a few minutes, and when she seemed to control her emotions, Marcy took her elbow and said, "Come on, honey. We'll go over to my fire, and I'll get you some coffee."

Ruby looked up at Clint, and he said, "That's a good idea. You go with Marcy. I've got to help with this wagon and take care of Cal. You go along now, and I'll talk to you later."

It was difficult for Clint to believe that Cal's life had been snuffed out so suddenly and in such an impossible way. He had gotten to know Cal well enough to feel he could accurately guess what his life had been before joining the wagon train. He was too fast with the pistol he wore for Clint not to believe he had had plenty of practice. And the way he dressed should tell anyone that he was more comfortable in a saloon, at a card table, than on a farm or ranch. Clint suspected Cal's incentive to travel all the way to Oregon might have something to do with the law. Clint didn't care. Cal had become a friend. He would miss him, and he felt especially sad that Cal had chanced upon the good fortune of meeting Ruby, only to have all their plans to build a farm in Oregon destroyed.

Peter Gilbert helped him lower Cal's body into the grave Clint had dug while most of the other men were working to get Ruby's wagon upright. "That sure is a shame," Gilbert commented as he and Clint filled in the grave. "Poor little Ruby, I expect she's the first woman who's been widowed twice on the Oregon Trail before she ever got to Oregon."

"I expect so," Clint conceded. It caused him to wonder

why she was the victim of so much bad luck and what was going to happen to her now.

"I reckon that'll do it," Gilbert decided when the grave was completed. "I reckon I'll go see if I can help with the wagons."

"I'll be up there in a little bit," Clint said. He stayed to tidy up the mound of dirt as best he could, knowing Ruby would soon be down to see it. He hadn't delayed the burial because he didn't think it would do for her to see Cal like he was when they found him under that wagon. Cal's grave was not the first one in the small little plot at the bottom of the hill. There were two others, and there would probably be others to join Cal, to get so near before failing. He shook his head in disgust then and mumbled, "And we ain't even passed the toll gate yet. I reckon they'll want five dollars from a dead man, too."

It was another full day before the rest of the wagons were safely down Laurel Hill and ready to get underway again. At supper that night, Fancy Wallace asked Ruby if she would eat with her. Ruby told her she appreciated the gesture, but she would be all right alone. Fancy insisted, however. "I've known Cal Nixon a long time and there's some things I think you need to know about Cal. We talked about you and him the other night after you went off to bed. He always liked to play cards, and he was good at it. So, I asked him what he was plannin' to do when you and him got to Oregon City." She paused then, when she saw Ruby's complete interest.

"What did he tell you?" Ruby asked.

"If I remember correctly, he said, 'Well, Fancy, I'm plannin' to file my claim for some land I can farm. I'm gonna work my ass off to make that woman the happiest woman in the world, 'cause she deserves a good husband.' He mighta said some other things, too, but I remember that word for word."

Huge tears began to form in Ruby's eyes, and she couldn't speak for a few moments. When she could, she said, "Thank you, Fancy. Thank you for tellin' me that."

"Just wanted you to know what kinda man you were married to. Now, come on and help me cook up some side meat. You need to keep your strength up. I gotta cook for Lemuel, anyway. But don't worry, he ain't gonna eat with us. A delicate little woman like you might have a stroke if you was to watch him eat. He's gonna drive your wagon on into Oregon City for you, though, so we'll feed him."

"Thank you, Fancy," Ruby said again. "You're a good person."

"Careful," Fancy cautioned and looked around as if someone might hear. "I can't afford to let that get out."

"Clint told me he would take me to see Cal's grave after supper," Ruby thought she should tell her.

"Good idea," Fancy said. "I won't keep you, but we better get the skillet out if we're gonna eat."

As he had promised, Clint found Ruby at Fancy's wagon and walked with her back to the little cemetery plot close by the bottom of Laurel Hill. "Well, here it is," he said when he led her up beside the grave. "You want me to leave you here a few minutes by yourself, so you can say good-bye?"

"No," she said. "I'd like it if you'd stand here with me. I think Cal would like it if you did."

"All right," Clint said and stepped up beside her. She put her arm around him, and they stood there for several minutes in silence. He could hear her whispering something, but it was not loud enough for him to hear. When she was ready, she dropped her arm and turned around. With tears streaming down her cheeks, she walked quickly away. He didn't follow her right away but stayed a few moments longer to look down at the grave and promise, "I'll take care of her." Then he hurried to join her.

As if the foul weather had been planned just to demonstrate what a miserable trip the Barlow Road could be, the skies cleared, and the sun broke through soon after they bade Laurel Hill good-bye. Even then, it was three days before they reached their destination, Oregon City. The town was built on the Willamette River at Willamette Falls, near the river's confluence with the Clackamas River. Like he had with previous wagon trains, Scofield led the twenty-seven wagons into camp on the Abernethy Green beside the city. It was a large open pasture owned by, and named for, the first governor of the Oregon Territory, George Abernethy.

The settlers were too late to receive the benefit of free land, as had first been offered, but they were well aware of that before they left Independence. That land offer was withdrawn five years before they set out on their journey. It was their hope that the price set on the land after 1855 was still at the cheap price of a dollar and twenty-five cents an acre. They found out at the federal land office that there was still plenty of land available in the Willamette Valley, even though there was a slight increase over the dollar-twenty-five price. It was still cheap for prime farmland. Anxious to finally settle on their own land, most of the emigrants gambled on the plots they filed on without riding down the valley to actually see the land. John Zachary and Emmett Braxton were among that group. Based on the land office's maps, they selected two adjoining parcels, just as they had in Missouri. When Scofield asked John if he wasn't worried about filing on a property he'd never seen before, John answered honestly. "This whole thing we just did was a helluva gamble, but we made it. So, filing on this property is just another gamble I feel like we'll win."

Buck Carrey and Doc Meadows walked out of the land office door then and stopped to say good-bye. Not surprising, like John and Emmett, they filed on plots side by side. "You fellows are gonna have to play a helluva lot louder if we're gonna hear you now," Emmett joked as they shook hands.

The wagons became fewer and fewer on Abernethy Green as friendships, hardened on the forge that was the Oregon Trail, were set to go their separate ways. Although having experienced it before, Clint could feel the sense of sadness that descended upon the travelers at trail's end. For that reason, he generally busied himself with his horse and Ruby's wagon. Tim and Amy Blake made a special effort to seek him out, however, to express their gratitude once again for his rescue of Amy. They made it a point to offer condolences to Ruby again for the loss of her husband. When they said good-bye and left, Clint asked Ruby, "Are you holdin' up okay?"

She gave him a sad smile and answered, "Yes, I'm okay. It's just kinda sad, though, I feel like I'm sayin' good-bye to friends I've known all my life." She tried to brighten up her smile and said, "I've got to decide what I'm gonna do now." She paused again, then asked, "Can I file a claim for a piece of land, like the families do?"

“Yeah, you don’t have to be married to file. Is that what you wanna do?”

“I don’t know, I guess so. I’ve got enough money to build a little shack and raise something to eat. I’ve got some money I sneaked outta Ralph’s hidin’ place, and Cal had some money. It’s gonna be tough alone, but I don’t know what else to do.”

“Since you ain’t really sure what to do, can I make a suggestion?” She shrugged in answer, so he continued. “On one of our first trips out here, Scofield’s brother, my Uncle Garland, and his family came with us, and they filed a claim on a piece of land to start a horse and cattle ranch. The plan was for Uncle Clayton and I to settle there with ’em after a few more trips guiding emigrants. For now, it’s home between trips. The ranch has done well and there’s plenty of room for everybody, and that includes you. I know you’d like my Aunt Irene and my niece, Janie. She’s thirteen now. I know they’d all welcome you, so whaddaya say?”

She found it impossible to speak. So profound was her relief that she almost sank to the ground. She could only respond by nodding gratefully, over and over.

Clint was with Scofield, looking after the horses they had picked up along the way, when they heard the shots. Since most of the wagons had pulled out, it was easy to determine the shots had come from Fancy’s. They both ran at once to determine the cause. When they got to her wagon, they found her standing there behind the wagon, her revolver still in her hand. Lemuel was lying face-down with two bullet holes in his back. She turned when they ran up and calmly stated, “I caught him about to run off with the satchel that has all my money in it." Neither Clint nor Scofield said anything, although both were thinking the same thing.

Scofield walked over to determine that Lemuel was dead. "He's dead, all right," he pronounced. "Made a run for it, did he?"

"That's a fact," Fancy said. "I told him to stop, but he didn't."

They waited there with her until a deputy sheriff arrived to investigate the shot and Fancy repeated her simple explanation. The deputy questioned them, but they told him they were not witnesses. He decided to accept Fancy's version of the story and told her he would have the undertaker pick up the body. "I'll be at the hotel, if you need me for anything else," Fancy told the deputy. The incident was neither a shock nor a surprise to Clint and Scofield. It more or less confirmed a speculation quite a few in the wagon train had held.

"Well, that pretty-much wraps up another trip, don't it?" Scofield remarked as they walked back to the horses. "We can drive these horses on down the valley to the ranch. I expect Garland has been lookin' for us to show up any day now." Scofield's comment caused Clint to picture his uncle Garland, an older version of his uncle Clayton. He would be pressing Scofield to retire from the wagon train business and help him run the ranch full time. Clint wondered, himself, if Scofield was ready to settle down on the ranch.

Scofield didn't say anything more for a while before asking, "Is Ruby gonna be able to make it on her own? I swear, I worry about what's liable to happen to her."

"I promised Cal I'd look after her," Clint replied.

"Well, now, is that a fact? How you gonna do that?"

"I reckon I shoulda talked to you about it first," Clint said. "But I figured I'd take a chance on it." He went on to tell his uncle that he had suggested to Ruby that she should move onto the Scofield ranch. "I wasn't sure if we were gonna go back east this year to organize another train or not. I figure that would be your call. That little cabin I'm buildin' down by the creek would be just right for Ruby with a little fixin' up."

Scofield just looked at him and smiled for a few seconds before he responded. "You know, I was wonderin' whether to talk to you about a trip for next spring or not. I wasn't sure I wanted to make this trip again. So why don't we wait till after winter's over and we'll both decide if we wanna do it again or not. All right?"

"Suits me," Clint answered.

"'Bout this thing with Ruby," Scofield continued. "I was thinkin' about askin' her if she'd like to move onto the ranch with the rest of the gang. I figured it'd be good for her to have family around her, even if it's a crazy family like ours. I'm pretty sure Irene would love to have another woman to help out and give her some company. And Irene would be good for Ruby, too." He paused and nodded thoughtfully before going on. "So, you went ahead and told her she'd be welcome to stay with us without checkin' with me first." Clint shrugged, defenseless. "I reckon you musta had one of your 'feelin's' again," Scofield said.

"As a matter of fact," Clint replied.

Keep reading for special excerpt!

NATIONAL BESTSELLING AUTHORS
WILLIAM W. JOHNSTONE
and J.A. Johnstone

BRANNIGAN'S LAND

First in a Brand-New Series!

Ty Brannigan traded his tin star for a cattle ranch. But the men he left to rot behind bars have their own hash to settle with him . . .

KEEPING HIS OWN PEACE

Once a respected lawman in Kansas and Oklahoma, Ty Brannigan ended his career as town marshal of Warknife while he was still young enough to marry, start a family, and raise cattle. Now nearly sixty, he's a proud husband, father of four, and proprietor of the Powderhorn Ranch on the outskirts of his old stomping grounds. It's been close to twenty years since Brannigan hung up his six-guns. Now he's more content wrangling cows than criminals.

But for every remorseless outlaw Brannigan put in jail, noosed, or left to the vultures, he made even more enemies. Thieves and killers looking to settle old scores have tracked the ex-lawdog to his ranch. They've made the mistake of targeting his wife and children—only to discover that Ty Brannigan enforces his own law with a lightning-fast draw and a deadshot aim . . .

Look for **BRANNIGAN'S LAND, on sale now where books are sold.**

Chapter 1

"What do you think, honey?" Ty Brannigan asked his oldest daughter.

"Just incredible, Pa. I don't know that I've ever seen a finer horse anywhere."

"He is something to look at, isn't he?"

"He sure is." MacKenna Brannigan lay beside her father near the crest of a rocky-topped ridge in the foothills of Wyoming Territory's Bear Paw Mountains, a spur range of the Wind Rivers, near Baldy Butte. Ty and MacKenna were peering down into the valley on the other side of the ridge. "I could lie here all day, just staring at him and his beautiful harem not to mention those six colts of his."

Tynan Brannigan, "Ty" for short, adjusted the focus on the spyglass he held to his right eye, bringing the big, impressive black stallion into sharper focus. The horse milled on the side of the next ridge, a couple of hundred feet up from where his harem languidly cropped grass with their foals along Indian Lodge Creek.

The big horse was watching over his herd, keeping an eye out for predators or rival herds led by stallions that might very well prove to be the black's blood enemy. He was having a good time performing the otherwise onerous task. The stallion ran along the side of the ridge then stopped abruptly, swung to his right and dashed up the steep ridge to the very top. He ran along the crest of the ridge first one way before wheeling, mane and tail flying, the sunlight glistening beautifully in his sleek, blue-black hide, and running back the other way before swinging down off the crest and galloping full out down the side toward where his harem lifted their heads and turned to watch him, twitching their ears incredulously.

Ty and MacKenna were several hundred yards from the big black, but Ty could still hear the thunder of the horse's hooves and the deep, grating chuffs the horse made with his powerful lungs as he ran.

The black slowed at the bottom of the ridge, near the stream, then went over and nosed one of the mares—a beautiful cream with a blond mane and tail. He nosed her hard, brusquely but playfully, then nipped the rear of one of the younger horses, a half-grown gray. The gray bleated indignantly. The stallion lifted his fine head and ripped out a shrill whinny. He put his head down, reared high, pawed the ground, then lunged into another ground-chewing gallop, making a mad dash up the ridge again.

MacKenna, who at seventeen was in full flower of young womanhood, lowered the field glasses she'd been peering through and turned to her father, smiling. Her long hair was nearly as black as the stallion's, and it shone in the high-country sunshine like the black's did, as well.

Her lustrous hazel eyes—her hair had come from her Spanish mother, but her eyes were the same almost startlingly clear blue-green as her father's—flashed in delight. Her plump red lips stretched back from her even, white teeth. "He's showing off, isn't he? He's showing off for the mares!"

Ty chuckled and lifted the spyglass again to his eye, returning his gaze to the black as the stallion stopped suddenly halfway up the ridge then turned to stand parallel to the ridge and peer off into the distance, ears pricked, tail arched, again looking for danger. "He sure is, honey."

Ty was glad he and MacKenna were upwind of the beautiful stud and his harem. If they'd been downwind, the black likely would have detected him and the girl and hazed his brood out of the valley where Ty and MacKenna, having a rare father-and-daughter ride alone together, lay on the side of their own ridge, admiring the lovely, charismatic, bewitchingly wild black stallion.

"They're just like boys, aren't they—wild stallions?" MacKenna said, playfully nudging her father in the ribs with her elbow. "Showing off for their women."

"Just like boys and men, honey," Ty agreed, chuckling. He turned to look at MacKenna who was peering through the field glasses again. "Would you like to have a horse like that, baby girl?"

MacKenna, named after Ty's long-dead mother, lowered the field glasses and turned to her father. Her thin black brows furled with speculation. Finally, she shook her head. "No." She turned to gaze with her naked eyes into the next valley. "No, a horse like that needs to be wild. Breaking or even gentling a horse like that . . . civilizing him . . . would ruin him." She glanced at her father. "Don't you think, Pa?"

"I couldn't agree more, Mack."

"How did you find this herd, Pa? I've never seen wild horses out here."

"Matt and I were hunting yearling mavericks on open range a few weeks ago, and we stumbled on several stud piles." Matt was the oldest of Ty and his wife Beatriz's four children, all of whom had been raised—were *being* raised, with the youngest at age twelve—on their Powderhorn Ranch in the shadow of several tall bluffs and mesas that abutted the ermine-tipped, higher peaks of the Wind Rivers.

MacKenna furled her dark brows again, curiously this time. "Stud piles?"

"Big piles of horse apples the herd leaders leave to mark their territory. Apparently, that big fella moved his herd in here recently. I've never seen stud piles in these parts before. Down deeper in the breaks of the Snowy River and in the badland country north of town, but never here."

"So, they're new in these parts," MacKenna said, smiling in delight and gazing into the next valley through her field glasses again. "Welcome, Black . . . ladies and youngsters." She turned to her father. "Thanks for showing me, Pa. It leaves you with a nice feeling, seeing such beautiful, wild beasts, doesn't it?"

Ty smiled and placed a big, affectionate hand against the back of his daughter's neck. "Sure does, baby girl."

MacKenna shook her head again. "No, it wouldn't be right to try to tame a horse like that. Just like some men can't be tamed, some horses can't either."

Her eyes acquired a pensive cast, and she lowered her gaze.

Damn, Ty thought. He'd brought her out here—just

him and her—to try to take her mind off her heartbreak, not to remind her of it.

"Oh, honey," he said, sympathetically. "He's not worth how bad you feel."

He meant the young, itinerant horse gentler, Brandon Waycross, who had once worked for Ty. MacKenna had tumbled for the rakishly handsome young man, five years her senior, one summer ago, and only a few months ago he'd broken her heart. Though they hadn't made any formal plans, and MacKenna had never confessed as much, Ty knew that MacKenna had tumbled for young Waycross and had set her hat toward marrying the young man.

"I hope he is, Pa. Or I'm a fool, because I sure do feel almighty bad."

"Even after what he did?"

MacKenna drew her mouth corners down and nodded, her now-sad gaze still averted. "'Fraid so." She raised her eyes to Ty's. "I don't think he meant to betray me with Ivy. Some boys just can't help themselves."

"Don't make excuses for him, MacKenna. He's not a boy anymore. Brandon Waycross doesn't deserve you. You hold tight, baby girl. You're gonna find the right man—a good, kind, loyal man. That's the only kind to share your life with."

"Sometimes I feel like Ma got the last one of those," MacKenna said, then leaned toward Ty and planted an affectionate kiss on his cheek.

Ty smiled, sighed. "Well, honey. It's getting late and we've got an hour's ride back to the Powderhorn. Don't want to be late for supper or your mother will send us each out to fetch our own willow switches."

"Ouch!" MacKenna said, grinning. "She doesn't hold back like you do, either, Pa!"

"Believe me—I know!" Ty grin-winced and rubbed his backside.

He crawled a few feet down from the lip of the ridge, so the stallion wouldn't see him, then donned his high-crowned brown Stetson and rose to his full six-feet-four. At fifty-seven, having married MacKenna's mother when she was twenty-one and he was thirty-six, Ty Brannigan still owned the body of a Western horseman—tall, lean, broad-shouldered, and narrow-waisted.

Just by looking at him—into those warm eyes, especially—most would never have guessed he'd once been a formidable, uncompromising lawman in several formerly wide-open towns in Kansas and Oklahoma—a town tamer of legend. Ty had been the town marshal of nearby Warknife for three years and had cleaned out most of the hardcases during his first two years on the job, before meeting Beatriz Salazar, a local banker's daughter, falling head over heels in love, and turning in his badge to devote the rest of his life to ranching and raising a family.

It had not been a mistake. Ty did not miss wearing the badge. In fact, he treasured every moment spent working with his wife and their four children, now between the ages of twelve and nineteen, on their eight-thousand-acre spread, even when the work was especially tough like in spring with calving or when Ty was forced to run rustlers to ground with his old Henry repeating rifle and his stag-gripped Colt .44, holdovers from his lawdogging days. That Colt was housed now in its ancient, fringed, soft leather holster and thonged on his right thigh. The Henry repeater was sheathed on the coyote dun standing ground-reined with MacKenna's fine Appaloosa that Brandon Waycross had helped her gentle.

Ty didn't like wearing the guns, but they were a practical matter. Wyoming was still rough country, and over Ty's years as a tough-nosed lawman who'd sent many men to the territorial pen near Laramie, he'd made enemies. Some of those enemies had come gunning for him in the past, to get even for time spent behind bars or for family members who'd fallen victim to Ty's once-fast gun hand. When more enemies came, and he had to assume they would, he owed it to his family to be ready for them.

So far, the Brannigan family plot on a knoll east of the big main house, was occupied by only one Brannigan—Ty's father, Killian Brannigan, an old hide-hunting and fur-trapping mountain man who'd lived out his last years on the Powderhorn before succumbing to a heart stroke at age 90. Ty didn't want to join his father just yet. He had too many young'uns to raise and a good woman to love. At age forty, Beatriz was too young to lose her man and to have to finish raising their four children alone.

"Come on, baby girl," Ty said, extending his hand to MacKenna. "Let's fork leather and fog some sage!"

MacKenna accepted her father's hand; Ty pulled her to her feet. An eerie whining sound was followed closely by a resolute thud and a dust plume on the side of the ridge, ahead and to Ty's right. He'd felt the bullet curl the air just off his right ear before the crack of the rifle reached him.

"Down, honey!" Ty yelled, and threw MacKenna back onto the ground, throwing himself down on top of her, covering her with his own bulk then rolling off of her, pulling her on top of him again and rolling first her and then himself over the top of the ridge to the other side.

As he did, another bullet plumed dust within feet of MacKenna's left shoulder, turning Ty's insides into one taut, cold knot, sending icicles of terror shooting down his legs and into his feet.

"My God, Pa!" MacKenna cried when Ty had her safely on the other side of the ridge from the shooter. "What was *that*?"

"Keep your head down, honey!" Ty said, placing his left hand on her shoulder, holding her down, while pulling his stag-gripped .44 from its holster with his right hand.

"Who's shooting at us, Pa?"

"Your guess is as good as mine!" Breathless, Ty edged a cautious glance over the lip of the ridge and down the other side.

His and MacKenna's horses had run off, the coyote dun taking Ty's rifle along with it. Fifty yards beyond where the horses had stood was a wide creek bed choked with willows, cedars, and wild shadbark and juneberry bramble. The shooter must have fired from the creek bed, hidden by the bramble. Ty saw no sign of him.

Turning to MacKenna, who now lay belly down beside her father, her face blanched with fear as she gazed at him, Ty said, "You stay here, Mack. And for God sakes, keep your head down!"

Ty started to crab down the side of the ridge. MacKenna grabbed his arm, clutched it with a desperate grip. "Pa, where you goin'?"

"I'm gonna try to work around the bushwhacking coward! You stay here." He set down his gun to pat her hand that was still clutching his left forearm, and his normally mild eyes sparked with the hard light of a Celtic war council fire. Messing with him was one thing. Messing with his family was another thing altogether. "Don't you worry. I'm gonna get him, Mack!"

He remembered the bullet that had plumed dirt just inches from her shoulder.

MacKenna, as tough as the toughest Brannigan, which would be old Killian, hardened her jaws as well as her eyes and said, "Okay, Pa. Go get him!"